TANGLED INNOCENCE

EGOROV BRATVA
BOOK 1

NICOLE FOX

Copyright © 2024 by Nicole Fox

All rights reserved.

No part of this book may be reproduced in any form or by any electronic or mechanical means, including information storage and retrieval systems, without written permission from the author, except for the use of brief quotations in a book review.

❦ Created with Vellum

ALSO BY NICOLE FOX

Zakrevsky Bratva
Requiem of Sin
Sonata of Lies
Rhapsody of Pain

Bugrov Bratva
Midnight Purgatory
Midnight Sanctuary

Oryolov Bratva
Cruel Paradise
Cruel Promise

Pushkin Bratva
Cognac Villain
Cognac Vixen

Viktorov Bratva
Whiskey Poison
Whiskey Pain

Orlov Bratva
Champagne Venom
Champagne Wrath

Uvarov Bratva
Sapphire Scars

Sapphire Tears

Vlasov Bratva
Arrogant Monster
Arrogant Mistake

Zhukova Bratva
Tarnished Tyrant
Tarnished Queen

Stepanov Bratva
Satin Sinner
Satin Princess

Makarova Bratva
Shattered Altar
Shattered Cradle

Solovev Bratva
Ravaged Crown
Ravaged Throne

Vorobev Bratva
Velvet Devil
Velvet Angel

Romanoff Bratva
Immaculate Deception
Immaculate Corruption

Kovalyov Bratva
Gilded Cage

Gilded Tears
Jaded Soul
Jaded Devil
Ripped Veil
Ripped Lace

Mazzeo Mafia Duet
Liar's Lullaby (Book 1)
Sinner's Lullaby (Book 2)

Bratva Crime Syndicate
Can be read in any order!
Lies He Told Me
Scars He Gave Me
Sins He Taught Me

Belluci Mafia Trilogy
Corrupted Angel (Book 1)
Corrupted Queen (Book 2)
Corrupted Empire (Book 3)

De Maggio Mafia Duet
Devil in a Suit (Book 1)
Devil at the Altar (Book 2)

Kornilov Bratva Duet
Married to the Don (Book 1)
Til Death Do Us Part (Book 2)

Heirs to the Bratva Empire
Can be read in any order!

Kostya

Maksim

Andrei

Princes of Ravenlake Academy (Bully Romance)

Can be read as standalones!

Cruel Prep

Cruel Academy

Cruel Elite

Tsezar Bratva

Nightfall (Book 1)

Daybreak (Book 2)

Russian Crime Brotherhood

Can be read in any order!

Owned by the Mob Boss

Unprotected with the Mob Boss

Knocked Up by the Mob Boss

Sold to the Mob Boss

Stolen by the Mob Boss

Trapped with the Mob Boss

Volkov Bratva

Broken Vows (Book 1)

Broken Hope (Book 2)

Broken Sins *(standalone)*

Other Standalones

Vin: A Mafia Romance

Box Sets

Bratva Mob Bosses (Russian Crime Brotherhood Books 1-6)

Tsezar Bratva (Tsezar Bratva Duet Books 1-2)

Heirs to the Bratva Empire

The Mafia Dons Collection

The Don's Corruption

MAILING LIST

Sign up to my mailing list!
New subscribers receive a FREE steamy bad boy romance novel.

Click the link below to join.
https://sendfox.com/nicolefox

TANGLED INNOCENCE

"What do you mean, 'You gave me the wrong sperm sample'?!"

But the doctor says he isn't joking.

Instead of being my sister's surrogate...

I'm accidentally carrying my boss's baby.

A few months ago, I agreed to be my sister's surrogate.

Then she died in an unsolved accident.

I swore I'd keep her child and raise it on my own.

But as it turns out, there was a mix-up at the clinic.

Instead of carrying my future nephew...

I learned I'm pregnant with my boss's child.

But Dmitri isn't just my boss.

He's also the one who killed my sister in the first place.

TANGLED INNOCENCE is Book 1 of the Egorov Bratva duet. Dmitri and Wren's story concludes in Book 2, TANGLED DECADENCE.

1

WREN

"What do you mean, *You gave me the wrong sperm sample?*'"

I can't quite believe what I'm hearing. I take a look around the room to check my surroundings and confirm that this is in fact reality and not just some terrible, twisted, Häagen-Dazs-fueled nightmare.

Unfortunately for me, everything seems to be in order.

The placard on the wall reads **SAEDER & BANKS FERTILITY CLINIC OF CHICAGO** in a sleek, modern font. The fluorescent lights overhead sound like buzzing mosquitos, casting pale white light over every inch of the exam room. There's not a speck of dust to be found. Normally, I'm the last person to complain about a clean room, but in this case, it's just contributing to the sense that none of this is real life.

I pinch myself. It hurts.

Shit. Maybe this is real after all.

Dr. Saeder blinks down at me. Or up, rather. He's perched on his gleaming black wheely stool and I'm sitting on the edge of the exam table with my feet dangling in the air like a naughty kid in the principal's office. He looks like an ancient tortoise from this angle, all bristly nose hairs and beaked nose and bulbous eyes magnified to ridiculous proportions by his Coke bottle glasses.

He clears his throat and starts again. He's one part weary and ten parts terrified that I'm about to sue his ass into the next dimension—which is reasonable, because I'm sure as hell considering it. "As I explained, Ms. Turner, there was a mix-up in the labeling system for donor samples at our offsite lab facility. At the intrauterine insemination stage of proceedings for a surrogacy pregnancy such as yours, the biological…"

He drones on and on, but I'm not really hearing him. I processed it the first time he explained things—well, processed it *logically,* at least. Emotionally, I'm light years away from coming to grips with the bombshell that the not-so-good doctor just dropped on me.

I'm pregnant with the wrong man's baby.

There isn't a therapist alive who's qualified to deal with *this* ol' satchel of trauma. Thanks a lot to the sperm clinic from hell.

It's not like I didn't have enough of the stuff already—trauma, that is, not sperm. When your sister and brother-in-law get viciously murdered a month before you're supposed to start carrying their baby for them, you end up with enough baggage to last a lifetime.

Today was supposed to be a good day, dammit. Well, as good of a day as you can have in the immediate aftermath of a tragedy like the one that stole Rose and Jared from me. I was supposed to come in and get final confirmation that my eggs were properly fertilized. That the baby Rose had spent her entire life dreaming of would finally be hers, albeit not quite in the way she'd always imagined.

Rose was always the girlier of the two of us. She was the one directing her Barbies in theatrical performances and whipping up Easy Bake brownies for anyone who asked.

I'd have chugged orange juice and toothpaste before doing anything quite so feminine. While she was straightening doll hair, I was climbing trees and feeding those brownies of hers to any squirrel that would come close enough.

But we made it work, her and I. When Dad kicked us all out and Mom fell to cancer, we were all we had left. I came back home for the funeral and never really left Chicago after that.

It was good to be back near my sister. She understood how I grew up, all the little wounds to the heart that I suffered along the way to adulthood.

And I understood her just as well.

Which is why I was the first one she came to when she found out that the baby she'd always wanted so badly wasn't ever going to be hers.

"I'm barren, Wren," she'd said to me. I remember those words exactly because of how ridiculous they sounded. They belonged in a Jane Austen novel or in a cheesy grocery store checkout aisle bodice ripper.

Not on the lips of my sister.

Not on Rose.

But she didn't need jokes then. She needed a hug—which is what I gave her in those first tear-drenched moments—and love, which is what I gave her in every second that followed.

She needed something else, too. It took her a while to work up the courage to ask me. But I'll never forget that moment, either.

"Do it for me. Carry my baby. Will you, Wren?"

Back in the fluorescent-soaked present, I close my eyes to ward off the tears. I've cried enough in the last few weeks, thank you very much. This exact room has seen its fair share of those tears.

Even though things with the surrogacy have gone well—up until now—that doesn't stop the sadness from sitting heavy on my chest, always ready to reach up and clamp my throat closed for a little while, just for shits and giggles.

Grief is a cruel, petty bitch.

"... you understand, Ms. Turner?" Dr. Saeder finishes. "Ms. Turner?"

I sigh and open my eyes again. There are three of him in my field of vision, blurred and split up by the unshed tears. When I blink, they coalesce back into one.

And at the sight of him, I get *mad*.

I don't get mad often. For all that Rose was the princess of us two Turner girls, she was also the one more likely to melt down into a temper tantrum. And when she did, it was *fierce*.

"Hurricane Rosie," my mom used to call it. "The forecast is rain and thunder—lots of it."

Sure enough, she'd cry and scream like a storm cooked up by the devil himself. Hands pounding the ground, cheeks red and wet, the whole nine yards. She'd let her rage out like that —and when it was gone, it was like it had never even happened. She'd just smile again and go right back to her dolls.

Me, though… I turned my storms inwards. I kept 'em close and buried 'em deep. It felt safer that way.

But Hurricane Rosie isn't ever coming back, is she? And after a lifetime of keeping the hatch closed on my own thunderstorms, I figure I've earned the right to let out a clap of lightning or two.

"What I *understand,* Dr. Saeder, is that you and your staff have made an incredibly serious mistake that is about to change the course of my life irreversibly," I grit out, my voice wobbling dangerously.

Dr. Saeder's eyes open wide and he scoots back a bit on his wheely stool like he wants to stay out of arm's reach. Not a bad idea, honestly. There's no telling what I might do next. "Now, Ms. Turner, I think 'irreversibly' is a bit of a strong word. There is always the option of ab—"

"Don't."

He freezes and the words die on his tongue. The only sound in the room is the irritating fluorescents—*my God, I wish they'd just shut up already!*—and the sound of his gulp.

"Don't you *dare* suggest I get rid of this baby," I continue. I jab a finger in his direction. "My sister is *gone.* I *buried* her, Dr. Saeder. She and her husband are ashes six feet under the ground right now—and you want me to get rid of the only piece of them I have left? You want me to put this baby there, too? I. Don't. Fucking. Think. So."

He gulps again. His throat is so scrawny that I can see every inch of the motion. "V-very well, Ms. Turner. I only meant to explain your opt—"

When the doors open on the twenty-seventh floor, they deposit me into the offices of Egorov Industries. In case any visitors are ever uncertain where they are, there's a sign over the receptionist area that has **EGOROV** in absolutely massive letters.

That's par for the course.

Because the man who lent his name to this company has an ego to match.

Right on cue, when I reach my desk, the door to his office opens… and Dmitri Egorov emerges.

Let no one say he's not a looker. He is—even *I* can't deny that. Windswept hair, almost black but with a mesmerizing hint of auburn to it. Chin chiseled out of marble. Eyes light gray, piercing, observant, arrogant.

Unlike the stinky men on the elevator, his mint-and-cedar cologne is perfectly calibrated to seduce and intimidate—and unfortunately for me, it's pretty good at both tasks.

Because I *know* he's an egotistical maniac and yet I *still* find myself wondering what his body looks like beneath the Brioni suit he's wearing.

And if *I'm* a sucker for it, you already know that the rest of the women in this office—or really, in this entire zip code—have been reeled in hook, line, and sinker. Half a dozen perfectly coiffed heads are popping up over the cubicles at the mere sound of Dmitri's office door opening.

They're all hoping for a glance, a smile, a kind word from him.

Keep on hoping, sisters, I wanna tell them. *Dmitri Egorov doesn't know the meaning of "kind."*

But my God, if there were ever a day for him to give me a break, it'd be today, right? I just don't know how much more I can take.

The look in his eyes, though, says "mercy" is not high on his to-do list.

"Ms. Turner," he drawls icily. He flips up his wrist and checks the gleaming Patek Philippe watch he chose today. The embroidered initials on his tailored shirt cuff—*D.E.* in a villainous red thread—flash at me like a wink. "I wasn't aware that work began at 10:07 A.M. on Tuesdays."

"And I wasn't aware that 'D.E.' stood for 'Douchebag Extraordinaire,'" I mumble under my breath.

"What was that?" he asks as I get closer.

I sling my bag into the chair behind my desk and paste on a smile. "Nothing, Mr. Egorov. I'm sorry I was late this morning. I had a doctor's appointment. I did request time off…" Peeking down at my planner, I look at the date and finish, "three and a half months ago."

He pauses. His cologne is stronger up close. Mint and cedar, like a winter forest. I do prefer it to Dr. Saeder's cloying aftershave, though I'd never admit that to Dmitri's face.

"It's a bad day to be insubordinate, Ms. Turner."

My smile stays plastered in place. It's one of those smiles that, if he paid any attention at all, he'd see is hiding a barely-closed box of screams and violent fantasies about wiping that smug smirk right off his face.

But luckily for me, Dmitri doesn't care about silly things like "other people's emotions." That would just be a very big waste of his very important time.

"Insubordinate? Who, me? I don't even know the meaning of the word."

"You apparently don't know the meaning of the word 'timely,' either. Should we step into my office and practice reading a clock together?"

Apropos of absolutely nothing, my mind immediately fills with images of all the things he and I could do if we "stepped into his office."

I could plant his toned ass in his chair, wrap his tie around my fist, and shove his face up my skirt to see how well he can tell time with a face full of lady bits.

I could knock him flat on the ground, rip open that infuriatingly well-tailored button-down shirt, and graze my nails down his abs while riding him 'til the cows come home.

I could make him devour me.

I could make him worship me.

I could make him beg me to let him finish—and beg me and beg me and beg me, just for the sheer pleasure of leaning down, brushing my glossy lips up against the shell of his ear, and whispering one of his favorite words right back to him: "No."

" … Ms. Turner?"

For the second time today, there's a man snapping his fingers in my face and asking if I can hear him. Admittedly, this one is much easier on the eyes than Dr. Saeder.

But despite my little hate-crush on the bosshole from hell, I don't intend to be any nicer to Dmitri Egorov than I was to the incompetent doctor with the nose hair of a wildebeest.

"I'm as capable of hearing you as I am of telling time, *Mr. Egorov.*" I throw a little extra sauciness on his title.

"Hm." He tilts his head to the side and looks at me from a new angle. An inexplicable softness passes over his face. On anyone else, it wouldn't even be noticeable. But it's such a departure from his usual "hell hath no fury like mine" broodiness that it captures my attention. "Is something wrong, Wren?"

Wren. When he says it like that, with that tone and that look in his eye, I can't help but shiver.

It's wrong for a man to look this beautiful and be this cruel ninety-nine-point-nine percent of the time… then turn around and be nice on the worst day of my life.

I'm *thiiis* close to breaking down and telling him everything. Rose. Jared. The baby. The mix-up. The last time I saw a positive sign on a pregnancy test and the nightmares that followed that. Hell, give me half a dirty martini and I'll start unloading on him about when Susie Coleman wiped a booger on me in first grade.

But I can't.

Because he's my boss.

Because he doesn't *actually* give a shit, even if he's doing an awfully good job of pretending like he does right now.

Because he's rich and dangerous and too handsome to waste his breath asking after the problems of the feeble little mortals like me who flit around and do his bidding.

So I take a deep breath and give him the only reasonable answer I can afford to give: "No," I murmur. "Nothing's wrong. I'm fine."

He surveys me for another long minute, that perceptiveness lingering in his silver eyes. He sees more than he lets on, I think. Or at least, it feels that way.

I feel naked. Exposed. Trussed up like a butterfly on a pinboard, completely at his mercy.

And that softness… that tiny, almost-imperceptible tenderness in his face that says maybe there's a human with a beating, bleeding heart buried somewhere beneath the flawlessly symmetrical bone structure… it stays for just one moment too long.

I turn away. I can't let him look at me anymore. "If you need anything, sir, I'll be at my desk."

Then I brush past him and into the guts of Egorov Industries. I don't dare look back. But I can feel his eyes follow me all the way.

∼

The rest of the day is a fight to keep my tears at bay enough for me to read the words on my computer screen. I tend to Dmitri's emails, file his papers, prep for his meetings and his travel and his many charity galas.

My work wife slash bestie, Syrah, pings me on the company chat channel late in the afternoon to ask if I want to hit a happy hour after work.

SYRAH MEHRA: *If I don't get a margarita or five into my bloodstream ASAP, I'm going to put a staple in my eyeball.*

My first instinct is to wince. I'm not gonna be having margaritas for a long time, am I? But Syrah doesn't know that. I'd planned on keeping the whole surrogacy thing under wraps for as long as possible at the office.

SYRAH MEHRA: *So are you in or are you in???*

Biting back my first half-smile of the day, I type back, *Lol, so dramatic. As if your bloodstream isn't pretty much pure margarita at any given hour of the day anyway.*

SYRAH MEHRA: *Guilty as charged. Sue me. I like Mexican food.*

WREN TURNER: *Gonna have to pass today, though. I have a thing after work.*

I feel weird as soon as I hit send on the message. A "thing" … Is that the best way to describe going to potentially meet the man who impregnated you from afar without your knowledge? I don't think English has had the need to dream up such a word yet. I may be venturing into unexplored territory here. First woman on the moon type shit.

My fried-to-hell brain conjures up a brief image of one of Dmitri's sperm cells planting a little flag in my womb and I bust up laughing.

Mostly because, if I don't laugh, I'll cry.

SYRAH MEHRA: *a THING??? As in, like, a date????!?!!*

She follows it up with a frankly impressive string of emojis depicting how she thinks my night will go. There are a few too many eggplants, peaches, and water droplets for my liking.

WREN TURNER: *lol. Not a chance. I'm planning on being a bitter old spinster with all my cats and knitting.*

SYRAH MEHRA: *I've been to your apartment, babes. You don't have cats and you don't knit. And you're too hot to be bitter and lonely. I could set you up with someone if you want. I've got a cousin…*

WREN TURNER: *First off, you have a thousand cousins, and my answer for all of them has been the same: thanks but no thanks. I love you but I'm just not in a space to be looking for romance right now.*

SYRAH MEHRA: :(*I know. I'll drop it. I just want to make sure you know how special and perfect you are. You're gonna make some guy feel so lucky one day.*

WREN TURNER: *<3 love you. Gonna wrap up and get out of here. Drink a marg for me.*

I sign out of the chat and sigh. It only takes a little bit of time to organize my things and clear my desk. Turns out grief is actually kinda good for productivity, because I got a lot of stuff done. Dmitri hasn't been back to the office since our cringe-inducing encounter this morning, but even he wouldn't be able to criticize today's effort.

I open the desk drawer to drop in a sheaf of papers and something catches my eye. My heart leaps into my throat immediately, but I can't stop myself from reaching in and pulling out the gilded picture frame.

I don't really need to look at it—I pretty much see this picture every night before I go to sleep like it's tattooed on the back of my eyelids.

It's me and Rose on her wedding day, wearing matching silk bathrobes as I toy with her hair. We're looking at each other in the mirror and there's just something in her gaze and in mine that screams "love."

Come to think of it, it's weirdly akin to the tenderness in Dmitri's eyes from earlier.

I shake that thought off immediately. Dmitri Egorov is not physically capable of loving anyone like I loved Rose—except for maybe himself.

But this…

Fuck, I can remember this day. The room smelled like Rose's vanilla perfume and the roses set up on the vanity. She was so happy. This was before the endless procession of doctors, before dozens upon dozens of negative pregnancy tests, before the verdict that conceiving was gonna be a no-go for her.

There was nothing to be sad about. The future was bright and beautiful and rose-scented. Pun intended.

The longer I look at the picture, the more my heart seems to be strangling me from the inside out. So I quickly tuck it back in my desk and slam the drawer closed. But it's not fast enough to stop a single rogue tear from racing down my cheek and dropping onto the empty desktop.

I wipe it away, grab my purse, and stand.

I have a meeting with my baby daddy to get to.

∼

When I get to Lifelines Bistro, I order a margarita immediately. If I don't, I'm gonna have a nuclear meltdown. My nerves are frayed beyond belief and I can't stop my hands from shaking.

Alcohol usually does the trick in these kinds of situations.

Unfortunately, no sooner have the words "make it strong" come to the tip of my tongue than do I remember that the entire reason I'm here in the first place precludes me from getting drunk at all.

So with a sigh, I amend to say, "Make it... virgin."

I pick a table in the corner with a vantage point of the front door and sit down. It's quiet in here tonight, which is a little weird for a Chicago Business District bar on a Wednesday at happy hour, but that's one of the reasons I picked it.

I want as few onlookers as possible to witness what might be the most awkward conversation of my life.

Uh, yeah, so we don't know each other, sir, but it seems like we're about to have a baby together.

Cue cringe vomiting.

The virgin margarita disappears down the hatch before I even realize how fast I'm drinking it. I need something to distract myself, even if this is placebo alcohol.

I order another one, mostly just to have something to do with my hands, and that goes down even easier. The thorny, recurring thoughts that have plagued me all day seem to retract their claws a little bit more with each and every sip.

Mocktail or not, it's helping.

I watch the door like a hawk, sparing an eye for the time on my phone every now and then. But fifteen minutes passes by, and no one shows.

Thirty minutes. Nothing.

I'm wearing a scarlet red blouse, just like I told Dr. Saeder to let the sperm donor know, so I'm pretty hard to miss. But as 5:45 P.M. comes and goes, I start to lose faith.

Maybe this was silly. What am I even hoping to gain from it? A co-parent? Someone to replace the role that Rose and Jared were supposed to fill? *Hell* no. Truth is, I don't even want this mystery man to have anything to do with this baby.

I just…

I don't even know. I just want to *meet them,* I guess. To look my baby's father in the face so I understand what kind of person has somehow snuck into the most intimate part of me.

But that's dumb, isn't it? It won't change anything. It won't bring back my family or make my life any less difficult.

This mystery man, whoever it is, can only make things harder.

I'm gathering my bag to go home so I can at least eat some ice cream and put this day from hell to bed when I accidentally knock my phone off the table. I bend down to scoop it up…

But before I can, a huge male hand grabs it from the floor for me.

Horror fills my gut before I even look up. It takes me a moment to understand why.

That scent.

Mint and cedar.

There's only one person in the world who smells exactly like that.

So, with my heartbeat pounding in my temples and the blood rushing in my ears, I drag my gaze from the tiled floor…

Past a pair of gleaming leather loafers…

Skimming up over muscular legs in well-fitted charcoal gray slacks… and a baby-blue-shirt-clad midsection I was fantasizing about literally this morning…

To look in the eyes of the last man on this planet that I would ever want to be the father of my baby.

Dmitri Egorov looks down at me and smolders.

"Seems like you and I have a lot to discuss, Ms. Turner."

3

WREN

This can't be it, can it? He can't possibly be my baby's father? That would just be too cruel for words and fate can't be that vindictive a bitch. I mean, surely I've maxed out my quota of bad luck for one lifetime.

Dmitri probably just walked into Lifelines, saw me, and decided to fuck with my head like he usually does. A little after-work entertainment.

I mean, why not? He's a god amongst men and deities tend to pursue their own twisted pastimes. Torturing mortals being one.

"'Discuss'?" I repeat in a croaky, pipsqueak voice that makes me sound like Elmer Fudd. "Did I miss something in the board meeting today? I took extensive notes. I even—"

"Why are you here?" he interrupts impatiently.

"I'm, er… meeting someone."

One eyebrow arches gracefully as he slides into the table I was just attempting to vacate. "Sit back down."

I stare at him uncertainly. "I really can't—"

"Your meeting has begun." His gaze flickers over my chest. "Red is eye-catching, but green is more your color."

I stiffen instinctively. *Oh, God.* I fall into the booth opposite him and reach for my empty glass, wishing that it was full of something other than virgin anything. *This situation requires hard freaking liquor and lots of it.*

I stand corrected: Fate? Yeah, she's a cruel bitch.

And apparently, she's not done with me yet.

"*You* are my sperm donor." It feels weird saying the words out loud to Dmitri. It's like talking to your mother about sex.

His expression is a cross between annoyance and discomfort. He puts his forearms on the table and clasps his hands together. *Why do I feel like I'm being judged?* "I'm no donor, Ms. Turner. It seems that I was subjected to the same spectacular incompetence that you were."

My hands keep skirting around the table, looking for something to hold onto. *Stop fidgeting, for Christ's sake! Act cool!* "I didn't peg you for the kind of man who wanted to be a father."

Shit. Did I just say that?

Out loud, no less?

He leans forward on his elbows, his lips curling into a half-sneer. "And I didn't peg you for the type of woman who was capable of being a mother."

It's like he's just poured a bucket of ice cubes down my back. That piercing gaze of his skewers me unapologetically, waiting for a reaction.

Well, *screw him*—I'm not gonna give him the satisfaction.

"I handle your bullshit all day long. Compared to that, a baby's gonna be a piece of cake."

His upper lip stiffens and he leans back. I'd like to consider that a retreat, but if there's anything I've learned about Dmitri Egorov in the last fourteen months that I've worked for him, it's that the man never backs down.

You don't amass a billion-dollar company at the ripe old age of thirty-six by being nice and deferential. At this point, I'm starting to think that no one gets *anywhere* by being nice and deferential.

It certainly hasn't done me a damn bit of good.

"Just because some of my DNA has inadvertently found its way into your womb, Ms. Turner, doesn't make you any less my employee. It doesn't make me any less your boss."

My jaw clenches. "I'm off the clock."

"I told you when I hired you: this job is twenty-four-seven. Much like this second job you've decided to take on." He tilts his chin toward my belly just in case I was unclear on what this "second job" might consist of.

My heart is thrumming hard against my chest. I'm so sick of playing it cool. I've got a breakdown percolating in the center of my chest and the pressure to release is building. His presence is not helping matters whatsoever.

Of all the men in the world, why did it have to be him?

"What are we going to do?"

I want to cry, but those sterling silver eyes of his leave zero room for vulnerability. "Let me make one thing clear, Ms.

Turner: there is no *we*. There is you. There is me. And then there's the fetus."

The word makes me flinch. *Fetus.* It's cold and clinical; it doesn't capture even a fraction of all the emotions bound up in this little bundle inside of me. "Let *me* make one thing clear, *Mr.* Egorov: I'm keeping this baby."

His lips twitch. "Why?"

"'Why'? Is that a real question?"

He presses forward, sending a fresh wave of his scent wafting toward me. "That sorry excuse for a doctor made a stupid mistake. This is not the route that either one of us was planning into parenthood. So why continue with it?"

For the first time since my pregnancy was confirmed, my hand lands on my stomach. "Because, mistake or not, this baby is *mine.*"

My forearms erupt in goosebumps. *Mine:* it's not a thought I had at all in the months preceding Rose and Jared's deaths. It was always *their* baby, never mine. There was never a moment when I felt any sense of possession over the child I'd agreed to carry for my sister and brother-in-law.

Then again—back in those days, I wasn't pregnant yet.

And they were still alive.

Things have changed.

"Wren." My eyes snap to Dmitri's. It throws me for a loop any time he says my first name, and now, it's happened twice in one day. "Be reasonable. You can have another baby under better circumstances. I'd pay for the procedure myself, if that's what it takes."

Hot color rushes to my cheeks. I'm undecided on if I'm more shocked or insulted by the offer. "I presume that, since you were using the same fertility clinic as me, you wanted to have a baby, too." He says nothing apart from flattening his lips into a thin line. I take that as a yes but with caveats. "And yet you seem intent on trying to convince me to get rid of this baby. Am I to assume that this is not about the baby at all? This is about *me*?"

He reclines in his chair and starts tapping the table with one finger. In the quiet of the cafe, it feels unnerving. I can only assume that's intentional.

"I'm not good enough to carry your baby?" I press. "Is that it?"

His eyebrows cave inwards in a deep scowl. "If it were solely a biological question of carrying my baby, I'd tolerate—" *Tolerate, jeez, what a gentleman.* "—having you as my surrogate. But I'm guessing you're not willing to relinquish your maternal rights."

"No," I snap forcefully. "I'm not."

He nods. "Which is precisely why I'm suggesting that it might be simpler to just end things here. So that we don't have to resort to the hassle of coparenting."

Coparenting.

Coparenting with Dmitri Egorov.

That's the stuff of nightmares.

"Jesus," I mutter under my breath. "Where's the waitress? I need another drink."

Ironically, the moment Dmitri glances towards the bar, a waitress materializes not even five seconds later.

"Vodka for me," he orders with a smile that doesn't quite touch his eyes. "And for the lady—"

"Rum and Coke. Hold the rum."

The waitress doesn't look amused by my lame joke, but Dmitri does, if only for a moment. If his mouth relaxes any more, he might be in danger of smiling. And that's saying something, because a smile from Dmitri Egorov is like sighting fucking Bigfoot.

The waitress throws some seriously suggestive side-eye at Dmitri as she leaves. But I'm pretty sure he doesn't notice because he's focused solely on me.

His attention doesn't feel like the flattering variety, though. It feels more of the *how-am-I-gonna-handle-this-inconvenient-little-problem* variety.

"Listen… I'm not looking for a co-parent," I say haltingly. "If that's why you thought I wanted to meet, it's not. I guess I… I just wanted to know who the father of my baby was."

He's staring intently at me through half-lidded eyes. "I'd like to reiterate: I am not a sperm donor; I am the *father*. You don't get to meet me and walk away and never have to think about me again."

I snort quietly. *Fat chance of that.* Even if he weren't the baby daddy I never wanted, Dmitri is still the bosshole from hell. And somehow, fate has seen fit to tie us together in one of the most intimate ways possible.

The most ironic thing about all of this? Fate has me knocked up with Dmitri Egorov's baby and we skipped right over what would have been the fun part. Which is what I'm sure would have been hot, sweaty, passionate sex. The kind of sex that involved his teeth marks on parts of my body. My claw marks on parts of his.

I meet that severe scowl of his with an unblinking gaze of my own. "Yeah, well, *ditto*."

In Egorov Industries, he's my boss and I'm his subordinate. But right here, right now? We're on equal footing. I'm not about to let him intimidate or manipulate me into letting him have all the control.

I guess coparenting has already begun.

I want to vomit at the sheer thought of it.

His lips press together in a hard line and he glances at his Patek Philippe as though this meeting has been a gigantic waste of his time.

"So we find ourselves at an impasse."

I shrug. "Guess so."

"First thing's first: we need to make sure."

Frowning, I start tapping at the table with my nails just like Dmitri was doing a moment ago. "Sure of what? Dr. Saeder confirmed it this morning."

Dmitri's lower lip curls with contempt. "You mean the same inept, ancient reptile who mixed up our samples? Forgive me if I'd prefer a second opinion."

I bite back a laugh. "Point taken. It's just that they ran several tests—"

"The tests wouldn't be for you; they would be to prove paternity. I need to make sure the child you're carrying is actually *mine*."

Mine. It's weird enough when I say it; it's ten times weirder when he does.

There's a whole lot of possessiveness there already. I can feel it skittering along my spine and, weirdly enough, it doesn't feel totally paternal. Nor is it affectionate. More like… business-minded. Like we're discussing his intellectual property, not his possible child.

I suppose that's the last hope I can cling to. If it turns out he's not the father, then I can continue with this pregnancy without the burden of an arrogant, demanding, billionaire baby daddy strapped to my hip for the next eighteen years.

If it turns out he is the father… well, then surely that entitles me to a few extra months of maternity leave, right?

The waitress comes back with our drinks. My Coke on the rocks is offered without so much as a glance in my direction. But Dmitri's vodka is set down with a smile that makes me want to roll my eyes until they never come back down.

"There you go, sir. Anything else I can get you?"

Those silver eyes slide to me. "Are you hungry, Wren?"

"N-no," I stutter out of pure panic. I was mentally prepared for drinks with a stranger, not a whole meal with my boss. My survival instincts have already kicked into flight mode. *Run far away and never return,* they're screaming. I just want to get back home to solidify my butt imprint on the sofa and finish up the half-eaten tub of Häagen-Dazs that's calling out to me from the freezer.

I might have to take it easy on the fancy ice cream now that I'm with child, though. Babies are expensive.

"I'm good," I add so as not to be rude. Then, reluctantly, "… Thanks."

His face ripples with what I can only assume is relief. I try not to take that personally. Just because he handles curveballs with an immaculate poker face doesn't mean he isn't just as worried and uncomfortable as I am.

"This is why you seemed off this morning." There it is again: that softness in his face, same as I saw earlier today.

Just like then, it makes me terrifyingly uncomfortable.

My stomach twists. "Yes… I had just found out."

For a moment, I consider telling him about everything that brought us here. About how this pregnancy was never meant to be about me. It was all for them: the last two people in the world that I could call family.

But I clamp my mouth shut at the final moment and reach for my Coke instead. There's no point in sharing the personal shitshow that is my life with Dmitri Egorov.

For one, he definitely doesn't care.

For another, he's still my boss.

And whichever way this paternity result goes, I *need* to keep this job.

"Hand me your phone," Dmitri commands abruptly.

"Excuse me?"

"I'm giving you my personal number. If anything comes up—and I mean *anything* at all—you call me."

"Um, I thought you wanted a paternity test first?" I say, blinking stupidly. "We don't know if the baby is yours yet."

He lets out a little sigh that has my nether regions tingling. "Until we do, I'm working under the assumption that it's mine. And I *always* take care of what is mine."

Mine. What a word. It morphs into something more and more terrifying every time one of us says it.

That tingle spreads slowly until it blankets all of me and sinks lower, lower, lower. It's a dangerous feeling. But what's even more dangerous is the thought that comes with it. As I stare at this infuriating, gorgeous, bossy, protective, rich, arrogant, too-full-of-contradictions-to-be-summed-up-in-one-adjective man, all my mind can conjure up is…

As far as baby daddies go, I could have done a lot worse.

4

DMITRI

"Mr. Egorov."

My mood is bad enough as it is. Seeing this human tracking device lurking in the foyer of my penthouse does not help at all.

"Dante," I spit at him. "Is there a reason you're here?"

"I brought over some Italian spices for Miss Zanetti, courtesy of Don Zanetti."

My Italian has improved over the years, but Don Vittorio Zanetti speaks his own kind of language. "Italian spices" is code. Translation: *I've been sent to check on the Italian princess to make sure this living arrangement sticks.*

I drop my coat into the vanishing cupboard and stride past Dante, who has the gall to follow me into the main living room without invitation. This is the second time this week he's stopped by. I' have enough spices to last me a fucking lifetime.

"Beatrice!" I call out.

Bee twirls into the living room from the arched doorway on the right. She's wearing a slinky silver bathrobe cinched at the waist. "Baby! I thought that was you."

She gallivants into my arms, ignoring Dante, who stands off to the side, blending in with the furniture. She drops a peck on my cheek and slides her hands over my chest. "Hm, I love when you come back home smelling of sweat and money."

Usually, I'm better at playing along with her little charade. But today, my head is throbbing and my patience is wearing thin.

I twist her around and point with my chin. "Your father's lapdog is here."

She laughs. "Yes, I know. I've already thanked him for the spices, and yet he hasn't left. The only reason I can think of for why he's still here is to see you, my love. I think he likes you more than me."

"That would be a first." Dragging my eyes up to face the pale, scrawny man in front of me, I ask, "Well? Do you have anything to say to me, Dante?"

Those dispassionate, watery blue eyes of his betray nothing, but his Adam's apple bobs up and down. "As I said, I only wanted to bring you Don Zanetti's regards, Mr. Egorov."

Bee tilts her head to the side and coos at Dante like he's a baby. "Aw, how sweet. See, Dmitri? Daddy likes you, too."

I grit my teeth and keep my distaste hidden behind an emotionless straight face. "Consider his regards received and returned in kind. Now, if you'll excuse me, it's been a long day and I'd like to relax with my fiancée."

"Of course, sir. Good evening to you both." Dante clears his throat and bows out of the room.

Bee and I wait in our carefully coordinated pose, arms looped around each other's waists. From the foyer, the elevator's automated voice chimes out, "Doors opening... Doors closing."

As soon as I hear the telltale metallic whoosh, I let my arm fall from Bee's hip and we both exhale in unison.

"Thank fucking God," she mumbles, springing away from me. "I've got a hot date tonight, and the last thing I want is to scare her away by smelling like some big, scary man."

I laugh as she dances away and disappears through a doorway in a flash of silver. The vodka I drank earlier is still singeing its way down my throat, but I move to the bar anyway and pour myself another dose in one of the crystal tumblers that Bee gifted me for our "second anniversary."

When she shimmies back into the living room, I'm almost done with my drink and she's dressed in a slinky pink dress that demands attention. Beatrice Zanetti has never been one for subtlety, that's for damn sure.

"Zip me up, will you?" she requests, cavorting around as she pulls her hair in front over one bare shoulder.

"Who's the lucky woman?" I ask uninterestedly as I tug the zipper up to the nape of her neck.

"The hot waitress from last week. The blonde who does that lip bite thing I was telling you about." She spins in place and starts finger combing her hair back to proper order, eyes going all foggy and dreamy as she thinks about her newest conquest.

She's bubbly tonight, which means she's excited about this date. I'm not sure why that irritates me so much. Probably because I'm stuck with a shit ton of complications while she gets to go out on the town and frolic.

"A second date with the same woman? Did hell freeze over?"

Cackling, Bee punches me in the shoulder. "Hey, I dated that ballerina for a full three weeks last summer. I might've even gone for four if she hadn't decided she liked men better."

"Pity." I return my attention to my vodka. It's the best money can buy—clear as glacier melt and just as bracing. I twist it this way and that in my tumbler, watching how it refracts the light into a million little shards.

Normally, it puts me at ease. It's not doing the trick tonight, though. Instead of numbing out the thoughts, it's making them louder and more chaotic.

Bee's smile dwindles as she regards me. "I fucking hate it when you stare at me," I mutter.

"What crawled up your ass and died tonight?" Instead of leaving me to stew like I deserve, she pulls out the bronze barstool next to me and parks her Prada-clad ass down on it.

"Nothing. Leave it alone."

"Never." She drills her nails against the marble countertop. "Remember that promise we made to each other when we were teenagers?"

"No."

"*Dmitri.*"

I scowl and set the tumbler down a little harder than I intended. "Why do you always bring that up?"

She smirks, her amber eyes flashing with mischief. "Because I like making you say it. Go on—you know you want to."

"*Blyat',* Bee. You realize we're in our thirties now, right?"

"I'm waaaitiiing..." she sing-songs.

"Fucking pest," I mumble under my breath half-heartedly. "We promised—"

"Nuh-uh-uh. The whole thing. Spare no detail."

My eyes roll with irritation. "We *pinky* promised—" Bee chuckles delightedly at my correction. "—that we were always going to have each other's backs."

"That's right." She nods in gleeful triumph, just like she always does when she coerces me into playing along with her. "You and me. Mafia mates for life. Bratva buddies forever." She holds out her fist expectantly. "Come onnn, she's waiting for a bump."

I glare at her tiredly and graze my knuckles against hers. "I used to think that you'd tone down as you got older, but I stand corrected. You just get more annoying with age."

Bee bats her eyelashes at me. "Aw, that kinda reminds me of the speech you made right before you proposed. I won't make you recount that one, but just know that it lives in my heart forever. So tender. So vulnerable. So—"

"For the love of fucking God, Bee, give it a rest. I'm not in the mood."

Still grinning from ear to ear, she gives me a sympathetic look. "Then therapy is in session, baby. Tell me what's going on and don't sugar coat anything."

"That bristly old fuck from the clinic called."

"Dr. Saeder? Oh, such a gem. How's his wife doing? Her arthritis was out of control the last time I—" I fix her with a glare that sends her trailing off wide-eyed. "Jeez, okay. We're not talking about Dr. Saeder's wife right now. Noted."

"Not unless it's about arranging a delivery of condolence flowers," I growl. "Because I'm contemplating making a widow of her soon."

Bee straightens up and starts chewing on her bottom lip. "Uh-oh. What happened?"

"My sample was mislabeled at the lab. It's already been used on another client. And… the insemination took."

Her jaw drops; her rapping nails go still—even her breath catches in the crook of her throat. I can only laugh miserably, because that pale-faced, wide-eyed, *this-can't-be-real* expression must be exactly how I looked when I got the call from Saeder earlier today.

My God, was that really today? It's been the longest day of my goddamned life.

But something tells me the days ahead are only going to feel longer.

"You're fucking with me," Bee breathes at last.

I down the dregs of my vodka. "I wish I was."

Her eyes dilate. "*Fuck*. She doesn't even know—Aw, goddammit, she has to be made aware of the situation she's getting herself into. Contracts need to be drawn up; NDAs need to be signed!"

"I'm aware," I growl. "Believe me, I'm very well aware."

She peels her hand off mine, leaving behind only the imprint of her nails. "Okay," she croaks, running her fingertips through her hair. "Okay. Oookay. This isn't ideal, obviously, but…" She turns to me, her eyes brightening. "—this does mean there *is* going to be a baby."

I shake my head. "Unfortunately, it's a lot more complicated than that."

"Are you going to tell me what that means or am I supposed to just start guessing?"

I bend over to snag the bottle from the bar and pour myself another glass of vodka. Everything else is going to shit, so I might as well get drunk, right?

"My sample wasn't inseminated into just any surrogate; it was inseminated into a woman who was using the clinic to have a baby of her own."

Bee's eyebrows flatten. "Fucking hell."

Cold laughter cracks through my lips, which only contributes to the miserable uncertainty hanging in the air between us. "That's not even the worst part."

Bee winces. "What could be worse?"

"The woman who was impregnated with my sample—she's on my payroll. Wren Turner."

She cocks her head to the side as the furrow between her brows deepens while she thinks. "Wren Turner…" she repeats. "Wren… Turner. Why does that name sound so—*wait*! Your *P.A.*?"

I raise my glass in a sardonic cheers. "That's the one."

"This is the green-eyed brunette with the great ass and the knockout smile?"

My forehead puckers. "Uh… sure."

Bee gawks at me open-mouthed before holding up a palm toward me. "Okay, hold on. So let me get this straight. You're telling me that the five-star, super-duper-accredited, state-of-the-art clinic we went to so that we could create a baby without actually having to fuck each other has botched up the surrogacy plan we established *very fucking carefully* and implanted your sperm into the womb of your personal assistant who is now pregnant with what is supposed to be *our baby with each other* but is really *your* baby with *her?*"

I incline my head infinitesimally. "That about sums it up, yeah."

There are a few seconds of silence and then the penthouse fills with the sound of her guffawing.

"Oh… my… *God!*" she gasps through her laughter, tears studding her eyes. "Talk about a cosmic fuck-up! Talk about a sick fucking joke! Talk about…" She breaks up again into more gales of laughter, hugging her ribs with both hands like she's going to explode if she keeps going.

While she cackles, I sit and drink.

And drink.

And drink.

When she's finally done and seated back on the stool next to mine, she wheezes. "Pass me the tissues, will you? I'm gonna fucking laugh-cry my makeup off." She dabs her eyes with the tissues. "*Well.* Doesn't this just go to show, huh?"

"Go to show what, exactly?" I demand irritably.

"Hell if I know." She shrugs, the ironic smile lingering on her face. "Definitely something, though. Maybe it's the universe telling us that you and I were never meant to have a baby together and we shouldn't try to cheat Mother Nature."

"Neither Mother Nature nor the universe need to tell us shit. You and I already knew it shouldn't happen. It's your father that needs to get the fucking message."

Bee's eyes tighten and darken, the way they always do anytime her father is mentioned. "Hell really would have to freeze over before that happened." She eyes the drink in my hand. "Gimme that." She downs it in one glug and wrinkles her nose as she deposits the glass back into my hand. "Fuck, that's strong."

I let my gaze go unfocused as I stare into the window over the sink. It's dark out, so I see our own faces reflected back at us. Mine is stony, shuttered, grim.

But as I look, Bee's melts and morphs into someone else's.

Into *Wren's*, from the moment she looked up and saw me approaching her at the bistro. The shock that bordered on horror. The nerves that bordered on panic. She was a ticking time bomb and I was a lit fuse coming to blow her world the fuck up.

"She wants the baby," I murmur, almost to myself.

Bee's jaw drops and she clutches my elbow again in both hands. "You already *spoke* to her?"

"I had to meet the woman carrying my baby," I explain, running a hand through my hair. "I didn't expect it to be *her*."

"Hm."

I hate when she makes that sound and she knows it. "What?" I snap, skewering her with an angry glare.

She plays it coy, shrugging innocently as she uncrosses and recrosses her legs. "Is this going to pose an additional complication for you?"

"I have no idea what you're talking about."

Bee smiles thinly and holds up her hands. "Oh my, did I touch a nerve?"

If she were anyone else, I'd bite her head off, but there's no point getting all worked up. Bee is the only person in the world who isn't in the least bit affected by my anger. As my oldest friend and ally, she's also the only person who's safe from it.

"Can I ask how the meeting went?" she ventures.

I'm already jonesing for another drink, but I resist the urge this time. "Did you not hear me? She wants to keep the baby. So I'd say not fucking great."

Bee's eyebrows hit the roof of her forehead. "Are you seriously telling me you tried to get her to agree to terminate the pregnancy?"

I pounce out of the barstool and start pacing. "It's not what any of us wanted! I mean, *fuck,* it's bad enough that I'm being forced into having an heir. I didn't sign up to have a baby with some random civilian woman. And I saw the look on her face when she realized why I was in that restaurant tonight. She doesn't want my DNA in her baby any more than I want hers in mine."

Bee swivels her stool in my direction, one eyebrow arched high. That expression usually means I won't like what's coming next.

"You know… this *could* work."

"Fucking hell," I mumble. "Don't start."

"I'm serious."

"I know you are. Which is why I'm pissed off."

She snorts. "Oh, no—you're pissed off because you don't have control anymore. And you *haaate* when things happen outside of your control."

I pause my pacing and narrow my eyes in her direction. "She's a problem, Bee."

"Might that opinion have a little something to do with the fact that you're attracted to her?"

Scowling, I twist around so I can pace away without having to look her in the eyes. "Quit with that bullshit."

She chuckles and jangles the bracelets on her wrists. "I know your type, Dmitri. And she's definitely your type."

"She's more your type than mine."

"Maybe. But the only reason I didn't hit on her at that gala was because of the way *you* looked at her. I know how you are: territorial."

I shake my head, still keeping my gaze rooted on the path my feet are walking. "You don't know me as well as you think you do."

"Oh, wouldn't you like me to believe that?" she scoffs. "The truth is, this unexpected little petri dish mix-up baby might be a blessing in disguise."

"You *want* this baby?" I gawk at her. "You're actually going to fight for a fetus that's not yours?"

She pops off her stool and sashays over to me. "Like it or not, we're getting *married*, D. What's yours is mine—which means that baby is mine, too. I don't really care how it happened; the point is, it *did* happen. So now, it's time to deal with the situation."

She rests a reassuring hand on my shoulder. I scowl and shrug it off. "You are a pain in the ass, Zanetti."

She blows me a kiss. "I love you, too, baby. Now, I'm already late for my date. I'll see you tomorrow. Good night, fiancé."

She grabs her purse and heads out while I walk my ass back to the bar and pour myself yet another drink. I'm not sure why I'm restricting myself anymore; it's not like Elena's here to wrinkle her nose at the smell.

She hated vodka—but she loved me.

That made all the difference.

I don't have the luxury of brooding about El, though. Not when I have a fake fiancée and a pregnant personal assistant on my hands. Beatrice was right: I do need a plan—and it starts with that miserable sack of shit, Dr. Saeder.

It starts with a paternity test.

It starts with figuring out if my pretty little assistant actually has the guts to carry a *pakhan's* heir.

5

WREN

"You okay, honey?"

I blink fast, flinching as Lory steps into my line of vision, drawing my focus with her big dreadlocks and even bigger grin.

"Hey, Lory. No, sorry... I'm just a little preoccupied."

She reaches out and gives my arm a playful squeeze. "Alrighty then, keep your secrets, girl. Can I get you anything? Oh, wait, I know." She digs a hand into her pocket and pulls out some candy. "I've got peanut caramel and salted almond. Take your pick. Can't go wrong."

I have to fight to make myself smile. I stare for way too long at the two pieces of candy on Lori's callused palm. The fluorescent lights above me make their wrappers shine a little brighter, almost as though they're winking at me.

"I-I'm good, thanks," I stutter after an uncomfortable length of time has passed. My voice sounds small. Like I'm scared of speaking too loudly. Like I'm worried about taking up too much space.

"Suit yourself, dear. Dr. Saeder should be here soon." Her forehead puckers and that smile dims. "I, um… I was real sorry to hear about your sister." Her voice is tissue-paper soft and tender. "She was a lovely girl."

"Yeah. She was."

"And I heard her… her husband passed away in the same accident?"

I swallow. It aches all the way down. "Yes."

"I lit a candle in church for the both of them. I don't know if you're religious or not, but—"

I blink away my tears. "I'll take prayers any day, religious or not."

Lory pats my knee. "I lost my mother a few years ago. The year after, my husband passed, too. It does get better," she promises. "It takes time, but it does get better." She gives me an encouraging wink and slips out of the room.

As soon as the door closes behind her, I pop off the examination table I've been sitting on until my legs fell asleep and start pacing around the room.

I've become insatiably restless this past week. Sitting still, sleeping soundly—those are things of the distant past. I can't even pretend I don't know why.

Though it has less to do with the fact that I'm pregnant and more to do with who I'm pregnant by.

Obviously, I'd expected work to be awkward and uncomfortable. At the very least, I figured there'd be tension.

But when I walked into Dmitri's office the next morning, he looked at me like nothing whatsoever had changed.

"Do you have the notes from yesterday's meeting, Ms. Turner?"

For a moment, I genuinely thought he was talking about our after-hours meeting at the bistro. *He wants my notes,* I'd thought. *Well, if he's asking...*

Bottom line: I don't want you to be involved in this pregnancy or the life of my baby because A) you scare the shit out of me; B) you're my boss; and C) I'm unreasonably attracted to your specific brand of douchebaggery.

So, considering the correct answer is D) all the above, I'd prefer we just forget the meeting ever happened and go back to quietly loathing each other. Cool? Cool.

It was only when he cleared his throat that I realized belatedly he was talking about business as usual. I gave him what he asked for, face burning bright red, and escaped back to my desk as soon as I could manage it.

Business as usual. I can deal with that. Or at least, that's what I thought I'd be dealing with, until Dr. Saeder called to ask when I could come in for the paternity test that the "father" had scheduled on my behalf.

Now, here I am, two days later... waiting.

Nothing about this feels like "business as usual."

The door swings open without a knock. I'm expecting Dr. Saeder, but in walks a Greek god wrapped in an Armani suit and a permanent scowl.

I stop short. "What are *you* doing here?"

"You have an appointment in a few minutes," Dmitri says, as if I'm not painfully aware of that fact. He walks over to the chair in the corner of the room and drops down like he owns it. "Where is that old turtle?"

I snort with laughter, if only because I've made the exact same comparison in my head countless times before. I cover it up with a cough and try to act stern. "If this is about the results of the paternity test, I haven't got them back yet."

"I'm aware. We'll get them in a second."

My knees buckles, so I decide to sit down before someone has to scrape a puddle of Wren off the floor. It was probably naïve of me, but I genuinely hadn't expected Dmitri to show up today. Wishful thinking, I guess.

Mine. The way his mouth looked as he pronounced that word flashes in my mind again. I shudder and shake the image away.

The fluorescent lights crackling above us feel almost ominous now. I could almost swear they're getting louder. I close my eyes for a moment and press my fingers against my temples.

"Are you alright?"

I drop my hands and look up. "Who, me?"

One eyebrow arches imperceptibly. "Do you see anyone else in the room with us?"

"I don't—no. I mean, yes, I'm fine. Just… overwhelmed."

Dmitri's resting face is usually a trademark blend of arrogant impatience and brusque steeliness that borders on apathy. But right now, there are lines at the corners of his eyes that

I've never noticed before. He's leaning in just a little bit, too, almost as though he's concerned.

"Getting what you want is not all it's cracked up to be, huh?"

"Gee, aren't you just a fount of optimism?" I mutter.

His lips twist upwards, but before it can morph into a proper smile, the door opens and Dr. Saeder slinks in, looking like he's one harsh sneeze away from peeing his pants in fear.

He offers me an uneasy smile and then he spots Dmitri, at which point urine becomes even more imminent. I'm pretty sure even his nose hairs are standing on end.

"Good evening, Ms. Turner." He directs one of those dramatic bows in Dmitri's direction. "Mr. Egorov."

"Are those the results?" Dmitri asks, cutting right to the chase.

"I-it is. Er, they are. Yes. Indeed."

"Well, go ahead. We don't need a fucking drumroll."

Clumsily, the doctor unfolds the paper in his hand and scans through the results. He pales visibly. That tiny little hesitation is all I needed. I close my eyes so the sound of blood rushing through my ears like a flash flood doesn't overwhelm me.

"Congratulations, Mr. Egorov," he mumbles weakly. "You're the father."

The blood thrums louder. "Maury Povich doesn't have shit on me," I whisper.

I peek at the other person whose life just changed irreversibly. Dmitri's jaw clenches tight. One hand curls into a fist as he gets to his feet and strides over to the examination table.

Is he going to throw a punch? Dr. Saeder certainly seems to think so, because he takes a few stumbling steps back and almost topples right into the sonogram machine.

"I want to know the sex. Today." Dmitri's voice is curt but quiet. Calm before the storm, if I had to guess.

"Er, well, uh—yes, yes, we can find out today."

"*What?*" I gasp. "As in—right now?"

"Right now," Dr. Saeder confirms, clearly relieved to still be standing with an intact nose. "Would you lie down for me, Ms. Turner?"

I recline back against the examination table robotically as Dmitri stations himself by my shoulder. He's looking at the screen, but I'm looking at him.

Is this really happening? Is he sticking around? Is he actually going to be involved?

Cold fingers and even colder wands poke and prod at my exposed belly. I stare up at the lights until my vision is just one big field of crackling black and white, that blood in my ears still rushing loudly. My heart is galloping so hard that I almost miss the part where Dr. Saeder tells us what I'm having.

"Wait!" I exclaim, sitting up a little. "Say that again?"

Dr. Saeder looks back at the screen and rolls the pointer over the pulsing little alien inside me. "It appears to be a boy."

"A boy," I breathe. "A boy."

All I can see now is the blue blanket that Rose knitted the week she thought she was pregnant. I still have it stored away somewhere in a box marked with her name. She was in the process of knitting a pink one, too, just in case, when she'd gotten her period. She cried for a week afterwards. I spent every day of that week at her side, telling her that she could try again soon. That it wasn't over yet.

"That blanket won't go to waste, Rosie," I whispered in her ear with my arm around her. *"You're going to have your baby boy one day. Just you wait and see."*

I'm vaguely aware of Dmitri snarling more questions from his spot at my shoulder. But I'm distracted by the heaviness that's gathering in my chest like storm clouds. I do *not* want to break down in front of either one of these men.

"I'll give you a moment," Dr. Saeder blurts unexpectedly before fleeing out of the room.

I bite down on my tongue and pinch the soft part of my elbow and stare at the screen as hard as I can, but it's still not enough to keep the tears from slipping down my cheeks.

The only thing I can do now is lie and pretend I'm fine.

I feel Dmitri's eyes on me, but I don't return the gaze. I don't want his scorn or his pity, though I'm not sure which of those two would hurt me more. I'm relieved when he turns and walks away.

But he only gets as far as the shelf and cabinets built into the far side of the room. I watch through tear-blurred eyes as he snatches a fistful of tissues out of the box and returns to my side.

Numbly, I hold a hand out to take them from him. My fingers shake in the empty air between us. I'm halfway to adding a mumbled "thank you," when he pushes my hand gently aside, bends over, and starts to dab the ultrasound jelly off of my stomach.

The gasp flutters out through my lips involuntarily. "Y-you don't have to do that." He just ignores me and continues. "Seriously," I insist. "I can do it."

I can't quite explain it but if he continues to do what he's doing, I might just have a full-blown meltdown. His eyes rise to mine. Under the fluorescents, the silver gray of his irises has turned a teal blue.

"Let it out," he says.

And that's all it takes. Three magic words and then *boom,* an ugly sob explodes out of my mouth, breaking open the floodgates. I lie there, crying desperately as Dmitri Egorov wipes my belly clean with a tenderness that does not in any way line up with the cruel, arrogant asshole I thought I knew.

By the time I'm done crying, I feel dehydrated and exhausted. At least my stomach's clean, though.

"Here." He hands me a glass of water. "Drink."

I take it wordlessly and finish the whole glass in one shot. He removes the glass from my hand before I can even offer it back to him. As nice as it is to have someone here with me, I'm wary of his presence. I'm nervous of his expectations.

Is his concern legitimate? Or is he just using it to manipulate me?

"Dr. Saeder mentioned that you've been having trouble keeping down your prenatal vitamins."

I glance at him through my eyelashes. With the lingering tears caught in them, he looks like an Impressionist painting, all vague suggestions of color and light and shadow. It's eerily beautiful. "Yeah. They make me nauseous."

He nods. "He's going to prescribe more options to see which ones are best suited for you. I want you to take them daily without fail."

I push myself upright. "I have too many as it is. I don't need all that."

Those eyes are so piercing they leave a tingle on my skin every time he looks directly at me. "This isn't a negotiation, Wren."

There he goes, using my name again. I wish it didn't make me shiver and melt at the same time the way it does.

"You're right; it sure as hell isn't. It's *my* body and *my* choice. You don't get a say."

His lips pull back in a half-formed scowl. "As long as you're carrying *my* baby, I do," he snarls. "In fact, consider your well-being my sole concern from now on."

I swing my legs off the side of the examination table and jump off it. Nothing about this scenario feels right.

Rose was meant to be my partner in this.

Not *him.*

"Speaking of which," he adds right before I can start unloading onto him, "I'm giving you a promotion."

I drop my coat and whirl around. "A what?"

"You're going to be my P.A.."

"Is it pregnancy brain, or did you just say that you were going to give me a promotion for a job I already have?"

"The job you already have encompasses my work at Egorov Industries. I need a P.A. *outside* of work—someone to handle all my personal affairs."

I flinch at the sound of that word. For most people, it's *"panties"* or *"moist,"* words that make your skin crawl without even trying. For me, it's *"affair."* Has been since I was seven years old and I found Mom curled up on her bedroom floor, crying into Dad's smoke-infused work shirt with the lipstick mark on the collar. The disgusting clicheness of it all didn't make it hurt any less.

"That's a bogus job," I snap. "It's just a way for you to control—" I stop short as the door opens and a male nurse I've never seen before walks in. He glances between the two of us awkwardly and then redirects over to the off-white cabinets in a way that strikes me as clumsy and confused. *Weird.*

I turn back to Dmitri distractedly. "I don't want you messing around with my life."

Dmitri's eyes are fixed on the nurse behind me. "It's a little too late for that, don't you think?"

I sigh frustratedly. "This may be your baby, but *I'm* the mother. If you want to be involved, we can work something out. But there's a way to do it that gives me space."

You'd think that would be considered a reasonable suggestion by anyone with half a heart, but Dmitri's lip curls in a stubborn sneer. "I—"

Bang. Clatter. Clang. I toss an annoyed glance over my shoulder at the clueless nurse who seems intent on lingering in the room for this faceoff.

"Hate to break it to you, Ms. Turner, but you're not going to get space. Not now that you're carrying my heir."

"I'm having a baby, not a prince."

His sneer becomes more pronounced as he takes a step towards me. "You're wrong about that." My skin tingles with unease. "In fact, you don't know how wrong you are."

I'm trying to formulate some kind of response when I catch a flash of movement from my peripheral vision. The male nurse—running at me with his arm raised. Something gleams in his hand.

Is that a knife?

Surely that's against hospital protocol.

6

WREN

God hits the *Slow Motion* button.

I see the gleam of the knife as it hurtles towards me.

I hear the crinkle of the definitely-not-a-fucking-nurse's baby blue scrubs.

I see every pore in his face, every acne scar, every hair he missed shaving. As he gets closer, his eyes wide and bloodshot, I note with a weird sense of unemotional detachment that I can really see pretty far up his nose from this angle.

Then God hits the *Panic* button.

That's a *knife* in the man's hand.

And that knife is coming for *me*.

He may be moving in slow motion right now, but I feel as though I am, too. I try to move my body—*Throw yourself out of the way, you dumb bitch!*—but my limbs are heavy and unresponsive. Even doing something utterly useless like screaming would cost precious energy that I simply don't have.

Oh, God—

The knife is arcing down for my exposed belly when I get knocked to the side by some invisible force. As soon as that happens, reality snaps back to normal speed.

Dmitri is a blur as he inserts himself between me and the nurse. His fist clamps around the man's knife-wielding hand, suspending it in midair. I see veins on each man's forearm bulging as they struggle over which way the blade will fall.

With a guttural snarl, Dmitri wrenches the nurse's hand hard. The knife goes clattering to the floor and skitters to a stop right at my feet. I look down at it and see myself reflected in the metal. I look really dumb with my jaw hanging wide open like this.

But before the knife has even stopped wobbling, I hear more commotion and I look up…

… to see that the nurse is pulling a gun out of his waistband.

A gun. That's a twist.

The only time I've ever seen a firearm is on television. It's a silly, abstract concept when you're watching it on a screen.

But there's nothing remotely silly or abstract about the gleaming black pistol waving around that single black cyclops eye of death.

If someone pulls the trigger when that eye is looking at me, I'll die. My baby will die. And after everything Rose, Jared, and I went through to make sure this baby had a chance to exist, I'm not about to risk losing him this soon.

I collapse to my knees behind the exam table. It's about as shitty as hiding spots get in terms of actually protecting me, and I can't see a damn thing, but it's better than just standing plastered against the wall like the loser kid at a school dance, gawking as two men grapple over whether my life ends today or not.

When I risk a glance back up, I see Dmitri and the nurse are fighting for control over the gun. The nurse is a big man, too, but his movements are clumsy and slow.

Dmitri, on the other hand, is like a panther in Armani. He stoops over and slams a hard uppercut into the nurse's gut. The man *oofs* in pain, Dmitri elbows his free hand, and for the second time in this longest minute of my life, a deadly weapon goes bouncing across the floor to land at my feet.

It's only when I instinctively reach for it that I realize my hand is shaking. I'm afraid to touch anything, least of all a gun that might go off in my hand if I do something stupid with it. So I toe it under the exam table instead.

"Fuck!" someone hisses as I hear the crunch of breaking bone.

Wincing, it strikes me that if Dmitri doesn't win this fight, I'll be a sitting duck. My eyes go back to the gun. *Should I...?*

But I'm not the only one who has their eyes on it. The nurse elbows Dmitri in the stomach and lunges forward. Ignoring the fear pumping through my body, I slide out of my hiding spot and reach to get it before he can.

But I'm too slow.

His hand lands on the gun before mine does. He looks me dead in the eye. His pupils are blown wide, swallowing his whole iris up in pure, bottomless black, as his lips curl into a sneer.

I freeze.

Oh, God, please...

That's when Dmitri appears at the nurse's back like a mirage. He grabs a fistful of the nurse's hair and pulls his head back, exposing his neck. I catch the gleam of the knife's blade before it slashes across the nurse's throat.

It feels cinematographic, almost cartoonish, the way the blood sprays out of his neck. A sprinkler of thick red going off. I feel its weight as it splashes across my face, warm and sticky and congealed.

The nurse's eyes, which were so fixated on me a moment ago, go blank. He collapses right in front of me, still leaking and twitching. How is it possible that one man could hold so much blood?

It's not real. It can't be real...

"Wren."

I flinch, backing away from the voice and the large presence that's hovering over me. The concept of having a voice is a distant memory right now, but if he or anyone touches me, I just might scream.

Dmitri kneels down in front of me. He's bleeding from his bottom lip but his face is otherwise unscathed. Why am *I* the one covered in blood?

"Wren, look at me."

He doesn't make any attempt to touch me. He just stays where he is, watching me with his eyebrows relaxed and his mouth a thin, grim slash. He's not even breathing hard.

"You're okay," he says gently. "You're safe now."

The blood is hardening on my face. I can *smell* it. That metallic taint.

I shake my head. "I-I'm gonna b-be… s-sick—"

Almost as soon as I say it, I duck to one side and throw up all over the gleaming white floors. I don't even have time to pull back my hair. But strangely, it doesn't get in my way as I deposit my guts onto the floor.

Even after there's nothing left to come out, I dry heave until my stomach starts cramping. When I finally stop, I realize that my hair didn't get in the way because *he's* holding it back.

And that soft, soothing stroke I can feel on my back? Yeah, that's him, too.

"Wren." His voice is so damn soft, so damn gentle. It actually does help me, at least a little. The fact that I can't see the blood or the body is helping, too. It's easier to pretend it's not *him* who's doing all this. "Stay where you are. I'm going to get you out of here."

That sounds pretty fantastic, all things considered, so I don't bother questioning it. I stay where I am, trying to make myself as small as I can to avoid the blood puddle on my right and the vomit puddle on my left.

After a few moments of shuffling and what sounds like Dmitri's fingers tapping on his phone, I see his feet reenter my field of vision. When he lifts me into his arms, my body goes slack like it's been waiting all this time for a signal to power down.

I'm vaguely aware of voices. I close my eyes and try to shut them out. *I'll be home soon. Everything will be fine when I'm back home.*

He smells nice. Mint and cedar. It's a dramatic improvement over blood, vomit, and ultrasound jelly, I can promise you that much.

I hear the *shoop* of a van door sliding open and I open my eyes again. I'm placed on the floor of an open trunk and Dmitri sits down next to me. The blood on his lip is still there, a tiny smear of crimson. It's bizarre how my fingers itch to wipe it away. A face that beautiful shouldn't have blood on it.

Then again, something about it makes him more human.

"I… I c-can't move," I whisper, wondering if he can even hear me or if I'm just talking in my own head.

His eyes follow my lips. "Yes, you can." His voice is calm and alert. "You're just in shock."

But that can't be true. I've been in shock before. The moment when I was told about Rose and Jared's accident—*that* had been shock. I'd stared at the policewoman they sent to break the news to me and said, "What?" She had to repeat the details of the accident in their entirety three more times before it finally began to sink in.

"I feel… heavy."

"It's the blood. I'm going to wash it off you now, okay?"

I blink at him. His face comes into high relief and I exhale sharply. Those silver eyes of his really are mesmerizing. I focus on them, because the only alternative is falling apart in the back of the van and wailing like a stuck pig, and I refuse to dissolve that far just yet.

He lifts a damp towel to my face and starts rubbing the blood off me. It's like he did with the tissues and the ultrasound jelly what feels like a lifetime ago, though it can't have been more than half an hour.

So much has changed since then, but the tenderness in his touch hasn't.

The care in his fingertips hasn't.

As he keeps cleaning my face, I backslide into a strange sense of déjà vu. Has this happened to me before?

No, not quite this, of course. But I do remember passing a damp towel over Rose's face a few years ago, the same way Dmitri is doing to me now. She was shaking with sobs as she gripped the edges of the bathtub.

It was her fifth miscarriage, her second that year. Her mind was spent, her body weak, but still, she kept banging her fists against her flat, bruised stomach.

"I hate my body!" she cried. *"I hate this body. It can't hold a baby. It can't grow a baby, so what the fuck is the point of it?"*

I was forced to hold back my own tears as I washed the blood from between her legs. *"Your body is strong, Rosie. And so are you. Strong enough to heal. And strong enough to get through this."*

But nothing I said could penetrate through her grief. She mourned each miscarriage like it was a fully-formed baby that she had carried nine months and pushed out whole.

Honk. Honk. Honk.

The blaring of horns just outside the darkly tinted windows of the van pulls me back to the present. Dmitri pulls his hand back and my skin aches for him to touch me again. I can still smell him on me, though—that copper scent of death twined in with the mint, with the cedar, with the tang of his sweat.

When I glance down, I notice blood is all over my clothes. *I'll never be able to wear this blouse again.* That's the only kind of thought I'm capable of processing right now: dumb, simple, irrelevant. *Not even the dry cleaners can get that stain out.*

Dmitri squints out the window. "We'll be there soon."

I glance through the tinted window behind his head. If I concentrate hard, I can make out the outline of buildings as we drive past.

It takes me a moment to place where we are. This area isn't right. The buildings are too big and intimidating, the streets are too pretty, the people are too well-dressed to belong to my part of the city.

"What's going on?" I croak. "Where are we going?"

"My place."

The unease in my chest stirs back up again. "I want to go home. *My* home."

He doesn't look my way. In fact, he seems intent on avoiding that for as long as possible. "For the foreseeable future, it's best you consider my place your home."

My throat tightens. I grip the window tightly, my knuckles turning white. "Why?"

Those silver eyes slide to mine. "Because what happened back there was not an accident or a mistake. It was an assassination attempt."

Assassination attempt. That's not a real thing. James Bond says stuff like "assassination attempt." That's what popes worry about, not personal assistants.

But here? Now? In my life? No freaking way.

Then again, I suppose it's not that crazy. Nothing makes sense anymore and it hasn't for a long time. So I do the only thing I can do under the circumstances: I ask the most obvious question.

"Who would want to kill me?"

He shakes his head. "Not you." His eyes snake down to my stomach. "My heir."

There's that word again. But this time…

I don't feel like laughing.

7

WREN

The van doors open to reveal sleek mosaic tile, glistening like fish scales. It's quite possibly the most beautiful thing I've ever seen, and we're not even inside yet. This is just the walled driveway that precedes the gilded façade of The Muse at Haven Crest.

Never in my wildest dreams did I imagine I'd be walking into the city's most luxurious penthouse condo building at all—much less with blood on my face and the taste of vomit on my lips.

I'm waiting for someone to stop me and turn me away at the revolving door. *I'm sorry, Miss—no lost causes, hot messes, or unpleasantly poor people allowed.* As a proud member of all three categories, I guess I'm triply denied.

No one could ever accuse me of underachieving.

But no one so much as bats an eyelid, either, as we walk through the massive, marble-drenched atrium towards the elevators. Five sets of brass double doors stand at attention in a neat row. Dmitri leads me to the centermost one and punches in a number that I don't catch.

I'm not doing a great job of retaining much of anything at the moment. My nerves feel like they've been rubbed raw, like they might snap at any moment.

"Doors opening."

I flinch at the weirdly sultry robot voice that welcomes us into the elevator. The bottom half of the car is padded in a jade green velvety fabric, while the top half is armored with infinity mirrors.

"Doors closing."

An endless procession of duplicates of my reflection stares back at me, blinking when I blink, moving when I move. But none of it feels like me. The girl in the mirror has way too many new lines on her face. She looks pale and exhausted and centuries older than her twenty-eight years.

I want to bang on the mirrors and ask, *Who is that?*

The answer comes to me a little too quickly: *Someone who's scared that this is only the beginning.*

"How long do you expect me to stay here?" I rasp, wrenching my attention away from the eerie reflections.

"That remains to be seen."

I don't like that answer one bit. But before I can demand just a teensy bit more info about the course of my life, please and thank you, I hear the robot seductress call out, *"Doors opening."*

The doors are indeed opening, parting to reveal a spacious foyer. An ash-gray carpet unfurls in every direction. I scan from left to right and see a black, petrified wood coffee table the size of a football field, surrounded by a black leather sectional sofa big enough to hold both teams that would play on said field. I see a bowl of lemons on a side table, a jarring pop of color. I see spiky, abstract art, beautifully tarnished mirrors on the walls, twisted black sculptures looming in the corners.

I keep coming back to those lemons, though. Everything else is drained of color, but the lemons shine like they're incandescent.

"Come on." Dmitri holds out a hand to me when I don't step out of the elevator.

I glance down at the carpet, suddenly worried about dripping blood onto it. His hand is huge in my field of vision. The nurse's blood is crusted dry on the back of his knuckles. I spy the hint of a tattoo on the underside of his wrist. I don't know how I've never noticed that before.

I follow the arm up to meet his eyes. It makes sense that his home is colorless—so are those eyes. They're brooding, utterly unreadable.

I swallow and raise a foot to step inside. But before I can set it down, a voice sings out, "Baby, is that you?"

A vision of a woman materializes from the open archway on the right. Her body is lithe as a model's, which fits the bill, considering she belongs on a runway in Milan somewhere. I never knew negative percent body fat was a thing until now. Nor did I know hair could actually be that shade of honey-blonde outside of a shampoo commercial.

The woman freezes at the threshold when she sees me. I'm expecting annoyance, suspicion, maybe a *Who the fuck is this?* All would be valid.

But instead, she gives me a smile. "Hello, Wren," she croons as though we've already been introduced. She glides forward gracefully, but doesn't offer me her hand. I don't blame her; I wouldn't want to touch me right now, either. "I'm Beatrice. Everyone calls me Bee."

I try to speak, fail, clear my throat, try again. "H-hi."

Judging from her designer clothes and perfect, olive-toned tan, she's definitely not the housekeeper. She looks too different from Dmitri to be related to him. So that leaves—

"I'm his fiancée, to answer the question you didn't ask."

My whole body constricts like it's trying to physically reject the word. *Fiancée?* He has a freaking fiancée, and I'm only hearing about it now?

But the more I look at her, the more sense it makes. Of *course* he has a partner. Very few men take on the responsibility of a child without having someone to share the burden with.

"I-I'm his..." I glance towards Dmitri, who is putting our coats away in a closet I didn't see. He's not even looking at me. "His... Um, I'm his—"

"You're his assistant," Bee interrupts helpfully. Dmitri floats to stand beside her. She nestles into his side and places a palm flat on his chest. *God, they look beautiful together.* "And you're the woman who's carrying our little bundle of joy. I'm honored to meet you."

My jaw flops open stupidly. Now that I know exactly how dumb that expression looks, I hate it, but I can't stop myself.

"Why don't you come sit down? I've got some tea and biscuits laid out."

Tea and biscuits? Is she Princess fucking Diana?

God, my head hurts. Was it just a little while ago that I was throwing up on a hospital floor while my would-be murderer bled out beside me?

Now, here I am, in The Muse at Haven Crest, being led to a Coco Chanel coffee table where, just like Bee said, a tea service has been laid out for me.

She has a feminine strut to her walk and a lovely lilt in her voice as she drapes an elegant hand toward the offerings. "I have honey and hibiscus and the more traditional Earl Gray. But if you would prefer coffee, I can whip you up a mug."

I lift my eyes to hers. She's exactly the kind of woman you'd expect to see on Dmitri Egorov's arm. Stylish, confident, carelessly beautiful.

"Wren?"

She says my name as though she's known me a long time. I shake my head to clear out the cobwebs. To try to, at least. "I, um… I don't think I can keep anything down right now, to be honest."

Bee nods. "Of course. You probably just want a hot shower and some clean clothes. Come with me; I've got you."

I look around for Dmitri, but he disappeared when I wasn't paying attention and left me with his ethereal fiancée. I have no choice but to follow her into the bowels of the massive penthouse.

All the interior details of this place are lost on me. It's just one beautiful thing after the next, so endless that I don't even bother trying to ooh and ahh over any of them.

What I do notice is the everyday stuff dotted here and there, almost as an afterthought. The framed engagement pictures of Dmitri and Bee hanging on the walls of the broad corridor she leads me down. The gorgeous pink stilettos lying discarded in a second sitting room next to a neatly-aligned pair of men's leather oxfords.

It hurts how beautiful it is.

It hurts that each of them look like they belong here.

It hurts how much I don't.

Bee swings open a door for me and steps aside to let me pass. "Here you go. Make yourself at home. There are fresh linens in the cabinet under the sink and I'll leave some clean clothes on the bed for you to change into when you're done showering."

She gives me a smile that doesn't betray even the slightest modicum of jealousy. Not that she has anything to be jealous of, but a lesser woman might resent the fact that a random stranger gets to carry her partner's child.

I know I would in her position.

She's already left before I remember that I didn't even thank her. With a self-pitying grimace, I pull the door shut and turn to the guest bedroom.

The first thing that catches my attention is the view. It's Chicago in every direction, Lake Michigan looming beyond in one huge, unbroken plane of blue-gray glass.

The second thing is the series of small, framed photographs standing on the sleek dressing table beside the windows. I squint closer.

Two young kids. The boy is dark-haired, silver-eyed, ridiculously beautiful. Easy enough to guess who that is.

The girl is blonde and pale with the same careless smile that she carried with her into adulthood. That's an easy ID, too.

Maybe that's why Bee can walk around in Dmitri's space, amongst Dmitri's things, and touch Dmitri's chest with that infallible air of ownership: they must've just been together so long that there was never any question of being with anyone else.

I slide my gaze down the line to the next photo. Same duo, but they're older in this one. She still has the softness of childhood but he looks like he's well on his way to being a man. The lines of his face are hardening into place.

The last photograph takes them into their teenage years. Dmitri looks handsome as ever and that cocked eyebrow of his says that he knows it. Bee is standing next to him, looking to the side and laughing at something out of frame. She's blossomed in the meantime; her long blonde hair almost touches her waist and, even in stillness, that laugh of hers is electric.

I'm not sure why tears jump to my eyes. *It's just the shock wearing off,* I tell myself as I duck into the bathroom and strip naked.

But maybe it's more than that.

Maybe, as I step under the rainfall showerhead in the huge, black-tiled stall, it's the panic of a fish flopping around on dry land, realizing that it's found itself somewhere it was never, ever meant to be.

I keep my head down and let the scorching water run all over me. It turns pink as it washes away the blood Dmitri didn't already clean himself. When I reach out to adjust the water pressure, I see that my fingers are still trembling.

"Fuck," I breathe to the empty bathroom.

Everything in here is soothing—the water, the temperature, the fruit-scented soaps that lather like a dream. But no matter how long I stay here, I can't bring myself to relax.

Because I don't belong here.

If anyone knows the feeling of not belonging, it's me. Dad didn't want me. My ex William didn't, either. That didn't stop me from thrusting my heart in both their hands and saying, *Here, have everything.*

I guess I shouldn't have been so surprised when they broke it.

Each time, I picked up the shattered pieces and promised myself that it would never happen again. I would make smart choices. I would be self-sufficient, independent, confident.

And yet here I am, in the middle of another man's marriage.

Again.

Giving up, I get out of the shower, satisfied at least that my body is clean, even if my head is still a mess. When I go into the bedroom, there's a small stack of clothes waiting for me on the bed. A pair of navy leggings and a white t-shirt, both softer than butter.

Once I'm dressed, I sit down at the edge of the bed and stare out at the city's jagged skyline. My apartment is out of sight, tucked away in the shadow behind a skyscraper.

"You're a long way from home," I murmur to myself just before the door opens and Bee enters.

"Ah, you're dressed. Wonderful."

I get to my feet anxiously, wringing my hands in front of my waist. "Thanks for the clothes."

"Of course." She stands in the doorway, leaning against the frame and watching me with a cool gaze that I can't quite decipher. "You're tired."

I clear my throat. "I can sleep when I get home."

"It's cute that you think you're going home after what just happened."

I frown. "He told you what happened?"

"Of course. He tells me everything."

I swallow hard and glance around the room. I have so many questions. *What do you want from me? Why does Dmitri keep referring to my baby as his "heir"? How are you so cool with the fact that I'm here in the first place?*

I have so many things to say that I end up saying nothing at all.

"Listen," Bee begins with a sympathetic sigh, "I know this is a lot. It must all be very overwhelming for you. But for right now, it's important that you get some sleep. If you're hungry, there's food in the kitchen or I can bring you a tray—"

"I can't eat."

Bea doesn't seem to mind my impatient tone. "Sleep then. And we can talk tomorrow."

Tomorrow. What a concept. I was pretty sure this was the last day of existence.

Beyond the window, the sky is darkening. And so is my mood. The attack at the hospital was horrific—but somehow, the idea of staying here tonight with Dmitri and his gorgeous fiancée feels equally bad.

"Please," I murmur, turning back toward Bee, "I have to go. Just let me leave and—"

"No." I flinch at the grating menace in his voice as he steps into the room behind Bee. "You're staying here tonight. That's final."

"But *why?*"

"The attack in the hospital wasn't an isolated incident, Wren." Dmitri's tone cuts like broken glass. "They will have eyes on you from now on."

I glare back at him, bristling. "No, I mean why as in, why are there eyes on me and my baby? Who are 'they' and why do they care about either one of us?"

"'They' are my enemies," he says in such a flat, cold snarl that I can't help but shiver. "And 'they' care because I'm the *pakhan* of the Egorov Bratva. What my enemies want more than anything is to destroy the future of my empire. Considering you're currently carrying said future in your belly, that means it's you they want to destroy. I'm the only one keeping you safe right now, Wren. I'm the only friend you have left. I'm the only chance you have to survive."

Bee's hand flutters over her fiancé's arm. "Dmitri…" she warns softly.

He ignores her and steps into the room, leaning in so close that I can smell his mint-and-cedar cologne and the vodka on his breath. "So you can spit in my face and run if you like. But if you do, they will catch you. And when they catch you, they'll kill you." His eyes drag down to my stomach as he adds, "*Both* of you."

8

DMITRI

"What are you doing?" Bee hisses the moment we're back in the living room.

"She was being stubborn. I was being straight with her."

"*'Straight'*? You were being *straight* with her?" She smacks my arm with the back of her hand. "Why are men so freaking clueless? This is, like, seventy-five percent of the reason I date women!"

I screw up my face into a scowl. "She's carrying my baby. She needs to know."

"Yes, but did she need to know like *that*?! She wasn't born into this world like you and me, D. She isn't used to seeing blood and guts on the floor. She's not used to having knife-wielding maniacs attack her in what is supposed to be a safe place. She was in shock when you brought her in—and you go and drop *that* bomb on her? I take back what I said: you'd have to get several orders of magnitude smarter before I'd even call you clueless."

Grinding my teeth, I turn away from Bee. But she's never been the kind of woman you can turn your back on. She whips around and plants herself in front of me again, hands fisted on her hips the way she's done since we were children. "Nuh-uh. No, no, and no. You don't get to tune me out, buddy. This is important. If you put her through much more, she could miscarry."

My first thought is, *Would that be so bad?*

The guilt sets in immediately after, though. That is my son she's carrying. It may not be ideal and fuck knows it wasn't planned—but it is what it is and I need to protect them both.

"What would you have me do?" I ask wearily.

"Great question. Thought you'd never ask." She tilts her head to the side and switches to a softer voice. "Make it right. Explain things to her. Give her some context. She needs to understand that you're on her side. That staying here of her own free will is what's best for her and the baby."

I let loose an exhausted exhale. "Fine."

I'm sweeping towards the open archway when Bee stops me. "Where are you going?"

"Where do you think?" I demand impatiently. "Did we not just discuss that I should calm her down?"

"No, not right now! *God*, clueless. Clueless. Clueless. I told her to sleep and she needs the rest. She's not going to be able to process anything you have to say now, anyway."

"Fuck me," I mutter, turning towards the skyline like the heavens might have some answers hidden there. "How the hell did this happen?"

Bee comes up to stand by my side. "There's no point in asking questions like that. It *did* happen. Maybe one day, we'll figure out why—but for right now, we just need to make this work." I throw her a curious, sidelong glance and she buckles ever-so-slightly under my gaze. "What? Stop looking at me like that."

"Why are you so invested in this?"

"The whole point of this was to make a baby, wasn't it?"

"Not like this. You're not in the least disappointed that this child won't be yours?"

She tries to hide her smile behind an adjustment of her hair, but I know her too well for petty little tricks like that to work. "Well…"

"You're relieved. You're fucking *relieved*."

A little giggle bursts from her lips. "Oh, come on, Dmitri! Can you see me as a mother? When they made me, they left out the maternal gene. I don't have the desire or the temperament to raise a human being. I'd just impart all my trauma onto them. This is for the best."

"You've got it all figured out, don't you? Everything's coming up Beatrice. Must be fucking nice."

She shrugs, innocent as a lamb by the looks of her. "It's a plan-in-progress, obviously, but it has solid bones. You need an heir; she wants a baby; I need to get my father off my back. This little bean solves all three problems. It's a win-win-win, and lemme tell you, those aren't a dime a dozen. We ought to be popping bubbly to celebrate."

I glower at her. "You don't think your father will get suspicious when my son is calling another woman 'Mom'?"

"That's not a hill I plan to die on, believe me." She taps a manicured nail against her button nose. "He can call Wren 'Mom' and I'll be 'Mama.' Or 'Mommy.' Or hell, 'Mother Dearest,' I dunno. Does it matter? That's a small detail."

"So our farce will hinge on an infant's ability to distinguish between Mother and Mama. 'Solid bones,' my ass, Bee. You expect us all to live a lie?"

Her eyes flash to mine, feisty as ever. "How is it any different from what you and I are doing now?"

"You and I have known each other our entire lives!" I remind her harshly. "We're as good as family. Wren is a wild card who might want more for herself than to lie to dangerous men for the rest of her days."

"It won't be for the rest of her days. Just until my father dies," Bee suggests. "The moment he conks out, we'll have a party, tell the whole world our truth, and live as a happy, dysfunctional throuple. It'll be bliss." Her smile grows wider in direct proportion to how my scowl is growing darker. "What? You don't like the throuple idea? Don't worry, I don't plan on having sex with you. Just her."

It's weird how fast I want to bite her head off for even suggesting such a thing. But I rein in my annoyance before I say something she'll make me regret later.

Bee must know I'm wavering on the edge of an outburst, because she does her damndest to push me right over said edge. "She's very pretty…"

"Bee."

"I'm just saying. Those dimples."

Don't remind me, I think with a grimace. Out loud, I say, "We need to lock her door."

"Abso*lute*ly not." Bee jabs a finger into my chest. "Did you not hear a word I said? We need to make her feel like she's a guest, not a prisoner. She needs to feel safe here. And that all depends on you not scaring her away with your big, bad boogeyman act." She bats her eyelashes at me. "You catch more flies with honey than with vinegar, baby."

"I'm a fucking *pahkan*. The hell would I want with honey?"

Her eyebrows flatline. "First of all, you might actually benefit from taking your crown off once in a while and remembering what life is like amongst us mortals. And secondly, you're not dealing with a *vor* or an ally or an enemy; you're dealing with the woman who's carrying your baby. If you don't put her at ease, then every day is going to be a knock-'em-down, drag-'em-out brawl. Things will be so much easier if she actually *wants* to be here."

I snort. "I don't see that happening."

"Fine. You want concrete reasons? How's this: the more stressed she is, the higher the chances of her miscarrying will be. If she's had to resort to a fertility clinic at… How old is she?"

"Twenty-eight," I supply without thinking.

"At the ripe old age of twenty-eight, it means she probably has fertility issues. Which means her pregnancy is going to be more delicate than normal."

"Fantastic," I mutter. "This keeps getting better and better."

Bee keeps jabbing her finger into my chest. "This is on *you*, oh mighty Lord Egorov. Don't fuck it up."

"Will you stop doing that?" I hiss, moving out of her attack range.

"I will when you start listening. So, no, probably not."

"*Blyat!*" I rub my chest where she's been clawing me. "Fine. I'll do my best to… explain shit to her. After she's gotten her rest."

"Can you do it with a smile?"

"Now, you're asking too much."

Bee laughs and tucks her talons away, temporarily satisfied. "I have a good feeling about all this," she muses with a satisfied nod. "I think it's gonna turn out just peachy."

I sigh and turn my gaze out the window. I can feel Bee scrutinizing me, wondering if I'm going to share with her all the things circulating through my head. Plans, possibilities, pregnancies I did and didn't ask for.

When I don't return her gaze soon enough, she pokes me in the side again. "Share with the class, Dmitri," she orders.

I stroke my chin as I turn to regard her. "If we take your father out, this whole ruse won't be necessary." Her throat bobs with a nervous swallow. "All you have to do is say the word."

"Would you really do that for me?"

"You know I would."

She closes her eyes for a moment and just breathes. When she opens them again, there's a vague sense of resignation there. "You know… I've wished since I was a very little girl that someone who could actually go through with it would make me that offer. Hell, I've thought about doing it myself.

But… you're in this fake, fucked-up marriage for your own reasons, you know? Through me, you get the Zanetti mafia. If my dad dies, that all goes up in smoke."

"I can live with that if it means you are free and happy, Bee."

She plucks some imaginary lint from my shoulder and smooths out the lines of my shirt, doting and primping on me the same way she has since we were children. "I appreciate the sentiment. But we've come this far. And I quite enjoy being fake engaged to you, if only because the jokes are endless. I'm sure you'll make an amazing fake husband."

I snort as she moves into my arms and hugs me tight. I kiss the top of her head fondly before she releases me.

"So—are you meeting the hot waitress again for a third date?"

Bee wrinkles her nose and bites on her bottom lip. "She's dust in the wind, my friend."

"Already?"

She laughs merrily. The light is back in her eyes now that we're not talking about her father anymore. "She got clingy on me the other night. I'm not looking for anything serious right now. I want fun and casual and la-di-freaking-da, you know?"

"Mm. And have you thought about what you'll do when that changes?"

She shrugs and tosses a flippant hand in the air as she starts to walk away. "I'll cross that bridge when I come to it. For right now, I'm happy playing the field." She pauses in the archway and glances down the hall towards Wren's room. "You'll make sure she's comfortable?"

"Yes. For your sake, though—not hers."

She winks at me. "That's love if I've ever seen it. See you tomorrow, lover boy."

The moment she disappears, my half-smile drops. *Make sure she's comfortable?* How the hell do I do that? My idea of making a woman "comfortable" involves plying her with good food, great booze, and a handful of mind-blowing orgasms before I send her on her way.

That strategy, foolproof as it's been thus far in my life, won't work here.

Which is why I call the only woman I can actually count on for advice in a situation like this—Rogan. She was married to one of my closest *vors* before he died in a confrontation with the Irish. The O'Gadhras have a lot to pay for and Misha's death is high on the list.

All in good time.

"Dmitri!" Rogan chirps when I answer. "To what do I owe the pleasure? You don't usually call at this hour of the night."

I drop down on the leather chaise and cut right to the chase. "You've had two children."

"Thanks for the reminder. Or was that a question? If so, yes. Keiron and Anya. You attended both their graduations, remember?"

I clear my throat uncomfortably. "Yes, of course. I'm calling to ask about your… pregnancies." I cringe at the sound of my own voice asking questions I never thought I'd have to ask.

There's a beat of awkward silence. "Is this about…?"

Sighing, I say, "Things have taken an unexpected turn."

I have trusted Rogan implicitly from the moment I stepped into her home to tell her that she was a Bratva widow. She sat opposite me in her living room, sheet-white and trembling in her hands. But she didn't shed a tear. Nor did she blame me for her husband's death.

"*He knew the life he signed up for,*" was all she said. "*As did I.*"

When I'd offered her a monthly stipend in perpetuity, her nostrils flared and her lips had pressed together in a thin, offended line. "*I don't accept charity, Mr. Egorov. If you're giving me money, I expect to earn it. So if you're not offering me a job, then you and your stipend can get the fuck out of my house.*"

Which is how Rogan Stanislav had entered my payroll as a fifty-seven-year-old woman and veteran of nearly three decades of stay-at-home-motherhood. How she came to be so essential to my operation is still a bit of a mystery, but I don't bother second-guessing it now.

Case in point: she was the one who made appointments for Bee and myself at the fertility clinic. She is—or, given recent events, *was*—the one working on finding us a surrogate who was, for lack of a better term, "Bratva-adjacent." Someone who understood on some level the risks of carrying a *pahkan's* child.

"'Unexpected turn'? What does that mean?" Rogan asks in her trademark, no-nonsense manner.

"It means that the clinic botched the whole fucking thing and my sample was used on the wrong person."

As usual, it doesn't take long for her to understand the gist of things. "So some poor, unsuspecting woman is pregnant with your baby and she has no idea what she's gotten herself into?"

"She knows now."

"Well—fuck."

"That about sums it up," I agree. Rogan's bluntness can be abrasive sometimes, but the last thing I need is more people bullshitting me. I get enough of that as it is. "She's at the Muse with Bee and me. I need to make sure she's comfortable."

"And you called the only woman you know who's been pregnant to ask? How flattering."

"That's why you're indispensable to me, Ro."

She sighs like I exhaust her, probably because I do. I can just picture her taking off her granny glasses and rubbing the bridge of her nose between thumb and forefinger. "I'll purchase everything she might need and send it over. Until then, make sure she sleeps well, gets lots of rest, and most importantly, give her a stress-free environment. I'll say that one more time for your benefit: *stress-free.* Now, tell me— what does she like?"

"What do you mean?"

"Oh, for fuck's sake, Dmitri. In terms of clothes, does she like pants, dresses? Does she have a preference when it comes to color or fabric or fit? What about food? Are there any cuisines she prefers? Snack foods that she enjoys?"

"I don't have the faintest fucking idea, Ro."

"Well, find out and let me know." Her voice is alert and clipped. I hear the scribbling of a pen and the typing of a keyboard roar to life in the background as she gets to work. "Oh, and Dmitri?"

"Yes?"

"Congratulations. Parenthood is one hell of an adventure."

9

DMITRI

Egorov Industries is still and silent at this time of night. The only people moving around are the cleaning crew, who are just finishing up when I arrive. Most of them barely notice me as I move quietly through the halls, but a few stand at attention when I pass.

As I approach my office, I notice a woman rifling through Wren's desk drawer. "Snooping is not in the job description," I snap.

"Jesus, Joseph, and Mary!" the woman cries, upending a stack of papers and sending them fluttering in every direction. "Sir… I didn't see you there."

"If you had, you wouldn't have been caught with your hand in the cookie jar, would you?"

Her cheeks flush. "I-I was just straightening up…"

"Spare me." I hold up a hand to silence her excuses. "Put the papers back on the desk and leave. This is your first and last warning."

She nods frantically, chin wobbling like a bobblehead. The moment the papers are stacked back on Wren's desk, she grabs her cleaning cart and pushes it down the hall. I sit down in front of the desk and scan.

Her computer screen is framed with Post-it Notes. Mostly to-do lists and task reminders, though I catch a few affirmations in there. **Patience**, reads one.

I snort—I have a feeling that might be directed at me.

I start going through her drawers. Most are filled with generic files, company stationery, printer supplies. But one contains a wealth of junk food, including a five-pound bag of gummy bears.

Beneath that…

"Well, well, well," I murmur to myself. "What do we have here?"

I pick up both books from the bottom drawer. The pages are yellowing, the covers well-worn from endless rereads. Both feature handsome, shirtless men with their muscled arms wrapped protectively around women who seem to exclusively dress in torn blouses three sizes too small for their bosoms.

The thinner book is titled **The Ballad of the Blood Rose.** I crack it open to a random page and take a look.

… Esme tried not to look in Cedric's direction. It was harder than she would have imagined to keep her eyes averted. Especially when her body, her heart, her very soul cried out for him with reckless abandon. She hadn't said more than two sentences to him since the last harvest, but those two sentences held a lifetime's worth of longing in them. It was almost supper now. If she didn't go in now, Mama would be out soon, looking for her. She didn't

want to be caught staring at Cedric again. Not after the last time...

I flip to a different point in the book.

... muscles rippled under the fading light. Sweat glistened like beads of molten silver on his divine body. Esme tried to calm her racing pulse, but all she could feel was her own desire. And there was nothing calm about it.

"You shouldn't be here."

"I wanted to thank you for helping me yesterday."

Cedric's eyes danced over Esme's body without shame or apology. "But that's not really why you're here... is it?"

He moved forward, forcing Esme back against the barn door. She could hear Trotter neigh from the corner stable. He never did like the rain.

"What do you really want with me, madam?"

Esme's heart fluttered with anticipation. She knew she ought to be scared, but curiously enough, she wasn't. She felt as though her whole, boring, cloistered life had been building up to this moment, like a caterpillar preparing to emerge from its chrysalis, born anew.

"I want... you."

Cedric's eyes flashed like summer lightning and Esme's nether regions trembled in response. "I can offer you neither love nor romance," he warned, drawing closer and closer. "But if you want me to take you roughly right here, right now... that I can do. Just don't ask for more."

Esme knew instantly that that's exactly what she wanted. More.

More of him. More of life. More of everything.

But if telling the truth was going to rob her of the excitement and adventure of this forbidden moment, then she would lie happily and freely. She would tell him what he wanted to hear so that he could tell her the same in return.

Esme was done being the perfect daughter. She was done being a good girl. For the first time in her life, she was going to take what she wanted.

And what she wanted... was Cedric.

"Jesus," I mutter, snapping the book shut. "Who knew?"

I tuck the books back in the bottom drawer—but as I do, one more thing catches my eye: a flash of silver, tucked in the very back, almost out of sight.

I fish it out to find it's a photograph. Wren is on the left, her arm looped around the waist of another woman who has her same chin. Neither woman is looking at the camera, nor showing any sign that they even know it's there.

The look on Wren's face as she smiles down at the other woman in the frame is magnetic. It's love, pure and simple.

What would it take to make her smile at me that way?

Disgusted at the thought alone, I tear my eyes from the frame and shove it back into the drawer. What the hell am I doing? Even with a gun pressed against my head, I couldn't tell you why I came to the office in the first place.

I stand back up with an irritated wince and stride to the dark windows that overlook the city.

I used to stay late at the office after Elena's death. I hated going back to my silent penthouse, and there was something about the spartan emptiness of this building at night that appealed to me.

Sometimes, I'd call Bee and listen to her ramble about whatever date she was going on that night. But more often, I'd just sit in my dark office and stare out at the city lights, the moving cars, the bustle of a world that was moving on without me.

Bee helped restart my life when it felt stuck. She refused to take no for an answer. Wouldn't let me waste away in grief.

"Elena wouldn't have wanted this for you, Dmitri. She would have wanted you to live," she'd told me on the first anniversary of Elena's death.

So I did live. But in all the wrong ways. I went out, I drank, I visited nightclubs with my brother and took home women whose names I neither remembered nor bothered to ask for in the first place.

And in the end, all I got out of it were a few fleeting moments of distraction.

Because none of those women got under my skin the same way that Elena did. Not a single goddamn one of them lingered in my head after they'd left my presence. As soon as they walked out of my door, they might as well have ceased to exist.

Remembering a woman after she was gone… that only happened once, and I married her.

So when the city's skyline starts to blur into a hallucinatory image of Wren's face—it feels invasive. It feels like a betrayal. To whom, though, I'm not sure.

Elena?

Myself?

Who the fuck knows?

"Fuck. I pull out my phone and fire off a quick text to my brother.

Where will you be later?

His reply comes back almost immediately, which means he's expecting something fun. My brother's never met a good time that he didn't say no to.

ALEKSANDR: *the Honey Pot prob. Or the Rec Room. but i probably wont be at either one til at least midnight*

DMITRI: *Drop in at mine before you head out. I have something I need you to do for me.*

ALEKSANDR: *booooo. boring. youre all work and no play these days*

DMITRI: *I don't have the luxury of playtime anymore. I've got an empire to run.*

ALEKSANDR: *you have no idea how glad i am that i was born second.*

DMITRI: *Be at my place in a half hour.*

My head is packed to bursting as I drive home. The whole time, I try to force Wren and her smile out of my head. But it's still there, even as I walk into my living room, feeling the weight of the day settle on my shoulders like boulders.

Ignoring the siren call of the minibar, I slip down the hall towards Wren's room. The door is unlocked, so I push it open quietly and step inside.

She's fallen asleep with the curtains drawn wide. Moonlight cascades into the room and pools around her where she's curled into a tight ball in the center of the mattress.

As I watch, she moans and thrashes the top sheet off of her, revealing that she abandoned the leggings Bee gave her. The only thing she's kept on is the thin white t-shirt that hugs the curves of her breasts. It's not enough to hide the twin points of her nipples or the tanned expanse of inner thigh leading up to where it meets her hip.

Fuck me. She's got a body that makes my mouth water. When was the last time I looked at a woman and felt this deep, animalistic need to possess her?

With Elena, there was never any question that she belonged to me. She fell into my arms and begged for possession.

But this woman is different. Even with my baby in her belly, I can feel her actively resisting me. Trying her best to put distance between us, to set boundaries, to erect wall after wall after wall.

That doesn't change the fact that she *is* carrying my child. And in a few months, her body is going to blossom.

I'm already inside of her.

She just refuses to accept that.

Clenching my jaw tight, I move to the bedside table and pick up her phone. I'm about to leave when she sighs. It's the softest of sighs, but the sound has my skin simmering.

I'm this close to doing something I regret when I catch sight of my reflection in the mirror hanging over the bed. My pupils are blown wide and my lips parted, revealing the black slash of my mouth.

I look reckless. Unhinged and untamed.

Turning my back on her, I walk out of her room fast. This strange preoccupation with Wren has to stop. If this living arrangement is going to work long-term, I'll need to erect some walls of my own.

My phone pings in my pocket.

ALEKSANDR: *I'm here.*

When I walk into the living room, Aleksandr is by the bar helping himself to a generous pour of vodka. "You're on time for once," I greet, clapping my palm against his shoulder.

He turns his dark hazel eyes on me and smiles. "Only because I know how crabby you can get when I'm late."

"Hasn't stopped you before."

He swivels the stool around to face me. "I heard about the attack at the clinic. I'm assuming that's why you asked me here this late?"

I clear my throat. "Something like that. I'll explain the whole thing to you soon. But for right now, I'm tapped out. I just need this to get done fast."

Aleksandr looks taken aback, but he nods. "Okay. Later it is. Just tell me what you need me to do."

I place the phone on the counter between us. "I need you to clone this phone for me."

He stares at the phone. It's obvious at first glance that it's not mine. The screen is cracked, the model is six or seven years outdated, and if none of that was a giveaway, the pink silicone case with **BREATHE AND REMEMBER YOU'RE PRETTY** engraved on the back would decide things.

He picks it up and gives it a tentative look. "Okaaay. I want to ask questions, but I won't."

"Smart man."

"Anyway," he says, setting his drink down, "it shouldn't be too hard to do. How urgently do you need this done?"

"A few hours. I want to put it back so that she doesn't suspect anything."

Aleksandr's eyebrows lift. "Okay—now, I'm asking questions. Why? What's the purpose here?"

Leaning back in my seat, I let shadows fall across my face, not by accident. Aleksandr knows me well enough to read my microexpressions, and the last thing I'm interested in is him poking and prying into my feelings.

"I want to make sure she keeps her mouth shut," is all I offer. It's partially true.

"So you want more than just texts?"

"I want everything. As much as you can get. I want it recording every last keystroke and piece of data that goes in and out of this device."

Aleks purses his lips. "It's gonna die on her more often. She might get suspicious."

I shrug. "I can deal with that. Put a tracker on it, too. I want to make sure I can find her just in case she decides to go waltzing off on her own."

"Do I even want to know who this chick is?"

I sigh. "No. Probably not."

10

WREN

I wake up to the rumble of my own stomach.

I'm not sure if it's a side effect of pregnancy brain or what, but it feels as though my whole body is no longer on my team. I woke up in the middle of the night, parched as hell, but when I went to get water, I could swear I saw Dmitri standing in the doorway and my knees buckled like a newborn baby deer's.

My stomach is just the latest traitor, robbing me of more precious seconds of dreamless sleep just to demand that I feed it.

I groan and spend a full ten minutes trying to ignore this inside-out mutiny, just so that I can stay in the room and not have to deal with whatever shitstorm is waiting for me outside the door of my citrus-scented refuge.

But when I can't ignore my hunger anymore, I tug on the leggings Bee gave me last night and peek into the hallway.

Everything's quiet. There's no sign of life. Which gives me the courage to tiptoe down the hall towards what I think is the living room.

I keep going past it until I hit the kitchen. It's just as impressive as the rest of this penthouse. The ceilings are high, the fittings sleek and modern, and I can see my own reflection in the gleaming black marble countertops.

I'm hunting for a glass, but all of the low drawers are a no-go, so I start to look higher, only to realize that the shelving in this place is set at a height more suitable for giants than for little old me. Even on tiptoes, I'm nowhere close.

I suppose that makes sense, though. Dmitri is a mountain of a man and his gazelle-like fiancée is probably close to six feet herself.

Lovely—just one more reminder that I do not belong here.

Gritting my teeth, I look around for something I can climb. I find a stool tucked under the bar and drag it toward the closest cupboard. Either it's absurdly heavy or my muscles are rebelling against me, too, though, because by the time I get it in place, I'm out of breath.

I take a moment to recuperate, then get back on track. I haul myself up onto the stool and lean forward, trying to find a groove in the side of the cupboard to pull since it's seamless and there are no knobs anywhere that I can see.

"My God, why do rich people make things so complica—*ahh!*"

The chair starts shaking as my weight pushes it off center. I reach out, but there's nothing to grab but empty air. My hands pinwheel wildly through space as I go, go, go…

Then something stops me.

No, not some*thing*—some*one.*

I peek open one eyelid to see an irritatingly familiar pair of silver irises grimacing down in my direction. "What the hell do you think you're doing?"

I wince inwardly. I honestly might've preferred to crack my head open on the tile floor, actually. This feels worse.

Dmitri sets me on my feet and keeps scowling down at me like I'm an idiot, to which I want to say, *Well... fair point.*

"This house is not short-people friendly!" I cry out instead, infusing as much indignation into my voice as I can under the circumstances.

That intense eyebrow pull softens just a little. It's as close to a smile as he ever gets. "Oh?"

"How is a *normal*-sized person supposed to reach up there! We can't all be gigantic ogres like you. Or supermodels with insane, Amazon woman proportions like your fiancée."

One side of his mouth twists up as he moves toward the cupboard I was trying to open. He pushes into it and it swings outward with a soft click, revealing a rack of glistening glasses.

"You could always ask for help," he suggests with amused sarcasm, probably because he knows damn well I don't want to ask him for anything.

"Whatever," I mumble, face burning. "Those cabinets are stupid. We poor people don't have fancy shit like that."

"You're not poor."

"How would *you* know?"

"Because I happen to know how much you earn."

"But you don't know what kind of other stuff I have to pay for."

He looks intrigued. "'Other stuff?'"

Yeah, "other stuff"—stuff like helping my sister pay for the fancy shmancy fertility clinic that she and Jared could by no means afford on their own. It was definitely worth the loan I'd taken out to cover the cost of testing, fertility medications, and egg retrieval.

Not!

Which reminds me: I've gotta speak to Dr. Saeder about a full refund. It is quite literally the least he could do. Not that I won't be paying for this decision in other ways for the rest of my life.

"That clinic wasn't cheap," I mutter under my breath. "There were others we could have gone with, but she had her heart set on this one."

"You get what you pay for, Wren," she tried to convince me. *"If we go to the best, then we're bound to get the best result."*

Ahh, the irony.

"'She'?"

My eyes snap to Dmitri's. "What?"

"You said that *she* had her heart set on this fertility clinic."

I cringe internally, cursing myself for slipping. I have no desire to discuss my sister with Dmitri. It's one of those sacred relationships that I hold so close to heart that I don't want to talk about it with anyone I don't trust.

And I sure as hell don't trust Dmitri Egorov. I don't even like him.

(Lust doesn't count.)

"I… misspoke."

One eyebrow arches incredulously. He's not even pretending to believe me, but I'm not about to cave in the face of something as silly as an awkward silence. Hell, I *thrive* in awkward silences. My whole damn life has been a breeding ground for them.

I fold my arms over my chest. "Are you going to feed me or not?"

Dmitri keeps his eyes on me long enough to make it clear that he's not letting me off the hook completely. This is just a temporary reprieve. Then he turns to the cabinets and pulls out a loaf of artisan bread and some cutlery.

"How about an omelet? I prefer bacon and cheese, but you strike me as more of a mushrooms and spinach kind of woman."

"*You're* going to cook for me?"

He pretends to look around. "Do you see anyone else offering?"

I pretend to scratch my chin with my middle finger. "Fine. Bacon and cheese, since you seem so set on judging me."

He chuckles under his breath. Meanwhile, I park my ass on one of the high chairs and watch him retrieve supplies from the recessed refrigerator as the pan heats up.

He sets a bowl of fruit and a glass of orange juice in front of me without a word, then turns back to start cracking eggs into a bowl one-handed. I guess I shouldn't be so surprised that he's graceful and talented in the kitchen.

What I *am* surprised about is how my ovaries seem to feel about that.

Just one more mutineer, I guess. *Et tu, Brute?*

As he cooks, I keep waiting for Bee to show up. But the apartment remains silent except for crackling eggshells and the cozy spitting of oil in the skillet.

"So, about yesterday." He glances over his shoulder at me. "I probably should have found a better way of telling you about… things."

I shudder. "You're saying that wasn't just a bad dream?"

"I'm afraid not."

I groan as I drop my face onto the counter. The cool marble feels good against my flushed forehead. "Mob boss. That's a real thing, then. *You're* the real thing."

"Bratva *pahkan*. It's Russian. Much different."

"And *waaay* better, obviously," I quip sarcastically. He smirks and starts cutting out slices of sourdough bread. "Wait!" I gasp as a startling question hits me. "Is *that* why the two of you wanted to use a surrogate? Because you thought it would be too dangerous for your fiancée to carry a baby?"

He blinks at me for a moment. "Something along those lines."

I frown. "That wasn't very convincing."

"We have our reasons for wanting to use a surrogate. I'm sure you have yours."

It's a very subtle and very smooth reminder that if I insist on asking questions, he's going to come at me with questions of his own. Obviously, I'd prefer to avoid that.

But still, we're not exactly on equal footing here. I don't have a partner in the picture; he does.

"Listen, I really don't want to get in the middle of your relationship."

"You met Bee last night. She's happy to have you here."

"Yeah, which is *weird*!" I exclaim. "I mean, is she aware that I'm not a surrogate? This baby is *mine*. I'm not gonna push him out and hand him over, which is what I'm assuming she expects to happen."

"I wouldn't make assumptions about Bee," he says, every bit as calm as he is cryptic. "The woman will surprise you every time."

He inserts the sliced sourdough into a toaster and pours the omelet mix into the hot skillet. I stare at his broad back, trying to figure out why his life feels like a thousand-piece puzzle that I'm struggling to put together.

The thing is, I'm freaking phenomenal at puzzles. So if I'm struggling, it's because there are a few pieces missing.

Correction: there are a few pieces he's *hiding*.

Then again, I'm hiding a few pieces about my life as well. The difference is that I'm not expecting anything from him or his fiancée. But even though nothing explicit has been mentioned yet, I get the feeling that there's going to be a lot expected of me.

And I'm not about to agree to anything that puts me smack dab in the middle of another couple's relationship. I fell into that trap once, based on blind trust and naivete. But I'd have to be a total idiot to enter into an arrangement like this with my eyes wide open.

Fool me once, et cetera. However that stupid saying goes.

The smell of cheese and bacon bubbles up in the kitchen, making my mouth water. A few seconds later, Dmitri slides over a large plate stacked with a very impressive cheese and bacon omelet and two pieces of perfectly toasted sourdough. "*Priyatnovo appetita.*"

"What?"

His smile curves up again. "It's Russian for 'bon appetit.' Which is French for 'enjoy your meal.'"

"I know what 'bon appetit' means, asshole." I turn my sneer down at the omelet and it melts away with a begrudging sigh. "This does smell amazing, though."

I drag my fork through the cheesy goodness. It takes every last scrap of willpower I have not to moan when it hits my tastebuds.

Culinary orgasm, here I come. The second bite goes down the hatch before the first one is even finished. I get a few more massive bites in when I look up and realize that Dmitri is just sitting there, watching me eat.

"Uh… aren't you eating anything?"

"No."

"Oh. Er, well, you don't have to stay and keep me company."

He shrugs. "I don't mind."

Weird. I'm not sure whether to interpret that as concern or distrust. "I'm not gonna steal the silverware, if that's what you're worried about."

"That's the least of my worries, Wren."

I'm too hungry to feel self-conscious, so I clean my entire plate and chug my way through the orange juice. "What time is it?" I ask when I'm done, dabbing my mouth with one of the cloth napkins on the side.

"Almost eight."

"Shit! It's later than I expected. I want to stop off at home to change before heading into the office. Do you mind if I'm a little late to—"

"You don't have to stress—"

I jump off the high stool. "Great. Thanks."

"—because you're not going into work today."

I stop short. "Excuse me?"

Dmitri pushes off the counter he was leaning against and grabs my empty plate. "You'll stay here today and rest," he throws over his shoulder casually as he walks my plate to the sink.

I round the center island to square up with him. "Are you serious?"

He drops my plate into the dishwasher. "You're not going anywhere until I can contain the threat to you and the baby."

"How long will that take?"

"As long as it takes."

"I can't—You aren't—You can't expect me to stay here indefinitely!"

He doesn't even bother to look at me as he scrubs my fork under the faucet and adds it to the dishwasher. "You'll be fine. It's comfortable here. There's plenty of room and I'll make sure to provide for all your needs."

"That's not the point. This isn't my home; it's *your* home. I'm sure your fiancée doesn't want me around long term anyway."

"On the contrary," he says calmly, "she's the one who suggested it."

My forehead wrinkles in confusion. "Dmitri—"

He drops the knife into the sink with a clatter and spins around to face me so suddenly that I almost scream. His face is dark and stormy. "What happened yesterday could happen again. Do you really want to take that chance because you're too stubborn to accept some help?"

How is he making *me* out to be the unreasonable one? How am I actually *falling* for it?

I decide to try a different approach. "You need a P.A. You're underestimating how much work I do for you on a daily basis."

"I already have someone filling in for you while you're away."

My hackles rise instantly. "You can't just give my job away because I'm pregnant. That's discrimination!"

He actually has the gall to look amused. "We're throwing around big, legal words now, are we?"

I take a step towards him, fist raised. "I can sue your ass."

"You're welcome to try. I have an excellent legal team."

I glower at him. "Just because I'm pregnant doesn't mean I'm incompetent. I can do both."

"This isn't a question of your competence. This is a question of your safety."

"I have bills to pay!"

He's not fazed in the least. "I'm not stopping your salary. You will still get paid on the first of every month as normal. But your only job will be putting your feet up and staying safe."

He's making it very hard to find reasons to reject this bogus proposal of his. "What am I supposed to do here all day?"

"The apartment has a gym, a theater, a game room, and a library. I'm sure you'll find something to occupy your time."

"What if I want some fresh air?"

"The balcony's just over there."

I scowl. "What if I want to go for a walk in the park?"

"I'd suggest you use your imagination."

We stare each other down for so long that my eyes start to water. It's the most intense staring contest I've ever had to endure. He wins in the end.

"Can I at least have the access code to the apartment?"

He rolls his eyes and heads out of the kitchen, forcing me to trail behind him. "I wasn't born yesterday. Now, if you'll excuse me, I have to get to work."

I feel like jumping right out of my skin. I'm raring for a fight, but Dmitri's glacial calmness is making it very difficult to keep up the same indignant momentum. He twists around abruptly and I nearly walk into his chest.

"If you need anything, text me on the number I gave you. I'll send over a couple of things you might need. Including a footstool."

For a moment, I'm genuinely stumped. "A footstool?"

"So you can reach all the high cabinets. Let it not be said that Dmitri Egorov discriminates against pint-sized people."

With that, he's gone.

"I'm not short, asshole!" I hurl at his back. Sighing, I drop to a pitiful seat right on the floor of his kitchen, my head hanging between my knees. "Not *that* short, at least."

11

WREN

It's been two days since I've seen either Dmitri or Beatrice. They've turned into phantoms in their own home. There are coffee beans on the counter every morning when I go into the kitchen for breakfast. Worn pairs of shoes thrown to the side of the corridor each night. I even catch the faint scent of some bougie perfume percolating in the air most mornings. But I never actually *see* either one of them. They're gone before I wake up and not home until long after I've fallen back asleep.

At first, it was a relief to have the penthouse to myself. But the relief was short-lived. And as it disintegrated, I was reminded of why I went back to work so soon after Rose and Jared's funerals.

The worst thing for grief is silence. And there's a helluva lot of silence to be found in this penthouse. Every room is full of the stuff.

So even if Dmitri and his fiancée are my only options for human interaction, I'd take it.

Not that I have the choice.

My only lifeline to the outside world is my phone. So of course, I've clung to it like an unhealthy crutch. Between texts to Syrah, who I've realized is my only friend, I've been combing through my photo library, staring at albums that I haven't looked at since long before their deaths.

To the shock and bewilderment of armchair therapists the world over, it's not making me feel much better.

My phone buzzes in my hand.

SYRAH: *hi sunshine. how you feelin today? are you on meds? work is boring as fuck without you.*

I hesitate. It's not like I can tell her what's really going on, so I've led her to the impression that I'm deathly sick. I hate lying, though.

WREN: *no meds yet. but i think im gonna see a doctor. feels like its getting worse, not better.*

SYRAH: *blech. does that mean ur not going to be in tomorrow either?*

WREN: *ill be lucky to get into work this week at all. miss you though.*

SYRAH: *how about I stop by after work with some hot soup?*

WREN: *thats sweet but i don't want to infect you. pretty sure this thing is contagious.*

SYRAH: *dont tempt me. a few sick days to veg out on the couch sounds amazing.*

SYRAH: *shit, gotta go. big boss is coming this way*

I start to type out, *As in Dmitri? Have you seen his new PA? Does she look competent? Is she pretty?*

I grimace and backspace. *Is she pretty*—God, I disgust myself. What does that matter? Why do I even care? Quickly, I delete the last part and press send.

SYRAH: *yup. looks like my sorority sister.*

Yup? As in yup, it's Dmitri, or yup, she looks competent? Also, quite annoyingly, Syrah's description in no way tells me if the new girl is pretty or not.

Sighing, I close the text thread and pull up my photo library again. I've scrolled all the way back to 2019. Rose and I were big into selfies that year. Her, because she and Jared were in the throes of googly-eyed young puppy love, and me, because I had finally moved out of the apartment I shared with her and into my very first grown-up apartment and I wanted to document every moment of my newfound independence.

I pull up a picture of the three of us shortly after we finished hauling all my junk into the basement unit. Jared's face takes center stage, blown up disproportionately because of how close he is to the phone. Rose is at his right shoulder and I'm on his left. All three of us look sweaty, grimy, and disgustingly happy.

My heart aches as I stare at those frozen smiles. "If only you knew what was coming," I whisper to the three oblivious fools on my screen.

Emotion wells up in my throat as I keep scrolling. Jared painting my bedroom. Rose baking a batch of brownies in my newly christened oven. The invincible cactus they bought me because I've never met a plant I didn't kill (though I did in fact kill the cactus, too).

I still remember the way Rose hugged me that night, just before she and Jared left to go back to their place. *"I'm gonna hate not having you in the next room."*

I laughed. *"Your apartment is a two-minute walk down the street."*

"Not the point. We've lived together all our lives. It feels weird breaking tradition."

"It's time to make that second bedroom a nursery. I'm ready to live on my own and you're ready to live alone with your husband for the first time ever."

Jared had given me a wink. *"We're still gonna miss our third wheel. We invested in a really comfy futon for a reason. Any time you're lonely, there's still plenty of room at our place if you wanna crash."*

Jared was so good like that. He never made her feel like she had to choose between us. From the moment he met and fell in love with Rose, he accepted that I was going to be along for the ride.

Maybe that's why it didn't feel like such a stretch to come to me when they realized that their chances of having a baby would be next to zero. We did so much together those last few years.

So why couldn't having a baby be a group effort as well?

"No!" I growl out loud, trying to shake the memories out of my head. "No, I'm not going down that rabbit hole again."

I swipe back to my texts and start angrily typing into the empty conversation thread I'm about to start.

WREN: *I've been trapped in this gilded cage for almost three freaking days! I want OUT!!!*

I stare at the text message. Are the two extra exclamation points a little too much? I don't want to come off as unhinged.

You know what? Fuck that. He locked me in this pretty prison and I'm worried about coming off unhinged? I *should* be unhinged, the way he's treating me. Being hinged would be the unreasonable option.

I smash **Send** with a vengeance and my message swoops away, out of my control. Then I set my phone down on the table, prop my head up on my fist, and stare broodily at the screen, waiting for three little dots to pop up so I can start directing psychic hatred in Dmitri's direction.

But nothing happens for a long time.

I see *Delivered* underneath my message. Somewhere out there in the city, Dmitri's phone is lighting up with my words.

"Come on," I mutter, gnawing at the inside of my cheek. "Come on…"

Three dots. They dance and dance and dance, and then…

DMITRI: *I'm in the middle of a meeting.*

WREN: *you're the boss. no one's gonna care if you're on your phone. also, I should be at that meeting too. is this the one with Belgium?*

DMITRI: *It's nothing to concern yourself with. Don't stress.*

WREN: *"don't stress"? how about "don't be an asshole!" i need something to do! i need a job!*

DMITRI: *The penthouse could use a good clean.*

WREN: **Middle finger emoji**

DMITRI: *I'll take that as a no.*

WREN: *i want my job back.*

DMITRI: *We'll discuss it when I get home.*

I can feel his absence like a sudden cold front ripping through the apartment. I hate how much it bothers me.

Grimacing, I resist the urge to go back to my photo library. All that'll do is bum me out further. So instead, I spend the rest of the day napping, snacking, and watching Old Hollywood movies in the theater room.

I emerge from my little dungeon only when it's dark outside and my body is craving food. The cupboards are stocked like something out of my dream. The selection is almost suspiciously good, like Dmitri scraped the inside of my head for ideas and pasted it all onto a grocery list.

But, c'mon, no freaking way. There's no chance on earth he took the time to figure out what kind of snacks I like to eat. I'm just being pathetically swoony. An extended dose of Cary Grant does that to a girl, I guess.

I'm rooting around in the fridge when I hear the distant voice of the sexy elevator robot sound out.

"Doors closing."

The heavy thump of his footsteps has me straightening up fast and closing the refrigerator door. I'm still fixing my crusty pajamas and rat's nest hair when he sweeps into the kitchen in one of his dark navy Burberry suits and a brown leather satchel. The navy draws out the bright silver in his eyes—not that I'm about to let that distract me.

"You came home."

He grabs a glass and pours himself some water. "I said I would."

"Men say they'll do a lot of things. In my experience, most don't get done."

The glass makes a soft chiming sound as he sets it down on the marble countertop. "The men you know, maybe. I am not them."

"Although," I muse, pretending he didn't say anything, "in my experience, the men I know don't kidnap me and force me into insane surrogacy deals, either. So I think I'll learn to live with the lack of follow-through if it also comes with a lack of abduction and coercion."

"Do you want to talk about the differences between me and your dating history," he drawls, "or do you want to talk about a job?"

I purse my lips in annoyance. "I don't want *a* job; I want *my* job back. You can go ahead and get rid of Sister Lynette."

"Who?"

"Never mind," I mumble. "I'm just saying that—"

"Do you know what's at stake here if you don't take my warnings seriously?" he interrupts. My heartbeat picks up a little as he stalks closer to me, his hand sliding over the marble counter. "Do you know how dangerous not listening to me would be for you?"

I swallow hard, trying to remember the argument points I've been rehearsing in my head all evening. They sounded so good in the mirror earlier. Now, they all feel tinny and flimsy and distant and dumb.

"I can listen."

He tilts his head to the side, eyes glistening, and regards me quietly. The silence persists for long enough that I can hear my own heartbeat throbbing in my ears before he finally speaks. "Then kneel."

I do a double take. "Ex*cuse* me?"

"You heard me," he says curtly. "Kneel."

I stare at him in disbelief, my jaw flexing wildly. "I absolutely will *not*."

"Not much of a listener, then."

"I'm prepared to listen," I snap. "I'm just not prepared to blindly obey like some insipid doormat."

"Even if obeying will keep you and your baby alive?"

"Don't do that," I hiss. "Don't conflate my safety with my sense of autonomy."

"I might have to, if your autonomy puts you at risk. And considering you don't fully understand the stakes, it inevitably will."

I pull myself up to my full height. "Screw you."

I'm expecting—maybe even hoping—for some anger. Some pushback. But he meets my exasperation with weary calm. "As I said, you're not ready." He deposits his satchel on the center island and opens the clasps. "Which is somewhat surprising considering how much you seem to enjoy dominance."

I freeze. "What is that supposed to mean?"

"Would you have obeyed me if I were standing in front of you shirtless? Maybe with sweat glistening like beads of silver on my… well, would you say I have a 'god-like body?'"

There's heat spreading up my cheeks. Why do those words sound so familiar? More importantly, why does it feel like he's quoting from something?

I get my answer when he pulls out a couple of books from his briefcase and places them on the table. "There. That should help your boredom."

My romance novels.

"How did you—" I stop short when it hits me: I wasn't crazy when I was perusing the pantries. He *did* do his research. "You went through my desk."

"It's my company; therefore, it's *my* desk," he corrects icily. Those silver eyes are sharp and extremely amused. "I'll give you your privacy now. I'm sure you'd prefer to be alone with Cedric."

With that, he walks off, leaving me standing there, feeling angry, embarrassed—and honestly…?

A little turned-on.

12

DMITRI

"I've never met the girl, but she's impressing me." Rogan's periwinkle eyes are magnified to alien proportions by the huge, blue-rimmed glasses she's wearing. I feel like she can see into my thoughts.

"How exactly?" I ask, despite "talking about Wren" falling at the very bottom of my to-do list.

"She kept things running smoothly. And considering your hellaciously stupid schedule, that's saying a lot."

This is not what I need right now. I don't need to hear about all the shit that Wren does well. I need to hear about all the stuff she does *badly*. I need a long and comprehensive list of all her sins, her flaws, her most annoying qualities.

Her infuriating stubbornness, for one.

Her complete inability to listen to orders, for another.

And while we're at it, there's the way she chews on her bottom lip. The way her hair curls on its way down to her breasts, like the locks are every bit as desperate for a touch of her silky skin as I am. Her eyes and her dimples and the curve of her throat where it—

Goddammit. I've completely lost the plot here.

As per fucking usual.

Rogan hasn't noticed, though. "I like the way she's rearranged the filing cabinet in here, too. And—"

"If you're looking for charter members of your Wren Turner Fan Club, look elsewhere," I snap, glowering at the brief I've been trying to read over Rogan's gushing.

Her eyes pinch together and her glasses slip down on the bridge of her nose. "My goodness, someone's crabby today. Have you had lunch?"

"Rogan."

"Or do you need another cup of coffee?" she continues blithely. "I can spike it for you, if you prefer. Whiskey, bourbon, horse tranquilizers—you name it, you got it. Whatever you need to take the edge off."

"What I need is for you to stop talking about Wren."

Rogan pushes her glasses back up and flashes a cheeky grin. "What are you more annoyed about: your assistant getting knocked up with your baby or the fact that you didn't get to do the 'knocking up' part yourself?"

Fucking hell. Now, I almost wish Wren was back so I don't have to deal with Rogan's scathing, way-too-observant honesty.

"Make yourself useful and get me some coffee."

"Fine. But I know you're trying to get rid of me," she remarks as she heads for the door.

"Nothing gets past you," I drawl back sarcastically.

She opens the door and pauses on the threshold to look back over her shoulder. "Oh, heads up: your brother is heading over with a head full of steam. Looks like he's got something important to say." She turns her back on me but I can see the apple of her cheek as she smiles. "Hello, Aleksandr. I'm getting Dmitri coffee. Would you like some as well?"

"Nix the coffee, Ro. We've got bigger fish to fry." He flies through the door but makes sure to shut it behind him. "Look alive, big brother. I've got news for you."

I arch a brow and set my papers down. "Good news?"

"I'd say this qualifies," he confirms with a self-satisfied smile. "I turned that sad excuse for a fertility clinic upside down looking for any clues that might tell us who the attacker was."

"And…?"

"The so called 'nurse' that attacked your woman—"

"She's not 'my woman!'" I snarl before I can stop myself.

Aleks holds up two hands and recoils in alarm. In his defense, my anger was a bit disproportionate. I blame Rogan. "Alright, Jesus, you're touchy. Fine—the fucker that attacked your in-no-way-emotionally-attached-and-definitely-not-'yours' baby mother isn't actually a registered nurse at the fertility clinic. He was signed in on the day of the attack about twenty minutes before he walked into Wren's examination room."

"Signed in by whom? And why?"

His shit-eating grin stretches another tooth wider. "Great questions. You can ask him yourself. Bastard's name is

Vincent Byrne. He's in the interrogation room right now, under the bowels of this building, waiting for you to torture the information right out of him." Leaning back smugly, he folds his arms over his chest. "Ta-da. You're welcome."

I close the briefing folder and stride for the door. Behind me, I hear the telltale thud of Aleks kicking his feet up on my desk and the accompanying crackle of foil as he opens a candy bar.

"That's a shit thank you!" he calls after me.

I pause at the threshold, rippling with pent-up energy that I can't wait to unload into this miserable *mudak's* face with my fists. "If you're waiting for my undying gratitude, keep fucking waiting."

Aleks is unfazed. "I'm just sayin', it wouldn't kill ya, y'know? *'Great job, Aleks. You're indispensable to me, Aleks. Couldn't have done this without you, Aleks. Aleks, you're so handsome and dashing and your penis is so—"*

"Shut up."

Finally, his smile deflates. "'Touchy' doesn't even begin to cover today's mood," he mutters to himself.

I growl in frustration, but I don't bother replying. How could I? It's not like I can explain to anyone why I'm so annoyed. What the fuck am I supposed to say?

That I woke up with the most painful, throbbing erection of my life, thinking about my P.A.-turned-baby-mama this morning? That, even after I'd managed to rub one out, I didn't feel satisfied in the least?

That I had a nightmare about being chained in place and having to watch as a fictional fucking fool named Cedric carried her off on a white horse with his idiotic Fabio hair flapping in the breeze?

Hell. Fucking. No.

I hear Aleks falling in step behind me, but I don't turn around. He knows me too well; he'll clock the turmoil on my face and have some pretty good guesses as to what might be causing it—and the last thing he needs is more ammo.

The elevator doors open onto ground floor parking. Aleksandr and I sweep through the lot to the far end, where there's a heavy metal door that can only be accessed with a special access code. Once I've punched it in, the door unlocks with a loud *thunk* of three-inch-thick bolts and whooshes open.

I spent a couple million on this basement shortly after acquiring the building. It's built like a bunker, soundproof and impenetrable. Without the tube lighting along the walls, we would be walking through pitch darkness.

"He's in the first cell on the left."

I follow where he's pointing and step inside to find Vincent Byrne bound tightly to a chair with military-grade zip-ties. He's wearing his nurse blues but there are a couple of bloodstained rips in his uniform. Apparently, he thought he could fight back.

I grab the duct tape over his mouth and pull hard to wrench it off. He spits out a curse and directs his terrified gaze in my direction. His nostrils flare with anxiety. "W-what am I d-doing here?"

I look over at my brother. "You didn't explain?"

Aleks just shrugs. "Figured it was pretty obvious. How was I supposed to know that he's stupid?"

Sighing, I turn back to Vincent and bend down so that I can look him in the eye. "We should have known. Because only a stupid man comes after one of *my* people."

Tears glisten on the man's face, refracting the purple of his bruised eye socket underneath. "I didn't come after anyone! I—"

I backhand him across the face and he yelps like a stuck pig, then clams up and descends into a shuddering, downcast silence. "Speak when spoken to, *mudak*," I spit at him. "You did plenty, whether or not you were the one holding the gun. I'm sure you're aware of what happened at the Saeder & Banks Fertility Clinic on the morning of the…"

I look over at Aleks, who fills in, "Seventeenth."

"The morning of the seventeenth," I echo grimly. "Yes or no?"

Vincent's nostrils flare again and he wriggles on his plastic chair. "I… I heard… rumors…"

"You heard a hell of a lot more than that. Especially since *you* were the motherfucker that signed in the man who came after the wrong person."

His Adam's apple bobs up and down furiously. "I-I can't r-remember."

"I suggest you try. Otherwise, this is going to get very painful." I hold out a hand without looking and Aleks deposits the cold butt of a pistol into it. I flick off the safety and start to raise it to Vincent's temple. I'm not even halfway there before he starts screaming.

"Help! Help! He's going to kill me! Help me, please—anyone!"

I pause, gun suspended in the air, and watch him as he goes blue in the face. When he finally takes a breath, I grin at him.

Then I start screaming, too. I mock him in a cruel high pitch, wailing at the top of my lungs.

When I'm bored with it, I fall silent again and wait until the echoes of our combined voices have faded away. "You can scream all you want," I explain to him. "No one can hear you. No one's coming."

A desperate sob bursts out of his bleeding lips. "P-please don't kill me," he begs. "I have a family."

I sigh. It's fucking Prisoner Bingo in here. He's screamed for help and begged for his life. I'd bet a pinky toe that he's going to piss himself next.

It's what comes after that that matters most, though. Because after that is *information.* Real, useful, bona fide information.

That's what I'm after.

That's why we're doing this whole fucking charade.

"It was *my* family you helped to target," I inform him coolly. "If I hadn't been in there with her, that attacker would have succeeded in killing my unborn child. Does that seem fair to you? Does it seem just? Kind? Merciful?"

Spit flies out of the corner of his mouth as he struggles to breathe through his rising panic. "I-I didn't know what was going to happen! I-I was just paid to let him in."

I nod to encourage him. "That's good. Tell me more. Paid by whom?"

He whimpers miserably. "I don't know."

I lift the gun without warning and shoot him in the leg. The scream that rips out of him is inhuman.

Stooping down, I squeeze his cheeks in my free hand and force him to look at me. "Unfortunately, that's not an acceptable answer," I hiss in his face. I'm not sure he even hears me over his own screams, but he should've known from the start that it would always end like this. "Now, let me ask you again. Who paid you to let the attacker in?"

"H-h-he didn't give me a n-name! B-but I can describe him to you."

"Fine." I grind my teeth together. "Paint me a picture, Vincent. Don't leave out a single detail."

"He was tall! Really tall." More saliva slicks his chin. "And he had a-a-a crew cut. Blonde, I think. He was wearing a wifebeater and he had a whole b-bunch of chains."

"What about tattoos? Scars? Birthmarks?"

"Tattoos, y-yes! He had one on his bicep. A naked w-woman, or mermaid or something. And another tattoo on his forearm. It was a dog or a wolf, I think. I-I'm not sure anymore."

I exchange a glance with Aleks who immediately pulls out his phone. He taps the screen a couple of times and then twists the phone around to show Vincent and me. "Did it look like this?"

The picture on Aleks's screen shows a dead body with the tattoo of a fierce-looking Irish wolfhound on the forearm. It's smeared with the man's blood, but there's no denying the outline. Hell, it almost looks artistic like that. Intentional, as if the hound itself took a bite out of the man wearing the ink. There's a metaphor in there somewhere.

Vincent nods frantically. "Yes, that's it! That's the one."

"Fuck." Aleks scowls, putting his phone away and cracking his knuckles.

I straighten up, trying to contain the buzz of anger that's flowing just under my skin. "How much did you get paid for your troubles?"

Vincent tenses as the tone of the conversation shifts. He can feel us retreating from him, I'm sure. Sensing his time in this room has come to an end. He's right about that. But the end he's hoping for is not the one he'll receive. "My wife is pregnant. T-t-twins. I needed the—"

"How much?"

He's sweating from the head now. "Five thousand dollars."

I shake my head. "You should have asked for more." I raise my gun fast and shoot before he has a chance to realize that he's a dead man. The bullet strikes him in the forehead and he topples backward on the chair, landing on the cement floor with a dull thud.

As I walk out of the cell, I nod to the boys by the door. "Take care of the mess. Leave no trace."

Aleks meets me in the dim hallway and circles around to lean against the bare stone wall with his arms folded over his chest.

"He's been keeping an eye on us this entire time," I growl as the door clangs behind us, muffling the sounds of my men butchering the unfortunate Mr. Byrne into easily-disposed-of pieces. "It wasn't enough that he killed Elena. He wants my future, too."

"You really think this is him?" Aleks asks cautiously.

"This has Irish scum written all over it."

Stroking his thin beard, he muses, "It does. Just seems pretty stupid to come at you now, is all I'm saying. Everyone and their mother knows you're hitching our wagon to the Zanettis. We're untouchable once that happens."

"Bee and I aren't married yet. He's trying to hit now before I gain more power. He's playing the long game."

"It's not gonna work," Aleks says confidently.

"Damn right it won't. That leprechaun fuck took Elena from me. He's not going to get anywhere near Wren or my son." I unleash my right hook into the stone, feeling the satisfying crunch of skin splitting and hot blood flowing past my knuckles. "I'll make sure of that."

13

WREN

SYRAH: *update: he was **so** not worth the Brazilian.*

I snort with laughter and check the time. 10:00 P.M. I'm usually asleep by now, but my body's hopped up on sugar and restlessness.

WREN: *finished with your date already, huh?*

SYRAH: *the highlight of the night was the espresso martini I had at dinner. i shouldve had a few more. might have helped keep me awake during the sex.*

WREN: *oof. that bad?*

SYRAH: *im considering drawing a map to my clit with turn-by-turn instructions next time. maybe that'll help.*

WREN: *your poor vagina. when will the suffering end?*

SYRAH: *if you find out, let me know. hey btw, im passing your neck of the woods in a bit. wanna grab a drink with me? end the night right?*

Blech. I hate lying to Syrah. Especially because she's been such a godsend this past week. She's filled my life with hilarious IG reels, silly memes, and a whole bunch of random links that have kept me distracted through the torturously long days.

But every time I even consider telling her what's actually going on, I imagine all the follow-up questions she'll ask, and I decide that maybe silence is better.

WREN: *id love to but I can't.*

SYRAH: *youre still sick?! i thought you said you were feeling better this morning?*

WREN: *i was. im just tired really. kinda wanna stay in and rest*

SYRAH: *kk that's no problem. I'll grab a bottle of wine and drop in at yours for a bit. i can give you all the details about the penis that took a left turn at Albuquerque :D*

It's pathetic how much I want to hear about her date, albeit maybe not in so much anatomical detail as she might prefer. But how the hell do I explain to her that I'm not home?

WREN: *i do wanna hang out but I think im gonna turn in soon*

SYRAH: *youre really starting to worry me, boo. should I come with you to the doctors next time? clearly whatever he's giving you isn't working.*

Her concern makes me feel like even more of a schmuck. I've got only one friend in the world; why should I be scared of telling her the truth? Or at least part of the truth?

We can only do this song and dance for so long. So, with a sigh, I decide that now's the moment the music stops.

WREN: *actually, the doctor said that the bug i caught will exit my body in about seven and a half months.*

It's agony waiting for her dancing three dots to disappear and the text to arrive.

SYRAH: *Wait. Are you telling me what I think you're telling me!!?!??*

SYRAH: *OH MY GOD!!!*

The typing disappears abruptly and my phone starts vibrating in my hand. Smiling, I pick up her call and answer in my best, most professional P.A. voice, "Hello, Wren Turner speaking."

Syrah's screech nearly punctures an eardrum. It's a wordless wail of excitement for a while before she finally regains the power of words. "You're pregnant!"

"Yeah," I say with an amazed sigh at how good it feels to come clean. "I am."

"I literally cannot believe this. It's legit? Confirmed?"

"Confirmed. I am one hundred percent knocked up."

"Fuuuck," Syrah breathes, drawing out the syllables in a sing-song voice. "Okay, wow. Was not expecting that. I guess I figured when you didn't say anything after your last appointment, it meant that the insemination didn't take."

"I think I was just processing it," I admit. "The whole point of getting pregnant was for Rose and Jared. And now…"

"Shit. Yeah. *Jesus,* I can't imagine… How're you doing with all of that?"

Just when I thought I had a handle on my emotions, my bottom lip goes and starts trembling. "I'm still not sure. I guess I just need time."

"Of course. I mean, duh." She lets out a sympathetic little whimper. "Are you going to be at work on Monday?"

The truth is, I have no freaking clue. Things like that are way out of my control these days. But for some reason, I find myself nodding. "Yup. That's the plan."

"Good. I miss you."

Smiling, I grip the phone a little tighter. "Miss you, too, Sy."

"If you need anything, just ask, okay? I'm happy to make late-night ice cream runs if you need it. Pickles may or may not be included."

"You're the best."

"Obviously. Anyway, I'm almost home and I know you said you're crashing, so I don't want to intrude. Talk later?"

"Definitely. I want to hear all about this unfortunately curved date."

She laughs. "I'll spare no detail. Goodnight, hon."

After I hang up, I pull the blanket off my lap and lean in towards my bedside table where a bowl of M&M's is waiting to be devoured. I'm not even hungry; it's just something to do. Snacking as a hobby isn't quite rock bottom, but it can't be *that* far off.

I have no idea how I'm gonna spend another week cooped up in this penthouse, let alone the next few months. "Batshit crazy" is starting to sound like a best-case scenario.

"Doors opening."

I bounce to my feet at the faint voice announcing a new arrival to the penthouse, shimmy into a white slip dress that I found in the walk-in closet, and run into the hallway.

I can already catch a whiff of his honey-and-musk aftershave. My resolve rallies fast and suddenly, I make a split-second decision that's at least partially fueled by the shit ton of sugary snacks I've consumed all day to stave off the looming specter of soul-crushing boredom.

By the time I walk into the living room, Dmitri is reclining on the sofa with a drink in hand. He turns to me warily as though he's anticipating a fight. I stride around the sofa until I'm standing right in front of him.

Then, without a word, I sink down onto my knees.

His eyes flare in that delicious way that only he can do. I grit my teeth and stay where I am, my chin jutting out defiantly. "You wanted me to kneel," I explain softly. "I'm kneeling."

He regards me coolly, still saying nothing. I have no idea if he's annoyed or impressed. Either way, he's called my bluff—so now, I'm calling his.

"I'm ready to go back to work."

His jaw clenches. "Stand up."

I flinch. My instincts rebel, but I force myself to bite back the retort on my tongue and get back up again.

My bare legs are almost touching his knees. Is that a bulge I see at this crotch? *Don't look. Don't get distracted.* My vagina would very much like me to lose myself completely in that particular distraction—but then again, she's never been very good at making decisions, so I tell her to STFU and focus again on Dmitri's burning silver eyes.

"Turn around."

Excitement and anger flash through me. It's amazing how close together those two emotions can travel. But with my endgame in mind, I rotate around. My ass is almost certainly staring him in the face. Why did I have to pick the see-through dress? And on a day where I'm not wearing underwear, no less.

But as much as I would like to flip him off and walk away, I don't. Dmitri wants me to refuse to follow his orders so that he has an excuse to keep me trapped in this penthouse.

Well, if that's the case, he's severely underestimated how stubborn I can be.

I hear him moving behind me, the rustle of clothes, the ocean's tide of his even breathing—but even when I feel the warmth of his proximity, he never actually touches me.

"Anything else, *sir*?" I ask over my shoulder.

That 'sir' was meant to be infused with resentment and anger. A real "fuck you" without actually saying the words. But it comes out sounding like something else entirely. Almost like I'm trying to lure him between my legs.

If my pussy throbs any louder, he's gonna be able to hear it.

When he still says nothing, I pirouette slowly to face him once more. "Well?" I demand. "Do I have my job back?"

His eyebrows lift for just a second. At least he's given me easy access: if he says no, I'll just punch him in the nuts.

My hand is slowly closing into a fist when he nods. "Yes, you've got your job back."

I exhale heavily, triumph flooding through me like a breath of fresh air. I've actually managed to move the metaphorical mountain. Put some points on the scoreboard. It's still **Wren: 1; Dmitri: A trillion**, but that's better than where we were before.

Yay for me.

I wriggle back out of his reach as the tension in the room eases, like the walls, the lights, the furniture itself is all taking a relieved breath.

Dmitri kicks one foot up onto the coffee table and sips his drink. "You'll be showing soon. People will ask questions. Did you have a story in mind?"

I squirm in place. As nice as it would be to keep certain parts of my life private, it's not exactly realistic. "The truth, more or less. I'm a surrogate for my sister and brother-in-law. If anyone asks, I'll tell them that."

"They'll want to know more. That's a lot to ask of someone."

"It was," I concede. "But you only ask a lot of the people you're close to; the people you trust; the people you love."

Those silver eyes soften. "Do you regret saying yes?"

That's a tough one, especially considering the baby I thought I was making is not the one I ended up with. This baby won't have Jared's dark brown eyes or Rose's soft smattering of freckles. Instead, he might have the shape of my face, lit up by the bright and penetrating silver eyes of the man sitting next to me.

Somehow, I don't hate that as much as I thought I would.

"I don't regret saying yes to them. I just regret everything that happened after."

He finishes the rest of his drink and gets up heavily. "Goodnight, Wren," is all he says before he slips out of the living room.

I stare after him, wondering why I feel so unsettled. I regret losing Rose and Jared the way I did. I regret that they never got to have the family they always dreamed of having. I regret that, for all their effort and prayers, it amounted to nothing in the end.

But as for the baby I'm carrying… He may not have come into being the way I planned, but it was Dmitri's contribution that made this child mine. *Truly* mine.

And even though I probably should regret that…

I don't.

I can't.

I won't.

14

WREN

I haven't been this excited for a day of work in my entire life.

I'm up at the crack of dawn in anticipation of getting into the office. Pulling on a robe, I practically skip into the kitchen for some tea. I pop an Earl Grey tea bag into boiling water and walk it back to my room.

But I stop short when I see a black box perched at the foot of my door with a Prada stamp on the lid.

"What on earth…?" I whisper, looking around. I don't see or hear anyone, but there's only one suspect on my list.

Bumping my hip into the door to open it, I slip inside and set the tea down on the bedside table. Then I lift the lid off the box with trembling fingers and…

"Oh, *wow*."

The gorgeous black skirt-suit feels like butter under my touch. Nestled beneath it in layers of velvety tissue paper is a crisp white blouse with a chic, subtle ruffle down the sleeves.

It feels beyond superficial to freak out over a designer suit—but sometimes, freaking out is just what's on the menu. When Rose and I were kids, Mom used to make most of our clothes for us by hand. Even when we got older, we shopped in thrift stores, at yard sales, not at *Prada.* For the longest time, I honestly thought it rhymed with "ta-da," like a magician revealing his big trick.

The price tag for this whole ensemble must be astronomical. It makes me nauseous to even contemplate. But as I slide the coat onto my shoulders, I find myself beginning to understand the appeal.

The fit is flawless, tailor-made for my body. I feel strong in it. I feel powerful. I feel like an honest-to-goodness businesswoman in my own right. This suit was made for someone *with* a P.A. Not someone who *is* a P.A.

Since I don't have the right shoes, I slip on my thrifted Birkenstocks and step out into the corridor. It's still early, but I figure I'll wait for Dmitri by the door. We haven't discussed it or anything, but I'm assuming that carpooling makes economical sense, even leaving aside the fact that he probably intends to keep me within arm's reach for the entire day.

The plan is to stand in the foyer and wait for him, but I hear movement in the kitchen, so I follow it there.

He's sitting at the counter, scrolling through his phone and sipping on a mug of coffee.

"Good morning," I say timidly, lingering on the threshold.

He doesn't lift his head but he does raise his eyes for a moment. "Morning." Then he goes back to his phone.

"Um… thanks for the suit. It's beautiful."

"It fits?"

"Like a dream."

He sets his phone down and scans me. "And so it does." But when his gaze settles on my feet, a frown curdles. "Those shoes are a nightmare, though."

"I know they don't match, but I don't have—"

"Wait here."

He disappears and, a minute later, he reappears with a pair of gleaming black pumps with a modest heel. When he sets them down in front of me, I spy the Jimmy Choo logo on the insole.

"Are these your, er… fiancée's?" When he nods, I bite nervously at my nails. "You sure she won't mind me borrowing them?"

"Stop asking questions and try them on."

It feels strange to slip my feet into another woman's shoes. It makes me feel like I'm stealing. Cheating, even. "May I ask, uh… where is she?" I ask tentatively. "I haven't seen her since the first night you brought me here."

"She's on a work trip in Paris at the moment. She'll be back in a few days. Here—" He slides a plate of fruit towards me. "You need to eat before we leave." He pushes another plate towards me. This one is filled with my vitamins.

I frown. "I'm not a child, Dmitri. I can take my vitamins without having to be spoon fed."

"Is that so? Because I'm not a child, either—which means I can count. And for someone who's supposed to be taking these supplements three times a day, there are way more pills in your bottles than there should be."

I try my best not to wince, but I fail miserably. "How come I have to have breakfast and you can get away with a cup of coffee?"

"Because I'm not pregnant." He smirks at my irritated groan. "Now, listen: you're going to have security when you're out of the penthouse. I've put Jasper and Bronn on you."

I pick unhappily at the slices of mango arrayed on the plate in front of me. "Don't you think it's going to raise suspicion if I show up after a week of absence with bodyguards tailing me?"

"They'll be discreet. And as for your job description, it's… changed slightly."

I flick my gaze up at him, immediately wary. "What does that mean?"

"It means congratulations, you've been promoted. You are now head of my Personal Management team."

I gawk at him. "What? That's not a thing."

"It is now."

"It's a made-up title."

"Yes. But no one in their right mind will refute it. That's one of the benefits of having your name on the skyscraper."

My scowl isn't going anywhere, though. "What is the purpose of being the head of your personal minion whatchamacallit?"

"Personal Management team," he corrects. "The purpose is to justify your increased salary. It'll also serve as an explanation later down the line if people find out you're living with Bee and myself."

My eyes nearly pop out of my head. "Wait, wait, wait. You're actually finding ways to *legitimize* this weird-ass and *extremely temporary* arrangement?" I bound off the high chair. "That's crazy. And even if you do, let's face it: no one's gonna think it's normal that your personal assistant is now living with you and your soon-to-be wife. Title change or not, that's insane."

"This promotion makes you Bee's P.A., as well as mine. You'll handle all our personal affairs—galas, charity events, joint business investments, all of it. And given that you'll be working with us so closely, it would make sense that this is a live-in position."

"That's ridiculous!"

"It's the simplest way to explain our cohabitation." He throws back the last of his coffee like it's a shot of tequila. "Now, let's go. I have things to do at the office." He grabs his leather satchel and strides for the door, making it very clear that he does not intend to wait for me.

Fuming, I jump out of my Birkenstocks, wriggle into the black Jimmy Choos, and run behind him.

"This is a bad plan!" I cry out as I jog into the elevator just in time to avoid getting nipped in the butt by the closing doors. "No one in their right mind will buy it."

Dmitri turns those dangerous silver eyes on me. "I don't give a fuck who buys what. That's the explanation they're getting. They can take it or leave it." He purses his lips and rises up tall, as if that settles things. *God,* I hate how certain he is that he's right all the time. "Now, before I forget, I got you something." He proceeds to pull out a long blade that glimmers as it moves under the amber elevator lights. "Here you go."

He extends it towards me but I just stare at the way it gleams on his open palm. "That's a knife," I say stupidly.

"You're as observant as ever, Ms. Turner."

I grimace and back away from it. That edge looks *sharp.* "You're handing me a knife?"

"For protection. Your guards will always have an eye on you, but it never hurts to be prepared. We don't want a repetition of what happened at the clinic."

I gulp and find myself reaching reluctantly for the hilt. It's black leather, with inscriptions carved into the material. As daggers go, it's quite pretty. "Thanks, I guess. Am I supposed to know how to use it?"

"Two rules," he explains. His eyes soften and his mouth relaxes just a little. "If someone bad comes for you, aim the pointy end at them."

"And the second rule?" I sass back.

"Don't stab yourself." As we reach the ground floor and he steps through the opening doors, I swear I hear him add under his breath, "And for the love of God, don't stab me, either."

15

WREN

"All hail the head of Mr. Egorov's Personal Management team!"

"Will you keep your voice down?" I hiss.

Syrah finishes her curtsy and blinks innocently as she hands me a cup of iced tea. "Why bother? Everyone already knows."

"They do?"

She shrugs. "Office gossip. Word gets around fast."

I groan and drown my frustration in peach iced tea. "This tea is the only thing that's gone right for me today," I mumble miserably. "Thanks for getting it, by the way."

"Anything for my knocked-up work wife," she says with a wink. "I know how to take care of my boo." Settling into the seat next to me, she props her temple on her fist and gives me a meaningful look. "Sooo, time to spill. I wanna know everything. What does this job involve? Are you in charge of giving him sponge baths and back massages? Because I'd have definitely applied for *that* job if I knew it was up for grabs."

I put down my drink and scowl at her. "Shouldn't you be getting home?"

Syrah giggles. "I'm on my way out. Just wanted to stop by and say hi first. Or bye, rather."

I raise my cup in a sarcastic salute. "Bye."

"Alright, alright. I can take a hint." She looks around conspiratorially and drops her voice. "Does he know you're pregnant yet?"

"Uh…" Some lies are necessary, right? I mean, truth is a spectrum. Or a process. Or… shit, I dunno. "Er, no, not yet. Not as such."

"Good thinking," Syrah agrees with a wink. "He probably doesn't want the head of his personal management team yakking up all over the seating charts for his charity galas. But again, just so you know, if you ever need a stand-in, I'm happy to take on sponge bath duties."

I scrunch up a stray piece of paper and lob it at her. "Get outta here."

Laughing, she blows me a kiss and sashays off down the hallway. I turn restlessly towards the closed door of Dmitri's office. He told me that he had only one more Zoom meeting to finish and then we could head home. But that was over thirty minutes ago, and the door has stayed resolutely shut.

The first day back has been hectic as hell and I'm all-caps WIPED. As pretty as these Jimmy Choos are, I want to get out of them with a quickness because they might've actually been designed by Satan himself to torture poor, unsuspecting women like me.

I actually have a really nice pair of secondhand heels at home that I could have worn today. If only I'd been allowed out of the penthouse before now.

Which gets me thinking...

I sit up and look around. I can't see my bodyguards anywhere. It's well past six, so most of the Egorov employees have left for the day. And my apartment is only a short ten-minute walk from here.

I could make it there and back real quick, right?

I grab my bag and dash towards the elevators before I can be spotted by my annoying shadows. That includes my bossy baby daddy. Pun very much intended.

To my utter shock and delight, it's a clean getaway. I make it out of the building without any problem and, when I hit the streets, the fresh air feels like a cool hug.

Even the walk is exhilarating. It's pathetic how much I enjoy myself as I saunter down my go-to route to get back home. My house keys are burning a hole in my pocket. Weirdly enough, I underestimated how much I would miss my apartment. My pillows. My things.

"Hello, home!" I call out enthusiastically when I walk in.

The mess I left before leaving for work that day over a week ago is waiting happily for me. A half-eaten bag of chips lies almost insultingly in front of a bowl of half-rotted fruit that I probably should've been eating instead. Shoes are scattered everywhere, including the heels I wish like hell I'd have worn in place of these Jimmy Choos. Laundry waits in a monstrous heap dumped in one of the armchairs, and I could swear that it's staring at me balefully like I should feel guilty for not having folded it much sooner.

I jump out of Bee's borrowed heels and leave them stationed in front of the door. I deposit my bag onto the floor by the sofa. My jacket gets hung over the sofa and by the time I reach my bedroom, my clothes are halfway off.

Change of plans: I'm not rushing back to the office. Dmitri is gonna take forever and a half to wrap up work, anyway.

Besides, there's nothing quite like end-of-the-work-day nudity in your own home to make you let loose that sigh you didn't even know you were holding. Taking off my bra feels like doing crack cocaine.

Honestly, being in this place is already calming me down. Albeit not enough that I manage to forget about the silver-eyed pain in my ass who handed me a freaking *dagger* this morning like a special little snack for my lunchbox.

I decide not to be a bitch and send him a text message to let him know where I am, but as it turns out, my phone's died on me.

Again.

It's infuriating how often that's happened this past week. Usually, it takes a good eight to ten hours at least before my battery drains. But for some reason, I'm barely making it to midday now before it winks out.

"Whatever," I mutter, casting my phone onto the bed. "He's a smart man. He'll figure it out."

I fill the tub with warm water and what remaining bath salts I have left. I'm about to slip into the tub to relax when it strikes me that I can really help expedite the whole wind-down process if I dip into the drawer of my bedside table, which happens to contain a pack of condoms (unopened), some lube (unused) and two vibrators (both *very* used, and one of which is helpfully waterproof.)

Weirdly, I haven't been able to *ahem ahem* "relax" at the penthouse. Even when I knew for certain I was alone, it always felt like I was in Dmitri's space. Which is ironic, considering that being in his space makes me feel perpetually horny.

But maybe that's precisely why it's difficult to masturbate there. Because not only is *he* the one giving me major lady boners, but I'm also surrounded by his presence. Thinking of him *and* being in his home... It just feels a little too intimate. He has a fiancée, for Christ's sake! I have no right to think about her man and get my rocks off to him while literally crashing in their home.

I'm no homewrecker.

Well—not intentionally, at least.

I gather my supplies, then slip into the tub and bring the vibrator between my legs. I've just coaxed it into position and turned it on when his face jumps into my head.

Those deep and intense silver eyes... That marble jaw... A nose so sharp you cut a freaking cake with it...

No. Stop it!

My eyes fly open. He is not the man I want to be thinking about right now. Who's my usual go-to?

Uh... well, *technically*, it was him. But that was before I knew he had a fiancée, so it doesn't count. And those were hate-fueled fantasies that involved me sitting on his face 'til I suffocated him. Or sucking on his cock until his balls exploded. Or riding him hard before jumping off him just before he came.

Y'know, *those* kinds of fantasies. Very normal, tasteful, acceptable fare.

"Okay, an actor," I tell myself. "Any actor." I close my eyes again. "Let's get me a little... Chris Evans. Mmm, right...?" But almost as soon as it appears, Chris Evans's face starts melting like butter until he eventually morphs into...

Dmitri Egorov.

Goddammit.

At this point, though, the vibrator is doing its job with a vengeance and I apparently can't think of a single other human male. My body is pinging with pleasure, that familiar flood of heat and tightening, and my mental faculties have decided to take a quick vacation.

So Dmitri will have to suffice.

And no sooner do I accept my fate there than does the heat and tension ratchet up several notches. I buck my hips to the surface of the water as involuntary moans escape my lips.

"Dmitri..." I whimper. "I'm yours. I'm all fucking yours..."

I underestimated just how much my body needs a release. Five minutes in and I'm pretty close to erupting. Especially with all the nasty, dirty, sexy things Dmitri is doing to me in my head.

His fingers delve deep... His lips suckle and taste and tease... He's a hard, unwavering presence crushing me and owning me and—

BANG!

I jerk so hard that quite a bit of the tub water ends up on the tile. *Did someone just break into my apartment?!* I'm in full-on panic mode when my bathroom door is shoved open and Mr. Pain-In-The-Ass-Himself storms in.

And those silver eyes blare the truth, clear as day: *He. Heard. Everything.*

16

DMITRI

Her phone is basically a memorial.

The cloned phone in my possession is chock full of pictures, videos, and conversations with Rose. January 16th: that was the last point of contact between them. Over two months ago now.

I remember now that she took a week off at the end of January. I'd been annoyed as hell about it and made no secret of that fact. But she gave me no explanation, apart from the very vague, *"I have family commitments."*

In retrospect, I feel like a fucking asshole.

"Yo, bro," Aleksandr greets as he walks in without warning. "'Sup?"

"What do you have for me?"

He purses his lips and drops heavily into one of the chairs opposite me. "Once again, I see we are dispensing with manners. *'Hello, beloved younger brother of mine. How's it going with you? What is new in your world? You are looking especially handsome today.'* I'd take any of that."

"Must we do this every time?"

"You're the only man on the planet who gets *crabbier* when he's juggling two women," he accuses. "It's insane."

"I'm not juggling either one of them. One's a ploy and the other's a surrogate."

Aleks looks skeptical. "Does *she* know that?"

I'm eyeing the blue envelope in his hand impatiently. It's sealed at the top, so I know that Aleks probably doesn't know what's inside. Neither do I, though I'm itching to find out. "Did you look into her background?"

"Oi!" Aleks says, snapping his fingers in my face, which makes me realize I've been staring into empty space. "My eyes are up here." He rolls his eyes dramatically to prove his point. *"Men."*

"I feel less and less bad these days for beating you up when we were boys."

"Touché." Aleks chuckles and raises the envelope. "Shall I do the honors?"

I nod and he tears the flap open. My jaw is pulsing with anticipation. From the moment Wren told me about her sister, I haven't been able to expel the nagging suspicion that there is more to this story.

And that I might have more to do with it than either one of us has realized.

"Well?"

Aleks squints down at the papers as he shuffles through them. But slowly, the squint turns to wide-eyed shock. "Shit. Shit! *Shiiiiit.*" That's about all I need to confirm that my suspicions, my instincts, were right. "She's *his* sister-in-law?" Aleks asks, glancing up at me. "How is this possible? How is the world *that* small?"

"Fate's a cruel bitch. That's how."

Aleks's jaw goes slack as he tries to process through it. "Does she know?"

"Fuck no. And she can't know, either. Not until that baby is safely delivered."

He nods and looks back down at his papers. "Well, you want the good news? There doesn't seem to be a man in the picture. Seems as though she's been unattached for a while. Probably why she decided to stop waiting for a man and have this baby herself."

"She didn't want the baby for herself," I explain gruffly. "She was doing it for her sister."

Aleks's forehead wrinkles with confusion. "I don't get it."

"Her sister and brother-in-law were the ones who wanted a child. But because of Rose's infertility problems, Wren was donating her uterus and her egg so that they could have a baby."

"Oh. *Fuuuck.*"

What I can't get past is that, when she finally caved and told me why she wound up in Shithead Saeder's clinic, it was clear to me that she didn't actually want to tell me of her own volition. It was a concession on her part. She was *choosing* to trust me. Whether she realized it or not.

"That's kinda fucking awesome of her," Aleks muses quietly.

He's not wrong about that. It kinda fucking is. I stretch my hand out over the table for the documents and Aleks hands them over. I flip through them, picking up little sound bites of Wren's life as I go.

I grew up with this idea that everything in life has limits. Including and especially love. Elena used to call me her soulmate, but she still didn't want to have my babies. I considered Elena the love of my life, but I would never have given up my Bratva for her.

There were always lines. Always.

But in a single conversation, Wren Turner laid waste to that hypothesis.

She not only agreed to put herself through the discomfort and inconvenience of pregnancy, but she also agreed to hand over this baby that she helped create. She was giving her sister the most intimate part of herself and relinquishing every right she might've had along the way.

I could never do anything like that. If there was a child out there that I knew was mine, there's no fucking way I would step aside and watch someone else raise them.

"Fucking hell," I spit as I read more. "She was helping them *pay* for the damn process, too. She's got an active loan for the precise amount."

Aleks leans over the table to get a better look. "Jeez. She must have really loved her sister, huh?" Settling back in his seat, he adds, "That's gonna make things more complicated."

"Tell me something I don't know." I grimace as I keep reading. It feels borderline invasive. Like I've got Wren herself splayed out naked and vulnerable on my desk. Come to think of it, that sounds kind of…

Cut it out, asshole.

Chuckling he gets to his feet. "It's kinda funny, don't you think?"

"What is?"

I know that smile of his: it means he's about to make an observation that I won't like. "You've fucked so many women —and the one female in this city you haven't slept with is the one you managed to knock up."

I jab a finger toward the door. "Out."

Cackling, he heads for the door while I try not to obsess about just how cruel a bitch fate can be. Aleks might find it funny, but my balls don't agree. They're way past blue at this point. They're fucking black *and* blue.

Every spare moment I have, I'm fighting the image of Wren on her knees in front of me. Biting her bottom lip and trying to follow orders, even though she's fighting her very nature to do it.

The kneeling thing was a test. A passing whim. And yet when she finally did it, when she yielded, when she submitted, she did it in a dress I could see straight through, with a body I couldn't look away from even if it fucking killed me.

There was so much blood flooding to my cock that, for a moment, I'd almost taken leave of my senses and reached for her.

Thank God I didn't.

If I did it, if I touched her, that would have been it. I'd have ripped that dress right off her and bent her over the coffee table and crossed lines that could never, ever be uncrossed.

Which would have been a disaster.

But at that particular moment, I wasn't thinking about disasters or consequences or what I should or shouldn't do. I was only thinking, *I have to right this wrong.* Surely the fact that she was carrying my baby entitled me to at least one torrid, intense whirlwind of a fuck.

Just *one* time.

And then I'd be able to put this burning desire to bed.

"Anything else before I go, Your Majesty?" Aleks calls from the door.

I start gathering up the files. I'm planning on going over them with a fine-toothed comb when I arrive home. "Tell Wren to get her belongings together. I'll be out in a minute."

"Roger." Aleks peeks around the corner, then looks back in with a frown. "Uh, she's not here. Did she already go home?"

I bounce upright. "What do you mean, 'she's not here'?"

"Which part is the confusing one? She ain't here and her shit ain't here, neither. Aren't Jasper and Bronn her security detail? I saw them in the lobby when I came in, but that was like an hour ago."

"Fuck!" I spit as I stuff the file into my briefcase and grab the cloned phone.

"I put a tracker on her phone, 'member? You should be able to—"

"I'm already on it," I snap as I wait for the app to load and tell me where the hell my defiant little *kiska* has snuck off to.

"Well? Where is she?"

I grab my stuff and storm to the door. "I don't know how she did it, but she managed to get all the way to her apartment." I overtake Aleks in the corridor. "Tell Jasper and Bronn to go fuck themselves."

Aleks jumps sideways into the elevator with me before the doors close on him. "Don't stress. She's obviously safe."

"She won't be when I find her."

17

DMITRI

Wren's apartment is only a short walk from the Egorov building, but for some reason, it feels like she's far from my reach and I don't like that shit one bit.

Any number of things could happen in the ten minutes it takes me to get there.

What if that old prick, Vittorio, discovered our little ruse and sent Dante to get her out of the way? What if the Irish have eyes on her and they're planning an attack as we speak? What if they've already attacked and she's lying on her sofa with her throat slit and my baby already dead in her womb?

Jasper pops up in front of me, his face drained of color. "Boss—"

"I'll deal with you two later. Right now, I suggest you get the fuck out of my way."

He jumps to the side and lets me pass. Aleksandr shouts something after me, but I'm too incensed to hear and far too agitated to stop and listen. I jump into my car, which is the only one with the authority to park outside the building, and speed in the direction of Wren's depressing little hovel.

When I get there, I take the steps two at a time until I get to her floor. There's only one window at each stairwell, which means the hallways are powered by a sickly orange-yellow light that makes my skin crawl.

As I head down the corridor that leads to Wren's apartment, I notice a balding, middle-aged man standing at the wall, his ear pressed against it and a smarmy grin on his face.

What the fuck...?

He doesn't notice me until I'm standing right on top of him. And only when my shadow engulfs him does he recoil upright, his eyes bulging wide as he looks me up and down.

"What are you doing?" I demand.

Relaxing, he leers towards the surface he was trying to make out with a moment ago. "Walls are thin here, mate. The little filly in this apartment seems to be getting her holes drilled hard."

Is that sound I'm hearing a *moan*?

Is that *Wren's* moan?

I glance down at the pervert's crotch and realize he's hard. He's fucking *hard* listening to *my* woman masturbate. Or at least, she'd better be fucking masturbating in there—because if not, whoever she's with is going to die.

My hands ball into fists. "Enjoying yourself out here, are we?"

Given my death stare, he's starting to look a little uneasy. "Uh, er, I was just... Walls are thin... She was the one moaning like a whore on her off—"

My fist flies into his face so fast he never sees it coming. The pervert stumbles back, blood gushing from his nose like a faucet.

"You better get yourself to the emergency room," I hiss. "Looks bad."

He whimpers, staring down in disbelief at the blood in his palm. When I flinch toward him again, he lets out a strangled cry and hauls in the opposite direction towards the fire escape.

As soon as he's gone, I turn my sights on the door.

It takes hardly any run-up to splinter the thing to bits. I step through the wreckage and the moans cut off suddenly.

But not before I hear the last echoes of something that makes all my blood flow south.

The door hits the Jimmy Choos she's just left lying on the floor right in front of it. I can hear her moans clearer and clearer as I move into the bedroom.

"Dmitri... I'm yours. I'm all fucking yours..."

She's mine alright. But not in the way she seems to think she is.

When I burst into the bathroom violently, Wren sits up so fast that half the water in the tub sloshes over the edge and runs up to my shoes.

"What. The. Hell?!" she gasps. "Dmitri! Get out!" The mechanical sounds of her vibrator are thumping against the floor of the tub where she dropped it. She roots around for it and turns it off quickly, her cheeks flaming bright.

I don't budge. "You were supposed to wait for me."

Her jaw is set stubbornly as she pulls her knees up to her chest. Joke's on her; I can still see the swell of her breasts, which is all I need to feel my pulse thundering below the belt. "Yeah, well, I *didn't*. Sue me."

"I'm gonna do a lot worse than that. Get out. We're going home."

Her cheeks are a fire hazard at this point. Only half of it is embarrassment. The other half is anger. "*This* is my home. It's where all my things are. My clothes, my books, my—"

"Your vibrators. Yes, I'm aware. Now, I don't intend to repeat myself. So you can either get out on your own, or I'm going to carry you out with my own two hands. I don't think we need to discuss which one I'd prefer."

Her jaw clamps shut and her eyes spark with fire. Fucking hell, she looks good with wet hair. "Keep your hands to yourself," she seethes.

She stands up defiantly and I'm faced with the full force of her nakedness. Her belly is still reasonably flat, for the time being at least. Her breasts are perched high and proud on her chest, the nipples hard and round and juicy. Those slim thighs of hers meet at her naked pussy which is glistening with beads of water and achingly alive.

She gets out of the tub, giving me a full view of her tight little slit. I'm so distracted that I almost forget to warn her that the floor is slippery. "Be care—"

Her foot hits the water and she starts to slide wildly to the left. I move without thinking—I jump forward and grab her, the entirety of her body smacking against my suit. I never thought I'd resent my Tom Ford two-piece so much; I want to feel her skin against mine, but I have to settle for this distant mockery of it.

The moment she's steady, she pushes away from me and snatches her towel off the hook. "Do I at least get the dignity of dressing in private or are you gonna stand here and watch that, too?"

I try to pretend like I'm not still imagining her naked body and all the depraved things I would do to it if I had the chance. "I'll be in your bedroom, packing a bag for you."

"Packing a bag?" she gapes. "But—what—*why?*"

"Apparently, I haven't made myself clear. From now on, you will be living with me. *Permanently.*"

18

DMITRI

"*Stronzo!*" Bee exclaims as she pokes her head from around the corner at the sound of Wren slamming the door closed. "The hell was that about?"

I dump my briefcase in the foyer and join her in the kitchen. "That was a temper tantrum by a stubborn little brat who has trouble taking advice."

Bee smirks knowingly. "Were you actually giving her advice or were you giving her orders? Because there is a difference and it is not an insignificant one." Groaning, I grab the glass of vodka she's nursing and take a not insignificant gulp of it. "Hey!" She eyes the glass for a few moments before her shoulders drop. "Fine. I'll pour myself another glass. Also, just FYI, I'm on her side by default."

"You don't even know what happened."

"Don't care."

Rolling my eyes, I sit down at the center island and take another sip of Bee's vodka. "Preparing for dinner tonight, huh?"

She fills the glass to the very top. "Yup. I need some liquid courage."

"Please. You're two parts brave. One part… well, alcohol."

"Har de har har." She scoffs. "I'm not brave. I'm a coward when it comes to my father." She stares down at the clear liquid in her crystal glass. "I *hate* these dinners."

I scrutinize the outfit she's chosen—a black miniskirt with a daring red halter that highlights both her flat chest and her flatter belly. "Not to further sour your mood, but is that what you're wearing?"

She looks down. "Why? It doesn't scream 'glowing and maternal'?"

"I'd say it screams 'hooker for cheap.'"

Flashing me a manicured middle finger, she says, "Asshole. I've got a whole other outfit planned. Something loose to back up the big reveal." She shudders. "Do we *have* to announce the pregnancy tonight, though?"

"Yes. Wren's already three months in. Soon, she's going to start showing and you're going to have to mimic her pregnancy as she gets bigger. Which reminds me… the package came this morning."

She makes a show of crossing her fingers on both hands. "Let it be Gucci. Let it be Gucci. Let it be… Fuck."

When she sees what I'm holding, her face crumbles to pieces. I don't have to look to know, since I checked this morning to make sure the order was correct.

"We've been over this, Bee. It has to be done." I temper my own frustration because I understand hers. I may have my own miserable part to play in this little charade, but at least it doesn't include prosthetics.

"Can't I just... not see anyone 'til the baby is born?" she begs as she fingers the plasticky swell of the fake pregnancy belly lying limply in the box.

"He expects us to be at family dinners on the fourth week of every month."

"So we'll get a doctor's note or something. We'll say that I'm forced to be on bedrest until the baby's born. Yeah!" Her eyes get more and more animated. "We'll tell him that the pregnancy is high-risk. That way, once this kid is born, we can also say that another pregnancy might kill me so we won't have to do this ridiculous dance a second time."

"Bee," I say patiently, "you know the stakes. If you don't go to him, he'll come here. That's worse."

Her face somehow falls even further, just when I thought she was running out of places for it to go. She drops her chin onto her interlaced fingers on the countertop.

"Just try it on," I encourage, nudging the box toward her. "It's made with the best material money can buy."

Bee's face is still hidden from view. *"Idumwansjfhosndnndifiebsnb!"*

"You'll have to repeat that," I drawl, tilting my glass back and forth so the vodka sloshes from side to side, not unlike the way Wren's bathwater went this way and that as I...

Cut. It. Out.

She drops her hands and looks at me with narrowed eyes. "I don't want to be pregnant. Even fake pregnant!"

Sighing, I push it in her direction. "You don't have a choice."

She snatches it from me angrily and holds it up against her stomach. "God, this feels wrong."

"You'll get used to it."

"Fuck you."

Suppressing a smile, I take her glass and offer it back to her. "Drink. You'll feel better once you're done. Then you'll have to chew through a pack of gum and some mints before we get to your father's estate. He can't smell alcohol on your breath."

She discards the fake belly unceremoniously. "Can you get it away? I can't bear to look at it anymore."

Sighing, I give her what she wants for the meantime. Once the box is packed away in the storeroom, I sit back down beside her. The glass of vodka is long since drained to the dregs. "Bee, need I remind you that this was your idea?"

"It felt like a good one at the time."

"It still is."

She wrinkles up her nose. "Don't take this the wrong way, because I do love you to death… but the thought of marrying you makes me want to cry."

I snort with laughter. "I'm not exactly jumping for joy myself."

She starts laughing, too, and by the end of it, she's dabbing her eyes with a napkin to keep the tears from ruining her makeup. "God," she sighs as her laughter subsides. "I'm sorry

I haven't been around this past week. Especially with Wren being here. I guess having her here made it so much more real and I needed to blow off some steam. I needed to lose myself in fun."

"Mm, and what's *fun's* name?"

She gives me a mischievous grin. "This girl I met at Wallflower. Arianne. Body like a goddess and a smile like you wouldn't believe."

"Planning on seeing her some more?"

She scrunches up her nose again as she shakes her head. "Nah. It ran its course."

"Good."

She does a double take as she twists in her seat to face me. "'Good'? You've never celebrated the demise of any of my relationships before."

"First of all, they're not relationships. They're flings—"

"Rude."

"—and second of all, we're in the home stretch now. We've got to sell this whole happy family story. And that means you're going to have to be a lot more discreet about your outings."

"'Discreet' is my middle name, asshole."

She's joking, but I'm not. "It's not enough, Bee. Flitting off to France for a weekend just because you feel like impressing some cocktail waitress? Buying out a theater because you want to win over the coat check girl at the opera? That shit can't happen anymore."

She pales as she realizes just how serious I am. "The whole point of our agreement is that I'm free to live—"

"I'm not saying this is forever. I'm saying that you need to play the game well so that your father doesn't suspect we're rigging it."

Her mouth clamps shut. I can tell she wants to argue, but simple logic is against her here. "Fuck," she breathes at last.

"We'll figure something out, okay?" I reassure her. "But we're at a critical stage. And it's not just you and me anymore. Wren's involved, too."

The moment I say her name, Bee's expression mutates. The hard line of her eyebrows relaxes just a little and her frown turns up slowly into a saucy smirk. "Getting fond of your pretty little baby mama, are you?"

"I'm just stating the obvious."

Her smile gets a little wider and just a smidge more superior. "If you say so. Speaking of which, you gonna tell me what happened with you and her just now? That door slam came with a *vengeance*."

I scowl as fresh irritation floods through me. "We were supposed to come back home together straight after work. She decided to go rogue on me and detour back to her place instead."

"Ah. So you stormed her place and dragged her back here like the caveman that you insist on being?"

I finish the last drops of my drink and nod begrudgingly. "More or less."

She shakes her head with that annoying pursed smile of hers. "You're really laying the honey on thick, huh? Glad to know you were listening to me."

"The fuck am I supposed to do?" I snarl. "I cook for her; I buy her books; I give her gifts. She's got a closet full of designer brands and a kitchen stocked with every brand of junk food she likes. And she likes *a lot* of junk food."

Bee looks deeply unimpressed as she stares at me in disbelief.

"What?" I snap at last.

She lifts her hands and starts slow clapping. "Wow. Amazing. You're doing a fantastic job."

"I loathe sarcasm."

"That's the pot calling the kettle—"

"Let me clarify: I hate when *you* use sarcasm on me."

She scowls and punches me in the arm. "Well, tough. I'm not Elena." As soon as the words leave her lips, she goes ghost-white and clamps her lips closed tightly. "I'm so sorry. I shouldn't have."

"No, no," I growl. "Tell me. What did you mean by that?"

Sighing, she starts playing with the condensation ring that her glass left on the marble, her eyes hooded and downcast. "I guess I just meant that she never really criticized you. She let you off the hook all the time. She went along with everything you said and every decision you made, even if she didn't agree with it."

I stare at her with wide-eyed disbelief. "Why would she do that?"

Bee shrugs. "I'm just speculating here, to be clear. But if I had to guess… I'd say that she probably loved you so much that she wanted to avoid conflict. I've just never agreed with that kind of mindset. Differences of opinion, arguments, honest conversation—that's what makes a relationship strong. That's what makes a relationship *real*. Cracks are how the light gets in, y'know?"

"Our relationship was real," I rasp. "It was very fucking real."

Bee's expression doesn't change. Call her many things, but she's no coward. She doesn't wilt in the face of my anger. She never has.

"I know it was, Dmitri. That's not what I was trying to say."

"What *were* you trying to say?"

She gives me a small, thin smile. "I would explain, if I weren't terrified that you're gonna bite my head off if I do."

At last, I sigh and relent. "You haven't been terrified of that since the day we met."

She rests a friendly hand on my forearm. "You loved Elena and she loved you. But sometimes, it felt like you were in love with the version of her you'd created in your head. And she did the same."

"I have no fucking clue what that means."

She shakes her head and gets off her high chair. "It doesn't matter. I'm sorry; I shouldn't have said anything at all. I have to get ready for the charade. Meet you back here in, like, fifteen."

"An hour it is."

She rolls her eyes and gives me another middle finger. "You think you know me so well."

When she's gone, I'm tempted to pour myself another drink, but I doubt that turning up to the Zanetti estate drunk off my ass will improve the already-fraught relations with Don Vittorio. Instead, I walk over to the window that overlooks the city and try to get myself into a Zen mindset in preparation for—

I twist around as Wren stomps into the kitchen. She takes one look at me and stops short. "I came to get something to eat," she explains nastily. "That is, if Your Highness allows such indiscretions."

I sweep a kingly hand toward the kitchen, smirking at her anger. "Everything the light touches is yours."

Her face screws up with irritation. "How generous of you. We subjects are all so lucky to serve such a kind and benevolent tyrant."

She stalks off towards the fridge and proceeds to stare at its contents for a while before she ultimately pulls out a bar of chocolate and a carton of milk. I watch her move, vibrating with agitation as she flits around the kitchen. Her jaw keeps flexing from side to side aggressively, no doubt fighting the urge to tell me to go to hell.

Finally, she succumbs. She whirls around and spits, "I *like* my apartment. It was the first place I ever had to myself."

Her eyes are all fired up and for some sick reason, it's getting me fired up, too. But instead of getting angry, I'm just getting hard.

"Consider this a step up then."

She gestures to the kitchen. "This isn't my apartment and it's certainly not my home! This is the home you share with your fiancée! And I'm not interested in playing third wheel."

"You seemed pretty content to play the third wheel with your sister and brother-in-law."

Even as I say it, I cringe. It's a low blow. A *very* low blow.

Wren's jaw drops but the fire in her eyes burns a little brighter. "You're an unbelievable asshole."

"And you're a stubborn little girl who can't seem to understand the fact that all I'm trying to do is *protect* you."

"Protect me? Or control me?"

"Sometimes, they're one and the same."

She takes a feisty step toward me, brandishing a teaspoon like a broadsword. "Tyrant."

I step right up to meet her. "Brat."

Fuck, how is it that she already smells like chocolate? All I want to do is lean in and take a bite out of her. Something ripples across her eyes. A similar realization that has her stumbling back a little, forcing some distance between us.

"Just… leave me alone," she mutters weakly, studiously avoiding my eyes.

"You can kick and scream—you can turn this place upside down if you choose to—but none of it will change the fact that this is your new home." I hesitate, both of us churning with more things we desperately want to say but refuse to let loose into the world. "Now, if you'll excuse me, Bee and I have a dinner to attend."

Then I walk out of the kitchen before I do something really stupid.

Like kiss her.

19

DMITRI

"This blouse makes me look like a grandma," complains Bee.

I keep my eyes on the road. "I don't know any grandmas who wear miniskirts or four-inch heels."

"Well, I had to compensate for this billowy potato sack of a shirt, didn't I?" she snaps. "I don't even know why I own it. I can't even remember buying it."

"That's because *I* bought it for you. Your wardrobe needed some filling out. Especially to accommodate your fake pregnancy stomach."

She twists in her seat, jaw agape in horror. "You went into my closet?"

"Had to be done."

"You never go into a woman's wardrobe without permission. That's a sacred space, Dmitri Egorov."

She's an alley cat backed into a corner right now, all bristling fur and bared fangs. But I've known Beatrice Zanetti long enough not to take it personally. It's just a natural reaction, born out of our nearing proximity to her father's estate. Every foot closer to him makes her another fraction wilder, crazier, more afraid.

She squirms in her seat. "I need a smoke." She quit smoking ten years ago, but she always starts craving cigarettes whenever she sees those intimidating black gates. "Do you think Little Miss Fake Boobs will be there?"

"She was at the last three dinners. Safe to assume that streak will continue."

She starts mumbling unintelligibly to herself, though I do manage to catch a couple of words here and there, mostly variations on the same theme. "… *fifteen* years younger… fucking ridiculous… pathetic… embarrassing…"

The gates swing inward as we approach and I steer us to a stop in the circular courtyard. The façade of the mansion is typical Italian Renaissance, all fluted columns and ornate pilasters, pediments, entablatures, arches, domes, with an extra bluster of self-importance layered on for good measure. *"Why have bare marble when you could paint gold leaf on* top *of bare marble"* seems to have been the guiding philosophy here.

Then again, when you meet the owner of the mansion, it makes perfect sense.

The butler shows us into the grand living room, where Vittorio Zanetti reclines on a gold velvet sofa, surrounded by his usual army of sycophants. His brother and consigliere, Alberto, is on his left, indulging in red wine and the company of a giggling, scantily clad brunette. His underboss, Valentino, is on his right, leaning forward and rolling joints on the gold-legged, glass-topped coffee table. Dante lurks somewhere in the shadows.

Bee sighs tiredly beside me. "It's always the fucking same," she mutters just before Vittorio spots us.

"*Figlia!*" he cries, throwing his arms out in welcome. "My daughter! How wonderful it is to see you."

He leaps up and embraces Bee tightly while she stands stiffly in place, her smile a mere ghost of what it usually is. "Papa."

He raps her lightly on the cheek with many-ringed fingers. "What is this hideous blouse you are wearing? How can I say I have a pretty daughter when you dress like a *paisano*?"

She just about manages to quell her scowl. "Perhaps you could say you have a smart daughter instead?"

"Ha!" he bellows. "Women don't need to be smart. In fact, it is better if they are not. Like your mother, my dear. She was the perfect woman. Beautiful as a rose... and stupid as a doorknob."

As Vittorio turns back to reclaim his seat on the sofa, Bee's face twists with anger. "You—"

"Thank you for having us tonight, Vittorio," I interrupt, throwing my arm over Bee's shoulders and reeling her against me.

Vittorio regards me coldly with his watery, pale blue eyes. His smile is tempered, more calculating than sincere. "Son-in-law. Dante tells me you've been keeping my daughter happy."

If I clench any tighter, I might just break my jaw. I take a deep breath and blow out some of the tension. "I'm relieved to hear Dante is satisfied with the state of my relationship."

Vittorio glances towards Dante, who is prowling in a dimly lit corner like the freakish little ghoul he is. "There is such a thing as being *too* happy, though. Women have many desires, not all of which can be encouraged. I heard you went to France recently, dear daughter."

"Steady," I whisper to Bee out of the side of my mouth.

"Just for a few days, Papa."

Vittorio doesn't even grant Bee a glance. He just sits back and runs a hand over his massive paunch. "I never let my women out of my sight. Even when they are not with me, they are watched. Women are fickle things, Dmitri. They have weak minds and even weaker control of their urges. You must not allow her to run rampant, yes? You are *pakhan*. You are the man. You must show her where the power lies."

He flicks his gaze over to the bored twenty-year-old who's twirling a lock of golden hair between her manicured nails.

To my eyes, she looks like a child.

To Vittorio's, she must look like prey.

"Look at my little dove," he purrs. "So pure, so pretty. That beauty must be protected, yes? For if she disobeys me, is it not my fault for making her feel like she has the option to do so?"

The only way I manage to stand there and tolerate his nauseating speech is by picturing me throttling him, my hands locked around his neck as the life melts out of his eyes.

One day. Perhaps even one day soon.

"We have an announcement to make!" Bee blurts without warning.

I glance at her in alarm. "Now?"

"Yes, fucking now," she hisses to me. "Before I murder him in front of everyone." Then she plasters a smile on her face and raises her voice. "I'm pregnant."

Vittorio's eyes bulge. "Pregnant! You're sure?"

Bee nods frantically. Too frantically, in my opinion. "Positive. We had it confirmed yesterday."

"Ah-ha!" her father cries, heaving himself up to his feet for the second time. He toddles forward and clasps my hand, forcing me to let go of Bee. "See?" he spits at me as if his own daughter isn't standing well within earshot. "I told you that you could fuck those disgusting urges out of her, did I not?"

Bee flinches next to me. When I peer over, she's got her lips pressed together in a thin, brutal slash.

"This is great news," Vittorio exclaims loudly. "I'm sure it will be a boy. A grandson! A continuation of my legacy."

"*Your* legacy?" Alberto drawls, eyeing me with a dagger-like stare. "Seems to me that our alliance with the Russians means that this baby is a continuation of the Egorov Bratva's legacy."

Vittorio's smile doesn't drop, but I can see how it freezes on his face, an icy rictus of fake joy. "Pah! Nonsense. Come! Let us celebrate with dinner, with good food and good wine. We can toast to my grandson." He clicks his fingers to the clueless blonde behind whom Dante is prowling. "Come, my pretty lamb. Lead the way. You are so much prettier when you are in front of me."

She sashays to the dining room, switching her hips as she goes. Vittorio follows, slaving like a rabid wolf, and the rest of the sycophants fall in line behind him. Only Bee and I hang back a little.

"Jesus Christ," she gasps, as if the air in here is thin and lacking. "That was worse than I expected."

"You did it," I say quietly. "You *can* do this, Bee."

"Without killing him? I'm not so sure."

"I am. Do you know why?"

She looks me deep in the eye and in that one glance, I can see just how much weight she's carrying. She's lived under her father's shadow for too damn long. "Why?"

"Because I'll be right here with you."

20

DMITRI

Zanetti dinners are unbearably long and tortuously boring. Conversation revolves around two primary topics. One is the glorification of the white, Italian, Catholic male, who is surely the finest of God's many creations, to hear Vittorio tell it.

The other is the defamation of anyone who doesn't fall in that category.

Minorities, other ethnicities, and God forbid, *women,* are the recipients of one insult after the next. Each of the seven courses is brimming over with jokes at the expense of everyone who's ever lived who isn't straight out of Hollywood casting for an Italian mobster.

Vittorio has just finished laughing at a joke Valentino made at the expense of a paraplegic Muslim lawyer with one foot in the Chicago underworld when he turns to me. Bee is brooding on my opposite side, nursing a glass of fruit juice with obvious distaste.

"We must ensure Beatrice's total protection now," he intones suddenly, shifting the subject in whiplash fashion and sending a plume of prosecco- and prosciutto-laced breath in my face. He's long past tipsy and well on his way to drunk, but unfortunately for all of us, that only makes the *mudak* talk louder. "Now that you've managed to plant a little Russian runt in my daughter's dried-up old womb, we must ensure it stays there."

"I'm doing everything there is to—"

He slams his palm against my back. "*Che sorpresa,* no? I didn't think this would happen before the wedding. Already trying to rob me of my kingdom before you've even put a ring on my daughter's finger. Sly Russian bastard, aren't you?"

"It's not a robbery if it's freely given," I point out icily. "As per the terms of our alliance."

Vittorio scowls as he picks up his glass of prosecco. "I'm aware of the terms of our alliance, Egorov. I still don't have to fucking *like* it." He hiccups loudly. "I want my grandson to take my name."

Bee stiffens beside me, but she doesn't say a word. I rest a hand on her knee under the table and keep my focus on her father. "You expect *my* son to wear your name instead of mine? Perhaps you've had a bit too much to drink, Vittorio."

"A hyphenate is reasonable. Zanetti-Egorov. That is a fair compromise, yes. Especially considering you will be inheriting all my wealth and power after I am no more."

"I will consider it," I say curtly, though I have no intention whatsoever of letting Vittorio get a single grubby finger on what's mine from the afterlife.

"Yes, yes," he slurs. "Consider it. As long as you give me the answer I want. Ha! This is good… very good." He leans around me to look at Beatrice. "See, *mia figlia*? Aren't you glad I beat the devils out of you early? Would you have been carrying the heir to not one but *two* mafias if it had not been for your papa?"

I redouble my grip on Bee's thigh and squeeze gently. She plasters a pained smile onto her face. "No, Papa. I would not have."

He laughs, too amused with himself. "And *you*." He claps my back again and finishes off what's at least his tenth drink of the night. "It's a good thing that pretty little wife of yours died when she did. Thanks to those dirty Irishmen, I didn't have to kill her off myself. Ha!"

I'm considering how bad damage control would be if I were to grab the serrated steak knife on the table and plunge it into his windpipe when Bee's hand lands on my leg.

Breathe, she mouths to me.

Problem is, Vittorio is still going. "You just got yourself an updated model, Egorov. This one—" He jabs a fat finger at Bee. "—may have been deviant once, but at least her womb can hold a baby. That first wife of yours… How many years and nothing? Young and pretty doesn't mean shit if she can't do her job and *breed*, am I right? Am I fucking right?!"

The table erupts in cheers from the slobbering jackals in Vittorio's employ. I slide my chair back and get to my feet. I hear Bee's gasp loud and clear amidst the roar of voices that immediately subside when I stand.

Vittorio stares up at me, those pale blue eyes immediately cautious. I wonder suddenly if he's not quite as drunk as I thought he was. "Have I *offended* you in some way, young Dmitri?"

Adrenaline is pumping through my body like poison. One move is all it would take to end the sexist, racist, homophobic *kozyol* sitting next to me. I'd happily risk my life to watch Vittorio bleed out and die.

But Bee?

Risking *her* life is something I can't do.

"Not at all, Vittorio," I assure him, slamming my palm against his shoulder. "I just need to get my woman home. She needs to rest; the pregnancy wears on her."

The Zanetti don eyes me for a long, tense moment.

No one else breathes or moves.

Then, at last, he smiles that sloppy, drunken smirk of his and waves a hand toward the door. "Of course! Alberto, show them out." As we're walking out of the dining room, Vittorio's voice rises. "And if you need to blow off some steam, Dmitri, let me know. I know of some delicious little offerings you can try. The sweetest pussy you will ever taste."

I have only the energy to nod back in response before we get the hell out of there. Neither Bee nor I say a thing until we're back in my Porsche and driving back to the penthouse as fast as the engine will take us.

"Well," she exhales as though the simple act of breathing is costing her dearly, "that dinner definitely killed a few billion brain cells."

"I'm not sure how someone like you could have come from someone like him."

She laughs miserably. "That's the nicest thing you've ever said about me."

Laughter bursts through my lips and immediately, the atmosphere in the car changes. Bee relaxes, stops picking at her cuticles, and finds her breath again. "I'm sorry about what he said about Elena," she offers.

"Don't ever think you have to apologize for that fucker."

"I just wanna get in bed and sleep for days."

"Well, you're pregnant. It's understandable."

She smacks my arm with a girlish giggle and we fall into silence for the rest of the drive. She's no doubt thinking about the five pregnancy bellies tucked away in our storeroom right now.

As for me? I'm thinking about Elena.

And Wren.

And the fact that thinking about the latter makes me feel guilty for not thinking about the former instead.

My first indication that something is not quite right comes when the elevator reaches the penthouse.

Bee's forehead wrinkles. "Is that music…?"

"Doors opening."

The moment the doors part, we're rocked by a tidal wave of drums and bass blasting so loud through the in-built sound system that the crescendo dissolves into nothing but hissing, staticky feedback.

"What the…?" I know Bee's screaming but it sounds as though she's barely speaking.

I follow the bass into the living room, which looks like a nuke was dropped in the middle of it. Ripped pillows and couch cushions spew their cotton guts everywhere, and the tattered shreds of a duvet lie in a rat's nest pile amidst stacks of books missing chunks of their pages. Shelves are upended, glass trinkets broken, liquid sloshed over the walls.

And then there's Wren.

She's wearing a pair of far-too-short shorts and a tight pink tank top that make it painfully obvious she is neglecting a bra. She's also standing on top of my ruined sofa with a drink in hand, bopping her head along to the music. She looks deliriously, blissfully out of this world. Totally in another dimension.

I rush over to the sound system controls and kill the music. It dies instantly, though my ears remain ringing and the adrenaline stays humming in my veins.

"Explain," I demand, whirling around to face Wren. "Explain yourself right fucking now."

Surprise, surprise, Bee has decided to slink off to her room without a word. This is my mess to clean up, apparently.

Wren just gawks at me, completely unfazed, and takes a noisy slurp of her drink. Her lips are stained purple. It's weirdly mesmerizing, oddly beautiful. "What?" she asks innocently without bothering to get down. "You left me trapped here with nothing to do and no one to speak to. I had to find new and creative ways of entertaining myself."

"By destroying my living room?" I cast a hand in every direction, not even sure which disaster offends me most. "Are those my sheets?"

"I was trying to build a pillow fort." She shrugs and giggles. "It didn't work out so well."

I don't know where to begin. It's so blatantly disrespectful that I'm actually rendered speechless. The worst part is that I know she wants me to blow up. She's pushing every button I have and inventing a few more just for good measure.

She *wants* me to haul her off that couch, bend her over my knee, and spank her raw.

She *wants* me to pin her down and fuck the defiance out of her.

She thinks this is a game we're playing, a tug-of-war with no consequences.

She doesn't fucking understand anything.

"Well then," I grit. "Carry on."

Before I can give into all those temptations swirling through my head, I storm out of the living room as fast as I can.

The music starts up again, but at least this time, it's considerably less loud.

Not loud enough that I don't hear Bee's room door open, though. She pops her head out and looks at me with wide eyes. "Hormones, am I right?"

"You need to do something about her," I snarl. "Whatever I'm doing is clearly not working."

She snorts with laughter. "*Clearly.*"

"We need her to be more compliant."

The music turns up and I hear the distinct crackle of more glass shattering.

"*Riiight.* 'Compliant,'" Bee scoffs incredulously. "I hate to break it to you, buddy, but she's a feisty little thing. 'Compliant' is never gonna happen."

21

WREN

I wake up the next morning to find that the living room has been restored to its original condition.

The floor is clean. The stains are gone and the furniture restored. And the carpet smells of roses.

The first wave is guilt, because while Dmitri Egorov can and does have pretty much any material thing that the world has to offer, I'm fairly sure he doesn't keep a squad of magic house elves hidden in the hallway closet. Which means some poor cleaning staff spent the wee hours of the night undoing all the petty, spiteful damage I inflicted on his penthouse.

After the guilt comes annoyance. Then more guilt. I'm standing marooned between the sofa and the chaise lounge, wondering how far I'm going to take my little protest, when I hear someone behind me.

I turn and almost scream. Bee is leaning against the archway with a lopsided smile on her face. "That was quite the show you put on last night," she remarks. "A-plus for effort, that's for damn sure."

I flush anxiously, desperate to explain myself. Although I'm gonna draw the line at apologizing. "He doesn't listen to me. So call this 'passive resistance.'"

She chuckles. "There was nothing 'passive' about your little display last night."

I have no idea how to interpret that cryptic smile of hers. There's a lot hiding in the curl of her lips. "Fine. Maybe not so passive. But if being loud is the only way to force him to hear me, then I'm gonna be loud."

"Literally, huh?" she says with a glance toward the blown-out speakers embedded in the ceiling.

"That was just… letting off some steam."

"Hm. If you say so."

I frown. *What does that "hm" mean?* "Listen, this place is comfortable. I mean—" I gesture around me. "—it's a fucking mansion in the literal sky. But as pretty as it might be, even the most beautiful place on Earth becomes claustrophobic the moment you know you can't leave."

She arches her eyebrows but says nothing.

"So," I continue with a tight throat, "if you expect me to be grateful for giving me a room here, you can forget it. And if you expect an apology for last night, you can forget that, too."

She pushes herself off the wall and beams widely. "I like you, Wren. I think we're gonna get along famously."

I pause, utterly baffled by these people and the whiplash changes in their moods. "Um… okay."

"You hungry? I was just on my way into the kitchen to stuff a croissant in my face. Feel free to join."

She doesn't wait for me to respond. She just saunters past me to the kitchen, leaving a fragrant trail of jasmine in her wake. I stand in place for a minute, considering just how far my rebellion ought to extend. Then, because my stomach is churning hungrily, I sigh and follow her.

"Herbal tea or orange juice?" Bee asks as I step into the kitchen. "Pick your poison."

"Tea, please."

Is it my imagination or do her eyes flicker to my breasts for the briefest of moments? I cringe inwardly. It feels like they're getting bigger by the hour and her gaze just confirms it.

By the time we sit down opposite one another with a bowl full of croissants between us, the elephant in the room is looming closer than ever.

"Can I ask you something, Beatrice?"

"Bee, please," she insists with a horrified shudder. "'Beatrice' sounds like some old British broad who paints dainty little woodland creatures all day."

"Like Beatrix Potter?"

"Who?"

"Uh…"

She laughs. "I'm just pulling your leg. I know who Beatrix Potter is. My mom used to read Peter Rabbit and Benjamin Bunny to me when I was a kid."

It's strange: so far, Bee has been a phantom, a secondary character in this weird, surreal little story I'm living out. It's easier in some ways to keep her that way. If she stays flat and lifeless and two-dimensional, I can pretend she isn't real.

But when she talks about mothers and childhood stories, I feel a surge of fresh guilt. She's got a life, too. A life of her own. A world of her own.

And I'm intruding on it.

If nothing else, I'm feeling guilty that I masturbated to a fantasy of her fiancé literally last night.

"Out of curiosity and the desire to end this awkward silence we've found ourselves in, what did your mother read to you?" she asks.

"The Bible, mostly."

"Wow. Fun." She chews on a hunk of croissant. "Riveting stuff."

"It was her way of coping," I explain sheepishly. "She lost my dad and found religion."

Bee's half-smirk is replaced with a frown as she picks up her glass of orange juice. "I'm sorry. I didn't realize you'd lost your father."

"That's not exactly—I mean, well, yeah, I did. Just not in the traditional sense. He, um… left us."

Bee sighs longingly. "God, I wish my father had left me." She says it so dryly that I have no idea if she's being serious or not. Then she winces. "Sorry, that was probably an insensitive thing to say. I don't really have a filter sometimes. Just for context, my father's an asshole."

I burst out laughing. "So was mine."

The laughter takes the edge off things. Suddenly, it doesn't feel so weird to be sharing breakfast with my baby daddy's future wife. In fact, I'm not thinking of her in those terms at all. Right now, she's just a fellow woman that I'm on the precipice of actually liking.

"I'm sorry—I distracted you. You were about to ask me something?"

"Right." *And just like that, we're back to our regularly scheduled programming.* I take a breath, nervous all over again. "How are you so cool with me being here?"

She shrugs. "Because I'm not a jealous person. Never have been. You're here because you're carrying Dmitri's child. That doesn't change the fact that he loves me. I'm smart enough to know that he can be both your child's father and my husband and that those two things can exist in harmony with one another."

"There's just one thing…"

"Shoot."

"Where do I fit into that equation?"

"You are the mother of his child," Bee says frankly. "And I will be his bonus mom. As far as I'm concerned, it's double the love. What could be wrong with that?"

She says it so succinctly that I find myself questioning my own emotional maturity. Apparently, she's light years ahead of me. "That's very… evolved of you."

"Hardly. I'm a self-serving bitch." She gives me a cheeky wink. "You'll find out soon enough."

A chiming sound from a panel on the wall draws her attention. "Front desk," Bee explains over her shoulder when she sees me looking. She gets off her stool and presses a button to open the communication channel.

I can't make out the words in the fuzzy, indistinct crackle that follows, but apparently, she can, because her face goes pale a moment later. *"Here?* Right now? Uh…" Her eyes flit around the kitchen wildly, like she's looking for a place to take cover. "Uh… yeah… send him up." Her knuckles are as white as her face when she hangs up. *"Fuck."*

"Everything okay?"

She doesn't answer me. She looks at the intercom again and punches in a three digit code. "Dmitri, where are you? My father's on his way up." *The asshole?* "How the hell am I supposed to know…? He didn't tell you he was coming? Uh-huh… Okay…"

"Doors opening."

"Fuck, he's here," she whispers urgently. "Gotta go."

She hangs up and turns to me with an apologetic expression. "Wait here," she orders. "And don't get—"

But before she can leave the kitchen, a man appears at the open doorway. He's maybe an inch shorter than Bee, but somehow, he looks worlds bigger. His shoulders are wide, his belly even wider. A pair of light blue eyes land squarely on me.

"Hello, daughter," he croons to Bee without breaking eye contact.

"Papa." Bee's voice rises to a higher pitch. "This is a surprise."

"Can't a father drop in to see his pregnant daughter?"

Hold up—did he just say she was pregnant?

Her smile isn't anything like it was a moment ago. There's nothing remotely sincere about it. She doesn't correct him, so either I'm missing something or Papa here has been lied to. "Of course. Although I'm guessing you're really here for Dmitri…?"

He chuckles and the sound makes my skin crawl. As does the fact that he has neither looked away from me nor blinked since he materialized here. "Who is this?"

Get up, begs a voice in my head. *Get up and put as many doors as possible between you and this leering ogre of a man.*

But Bee told me to stay here. So I stay.

"This is Wren," Bee replies smoothly. "She's my P.A. Wren, this is Vittorio, my father."

He has a lopsided walk that favors his right side. "Vittorio Zanetti," he announces as he approaches, offering me a veiny hand with fingers like blistered sausages.

I'm not sure if I'm just feeding off Bee's energy or if it's real, but unease trickles down my spine as our hands meet. "Pleasure to meet you, Mr. Zanetti."

"Vittorio, please!" he insists firmly. "Don't make me feel old. I'm still a very young man." He still won't blink, but at least he lets go of my hand. "P.A., hm?" he says as his eyes slide down to my pajamas. "I'm not sure your attire is entirely appropriate, Miss Wren."

I flush self-consciously but thankfully, Bee jumps to my rescue. "I've asked her to be my live-in P.A., actually. So it's really more of a work-from-home situation. It's a crazy world these days, y'know?"

Vittorio's eyes widen enough for me to see every single one of the thin red veins that wind through them. "A live-in assistant? That seems… extravagant."

"I don't think so," Bee demurs nonchalantly. "I think it's efficient. I'm going to need a lot of help, especially now, and Wren will be here to help me."

His eyes flit back to me and all I want to do is get out from underneath that gaze. "All well and good. But if you had to hire live-in help, *mia figlia*, couldn't you have found someone who was buck-toothed and fat as a hog? It's not a smart move to hire a woman your husband will want to fuck."

My jaw drops. *Did he just say that? Out loud?!*

My cheeks feel like they're on fire as I spring out of my stool. "Sorry to interrupt, but if you'll excuse me, I have to—"

His eyes drop to my stomach and I freeze belatedly. *Shit.* I don't know why my pregnancy poses a problem—I just know instinctively that it does.

"You're pregnant." One eyebrow arches with interest, but there's a new coldness in his features that makes me shudder.

I want so badly to look at Bee for guidance, but I know if I do, my face will give me away. I might as well emblazon a giant **THERE'S FOUL PLAY AFOOT** stamp across my face. "Uh… yes."

Bee drifts over to stand beside me. "Actually, that's precisely why I hired Wren in the first place. It's no secret that I've always been a little wary about the idea of pregnancy and childbirth. I figured that going through the process together would be less frightening."

Vittorio's attempts at civility drop altogether. To be honest, it's straight-up terrifying. His eyebrows unify into one vicious slash and his lips pull back over his teeth. He looks seconds away from lunging for my throat.

"What kind of woman—what kind of *Zanetti* woman—fears childbirth? It is what you were made for."

Good Lord, is this guy for real? I'm so incensed that I forgot for a moment to be scared. "It's completely normal to—"

Bee clutches my arm and nods quickly. "Of course, Papa. I won't let you down. Dmitri is waiting for you in his office."

His eyes move to the place where Bee is gripping me tightly. Almost self-consciously, she lets go of me. Then he nods once and leaves the kitchen, taking his nightmarish presence with him.

But even after he's gone, my skin tingles and burns.

I turn to her slowly. In just a few short minutes, things have changed. The confident woman I thought she was is just a front, the first shield in her line of defense. There's so much I want to ask her, but I settle on the only question that feels tenable.

"Are you okay?"

She gives me a small nod and an even smaller smile. "I'll let you know after he leaves."

Then she practically sprints out of the kitchen, leaving me with a barely-touched croissant and the sense that this situation is a lot more complicated than I ever could have guessed.

22

WREN

I'm still in the kitchen when Vittorio finally leaves the penthouse. I'm so nervous to run into him again that I hide in the storeroom next to the pantry to avoid being seen. It's only when I hear the faint call of *"Doors closing"* that I breathe a sigh of relief.

Bee was kind when she called him an asshole. I'd have chosen some saltier adjectives.

I'm about to leave the storeroom when I notice a large box tucked to one corner. One half of the top lid is open and I just so happen to take a peek inside. Oh, okay, fine—I *choose* to take a peek inside.

"What is this?" I mumble to myself, peering down at the weird, misshapen, flesh-colored molds that don't seem to resemble much of anything. I pick one up and stare at it for a moment before the realization hits me like a slap in the face.

It's a *belly*.

It's a *pregnant* belly.

It's a *fake, pregnant belly.*

A whole box of them, actually. I stumble backwards in shock and confusion before I bump into the door, at which point I turn around and sprint as far away from the alien prosthetics as I possibly can.

The whole way back to my room, I'm thinking about what Vittorio said about Bee being pregnant. About how her reaction was just a tiny bit off, a little bit delayed and wrong and skewed for reasons I couldn't explain.

Now, though, I have an explanation.

Is she faking *a pregnancy?*

I check around the corner first before I duck back into my bedroom and seal the door behind me. Annoyingly, it's starting to feel more and more like *my* space. The longer I stick around, the more comforting this room becomes to me.

Stockholm Syndrome is alive and well in this place.

I spend a solid twenty minutes in the shower, watching the city buzz down below me through the half-frosted windows. My mind is turbulent, though the steam helps take off some of the edge. But even after I'm dressed, I can't shake the feeling of having Bee's father's deadly blue eyes on me.

It's men like him that make women feel like they need to carry around pepper spray in their bags.

Which reminds me: I may not have pepper spray in my bag, but I do have the knife that Dmitri gave me. I retrieve it and examine it flat in my palm for a moment. I'm not exactly a connoisseur when it comes to weapons, but even to my untrained eye, this one is beautiful.

I check one more time to make sure the door is firmly closed before I wrap my hand around the hilt and take a tentative slice through the air. That's all it takes to open the floodgates.

Then I'm Lara Croft all the sudden, slashing and stabbing my way through an endless slew of bad guys. I'm certain that I look well beyond ridiculous, but there's no denying that it feels good to fight back, even if it's just invisible enemies I'm gutting and fileting into little ribbons right now.

I don't have much in the way of agency these days. I'll take what I can get.

I'm twisting around mid-swing when the door opens. I freeze. So does Bee.

She stares at my raised arm and the knife in my hand as one eyebrow pops up her forehead. "Whoa there, cowgirl. I'm sorry—I knocked, I swear, but I didn't wait for you to let me in. Please don't stab me."

I drop my hand and set the blade down on the closest flat surface, blushing furiously the whole time. "Sorry," I mumble. "I was just… fooling around."

"Yeah, I can see that. Because there's no way that stance is going to be effective in a knife fight."

I look down at my blade. "You know how to use this thing?"

"You met my father. Wouldn't you keep a knife under your pillow at night if you lived under his roof?"

"I… I'm not sure if you're joking or not," I say, blinking.

She laughs and beckons for me to follow. "Come on. I came to ask if you wanted to watch a movie, but this feels like a better way to spend the day."

She leads me to the opposite side of the penthouse, to the room I've spent the least amount of time in: the gym.

The left side of the space is decked out with huge, spotless mirrors, byzantine-looking exercise machines, and an absurd amount of weights in every increment. The right side is mostly just open, with a padded floor.

Bee walks onto the soft padding and gestures for me to join her there. "Firstly, it's important that you think about that knife as an extension of yourself. It's not a knife at all; it's a part of your hand."

"Uh, right. I am cyborg; hear me roar. Like that?"

"Not quite," she says with a laugh, "but it's a start. Now, picture me as some creepy dude coming at you." Her father's wrinkled face pops into my head instantly, which must be obvious, because she immediately follows up by asking, "Are you picturing my father?"

"Well…"

Bee grins roguishly. "Don't worry. That's exactly who I picture, too."

∾

"So which one is next?" I ask as the *Star Wars* theme fades out from the TV speakers.

"Are you kidding? We're watching that again from the start. I'd do heinous things to Princess Leia in a gold bikini, I swear. Pity that her galaxy is so far, far away."

"Gold bikini it is then." Laughing, I grab a gummy worm from the bag she's holding out to me. "Thanks for today, by the way. It was really fun."

"Hey, it's the least I can do. Not only are you putting up with my fiancé, but now, you're forced to put up with my dad, too. I owe you."

We've spent most of the day avoiding conversation about anything remotely personal. But that was in the morning when Bee still felt like a stranger. Right now, she's feeling more like a friend.

"Speaking of your father," I start cautiously, "may I ask why he thinks you're pregnant?"

Bee empties the bag of gummies right into her mouth before flicking it onto the table. "We might need alcohol for this conversation. And by 'we,' I mean 'me.'" She sighs. "But since I'm too lazy to get up, I guess a sugar high will have to do." She turns to me and crosses her legs. "As I established in the morning, my father's an asshole."

"I… I did notice."

"Don't worry," she reassures me with a pat on the knee. "This is not a case of *'I can say it but you can't.'* That's the general consensus from any decent human being with eyes or ears who meets the man. In fact, being an asshole is probably the nicest thing you can say about him." Combing her hair out of her face, she says, "He doesn't believe in surrogacy, which is why Dmitri and I never told him that we were resorting to a fertility clinic to have a baby. As far as he knew, we were just trying the normal way. Or, as he would put it, the 'right' way."

"Gross."

She plays with her toes and nods forlornly. "Yup."

"Do you mind if I ask why any of this is his business?"

"He's got an empire of his own to pass down," she explains patiently. "And he's not about to hand it over to anyone who isn't born of his direct bloodline. To his eternal shame, he doesn't have a son. So a grandson is his next best bet."

The word *"heir"* keeps echoing in my head. "I'm sorry, but which century do we live in? Everyone keeps talking about this baby as though he's, like, the successor to a throne or something."

Bee shifts uncomfortably. "Well, he kinda *is*. Dmitri's and my baby was always meant to be the heir to both the Egorov Bratva and the Zanetti Mafia."

My eyes pop. "M-mafia?"

"You didn't think my father sold insurance for a living, did you?"

Now that she's put it that way, it seems obvious. *Of course* he's a mobster. He fits the archetype perfectly—scary, controlling, demanding, archaic as hell. I still take a few moments to process that.

"Okay, so let me get this straight: this isn't really about you and Dmitri wanting to have a child. This is about the two of you *needing* to have a child?"

She grabs a throw and hugs it to her chest. "Kinda."

My heartbeat is rising rapidly. "Except for one problem: you're *faking* a pregnancy. And the only baby that really exists…" I put my hands on my stomach. "… is this one."

"I wouldn't call that a problem, per se—"

"Bee!" She jumps when I yelp her name. "Are you trying to pass off *my* baby as yours?"

She's chewing hard on her bottom lip. When I do that, I look like a rabid hamster, but when she does, she looks like a Hollywood starlet. "Only to my father and his people," she assures me quickly.

There are so many holes in this plan that my head spins. "I don't get it. Why can't you just tell him that you can't have children? My sister had fertility issues, too. It's not uncommon and it's also not anything you need to be ashamed of."

"If only it were that easy," she whispers in a mournful, broken voice. "If only that would work."

It's taking a lot of effort not to devolve into full-on panic mode here. It's one thing to be forced into this weird little love triangle, albeit minus the love. But it's a whole *other* thing to know that we're actively deceiving a man who clearly wields a lot of power of the morbid and quasi-illegal variety.

"It *should* be that easy! It should work! Just say your body isn't cooperating with you. That's out of your control."

She shakes her head. "My dad's not the kind of man who just accepts that things are out of his control. He's made it clear what he expects of me. Marry well. Make heirs. Continue his legacy. That's the bottom line."

"And if you can't deliver?"

She looks undecided for a moment, caught between thoughts. Then she sighs deeply, and the next thing I know, she's stripping off the thin white tank top she's wearing. I get a glimpse of her tiny breasts and her unfairly toned stomach before she spins around.

And when she does, the gasp that escapes my lips is visceral and horrified.

"Oh my God, Bee…"

Her back is riddled with deep scars that slash from left to right, from right to left, up and down and down and up. I can count at least a few dozen at a glance, but there are so many more, each melting into the next. Thick, deep, pink, barbed-wire-like scars pleated over one another like cross-stitching.

She tugs her tank top back on and turns to me. "He had a name for the whip he used on me. He called it *'Absolution.'*"

My upper arms are covered with goosebumps and I feel physically sick. All the gummy worms I consumed during the movie are roiling uncomfortably in my stomach. "H-he *whipped* you?"

"There isn't an option of not delivering, Wren," she explains gently, as though I'm the one who needs comforting. "That's the result of saying no to Vittorio Zanetti."

I swallow back the bile rising to my throat. "He's not an asshole," I hiss passionately. "He's a monster."

She nods. "I don't disagree. But even the worst monsters can be slain. It just takes time and patience. And until then, we play the game."

Her eyes brighten with determination but I'm still feeling pure panic. I'm in way over my head here; that much is super obvious. "Bee, you have no idea how much I feel for you… but—"

"You're scared for your child."

I nod, feeling like a bitch for turning the conversation around to my problems after what she just showed me. "I'm sorry—"

"Don't be sorry," she insists. "It's natural. And honestly? I think you're gonna be a much better mother than I could ever be. That's why I want you here: so that you can be the mother this child needs. I don't plan on taking your place, Wren."

"Except publicly."

She winces. "I know it's a lot to ask."

I keep seeing those horrible scars, those inhuman lashes. It makes my own skin crawl in sympathy pain.

It also makes me realize how high the stakes are.

"I want to help, Bee, but I just don't know how this is workable long-term. I don't want my baby to be in danger, but I don't want you to be in danger, either."

She opens her mouth to say something, but bites her tongue at the last moment. "Thank you," she murmurs instead. "That means a lot to me." Then she clears her throat and that graceful smile comes back on her face. "It's late. We should both get to bed."

I have no idea what's going through her head right now. Is she sad? Disappointed? Scared? As we mope out of the theater room, I'm on the verge of asking her when her head perks to the side. "Ah, Dmitri is home."

It's a cold reminder that this is *their* life, *their* home. I may be the mother of Dmitri's baby, but it's becoming more and more obvious that I'm the inconvenient accident in what is clearly an ongoing plan.

"I'll let you say goodnight," I mumble.

"Goodnight, Wren."

She steps into the living room and I retreat to my room in a hurry so I don't have to speak to Dmitri. But when I'm passing the second archway that overlooks the living room, I catch sight of the two of them.

And despite my best efforts, I hesitate.

Dmitri leans forward and kisses Bee on the forehead. It's the sweetest kiss I've ever seen. Affectionate, protective, and caring all at the same time.

Averting my eyes quickly, I rush to my room. But the image of Dmitri and Bee stays with me. Maybe that's why he seems so angry with me more often than not: he probably wishes that Bee was the one carrying his child, not me.

I collapse into bed without even bothering to take my clothes off. Everything feels so murky and messy, and I can't even escape to fantasies anymore because he's become a part of each one.

There's no way in hell that I'll let myself be the wedge that drives them apart. So as I lie in bed, tossing and turning, following every possibility down to its logical conclusion, I inevitably wind up in the same place again and again.

The only way to let them live…

Is for me to take my leave.

23

DMITRI

I'm woken with a blunt force pillow to the face. "The fuck…?" I groan, looking out in bleary confusion.

Bee comes into focus in front of me. I grimace and tug the same pillow she'd just thrown at me over my head. "Go away, Bee."

"We need to talk about Wren."

I grunt louder in answer. "I'm fucking *sleeping* here. Sunday's the only day I get to—"

She yanks the pillow right off me. "Oh, quit your bitching and sit up."

"I need to start locking my door," I grumble as I struggle upright.

"Go right ahead. I have the spare key and even if I didn't, you taught me to pick locks when I was twelve years old. You'd only have yourself to blame." She plants her fists on her hips. "Wren's having some serious second thoughts about this arrangement. Meeting my father yesterday just made it worse."

"Shocker," I mumble as I rub a knuckle in my eye.

"We need to consider telling her—"

"No."

"I'm not finished!"

"You don't need to finish." I drag my gaze up to meet hers. "I know what you're going to say and the answer is still no. We can't tell her everything."

"If she understands the situation, she might be more willing to stay. She might feel like she's a part of the group instead of an outsider here."

"We are not a group, Bee. There is no group. There is no anything."

"That's precisely what I'm trying to say," she insists in weary exasperation. "We could be. We so could be if we were just honest with—"

"I said *no*."

She makes a bleating noise that anyone who knows Bee knows means *you're so fucking annoying* and promptly rips the sheets right off the bed, pulling me to my feet along with them.

"Fucking hell." I scowl down at her. "What's gotten into you?"

"At least take her out today. That's an order."

I gawk at her incredulously. "You want *me* to take Wren? Out? Today?"

"Those are all the correct words in the correct order, yes. Congrats on your fantastic listening comprehension."

She's all fire and brimstone this morning, but I'm tired and in no mood for this shit. "Where? And why?"

"Anywhere they sell things. She needs new clothes, new things, new stuff for the baby. Honey as opposed to vinegar, remember?" Her eyes flash as she glares up at me. I've got half a foot on her and I still wonder sometimes if she'll get the jump on me one of these days.

"And shopping is the way to do that?"

"It's a freaking start!" she shouts, tossing my sheet onto the floor. "I'll go tell her to get ready. You can leave in half an hour."

"You're not coming?"

She doesn't slow down as she spins on her heel and charges to the door. "Sorry. Busy today."

The door slamming shut is almost deafening. I know Bee well enough to know that she's up to something; I just don't know what.

And I don't like that I don't know.

∼

When I walk into the kitchen twenty minutes later, Wren is sitting at the center island with a cup of tea and a plate of saltine crackers. I pause and frown down at the meager offerings.

"That's all you're eating?"

"Morning sickness," she explains miserably, walking her plate and mug to the island.

I watch her as she goes. She's wearing jeans and a loose-fitting white smock with thin straps over her shoulders. You can't even tell she's pregnant at all. Not that I'm looking at her stomach. I keep getting distracted by the way her ass looks in those jeans.

She sets her cutlery down in the sink and turns the faucet on like white noise to break up the awkward tension surging between us. "Bee tells me that you have some personal errands to run today and I'm supposed to assist," she mumbles. I scowl with irritation and Wren hesitates. "Because I'm the, you know, head of your Personal Management team."

I'm impressed that she manages to get through that title without rolling her eyes. "Let's just go," I sigh impatiently. "The sooner we start, the sooner we finish."

I stay on my phone as we take the elevator to the ground floor. Pavel is waiting for us just outside the building, standing at lazy attention in front of my silver BMW. There's a black Escalade parked right behind it with Anton behind the wheel.

"Where are Jasper and Bronn?" asks Pav as we approach, puffing on his vape.

"We're having a changing of the guard."

He exhales a cloud of apple-scented smoke in my direction, which I wave away with a grimace. "There you go again with all the royalty rhetoric. Don't you find it all a little bit… oh, I dunno… self-aggrandizing?"

I hold the passenger side door open for Wren. "If the shoe fits."

She screws up her face in distaste, but gets in silently. I shut the door and turn to Pavel. "I'll take the wheel. You and Anton follow us and keep a lookout."

He throws me a sloppy sailor's salute. "Aye, aye, captain."

The moment I'm behind the driver's seat, Wren shoots me a furtive glance. "So... what are these personal errands you need to run?"

"Shopping," I say dryly. "Which we will do silently."

I don't miss the way her face continues to sour in the rearview mirror.

But to her credit, she doesn't say a word until I pull into a premium parking spot along the Magnificent Mile. White stone buildings rear overhead as we're greeted at the door of a boutique clothing shop by Minka, a tall, willowy woman with platinum blonde locks far too perfect to be natural.

"Ms. Zanetti informed me that you would be arriving today. Welcome, Mr. Egorov."

"Good God," Wren whispers from behind me, gawking up at the awnings and the window displays teeming with gold and silver.

"What are you interested in seeing today?"

"The ladies' section first," I instruct gruffly. I start striding fast before Wren can bombard me with more questions, but she's right behind me, practically jogging to keep up.

"The ladies section?" she bleats. "Is this trip for *me*?"

"I have a full wardrobe and excellent taste. Draw your own conclusions."

She grinds to a halt and looks down at her outfit critically. "My clothes are fine! And even if—I mean, these aren't my best. But I have more options if you'd just let me go back to my damn apartment."

"I'd hardly call those 'options.'" I follow her eyes to see her checking out her reflection in the window and, to my discomfort, I find that I very much agree she looks perfectly fine. Edible, even. "Everything half-decent was brought to the penthouse for you."

"You're an asshole."

I sigh noisily. "Only *you* would find a way to turn a shopping spree into an insult."

"It *is* an insult," she insists. "You're saying I have bad taste."

"*I'm* not saying anything. I would have gladly sat this trip out. It was *Bee* who insisted I take you shopping."

That stops her in her tracks. Those pretty eyes of hers widen, just a little. "She did? But… why?"

"Fuck if I know. Her bleeding heart probably just wants to make sure you feel comfortable. Pampered. I assure you, this was only ever meant to be a gesture of goodwill. And it certainly wasn't my goodwill being gestured."

She twists in place, mouth going side to side with uncertainty. She glances over to Minka, who's looking into the distance a few yards away and doing a professional job of pretending she isn't eavesdropping on every last word.

"Oh, okay," Wren concedes with a sigh. "I guess it wouldn't hurt me to get a few new things."

I make a mental note to ask Bee what the two of them did yesterday. What they talked about. Something has shifted between them. I'm not sure what and I'm not sure how; I just know it has. The mere fact that Bee had insisted I take Wren shopping today is proof enough.

I love Bee to death, but the truth is, despite what I just said to Wren, she's no bleeding heart. In another life, maybe she would've been. But when you grow up in a family of sharks, you learn how to swim in bloody waters.

Wren moves towards a collection of handmade cashmere sweaters. She goes straight for the ivory palette, fingers the fabric longingly, and then moves on to the taupe.

Minka moves forward enthusiastically. "You may hand me anything you like, ma'am. It would be my pleasure to carry your selections for you."

"Oh." Wren looks very taken back. "Um, that's nice of you."

"Wonderful. Snowstorm or desert sand? Or would you like to take both?"

Wren's lips tic upwards like she's trying not to smile. "Hold on a minute." She pulls apart the sweater and starts shaking it out in search of something.

"What are you doing?" I ask while Minka looks on with all the patience that I don't have.

"Looking for a price tag."

"Our items don't, er… don't carry price tags, ma'am."

Wren drops the sweater and blinks, confused. "Huh? What? Why not?"

"Well…" Minka's eyes flicker to me and then back to Wren. "Our clients don't generally care, to be quite blunt."

She thrusts the sweater in Minka's face. "How much is this one?"

"Wren—"

"How much?" she insists over my warning growl. "Tell me a number."

Minka looks to me for guidance, so I just sigh and throw my hands in the air. Glancing back to Wren, she mumbles, "The Angelique sweater with Peruvian cashmere retails for four thousand, eight hundred, and seventy-nine dollars, ma'am."

I've never seen someone's jaw drop so fast or their skin pale so literally. Wren hurls the garment back onto the display like it's on fire and takes off away from it like she's fleeing the scene of a crime.

"Hell to the no," she calls back as she vanishes into the distance. "I'm good."

Poor Minka looks completely out of her element. Barely hiding my smile, I give her a nod. "We'll take the ivory and the taupe. Throw in the jade green, too."

"Yes, of course, sir."

"I have a feeling she's going to be difficult today," I continue. "So just take note of every piece of clothing that she admires, however subtly, and get it in every color."

"Understood, sir."

I spend the next hour trailing after Wren as she goes through the charade of interrogating Minka for prices, only to hyperventilate at every single one she's given.

"Ten thousand dollars for a dress! I could buy a first-class roundtrip to Asia."

"Three thousand for a blouse? Get fucking real."

"Five hundred dollars for a headband? You people are out of your goddamn minds."

Once we've circled the store, Wren turns to me indignantly and drops her voice. "This is ridiculous. There's nothing in here I would buy."

"But is there anything in here you *like*? If it's money you're concerned about, it goes without saying that I'm footing the bill."

Her eyebrows pinch together. "I'm not wasting money. No matter whose money it is."

"Very noble. Also, very stupid."

She rolls her eyes. "Can we please just go? I'm done here."

"Do you want to check out the childcare section? It's the floor—"

"No," she insists firmly. "I'm tired."

"So be it. I need to speak to Minka. Then we can leave."

She rolls her eyes and I leave her to her judgmental examination of the store. Bee's forced me on enough of these shopping sprees that I thought I knew what to expect of them. I'd been prepared for boredom, impatience, and annoyance.

And instead, what I'm left with is something that closely resembles… enjoyment?

What fresh hell is this?

24

WREN

Why do I keep looking over at the baby section?

I stand by my statement: this place is absolutely ridiculous. And yet… I find myself looking longingly at the gorgeous black silk pants and the soft cotton blouses with all this intricate lacework and wishing. Hoping. *Wanting.*

I'm a hundred percent sure that the baby section will carry items just as beautiful—and just as obscenely priced. Which is exactly why I don't need to venture anywhere near there.

But as Dmitri disappears around a display of elegantly dressed mannequins, my curiosity gets the better of me.

"Ah, what the hell? A quick browse won't kill me." Decision made, I bound up the spiral staircase two steps at a time until I reach the upper floor. As soon as I arrive, an involuntary gasp passes my lips.

It's baby heaven.

Well, not that, because that's a morbid and frankly pretty gross framing of things. But it's baby nirvana—er, baby paradise—look, it's a nice place for baby stuff, okay?

Even the smell up here is different. The women's section smelled of diamonds, if that's even a thing that can be smelled, and Chanel No. 5. This floor smells like daffodils, soft cottons, creamy lotions.

A weird sense of longing takes hold of me here. Sure, there were things I liked downstairs, but it was easier to say no to them because they were for me, and who am I to deserve nice things? But as I stare at a gorgeous mahogany crib with an intricate, platinum-plated mobile of the galaxy hovering over it, I'm finding that it's much harder to squelch the desire when it comes to my baby.

I want all these things for my son.

I want the ornate crib and the patterned baby blankets. I want the organically sourced onesies and the hand-carved rocking horse. I have no doubt whatsoever that Dmitri will buy it all at the snap of his fingers—which is exactly why I didn't want him following me up here.

I need to take some sort of ownership over my life and this baby or I'll end up deferring to him at every turn.

"Well, well." *That voice.* I'm immediately on edge as I turn to find pale blue eyes and a steadfast leer. "We meet again. Hello, little bird." Vittorio Zanetti swoops in so close that I take an instinctive step back.

"My name is Wren," I rasp.

"It's fitting, though, no? A beautiful bird, indeed. And don't you look just *lovely*. You're glowing, *amore*." His eyes travel up and down my body without any shame. My limbs feel heavy, like I'm encased in mud. Then something changes in Vittorio's eyes, the moment passes, and I can move and breathe again. "Where is Beatrice?"

"She was busy today. I'm running some errands for her." I sweep my hand over the store. "She needs a few things for the nursery."

"Ah, is that why you're here with her fiancé?"

My eyes dart past him towards the staircase. I'm suddenly wishing that Dmitri will show up soon and save me from this creep. "Bee insisted that he come with me to… to supervise."

I can only hope I'm being convincing, but I don't sound all that confident even to my ears, so Lord only knows how Vittorio is handling all of this.

"I'm sure he thoroughly enjoys supervising you."

The man can inspire chills in the dead of Chicago winter. "Er, right. If you'll excuse me—"

"Perhaps you can help me," he interrupts. "I'm here to buy a present for my future grandson. Since you and my daughter seem so close, I'm sure you can tell me what she likes."

I do my best to keep my face neutral. "I can certainly try."

"Wonderful." He turns and sweeps a grand hand around to encompass the whole floor. "Direct me to her heart's desires."

I glance towards the closest thing I can find. "She loves, er… rocking chairs?"

"Rocking chair it is then," he murmurs. His eyes sear through me again, hunting for something I can only guess at.

When his head tilts to the side, I close my own eyes and brace for impact. I feel it coming like a speeding car in the corner of your eye.

"Tell me, little bird: who is the father of your baby?"

Dmitri, where are you? I beam the thought telepathically throughout the entire store and pray that he's on my mental wavelength.

"You, uh, you wouldn't know him."

Vittorio chuckles, but there's a dark edge to his laughter, and to the way he keeps inching closer, hemming me in toward a towering display of mannequins that obscure all the lines of sight in our direction. "You're rather secretive about this baby, darling. One would almost think you had something to hide."

I may not be well-versed in the politics at play here—but I'm not stupid, either. He's trying to accuse me of sleeping with his daughter's fiancé.

Of course, the fact that I am in fact pregnant with Dmitri's baby doesn't exactly lend itself to a denial.

So I'm worried about myself, but I'm also worried about Bee. Her scars will forever be imprinted into my head. So pink. So many. So heartbreaking.

"This baby isn't actually mine," I hear myself saying like a fool. "I'm a surrogate."

A dark flicker tears across his eyes. "A surrogate?"

I want nothing more than to backpedal to some other, simpler story, but now that I'm here, there's no going back. "Yep, surrogate. That's me. Like she told you, Bee wanted an assistant who could go through the pregnancy process right along with her. The timing just worked out."

He clicks his tongue thoughtfully. "My daughter did always have strange ideas." He scrubs a hand at his chin. "Well, it's a busy day and there is lots to do. I'm sure I'll see you around, little bird."

God, I hope not.

He leaves me gripping the side of the crib to tether myself to reality and saunters away down the stairs. By the time I calm down, my palms are sweaty and I'm so beyond done with this shopping trip.

Luckily, Dmitri doesn't force me into another store; he just drives us home in silence with the car as empty as it was when we left this morning.

When we get back to the Muse, I find Bee in my room, unloading endless armfuls of clothing on my bed. T-shirts, shorts, leggings, the works.

"What's that for?" I ask in surprise.

She shrugs. "Let's just say I understand the need for comfy home clothing. There's nothing comfier than dudes' shirts. And this way, you can retire some of those worn-out rags you've been sporting around here. No offense to you, but I was starting to think a hobo was squatting in the guest bedroom."

I snort. "Some offense taken."

Bee laughs breezily. "Well, you'll forgive me sooner or later. I'm gonna grab a snack. Care to join?"

"Sure. Be out in a bit."

I'm still contemplating whether to tell her about running into her father as she dances out. I comb through the shirts she left me and marvel at how soft they are. She might have a point about retiring some of my older lazy day clothes. Many of them are just relics from old relationships at this point, and who needs reminders of a past that's better off forgotten?

Once I'm done changing into a pair of shorts and one of the long-sleeved shirts on the bed, I go to the kitchen.

Bee is cutting up an apple and Dmitri is, to my dumbfounded surprise, rolling out pastry. It's a sweetly domestic scene and immediately, I feel bad for intruding. "Uh, I can come back later?"

"Of course not." Bee looks shocked that I'd even ask. "Join us."

Dmitri glances up and freezes. He takes in the shirt I'm wearing and instantly, I realize that I'm not just wearing a random shirt; I'm wearing *his* shirt.

Why the fuck would Bee do that to me?

I wait for him to comment, but instead, he looks back down at his pastry. Though the kneading gets a lot more aggressive.

"So!" Bee says brightly. "How was the shopping trip?"

"It was fine," I mumble. "I didn't find anything."

"Yes, she did," Dmitri interjects. "Expect a delivery this evening."

I gawk at him open-mouthed. "Pardon me? What did you buy?"

He shrugs, slamming his fist into the dough with a vengeance. "Everything you looked at."

"Oh my *God*. How much did that cost?"

"You don't need to concern yourself with the bill."

"Yes, I do! I don't need you spending a ton of money on me. If I want something, I'll buy it myself."

"Except you didn't."

"Because I can't in good conscience wear anything that costs an entire month's salary!" I protest, feeling like more and more of a lunatic with every passing second. "That's just craziness."

Bee looks between the two of us with amusement. "Hate to break it to you, Wren, but we're kinda crazy here."

Dmitri slaps the pastry into a bowl and pushes it towards Bee. "Take care of that. I've got work to do."

She looks at him aghast, as if he'd handed her a scalpel and told her to finish up the open-heart surgery he was just doing. "What do you want *me* to do?"

"Blind bake it, add the filling and the upper casing, and then bake it again for ten minutes or so."

"But *you* usually do that." I've never seen panic on her face in a non-Vittorio-related situation, but this is as close as it gets.

Dmitri gives Bee a look that makes her wither where she stands. Even I take a step back and I'm not anywhere near the line of fire. Then, without another word, he brushes past me on his way out of the kitchen. He smells like flour, mint, and cedar.

"Do *you* know how to cook?" Bee asks desperately once we're alone again. "Because I will one hundred thousand percent mess it up."

I join her at the kitchen counter and offer a brave smile. "Have no fear; Wren is here."

She hands it over with relief. "Oh, thank God. I thought I was gonna have to go hungry tonight. Phew." She grabs a butter knife and stabs one of the apple slices she's just cut. "Want some?"

"Bee?"

"Hm?"

"Be honest: am I wearing one of Dmitri's shirts?"

She very pointedly does not look at me. In fact, she seems engrossed in the apple she's eating. "Uh… I think one or two might have belonged to him. But he doesn't really wear them anymore."

"*Bee!*"

"What?" she protests innocently. "I'm supposed to memorize the chain of custody for every garment in this household?"

"I can't be walking around your apartment wearing your husband's shirts! It's bad enough I'm carrying his baby."

She rolls her eyes. "*Please.* I already told you: I don't care about that stuff. I'm not a jealous person."

"There's such a thing as being too chill."

"No, as a matter of fact, there is not." She takes a big bite of apple and crunches noisily at me. "I had hoped this shopping trip would chill you out. No dice, it seems."

I pop the pastry into the oven and slam it shut. "And that's another thing! I didn't need a shopping spree."

"Uh, have you seen your wardrobe? You most *definitely* needed a shopping spree."

"Ouch. You're a snob."

She beams in a way that makes it impossible to stay mad at her, much to my irritation. "Why, yes I am, thanks for noticing. Listen, I know these things are expensive in your world, but to Dmitri, they're literally nothing. In any case, he likes taking care of his family. It's in his nature to provide. So… let him provide."

"It blurs the lines, Bee!" I insist. "It makes things… messy. Messi*er*."

"I don't see how."

"How about your *father*? Shall we start there?"

"I told you," she says dismissively, "you don't have to worry about Papa. I'll handle him. He's just got some very… traditional views on how a family needs to be created and some very offensive views on what a family needs to look like. I'll—"

"I ran into him today."

Bee stops short. Her cheeks and lips pale to the same sickening shade of pasty white. "You what?"

I nod. "At the department store. Dmitri was downstairs going behind my back and I was in the baby section when he just… showed up."

She swallows and tries to paste an easygoing smile on her face again, but it's too late. I saw the fear already. "What did he say?"

"He didn't come right out and accuse me of having an affair with Dmitri, but he might as well have. So I told him that I was a surrogate. I have no idea if he bought it or not."

She places her elbows on the counter and purses her lips in thought. "The bones of that story are true."

"He was not happy about the fact that I was out shopping with Dmitri. What if he drops in again? You really think seeing me walking around in Dmitri's shirts is gonna convince him that there's no funny business going on? He's already suspicious as hell!"

Bee cocks her head to the side to look at me. "You did the right thing, okay?" Patting my hand, she straightens up. "Let's not ruin this beautiful day by talking about my father. Let's just enjoy Dmitri's pie without him."

"I'm gonna go change first."

"So stubborn," she laments. As I'm leaving the kitchen, I swear I can hear her mumble something that sounds a lot like "… *made for each other.*"

25

DMITRI

The moment Bee steps foot in my office, I'm tempted to throw her back out again.

The shopping trip this morning was one thing. But giving Wren my shirts to wear around the house? That's crossing the line.

"Busy?" she asks, strutting over to my desk.

She stops short in wide-eyed alarm when I leap to my feet. "What are you playing at?" I hiss at her. I'm relishing how, for once, she actually reacts to my anger.

"Me?" Her lips are pressed into a thin line. "What did I do?"

I'm irate. She has the gall to pull this innocent Pollyanna crap on me? No. *Hell* no. I'm in no mood for this shit. Wren already has me feeling like my nerves are being flayed with a rusty butter knife. The last thing I need is Bee throwing her own edges into the mix.

"Need I remind you that this is *my* house and the only reason you have any kind of freedom at all is because you are under *my* protection?"

Her silence and submissiveness are short-lived. "Answer this: is the reason you're angry because I gave Wren a few of your shirts? Or is the real reason because you *liked* seeing her in them?

"Don't be ridiculous."

"You care about her!" Bee cries in my face, planting both palms on my desk and leaning up to meet me eye-to-eye. "Everyone with eyes can see it!"

"She's a walking womb. Nothing more than a means to an end. That is all."

Bee practically spits on the floor of my office in pure, undeniable disgust. "You think being cruel makes you a man?"

"No. Protecting what is mine makes me a man." I crack the knuckles of one hand. "And that includes you. Do you really think that playing these silly little games will keep you safe? Will keep *her* safe?"

Bee opens her mouth to say something, then thinks better of it. This is unlike her—this back-and-forth, hot-and-cold routine. She's normally hot-and-hotter. It takes me a moment, but eventually, I do recognize the flittering, skittering emotion on her face.

It's *fear*.

"What's going on?" When I speak this time, my voice is devoid of the fury it had just a moment ago.

"Nothing." She toes at the carpet, eyes downcast. I can feel her wilting away from me.

"Bee."

She glances at me and then away again as fast as she can. "I think Vittorio may have eyes on Wren. He was at the department store this morning."

My hands ball into fists. "What did he say to her?"

"He's suspicious," she admits. "Wren basically told him she was a surrogate to try to throw him off the scent. I just… I don't know if it worked."

"*Blyat'.*"

I leave my spot behind the desk and start pacing furiously, cursing in Russian under my breath. Bee stands stock-still, her face pale and her shoulders hunched. She looks like a lamb trapped in a cage with a predator.

"Don't bite my head off, okay?" she pleads tremulously. "But this is why I suggested we tell her the truth. The *whole* truth."

My blood is boiling. Bee looks like the lamb now, but Wren must've been fucking terrified…

And I wasn't there to stop it.

I've always been careful with Vittorio, no matter how much personal distaste I may have for the man. My grace, my formality—it was a necessary compromise, given how interlinked our lives always were. I stood to gain so much. He supported and backed my rise to *pahkan*. He's both Bee's father and, if I push him wrong, her worst nightmare. Most of all, he is the key to doubling my kingdom overnight. All I've had to do was play my cards right.

So, even when I'd have preferred to put the arrogant motherfucker in his place, I've stayed my hand; I've played the long game.

Now, I think I've played it *too* well. Made the motherfucker far too comfortable. Vittorio Zanetti needs to understand that he doesn't pull the strings.

I do.

I push past Bee and leave the office. "Where are you going?" she calls out after me.

I don't bother answering. She can draw her own conclusions; I've got shit I need to handle.

I pull out my phone and dial Aleksandr. He answers right away. "Yo, bro. What's—"

"Where is he?"

"La Vita Oscura," he answers immediately, dropping the cheery tone. "His little nightclub in River North. Showed up a couple of minutes ago."

"Do you have eyes on him?"

"Not right this minute. We left. Do you want me to double back?"

"No. I'll handle this myself."

∼

Within twenty minutes, I'm parking outside the gloomy facade of the club. A valet comes scurrying up to try whining to me about where I can and cannot leave my vehicle, so I throw five hundred dollars in his face without breaking stride.

He'll be in the Red Bar, I'm sure, just like he always is. The hostesses and servers greet me with choruses of "Good evening, Mr. Egorov," but just like with the valet, I ignore them all.

I'm here for one man and one man only.

Sure enough, he's sprawled in one of the leather armchairs with Alberto and a bevy of young women who are paid handsomely to pretend as though they're interested in what Vittorio has to say.

I make no secret of my entrance. All eyes flit to me at once. Vittorio's are bright and blue in the red-tinged darkness. Beneath them, his lips spread in a weak facsimile of a smile.

But I don't bother stopping. That's what he wants; that's what he expects. And I'm not playing by his terms anymore. He's going to come to me.

So I keep on going without stopping and find a perch in the Ice Bar at the back. In here, all the red lights are gone. It's cool, silvery blue everywhere, and the temperature suits me far better. I can see my breath pluming in the air as the bartender slides me a vodka neat across the frozen surface of the bar counter.

Almost as soon as the first tang of liquor hits my tongue, Alberto steps up next to me. "Dmitri, how nice to see you here. It's been a while."

I drain my glass, set it down, and lock eyes with the bartender. "Another."

In the corner of my vision, I see Alberto blink. "Would you care to join us?" he tries again.

I take up the drink once the bartender has replaced it with a fresh one and throw it back in one gulp again. Only then do I set it down and drag my eyes over to Alberto. "If I cared to join you where you were, Alberto, I would have done it. Tell Zanetti he can come talk to me here."

Alberto considers replying, then thinks better of it. He bows and disappears back towards the red rectangle leading to the other section of the club.

I don't have to wait long. I take this vodka slower, but I'm still not even halfway before Vittorio materializes in Alberto's place.

Gone is the fake smile he had when I passed him by earlier. Now, he's shivering with the cold and frowning grumpily.

He doesn't play stupid by asking why I'm dropping in on him unexpectedly. "I heard we just missed each other this morning," the man begins.

I grunt. "You didn't say hello."

"I did say hello… to your pretty P.A. Did you hire her for her credentials or her ass?" That crocodile smile of his twitches back to life. "Listen, I understand. You're a man. We are only human. And faced with something as tempting as fresh pussy, it's impossible to turn away." He smacks my back and chuckles in a way that makes my skin crawl. "I say, have as much pussy as you want. But make sure your whores will never carry your heirs."

"Wren's baby is not mine." The words taste so bitter coming out that I want to correct myself instantly. Refusing to take ownership of what is naturally mine feels wrong. Worse than wrong—it feels like a betrayal. "She's a surrogate."

"So I've heard. But perhaps that is simply what you want me to hear."

I pivot to face him head-on. "What are you accusing me of, Vittorio?"

The smile melts off his face. Those barren eyes glow with simmering fury. "I will not have some whore's whelp inherit my fucking empire!" he growls. "I will not tolerate—"

I get to my feet slowly. And as I draw myself up to my full height, Vittorio's words peter off.

I clamp my hand down on his shoulder. *Hard*. "We seem to be having a little misunderstanding here, Vittorio." I increase pressure on his shoulder until he winces. It takes only twenty-five pounds of pressure to snap a man's collarbone. I could do it without breaking a sweat.

I might.

"The fact is that I'm marrying your daughter. Beatrice Zanetti will soon be my wife. Our child—your grandchild—will be born in half a year. And the agreement we made will stand. Don't let yourself be confused or distracted by an unimportant woman whose existence in our lives is nothing more than comfort to your daughter." He tries to flinch out from under my grasp, but I just dig my hand in harder. "We have had a smooth relationship so far, Vittorio. For decades, we have made each other stronger. Let us not destroy it all by pretending as though you have a say in my affairs."

"Interesting choice of words," Vittorio snarls. "I'm starting to think I should never have agreed to marry my daughter off to you."

A smile curls around my lips. "You didn't agree to the marriage for her sake; you agreed to it for yours. Let's not pretend to be the doting father now."

I can feel, pulsing underneath my fingertips, the don's latent fury, the primal male need to strike back, to growl and fight and demand respect.

But Zanetti is no fool—we are alone in here and I will not hesitate to cut him down if he speaks wrong.

"There's still time," he tries. "The Irish need an heir, too."

It's a bold move, naming the Irish in my presence. Were Bee a different type of woman, I might've even felt threatened.

"Ah," I croon pleasantly. "We've entered the portion of the night where threats are exchanged, is that it?"

Vittorio can do nothing more than scowl at me, his eyes darting from side to side like Italian soldiers will pop out of the icy walls to keep him safe from me.

"Then let me return the favor: if you ever call any woman under my protection a whore again, you will force me to be uncivilized. And trust me, Vittorio, your body can't take uncivilized. Your mind won't withstand uncivilized."

A flush races up his face, leaving his cheeks blotchy. Putting all my weight on him, I lean in, just so that he can see the promise in my eyes. "This alliance works because I say it does. Remember that. Your life depends on it."

The moment I release him, he stumbles backwards out of arm's reach. Alberto is hovering in the corner, not that that scrawny fuck would ever dare to get involved in an altercation. This is new for him, too—he's not used to seeing me cross these lines, flex these muscles.

But I'm not about to play nice anymore.

Not when Wren's safety hangs in the balance.

"How quickly the young forget," Vittorio hisses from his safe distance. "I was the one who put you on the throne."

I laugh coldly. "You? You supported me once I already had the throne. That's a coward's move."

"How dare you? I've dismantled organizations many times greater than yours. I'd be careful about crossing me."

I arch my eyebrows. "That's a warning I'll return in kind."

"You can't move against me," he accuses, jabbing a skeletal finger in my direction. His breath is a foggy wreath, hanging around his puckered old man's mouth. "You wouldn't dare."

"Nor do I want to," I assure him. "Just as long as you don't give me a reason to."

His eyes flash their brightest yet. Apparently, of all the things I've said tonight, that insult is the most offensive. I'm turning from the bar when he starts talking fast, his words slurring with the strength of his passion. "No matter. I don't think I have to do anything. I'll leave you to topple your empire all on your own." He takes a step towards me, his nostrils flaring wildly. "Tell me: does your pretty little slut know that *you* were the one responsible for her sister's death?"

I do everything in my power to keep my body language from betraying me. But all I'm thinking is—

Fuck.

He knows.

26

DMITRI

My dark mood lingers into the night. Even the vodka I've been sipping on throughout the evening hasn't dulled my sense of restlessness. Between the business deals and the action comes the intelligence gathering, and that's the part I loathe most. Those stagnant moments where time stands still and there's nothing else to do but wait.

I've got one team on Vittorio. Another team on the Irish.

And so far—not so much as a drop of information.

The apartment is quiet. Bee is at home, but she's sticking to her room tonight. She tried to talk to me when I got back from her father's club, but I shut down the conversation immediately. I'm not in the mood to hear her prattle on about my so-called "feelings" for Wren.

If I have feelings at all, they're strictly primal, exclusively sexual. The combined result of months of celibacy and forced proximity to a woman who's actively challenging my understanding of what I thought I was attracted to.

"Shit!"

I walk to the open archway when I hear a suspicious thump, only to find Wren in the hallway with a stack of books in her arms, several of which are currently on the floor. That explains the thump.

"Raided the library?" I ask, brow arched.

She blushes. "Uh… guilty."

I lean against the wall and cross my arms. "Cedric must not have scratched the itch."

"It's not just provocative sex scenes, okay?" A swatch of hair falls over her face and she puffs it away angrily. "Some of those books have a legitimate storyline." Bending down carefully, she picks up the fallen books and adds them back to the top of her pile.

I don't miss the opportunity to ogle her ass, though I immediately curse myself for the mental lapse when I realize that's what I'm doing.

"Thanks for the help, by the way," she seethes sarcastically.

Sighing, I stand tall. "Come in here for a moment."

"Are you asking or ordering?"

"Whichever one gets you in here."

"Fine. Give me a second to put the books in my bedroom."

She stomps off down the hall and I watch her go, marveling at how she can turn even the simplest request into an opportunity for dissent. I never had to ask Elena twice for anything. More often than not, I didn't have to ask at all. She anticipated my needs and, before I even knew I needed something, there it was in front of me.

"Ahem." Wren presents herself in front of me again. "Private Turner, reporting for duty."

I step aside and gesture towards the sofa across the room. She promptly takes a seat in the armchair, because of fucking course she does.

I sigh again. This conversation might be harder than I anticipated.

Dropping onto the sofa, I cross one ankle over the opposite knee and regard her carefully. "In order for me to keep you safe," I begin, "I require a certain level of cooperation from you."

She frowns, already on guard. "What is this about?"

"I expect you to tell me things. What I don't want is to hear shit secondhand from Bee."

"Bee told you about Vittorio."

"Yes. But *you* should have told me about him."

"I didn't want to make a big deal about it," she mumbles, dropping her eyes away from me and finding a sudden fascinating interest in the stitching of the armchair.

"Vittorio is a veteran don with many years in this game, Wren. If he's interested in you, it is by definition a big deal."

For all that she's trying to play it calm, cool, and collected, Wren is rippling with signs that I'm getting through to her. Her breathing grows heavier; her hands wring in her lap again and again. I'm ready for more defiance, but then she surprises me.

Her eyes meet mine. "He's terrifying," she admits at last.

I wish I knew how to explain what it does to me to hear her say that. I have to urge myself to stay seated, to not go rip Vittorio's fucking head off right this goddamn second. It's like hot lava in my chest and in my veins.

She's so fragile and small and it's my job to protect her. She should never be afraid. She should never be touched. She should never be alone.

"You don't have to fear him," I rasp. "I swear to you—I will protect you."

Her chin trembles, another heartbreaking sight. "It seems to me that… you're gonna have to choose." Her voice is soft and uncertain. "You can't protect both me and Bee. She's Vittorio's daughter and—let's face it, I don't have to be having an affair with you. By virtue of the fact that I'm carrying your child and Bee isn't, I *am* the other woman."

"I can control Vittorio."

"You can't—"

"I can and I will," I snarl, still brimming over with that white-hot energy. "If you doubt that, you don't know me very well."

Wren just shakes her head sadly. "I beg to differ. I may have been invisible to you for as long as I've worked outside your office—but trust me, it didn't go both ways. I've watched you command every room you walk into. I've watched you manipulate, dominate, and charm your clients and investors and employees alike. I've watched you get every single thing you set out to achieve. It's all very impressive. It's all very intimidating. But it's still not the same thing as being able to control your circumstances."

She swallows, pushing down her tears in the same breath. "My sister believed she could manipulate her body into cooperating with her. She pumped herself full of drugs, did test after test, took supplements and hormones and a whole bunch of other shit. And when that didn't work, she tried to control her circumstances. If she couldn't have her own baby, she would engineer one that had Jared's DNA and some of her own. It was a great plan—but guess what? It didn't work. Some things are just out of our control, Dmitri."

The frustration is written all over her face. Her emerald eyes have turned into a glinty kind of jade. I'm angry again. I'm angry because everything she just said makes sense to me.

And a short time ago, it wouldn't have.

"I didn't ask you in here to have a philosophical conversation about life." I rise to my feet and look down at her. "I expect you to tell me things the moment they happen. I expect to hear from your lips first." I stare at her lips as I speak to drive my point home. "Am I understood?"

"No," she retorts, springing to her feet. "I don't understand anything about you right now."

She tries to storm off, but I lurch forward and grab her arm, then yank her toward me so hard she collides into my chest with a surprised *oof*.

"Let go of me!" she cries, fists beating against my abdomen.

I do the exact opposite: I pull her closer. My lips are so damn close to hers. Another millimeter more and they'll be touching. I bet she tastes so sweet.

"Let me say this plainly so you *will* understand: next time you keep secrets from me, I'm going to spank your ass so hard you'll have an imprint of my hand there for the rest of your life."

Oh, fucking hell—where did that come from? The intent was all right, but the shape it took was anything but. It took on a life of its own as it came past my lips.

But it's the most truthful thing I could've said, because it held *all* of me in it. My desire and my fury—both at her and for her—and everything in between.

Fear ripples through her eyes, but there are other things swimming in there, too. She rips herself from under my grip and stumbles backwards. Her jaw is set aggressively but her hands are weak, trembling, and confused.

For one endless second, she stays there. A scared little lamb in a world designed to devour her.

Then she turns tail and runs.

Fuck. I stand there long after she's gone. Her scent lingers. As does the heat surging through my veins.

Finally, I growl in disgust, head into my office, and lock the door behind me. Then I call Pavel, because the only thing that will get this energy out of my body is channeling it into work. Into keeping Wren safe—whether she likes it or not.

"Well?"

"I've had eyes on Cian O'Gadhra since the hospital attack, boss, as per your orders," Pavel reports. "But so far, nothing suspicious. He moves between his homes, his clubs, and his businesses. Everything looks aboveboard."

"Nothing with that blonde prick is aboveboard," I snarl. "I need you to step up surveillance. Just because it looks like he's uninvolved doesn't mean he is. Get some men into his clubs. I want inside intel."

"Yes, sir. I'll get right on it."

After he hangs up, I turn on my computer and pull open a file that I haven't looked through in a long time. Years, maybe.

Years. Is that even possible? There are some days when I wake up and, in those few oblivious moments before consciousness hits, I'm sure that if I turn over, I'll find Elena right there, breathing softly and sweetly.

I open it and stare at the first few pictures taken from the crash site. Elena's beautiful body, broken in a hundred different directions. Her eyes, staring unseeingly up at the sky. Her smile, frozen forever at twenty-eight.

I scroll down quickly before I end up punching right through the screen. But I'm no better off, because now I'm staring at *his* face.

Cian O'Gadhra.

His chilling blue eyes stare smugly back at me, taunting me with their indifference. He's the reason I decided to get in bed with the Zanettis. With Vittorio's assets under my banner, I'd have twice the manpower, twice the might, twice the power to annihilate the Irish scum.

Whatever it took to wipe Cian O'Gadhra and everything he loved from the planet, I'd do it. The world would one day thank me for clearing up that bit of pollution.

Except that I haven't. Not yet, anyway.

But his day of reckoning will come.

27

WREN

After checking the hallway yet again to make sure I'm alone, I give the elevator keypad my surliest frown. "Cooperate, you little skank," I hiss at it.

No response. I can see only my own scowling face reflected back at me in the polished chrome.

I'm fairly sure I have the first handful of digits of the access code memorized from spying on Bee and Dmitri coming and going over the last few days. But the final two are a little fuzzy. Either three-four. Or four-three.

I think.

hope.

I punch in the first six numbers, then stand there and try to guess which sequence to go for. "It's three first, then four. Gotta be. I'm one hundred percent positive. This is it. This is—"

"Access denied."

I could swear the robot has a little bit of sass in her voice, too.

"Bitch."

"Having a little argument with the elevator, are you?"

I whirl around to find Aleksandr standing at the left archway. He's chomping on a sandwich and grinning smugly at me.

Apparently, Dmitri has a brother. That was news to me. I met him this morning when he strolled in to see Dmitri about something he refused to specify. That was over an hour ago now and he's still hanging around like he owns the place.

He's like the smaller, boyish version of Dmitri. Jury's still out on how annoying he is. Dmitri has a significant head start, but I get the feeling Aleksandr doesn't bring a knife to a gunfight in that department, so to speak.

"What's the access code?" I ask pleasantly. "I keep forgetting the last two—"

"Can't fool me, sister." He smirks. "I wasn't born yesterday."

"This is ridiculous! I should have the access code!"

"You want a bite of my sandwich instead?" he asks, offering it to me. "Roast beef and mustard. I pan-fried the sourdough in a little bit of butter, too. Delicious, if I do say so myself."

"Pass," I mutter as I blow past him.

"You're missing ouuut!" he sing-songs. "This mustard is to die for. It's harvested by monks on the foothills of the Himalayas. Or maybe it's by elephants in Brazil. Can't remember. Anyway, point is, you'll love it. Tangy, slightly sweet, with a saucy little kick at the end."

I grimace. Dmitri's head start might not be nearly enough.

Turning my back on Aleksandr, I start raiding the pantry for my saltines. The nausea has receded a little the last few days, thank fucking God, but my appetite hasn't picked up in similar fashion. Probably because I'm so annoyed at my forced imprisonment.

"The hell are my crackers?" I mumble under my breath.

My first thought is that Dmitri moved them just to piss me off. Petty irritation is not usually his game—that seems to be Aleksandr's forte, if I had to guess—but I think my little detour to my apartment the other day really riled him up. He's been giving me the cold shoulder ever since. Leaving the penthouse before I'm awake and staying away from home until long after I'm asleep again.

Aleksandr is now sitting at the kitchen table, inhaling the rest of his sandwich. He's a noisy eater and apparently, no one ever taught him that it's polite to chew with your mouth closed.

When I feel my phone vibrate in the kangaroo pocket of my hoodie, I grab it and open the text message. My battery's already down to a forty percent charge, which is insane, because I literally took it off the charger an hour ago. It's like there's a parasite sucking the battery life away at triple speed.

SYRAH: *i want to be supportive but I hate this new job of yours. youre never at the office anymore! i miss my work wife. :(*

I quickly text back, *miss you too. more than you know. im not exactly having the time of my life over here*

SYRAH: *hope they're not riding you too hard. hows the fiancée? she a total bitch or what?*

WREN: *no, she's actually really cool. I like her more than him to be honest.*

SYRAH: *When are you gonna get back to the office?*

WREN: *i have no idea. their personal lives need a lot of managing. im sorry I couldn't hang out over the weekend. This job has a lot of overtime too.*

I feel super shitty lying to her about what's really going on, but the explanation feels way too messy to even begin to get into. It's simpler to just stick to the fabricated story, which ironically, makes me feel complicit in my own kidnapping.

I'm sure all this will play really well in court one day. Dmitri's lawyers will have a field day making me look like an absolute fool.

SYRAH: *surely you can ask for one night off though? We have the City Monkeys concert coming up, remember?*

"Shit!" I gasp out loud.

Aleksandr, who's busy licking his fingers, startles in alarm. "What? What's wrong? Did you not like the mustard?"

I ignore him and try to figure out how I'm gonna justify not being able to make the concert. I got nothing. Because there's no justification for missing that concert. Syrah and I bought those tickets *months* ago, and they weren't cheap.

WREN: *im gonna try to get the night off.*

SYRAH: *"try"??? Dude! The concert starts at eight. as in PM. as in there's no fucking reason why you should have to work at that time.*

WREN: *i know. you're right. ill handle it.*

But despite my confident text, I don't *feel* confident in the slightest. I glance towards Aleksandr, wondering if maybe he'll take pity on me and help me out. Time to play docile and sweet.

I join him at the table and make an effort to smile, but it feels like my face is gonna crack in two, so I scrap that and fold my hands politely in front of me. "So…"

"If you're gonna ask me for the code again, you can forget it. It's a no-go."

"Let me guess: your brother told you to keep an eye on me?" His gaze flickers to me before he pops open the can of beer in front of him. "Do you always do exactly what your brother tells you to do?"

"Yes." He says it without apology or shame.

"Why?"

"Because he's my brother," Aleksandr says with a shrug. "And he's my *pahkan*. It's a double whammy."

"So if he asked you to jump off a bridge, you would?"

He considers that thoughtfully. "Why does he want me to jump off the bridge?"

"Seriously?"

"That's a lot of judgment coming from the girl who agreed to be the living oven for her sister and brother-in-law."

He's got me there. "Shut up."

Chuckling, he leans back in his seat and props his feet up on the kitchen table. "Listen, Wrenny, the best way to get something you want is to ask."

I roll my eyes. "Have you *met* your brother?"

"I know he seems like a stubborn ass to you. But he's quite reasonable most of the time. Well, some of the time. Okay, not that often—but it does happen, I swear."

"Funny. I haven't experienced that side of him."

He slurps noisily at the beer and wipes his mouth with the back of his hand. It's almost charming how boyishly gross he is, actually. "That's different. You're carrying his baby. He gets a little intense when it comes to family, especially since we lost Elena."

"Elena?"

Aleksandr's face freezes. "Uh, y-yeah..." he stammers. "You haven't... heard about her?" When I shake my head, he plops his feet right back off the table again. "Fuck. Well, you didn't hear about her from me." He jumps up and starts to swiftly depart the kitchen.

"Wait!" I call after him. "Who's Elena?"

"What? I can't hear you."

"Aleksandr!"

"You're breaking up! I'm going through a tunnel! Bye!"

"Idiot," I grumble as I abandon my crackers and stand. Now, I'm doubly annoyed. One, because I want to go to this concert and Dmitri is undoubtedly gonna be a major ass about it.

And two, because I'm curious about who this Elena person is.

Since Bee's in the picture and seems to have been for a while, I'm guessing Elena wasn't a girlfriend? But then again, I have no idea how long Bee and Dmitri have actually been together for. Maybe Elena was the girl before Bee? Or maybe she wasn't a girlfriend at all. Maybe she was his friend? His sister? His colleague?

Or maybe this is none of my business and I shouldn't give a shit. What do I care about these people or their lives? I'm a pawn in it. They don't care about me as an individual. I won't do them the kindness of wasting my thoughts on them.

So instead of getting distracted by stuff that doesn't concern me, I decide to take Aleksandr's advice and just go and ask Dmitri about the concert. I don't have high hopes, but perhaps we can come to some sort of compromise if I ask nicely.

And perhaps pigs will fly past the window.

I cringe at the mere thought of asking permission. I'm a grown-ass woman, for God's sake. I shouldn't have to go ask Dad if I can stay out past curfew.

Still, I feel a vague sense of nervousness when I knock on his office door. "Enter."

It takes some effort to push open the dark mahogany door. I linger on the threshold, looking around as if for the first time. It's massive, of course, and it has a professorial vibe. Leatherbound books, crystal decanters of brandy, that kind of thing. A big desk just built for fucking his—

"Wren," he says in greeting. "What do you need?"

"Can I talk to you about something?"

He closes his laptop and gestures. "Take a seat."

It feels like I'm meeting the dean of admissions at some fancy shmancy university. A very hot, very young dean. A very tall dean. A very brooding dean. I bet he's the only man in the

28

WREN

IT'S CONCERT TIME.

I'm deliriously excited—not just because I'm getting out of the penthouse, but also because I get to spend some quality time with Syrah.

Of course, I'll have my surly "escort" to deal with, but even the Prince of Darkness himself can't dampen my mood.

Though he will certainly try.

My stomach has popped a little since I left the first trimester behind. Most days, I don't mind, but tonight, I don't want to look like a pregnant girl. I just want to let loose. I want to be *free*.

So I dive deep into my closet and pick a black leather miniskirt and a shimmering, silver blouse that's just flowy enough that I can tuck it into the skirt and it completely hides my belly. I go heavy on the eye makeup, but I keep it light on the rest of my face. Once my heels are on, I head to the foyer, hoping against hope that Dmitri won't flake on me at the last minute and condemn me to another miserable night of solitary confinement.

He's not in the foyer when I get there. Then again, he did say we'd leave at seven and it's only 6:50 right now. The man is punctual to a fault, so I'm not worried.

Okay, maybe I'm a *little* bit worried. Ruining my night seems like something he'd do just for shits and giggles.

"Doors opening."

The elevator doors slide apart and Bee enters the apartment. She's wearing a gorgeous, color-blocked maxi dress with a deep neckline that only she could pull off.

"Damn, girl!" she whistles when she sees me. "You look sexy as hell."

My cheeks flush with color. Stupid as it might seem, it's only just now occurring to me that my escort has a fiancée who might not be so keen on him escorting me to a sweaty, frothy, bump-and-grindy concert venue.

"Thanks. The City Monkeys are playing at The Eclipse tonight." I shuffle from side to side awkwardly. "Did, er… did Dmitri tell you that he was taking me?"

If it's news to her, she does a good job of waving it off. "Oh, sure, sure. He might have mentioned it."

"I'm sorry. I should have asked you if you wanted to come, too."

She *pshaws* away my apology. "Nonsense. I wouldn't want to intrude."

"You wouldn't be. At all. I mean, to be honest, I didn't even want Dmitri coming with me. It's just, he insisted and…" I cringe inwardly. Now, it sounds like I'm saying that her man was more interested in being with me than staying at home with her. "He's just worried about the baby, I think. Otherwise, he'd probably much rather stay here with you."

Bee fixes me with a strange, shifting smile. "I can assure you, he'd much rather be with you. And the baby, of course." She adds the last bit almost as an afterthought.

Nothing she's saying is really soothing my anxiety here. But before we can dig any deeper into the feelings at play, I sense footsteps.

Then Dmitri rounds the corner.

"Ready?" he asks as he strides into sight. He's adjusting the cufflink on his shirt, but when he looks up and sees Bee, he gives her only a cursory nod—which is bizarre, because she looks like an ethereal, angelic, siren-slash-succubus creature designed to lure men to blissful demise.

As his gaze flickers to me, though, he does a double take.

And he gives me the reaction that Bee truly deserves.

His eyes rake up and down. It'd be stupid to say, "Time stands still," so I won't say that—but I will say that the second hand on the clock on the wall sure doesn't seem to move anywhere for a while as Dmitri looks over every stitch of clothing I'm wearing like he can see straight through it all.

A fresh wave of anxiety peppers my skin with goosebumps. Does he have to look at me so hard? And so long? And does it have to make me feel so…

"What are you staring at?" I finally snap, shooting Bee a quick glance to remind him that he's gawking at me in full view of his fiancée.

He clears his throat and just like that, the scouring heat vanishes from his eyes. Time resumes as per usual. "That's a lot of eye makeup."

I scowl. "Gee, thanks."

Bee laughs pleasantly and resumes her sashay down the hallway. "What he meant to say is, you look hot. Have fun, guys!"

I look between the two of them. Something seems just a little bit off. *Are they fighting? Are they fighting because of* me?

I feel that prickly, uncomfortable onus settle over me again. It's the same heavy feeling I had years ago. The one I promised myself I would never have to feel again. The William Feeling™, I used to call it.

"Bee, why don't you come with us?" I have no idea if we can even get her in without a ticket, but I throw out the Hail Mary anyway because I'm sure Dmitri, rich as he is, can grease someone's palm and make it happen.

"Oh." She pauses and blinks, seeming shocked that I'd even ask. "Thanks for the invite, but I have plans tonight."

Dmitri arches a brow. "Plans?"

Bee combs fingers through her long ponytail. "Big plans. Matter of fact, I need to go get ready now. So, like I said, have fun without me!" She walks off before I can insist any more.

"Doors opening."

Wringing my hands, I step into the elevator with Dmitri, wondering what the hell is going on between them. Not just tonight, either—I'm talking in general. At first, I thought they had a very close, really healthy relationship.

Now, I'm not so sure.

I've lived with them for weeks now. But now that I think about it, I haven't really seen much, if any, intimacy between them. There was the time I saw Dmitri kiss Bee's temple, but there was a subtle stiffness there that's stuck out in my head ever since. It was two people acting out a script, not acting out their feelings.

Or is that just what you want to think? asks the prissy little bitch voice in my head.

I scowl and snap back to reality as Dmitri holds open the door of his black Porsche for me outside of the lobby downstairs.

"How long have you and Bee been together?" I blurt.

Something passes over his face. Like a shadow, almost. Close to a grimace. "A few years."

"But you've known each other a lot longer, right?" His gaze slides over to me questioningly. "There are pictures all over the penthouse of you and Bee together as kids."

He sighs, his fingers drumming on the car window like he wishes he could just slam the door shut in my face and end this conversation here and now. "Our fathers were rivals a few decades ago. Not in any significant way—no bloodshed—but it was tense. When the Irish started to rise in power, alliances needed to be made to preserve the status quo."

"It's like the United Nations of crime out here, jeez," I mumble with an overwhelmed whistle. "Irish, Italian, Russian—how do you keep track of who's doing what illegal stuff?"

His mouth twitches up in a facsimile of a smile. "Not all of it is illegal. You work for one of my many perfectly legitimate businesses. Now, get in the—"

"Sure," I say, standing my ground so he can't shove me in the backseat just yet, "but aren't they all just covers? Like, ways to explain where all the money comes from?"

"Partly." Dmitri rakes a hand through his hair. "Get in the car, Wren."

I exhale and do as I'm told. But as soon as he's around and behind the wheel, I start right back in on the line of questioning again. "So your fathers became allies and you and Bee became friends?"

Is he gripping the steering wheel a little tighter than necessary? Could be—who's to say for sure, though?

"Something like that. 'Friends' might be pushing it. She was a pain in the ass back then." He snorts. "Come to think of it, she still is."

I wonder if I'm bold enough to ask him who Elena is. I sneak a glance at his profile and quickly arrive at a conclusion: *nope*. But maybe, if I keep asking questions long enough, she'll just… come up naturally?

"So when did your friendship evolve into something more?"

He glances at me out of the corner of his eye. "You can ask Bee all these questions, since the two of you seem to get along so well."

Interesting. He seems almost resentful of my friendship with Bee. That's a twist. Honestly, every time I think I've got him figured out, he turns around and surprises me.

"Contrary to what you and all men seem to think, girls don't always gossip about guys when we're together."

He shoots me a sharp glance and I bite back my smile.

"But c'mon," I press, "don't hold out on me. I want to hear a love story. When did you know Bee was the one?"

His sneer could be measured on a Richter scale. "Don't tell me you're one of *those* women. The kind who believes in soulmates. True love. Fate. All that shit."

I shake my head. "That was Rose. She and Jared were meant to be."

"And you?"

I peek out the window as buildings and pedestrians flash past. A million lives unfolding all around us, and none of them could possibly be as weird as mine is turning out to be.

"Me? I was on track to believe all that naïve crap myself when I was younger," I admit in a near whisper. "But then…"

I trail off, wondering for a moment where William is right now. If he's still with his wife. If he's still playing at being a father.

"Then what?"

I cringe and jerk towards Dmitri. "Then I fell in love and I realized that fairytales exist only in books and movies."

"I sense a love story gone wrong," he murmurs.

I peek at him, wondering if I'm misreading the level of interest in his voice. *Of course you are,* chimes that prissy voice in my head again. *You* want *him to care. It's the same mistake as with William. He's a rich, powerful, older man and you think he'll fall for you eventually if you just fall for him first. You never learn, do you?*

"Shut up," I mumble to it.

Dmitri arches a brow. "Pardon?"

"Nothing." My cheeks heat up. "It's not really a love story if you delude yourself into thinking you're in love. And in my case, it didn't turn out so well."

I'd be lying if I said I'm sharing all this with no ulterior motive. But maybe, if I tell him a little about my past, he might open up to me about his?

I have no idea why I even care to know. This is none of my business. In fact, knowing will only make things more complicated going forward. The less involved I am in Dmitri Egorov's messy personal life, the better. And yet, when he asks, "What happened…?"

I can't help but answer.

"He… he turned out to be a different person than I thought he was." I squeeze the armrest of the seat as that familiar avalanche of emotion surges through me like lava flow. It recedes a moment later—not all the way gone, but not quite so overwhelming. "But everyone has their own heartbreaks. I'm sure you've had your fair share."

He doesn't reply to that. There's not even a grunt of acknowledgement.

The silence is killing me, so I ask, "Do you have any other siblings apart from Aleksandr?"

"No."

He turns the corner but the street is jam-packed. I can see the spires of the club from here. Beneath it is an ocean of people, glistening with piercings and glitter and leather and who even knows what else.

While Dmitri hands the keys to the valet, I start moving towards the end of the line. It's about a mile long. I already regret not coming earlier.

"Wren."

I swing around. He didn't even raise his voice, but I heard it slice through the cacophony of the crowd like nothing.

When I find him, Dmitri is standing next to the bouncer, glaring impatiently at me. "Where are you going? The entrance is right here."

I glance at the people in line. I'm already getting a few dirty looks, a few cleared throats as people prepare to declare me a line cutter and burn me at the stake like a witch. "Um…"

"Get over here."

Then he shakes the bouncer's hand, gives him a crisp nod, and gestures for me to walk in ahead of him. Sound swallows us up as we enter the club and I'm forced to lean in close to talk to him. He smells of whiskey and spice. And pheromones. A potentially lethal dose of pheromones.

"How did you get us in so fast?"

He blinks in bewilderment, like the question itself doesn't make any sense. "My name carries weight in this town. Take the stairs."

"The stairs?" I glance to my left in confusion. "The dance floor is down here. I told Syrah I'd meet her at the—"

"You won't be able to see her if you stay down here. You can sit in my box until she arrives."

I glance up at the rows of suites that look down over the dancefloor and the stage. "You have a VIP box?"

"You're surprised?"

"No," I say to myself with a sigh. "At this point, nothing surprises me anymore."

As we navigate through the packed space, I can't help but notice the looks that Dmitri gets. He is the kind of good-looking you just can't ignore. Every woman's gaze lingers on him, and most of them turn back for a second helping.

When they finally deign to recognize that he's got his arm draped around me, their eyes tend to narrow—not even in judgment, just confusion.

I keep peeking up at him for his take on the whole situation, but there's not much to see. He seems oblivious to the attention. But surely he must be aware of the effect he has on people, right? You can't slice through life this effortlessly without at some point recognizing that no one else has it quite so easy.

Or maybe you can; I don't know.

Maybe that's just life as Dmitri Egorov.

His box is amazing. It even smells different up here. Gone is the sweaty, boozy stench of the masses, and in its place is peach blossom air freshener and lavender incense. Carts stacked high with alcohol await us in the corner, stationed on either side of broad leather sofas with excellent views of the stage.

I catch a bevy of rich blonde hair and a vaguely familiar face in the crowd. But he's gone before I can figure out if it's really who I thought it was or not.

I shake my head. *Probably wasn't. I'm just in a weird mood tonight.*

"Thirsty?"

I stand at the edge of the balcony. "Yeah, I could use a drink."

He presses a hidden button beside the bar cart and, a few moments later, a waiter in a bow tie appears. The child in me is very impressed. Dmitri looks completely unfazed. In his world, it's normal to be waited on hand and foot. I wonder how long it takes to get used to something like that.

Dmitri's phone starts to ring and he glances at it impatiently. His eyes glaze over when he sees whoever's calling. "Give me a moment. I have to take this." He looks at the waiter. "Get the lady whatever she wants—as long as it's non-alcoholic."

I scowl at him as he leaves the booth. Not because I want alcohol, but because it's annoying that he thinks he needs to police me. I'm not about to start binge-drinking while pregnant, thank you very much.

The only one who sees my scowl is the waiter, though. He's smiling at me, one eyebrow hitched up with interest. "What can I get you, ma'am?"

"A big, fat vodka tonic. On the rocks."

He chuckles and takes a glimpse at the curtained door before his professional mask drops and a loopy, friendly grin appears in its place. "Unfortunately for the sake of the prank, I'm not interested in getting the shit beaten out of me."

I sigh. "Smart."

He inches a little closer and leans in conspiratorially. "But if you're looking for a high, I can hook you up with some great weed."

Oh. I smile awkwardly. "Um, thanks. That's nice of you, but I'm good. I was just kidding about the drink anyway."

He nods. "No worries. Just letting you know there's other options."

"I appreciate that. For now, I'd just like a virgin mojito."

His smile is boyish and charming. The lanky hair and kissable lips are giving pretty boy, but the stubble on his jaw saves him with a little dose of edge. Those eyes are searing, too. Almost translucent green.

"Gotcha." He starts to turn away, then pauses and turns back. "Y'know, if you wanna have some fun after the show, you could give me your number…?"

The door shuts. Neither of us heard it open, but we both definitely heard the thumping footsteps that can only belong to one man.

And unfortunately for this poor waiter, Dmitri heard what he was trying to do.

So much for not getting the shit beaten out of him.

That sleazy grin falls right off his face, replaced with sheer panic. "Sir—"

Dmitri holds up one huge hand that stops him in his tracks. "If you had to choose between your job, your life, or your balls… what would you pick?"

"Dmitri!"

He ignores me. "Answer. I suggest you do it quickly."

Amazing how quickly all that cocky, flirtatious, big dick energy evaporates in the presence of a true alpha male. "I'm s-sorry, sir. It won't happen again."

Dmitri takes a step forward and my skin tingles with anxiety. I can only imagine how the waiter feels. "It better not. Because if it does, I promise you, you will lose all three. Your job will go quickly. But your balls and your life… those will take a long, painful time. Got it?"

He nods fervently and stammers out, "I'll s-send another w-waiter with her drink."

"Smart man. I don't want to see your face again."

The green-eyed flirt sprints out of the suite while I just stare on in disbelief. "Was that really necessary?" I demand when we're alone again.

He advances on me, huge and fragrant and terrifying. "Any man who thinks he can lay a finger on you in my presence is a dead man, Wren. That one was lucky. The next one won't be." I'm quaking when he sighs and the storm clouds on his face part. "Now, I think your friend is here."

The distraction works. I turn back to the crowd and catch Syrah entering through the club's main entrance. I wave desperately but she doesn't see me. Shouting doesn't help, either. The music consumes every other sound.

"You can go down there."

I whirl around in surprise. "Really?"

"I'll be watching. You'll be safe."

I squint suspiciously. "That's… out of character."

He grimaces and rubs a hand over his chin. "This is me trying to… loosen the reins. Give you some freedom. A bit, at least."

I'm waiting for a catch, but it doesn't come. So I decide not to look a gift horse in the mouth. "Thank you," I murmur quickly before I slip out of the booth.

Syrah and I embrace excitedly when I find her. She drags me onto the dance floor immediately and we start pumping ourselves up for the band as the opener goes full tilt into their set. I throw myself into the dancing, reveling in the freedom of letting loose.

As the band segues into another song, I close my eyes and move my body to the beat. And even in the depths of my reckless abandon, I know he has one eye on me.

It makes me realize that I'm not free at all.

Because I'm not dancing for myself.

I'm dancing for *him*.

29

DMITRI

"Hello, old friend. I heard you were here tonight."

Ever since I got the call that Cian O'Gadhra was in the building, I knew, I fucking *knew*, that he would find me.

Which is the main reason I gave Wren permission to go down to the dancefloor on her own without me. Because as much as I dislike her being out of arm's reach, there is no way I'm going to put her in this Irish fuck's path if I can help it.

Cian's voice does something to my body. It's like all this energy, all this adrenaline, is congregating inside me, ready to combust.

Except that it *can't* combust. Not so publicly and certainly not so recklessly.

Not with Wren in the line of fire.

"Cian."

The Irishman has a deceptively charming smile. The kind of smile that you trust. Not that I ever trusted him—but Elena did.

Look what it cost her.

He's dressed simply tonight, in a white shirt with short, cuffed sleeves that puts all the tattoos down his fair-skinned arms on display. I see Gaelic characters swirling across his biceps. The shaven sides of his head gleam with the copper tint of his hair.

He floats to the balcony, leaning against the banister as though this is his box. He always did have an eye for other people's things.

"Great crowd tonight," he remarks, his gaze skittering over the throng of people down below. "Full of life, you might say."

I bite down on my molars. Everything he says is interpretable. He makes it impossible to suss out just how much he does or doesn't know. Is that a crack about Wren's pregnancy? Is it just an off-the-cuff observation? It's smoke and mirrors with this fuck. Always has been. Until the day I kill him, it always will be.

Downstairs, the band is playing hard. They have been for almost an hour and a half now. Which is about how long Wren's been down there. I search for her in the crowd but I can't spot her anymore. *I turn away for one fucking second...*

"Lots of beautiful women," he adds.

Is that another jab? Is he trying to say something with that sideways glance of his? Is he here to goad or to spy?

I've had enough time since Elena's death to give me some level of control. I couldn't say as much in the days right after she was buried. If he'd come waltzing into my vicinity then, I'd have separated his head from his body. Recklessness be damned, consequences be damned, the inevitable war that would ensue be damned.

Now, though, I just breathe and tell myself to proceed carefully. Every word matters.

He seems relaxed. Too relaxed, in my opinion. It's been years since we were last face to face, and we both walked away from that encounter with broken bones and bruises covering our entire body. The only reason war didn't follow is because of my newly-formed alliance with the Zanetti clan. Cian knew that escalating things would only end in the destruction of his organization. So he backed off. Practically disappeared.

At the time, Aleksandr called it a victory. But me? I knew that it was merely a temporary respite. A time for me to lick my wounds and get my head on straight so that when I confronted him again, it would settle things once and for all.

Now is still not that time.

But I can feel it in the space between us, gathering energy, reminding us both that our past has yet to be fully laid to rest.

"Is there something you came here to say to me?" I grit out.

"Just wanted to say hello to an old friend."

"'Friends' is a stretch by too much, O'Gadhra."

He wrenches his attention away from the performance to look at me with a mock crestfallen expression on his face. "You wound me."

"Not yet. But I will."

He seems amused by the threat. That would infuriate me if I weren't distracted by the fact that I still can't spot Wren. Her friend is down there, grinding provocatively with some big, hairy beast with piercings all over his face.

Could she be in the restroom? That has to be it. I need to get eyes on her immediately. Pavel and Aleks are both here, each manning a different entrance, and I'm certain that if they'd seen her roaming, they would have informed me already.

But what if Cian did something to them? What if he knew we were coming and prepared a strike? What if he—

The curtain rips open in the middle of my frenzied thoughts and Wren walks in. I sigh—relieved on one hand that she's fine, and irritated on the other hand that she's here. Impeccable timing, as always. The woman has a gift.

Cian turns around and Wren freezes. I'm having a hard time comprehending the look on her face. I'm still trying to puzzle it out when—

"Cian!" Wren cries. "Oh my God!"

She rushes forward and throws her arms around him. Around Cian fucking O'Gadhra.

What.

The.

Fuck?

"Ay there, pretty lass."

My body convulses from the inside. *Pretty lass.* He said that exact phrase every time he laid eyes on Elena. My fingers twitch but I refuse to curl them into fists. He may have his arms around Wren, but his eyes are on me.

Wren releases him first and takes a step back. Only then does oxygen fill my lungs, but it's filled with bitter, black smoke. This motherfucker is a walking danger sign and Wren ran right up to him as though they were best fucking buddies.

"I thought I saw you down in the crowd at the beginning of the night," she exclaims.

"It's been a while," Cian demurs as his smile goes soft and sympathetic. He raises a hand and places it on Wren's arm. "I haven't seen you since the funerals."

He was at their funerals?

Wren stiffens. "I didn't even thank you for coming, but I appreciated it, Cian. I was just—"

"You were mourning. Please don't apologize."

Every single word is drenched with sincerity. His eyes are soft with warmth; even his smile is somber. I could almost swear he *means* it.

Wren glances over to me. "How do you two know each other?"

"Oh, Dmitri and I go way back," he answers with a booming laugh. "In fact, I was close friends with—"

"Where's Syrah?" I ask forcefully, cutting Cian off. It's not exactly subtle. Wren looks confused and Cian chuckles under his breath.

"Oh, um… downstairs."

"She's probably waiting for you."

Wren's eyebrows arch. "Right, okay. I should go back down then." She turns to Cian. "It was nice seeing you again, Cian."

"You as well, lass. Take care of yourself out there."

He takes a half-step forward, but before he can hug her again, I step between them. "We're leaving the moment the concert is over. Better not waste any more time."

I'm blocking her view of Cian, so she has nowhere to look but at me. Her throat bobs. "Okay."

She gives Cian a parting wave over my shoulder and ducks out of the booth. I turn back to him with a glower. He's leaning comfortably against the railing, pouring himself a cocktail. "How do you know Wren Turner?"

"She's my assistant. Bee's as well."

"Isn't that something?" He wags a brow at me. "Does the sharing extend to the bedroom?"

I step forward, fantasizing about shoving him over the ledge. If we were more than one floor up, I'd do it, but at this height, the worst he'd suffer would be a broken leg. I want it to count when I do him in for good.

"Careful, O'Gadhra."

He holds up his hands. "I come in good faith, my friend. I just wanted to borrow your ear for a bit, matter of fact."

I know he's goading me, but I take a deep, steadying breath and nod. "Is that so?"

"I want peace. Peace between us. Peace between our men."

"'Peace'?" I repeat incredulously, striding right up to him until he's trapped between me and the balcony. "You dare say that word to my face?"

He flinches. "What happened with Elena—"

The moment he says her name, all that hard-won control that I've been fighting to maintain evaporates like fog under sunlight. My hand wraps around his throat and I shove him backwards, bending his spine against the iron railing. One little heave and he'd tumble down. The fall wouldn't kill him—but I'd be sure to follow behind and finish the job.

"You may think you can rewrite history," I snarl at him in a feral growl, "but *I* remember. I will always remember." I spin him around, throwing him backwards against the wall next to the exit. "Get out of my sight, Cian. You shouldn't have come here to begin with."

Cian straightens up, his hand going straight to his throat. I can see my claw marks there, indented into the sides of his neck. It gives me a fierce sense of satisfaction to see that I've drawn blood.

"You're making a huge mistake," he rasps. His voice is raw and weak.

"No. My mistake was letting you anywhere near Elena."

His eyes narrow. "I won't make this offer again."

I laugh coldly. "Good."

He scowls one moment longer, then shoves the curtains aside and disappears. I laugh louder as he leaves, but it feels as though I'm just trying to drown out my own worry.

My first thoughts should be for Bee, for the Zanetti empire I stand to inherit.

But the only thing on my mind is *Wren.*

30

DMITRI

She dances like no one's watching. Eyes closed, slender arms raised high in the air.

But someone is watching: *I* am. And also…

"Cian's still hanging around," Aleksandr mutters in my ear. "Back of the bar, corner booth."

Just like that, my moment of watching Wren's rapture in the music goes up in smoke. There are things that need to be taken care of. People that need to be reminded to stay in line.

"Should I get Wren or will you?" asks Aleks.

My instinct is to get her myself, but if Cian is lurking, then Cian is observing—and if Cian is observing, then he's gathering information he can use against us.

He may already know too much as it is.

"Get her and bring her to the car." I wait to make sure my brother reaches Wren, and then I leave the club and wait by the Porsche.

A few minutes later, they emerge from the throngs of concertgoers and meet me. Aleks quickly departs in his own vehicle. She's sheened with sweat, glistening like she's not quite real. More mirage than woman.

I turn away because the sight of her like that, gleaming under the street lights, stirs up a feeling in my chest I can neither name nor explain.

It isn't until we're driving away from the club that Wren twists in her seat to regard me with a curious look. "So, how do you know Cian? He said you guys were old friends…?"

I try and fail to control the twitching in my jaw. "I wouldn't go that far. He's an old business associate."

"Be more vague, I dare you."

"How do *you* know him?" I keep the question as casual as possible, but her gaze is burning a hole into the side of my face.

"He was friends with my brother-in-law. Jared used to hang out at this Irish pub downtown. O'Malley's. That's where he met Cian."

Of course. It makes sense now. It makes so much fucking sense.

"They were close?"

"Jared and Cian?" She thinks about it for a moment. "I wouldn't say they were best pals or anything. Just, like, drinking buddies." She waits for me to say something but I'm not about to go anywhere near that minefield. "Small world, huh?"

I nod. "Too small."

For some ridiculous reason, I actually weigh what it might mean if I told her the truth. Her beloved brother-in-law wasn't as pure as the driven snow. Very few men are, in my experience. But telling her that truth would also mean telling her the rest.

And I can't risk her running from me.

"Did you like the band?"

I glance in her direction. Is she trying to make conversation? We've been on the road for ten minutes now, but her cheeks are still flushed from all that dancing. "They were okay."

"Just 'okay'? My God, you really have no soul."

I shrug. "I prefer classical music."

"Fine," she grumbles. "Maybe you're more of an old soul than a no soul." She purses her lips as she gazes out of the window at the sidewalks. It's started to rain, just a light drizzle. It makes the city look like Wren does: flushed with sweat and all the more beautiful for it. "I tried my hand at classical music once. Took piano lessons for a couple of weeks."

That's news to me. It strikes me suddenly that, apart from the broader strokes of her life, I really don't know much about her. What's weird is that I *want* to.

"Didn't stick?"

"My lessons got… hijacked." Her voice hitches strangely on that weird. "Life intervened." When I keep looking at her, saying nothing, she sighs and concedes the rest of us. "My dad left us. Left me at piano, specifically, actually. He was supposed to pick me up after the lesson but he never showed. I was eight years old. Took a while before I actually understood what was happening."

Her face is calm, but her hands are a writhing, wringing mess in her lap. I offer her a soft, noncommittal hum and she finally looks up at me. "I thought that there'd been an accident or something. I assumed someone was hurt. I guess we were *all* hurt; I just didn't know it yet."

"Did you ever see him again?"

Her gaze bounces everywhere, never settling in any one place for long. Certainly not on me. The more her knee pistons up and down, the stronger my desire to place my hand on her thigh grows.

"Once," she admits. "On purpose, believe it or not." I stop the car at a traffic light. The red shines in, casting her face and hands in a crimson glow. Her leg keeps bouncing up and down, up and down. "Five-ish years after he peaced out, I overheard my mom talking to my aunt about how he was only living a few neighborhoods over. So me and Rose rode our bikes there and went looking for him. And boy, did we find him…"

The light goes green. I don't move. Rain keeps pattering softly on the roof of the car. "You spoke to him?"

She snorts. "The plan was to walk up to his front door and ring his doorbell. He would answer, see me standing there, and go sheet white. Maybe shit his pants, if we were lucky. Then I'd tell him that—" She twists in her seat to look at me. "—I had a whole speech planned. You want to hear it?"

I nod, not daring to speak.

"*Ah-hem!*" She clears her throat dramatically and stares at the windshield like she's putting on a play. "'*Oh, hello, Father. It's us, the daughters you abandoned. Remember? We just wanted you to know that we're fine. As it turns out, it took you leaving to make us realize how little we needed you. Because even when you were around, you weren't a good husband. Even when you lived at home, you weren't a good dad. I'm here to say, no hard feelings. You did us all a big favor when you left.'*

She takes a big breath when she's done and glances at me like she's waiting for a review or a standing ovation. "Then I was going to turn around with my head held high and walk away with dignity while he stood there ruing the day he decided to leave us."

I smile grimly and clap my hands. "Simple and devastating."

She returns a soft grin of her own. "I thought it was pretty good for a thirteen-year-old. Never actually got to use it, though."

"He didn't come to the doorbell when you rang?"

"No. But his new wife did." Her leg has now stopped bouncing. Somehow, that feels worse to me. Like the fight has left her altogether. "As it turns out, he had left Mom, Rose, and I in our three-bedroom house in Evanston to move five minutes away to another, almost identical three-bedroom house with *Helena* and her two little gremlins. Guess how old they were? *The exact same age as me and Rose.*"

"Fuck," I mutter.

It's strange—empathy has always been a foreign concept in my eyes. Something for lesser mortals to contend with.

But as rain slicks our windows and I press the gas to coax us back into motion, tires groaning on the wet asphalt, I feel a gnawing twist in my gut that must mirror Wren's own.

She laughs ironically. "'Fuck' is right. Go figure, huh? He didn't want different; he just didn't want *us*." Her voice drops to something barely audible. "We were his and he still didn't want us."

I'm pissed off three times over. I'm pissed off for the teenage girl who worked up the courage to confront the deadbeat father who had abandoned her.

I'm pissed off for the beautiful, heartbroken woman sitting next to me who's still feeling so much of what her younger self felt all those years ago.

And I'm pissed off at myself, for letting her draw me into this fucked-up web of her life. For making me *care.*

"Goddammit," she blurts suddenly, scrubbing her hands over her face. "I'm sorry. I don't know why I just told you all that."

"We were talking about classical music."

She grimaces. "Right. Piano lessons."

I park the car and come around to open her door. Just before I do, I catch sight of her sitting there. Her face is blurred by the rivulets of rainfall on the windows. She looks like an Impressionist painting, a beautiful smear of color and shadow. It's a perfect metaphor for the situation she and I have found ourselves in.

She's something I want more than I've ever wanted anything —but, stranded there on the other side of the glass, she's just out of reach.

When we step under the awning of the penthouse entryway, Wren turns to me abruptly. Her posture is awkward, uncertain. The dredges of smoky eyeshadow make the green in her eyes shine all the brighter.

"Uh, I just wanted to thank you. For taking me out tonight. It was… It felt so good to be out again."

Her gaze softens as she looks at me. The sidewalk is empty and the lights are dim and the rainfall is still shushing against the canvas awning just over our heads. And suddenly, alarm bells are going off in the back of my mind. *Mayday, mayday—get the fuck out now!*

She bites her bottom lip. Her eyes look huge. My heart thunders, thunders, thunders—

And I then take a step back. "I'm heading out."

"'Out'?" she repeats in confusion as I sweep past her into the lobby. "It's almost one o'clock."

"A *pahkan* never sleeps." I punch in the access code fast and step back to usher her into the elevator. "Bee's out tonight, too, so you've got the place to yourself. Goodnight, Wren."

"Doors closing."

The doors close on her stunned and confused face. "Fuck," I mutter to my reflection when she's finally gone. *"Fuck."*

I get just back outside before it strikes me that this particular *pahkan* has been run out of his own damn home by a pint-sized brunette with Bambi eyes and a simpering, tragic past.

I turn back and catch sight of my own reflection in the plate glass lobby doors. It takes everything I have to resist the urge to put my fist right through the mirrored surface.

Between seeing Cian tonight, watching Wren dance around, and whatever the fuck just happened in the car on the way home, I'm wired beyond belief, and not in anything close to a productive way.

Cursing under my breath, I charge back to the elevator and punch in the code for my floor.

I'm not a coward. I'm no weakling. I can stand to share space with Wren, despite the weird energy we exchanged tonight.

I'm heading straight to my bedroom when I hear a long drawn-out moan.

I freeze. There's no mistaking that sound. It's the sound of arousal and desire. It ignites my chest and fills me up from the inside. I'm rock-hard before my conscious mind has even finished processing what I'm hearing.

I look towards Wren's door, but it's closed and the crevice beneath it is dark. I take a couple of steps forward until I hit the living room.

And there she is. She's lying sprawled on my Coco Chanel couch with one hand between her legs. She masturbates like she dances—with her eyes closed and her lips parted slightly.

My cock strains hard against my pants. Wren moans as she touches herself. I can see the milky creaminess of her thighs as her fingers slide over her swollen lips.

Her skirt is bunched up around her waist and her blouse is in complete disarray. She's got one hand on her chest, playing with her own nipples as she clamps down on her bottom lip.

What I would give to bite that bottom lip myself...

As I stand there watching her, one thing becomes increasingly clear to me: I'm either going to have to kill someone right now, or I'm going to have to fuck someone right now. Those seem like the only ways to quiet the monsters in my head.

"Ahhh," she gasps again. "Hm... Dmitri..."

Dmitri?

Did she just say my name?

I take another step closer as her wrist action gets more and more aggressive. Without thinking about it, I unzip myself and pull my cock out. I'm so horny that not even my dry palm is an impediment.

I start stroking my dick while Wren fucks herself. The whole time, all I keep thinking is, *Say my name. Say my name again.*

She obeys like she can hear me.

"Dmitri… yes, yes… Fuck me like that… *Dmitri!*"

I have to grip the frame of the archway and lean forward as I come into my own hand. Only when the surge of tightening has finally receded do I dare release a breath again.

This may be a new low.

Standing huddled in the darkness, my own animalistic desire drying between my fingers… Too proud to go in. Too committed to walk away.

I hear her sigh from the next room. There's so much contained within that one pregnant sound. Relief? Satisfaction? Disappointment?

I have half a mind to storm in there and demand a full accounting of what was going through her mind while she got herself off. If she's going to come to fantasies of me, I should at least know what they are.

But instead, I retreat into my room and click the door shut silently. I came back up here to prove that I wasn't weak. That I could share space with her without crossing lines.

But the more space I share with her, the more obvious it becomes…

Wren Turner might just be my weakness.

31

WREN

Clack, clack, clack.

"What's going on?"

Blushing furiously, I keep trying to get the damn seatbelt to cooperate. "It's stuck," I complain. "Hold on a—"

"Let me help."

"No!" His hand freezes mid-air. Pretty sure I'm the color of watermelon right now, but I stick to my guns. "I can manage on my own."

I take a deep breath and fuss with the seatbelt one more time. There must be a god having mercy on me today, because finally, it slides over my chest easily and I can breathe a sigh of relief. Not because it's working, but because it means Dmitri doesn't have to touch me.

I turn away from him pointedly and pretend to be transfixed by city traffic as we drive to my very first appointment with this new OBGYN Dmitri intends to force on me.

"What was her name again?" I ask, if only because the silence is driving me nuts and the heat in my cheeks refuses to dissipate.

Dmitri's gaze stays fixed on the road ahead. "Dr. Liza Zaitsev."

"She sounds Russian."

"Very astute observation."

"Does that mean she works for your Bratva?"

"Yes."

I know why *I'm* being evasive and standoffish; I'm just not sure why *he* is. Unless of course we've both stumbled across the same problem: which is that the lines are getting blurred and it's becoming harder and harder to figure out what's real and what's not.

I woke up this morning with a mental list running in my head. It's a work-in-progress, as at the moment, there are only two points on the list, but that's fine, because they're both impossible to forget and easy to repeat. It's simple math, really.

Bee** + **Dmitri** = **real.

Me** + **Dmitri** = **not real.

Easy, right?

I just got a tad bit carried away after the concert. I was high on music and freedom and maybe the faintest hint of residual marijuana floating around the crowd. I was out and about and having fun for the first time in a long time.

Then I saw Cian and it just reminded me of old times with Jared and Rose. Let me rephrase that: it reminded me that he and I are still here and Jared and Rose are not.

After that unsettling encounter, I'd gone back to the dance floor and tried to lose myself in the music again. But something had changed. I wasn't dancing to have fun anymore; I was dancing to forget. So when Aleksandr came to get me, I didn't even negotiate for more time. I gave Syrah a tight hug goodbye and followed him to the Grim Reaper waiting in his blacked-out hearse by the curb.

I don't know how the topic of my dad came up. I don't know why I decided that sharing all that information with Dmitri was a good idea.

I just know that for once I didn't want to feel so alone.

And talking to him accomplished that.

Feeling less alone accomplished what followed: sprawling on the couch in Dmitri's living room and touching myself while I fantasized about him making good on his threat to spank my ass until he left behind a permanent imprint of his hand.

It wasn't until after I came that the guilt settled in. I was sitting legs akimbo in the home he shared with his fiancée—a woman I actually happen to like—and I was getting off to *her* man.

Honestly, how dare I?

So I spent the next day and a half avoiding Dmitri. That turned out to be a breeze, because he seemed just as intent on avoiding me. He probably just wasn't interested in hearing any more sob stories from my childhood.

It also seems that that's the status quo now. Or at least, I assume that that's why he's staring at the road with that stony scowl on his face. It says, *Closed for Business. Do Not Share Sad Tales. Do Not Even THINK Of Attempting Interpersonal Connection.*

"Why can't we just stick to Dr. Saeder?"

He barks out a harsh laugh. "Is that a serious question? Hell no. *Fuck* no. My son gets only the best and Dr. Saeder has proven to be far less than that."

I sigh and turn back to my window. I'm not sure why I'm resisting so much. It probably has a little something to do with the amount of control he currently exerts over my life. I guess questioning him from time to time allows me to feel as though I haven't lost all my autonomy.

As it turns out, I actually like Dr. Liza. She's a smart, middle-aged woman with thin, scanty hair faded to a mature gray. She goes through my entire history first before she examines me head to toe with patient professionalism. Once she's determined that I'm healthy, she moves on to the sonogram.

"There he is," she purrs with a smile, pulling the screen closer so that I can get a better look.

Dmitri leans in alongside me and I get a whiff of his dark, musky aftershave. I cringe away instinctively. I could swear his face twinges with something, but he's too far in the corner of my eye to be sure.

"Everything's okay?"

"Definitely," Dr. Liza assures him. "He's a healthy boy. And right on track for fourteen weeks."

"My God," Dmitri mutters under his breath. If I weren't so hyper-aware of him, I might have missed that awed little exclamation altogether. "There he is."

For once, his attention is focused away from me. I can stare at his face and take in just how shocked and amazed he looks. When I look back at the screen, it's with fresh eyes.

I've been so conditioned to think of this baby as Rose and Jared's that I haven't truly accepted that the little life force inside me is *mine*. Truly and completely mine.

At the end of this journey, I'm the one who will hold the title of mother.

It's breathtaking and terrifying in the same instant. Without thinking, I grasp the only hand available. The calloused warmth is like a cattle prod to the nervous system, though, which prompts me to snap out of my daze and realize that it's not Rose's hand I'm holding; it's Dmitri's.

"Sorry," I mumble, ripping it away.

He doesn't say anything apart from straightening up and thanking the doctor. We say our mumbled goodbyes and depart.

As we're driving away from Dr. Liza's facility, Dmitri clears his throat. "Are you hungry?"

I am indeed hungry. I'm also eager. A little too eager at the prospect of having lunch with him. That's precisely why I shake my head. "Not really. I just want to go ho—to the penthouse."

He doesn't try to change my mind. The drive back is filled with a pregnant silence, pardon the pun. The moment we're in the penthouse, I grab a box of Doritos and Oreos and retreat to my room.

I'm in there for an hour or so before I hear a knock on my door. I glance outside. The sun is only just beginning to set, so there's no way I can pretend I've already fallen asleep. Then again, I am pregnant. Surely I can get away with—

"Wren?"

I tense up immediately. It's Bee. Usually, I'd be happy to hang out with her, but right now, I feel like a homewrecking bitch who's been coveting her man. How can I even look her in the eye, knowing what I did on her couch?

"Wren, can I come in please?" she asks. "I know you're awake. You're not as quiet as you think you are."

Cringing, I sigh with defeat. "Come in."

She walks in with a satisfied smile on her face. "You should know I have amazing hearing. I'm half-bat."

"Like the kind that flies around at night?"

"Another thing we have in common. We're both nocturnal."

"Ah, that's good to know. You can be on night duty when the baby comes." I only meant it as a joke, but Bee's face twists uncomfortably. I can't tell what exactly has turned her off, though. Was it the assumption that she will be an active part of the baby's life? Or perhaps I just reminded her that I'm the baby's mother, whereas she will only ever be an exterior appendage—biologically speaking, at least?

Or maybe the sourness on her face has nothing to do with anything I've just said. Maybe she's just here to tell me to stay away from her man.

"I'm just kidding," I add with a forced smile that turns into a grimace.

"I knew that." She points at the edge of the bed. "Can I, uh… can I sit?"

"Of course. You don't have to ask. It's your house, not mine."

She sits down on the corner of my bed and slides flat, resting her chin on her folded arm. "Is everything alright with you?"

Frowning, I nod. "Yeah. Why wouldn't it be?"

"It's just…" She glances towards the door as though there's someone standing on the other side of it. And who knows? Maybe there is. Is she here because Dmitri sent her in to do recon on his behalf? "You've been a little off the last couple of days. Pretty much since the concert."

My heart plummets. "Oh, have I?"

She gives me a look. You know the one. The *you-know-exactly-what-I'm-talking-about-so-don't-play-dumb* look. "If there's something on your mind, something you're worried about, you know you can share it with me, right? I'm here for you, Wren."

I push myself off the bed and walk to the window. I genuinely can't look at her now. If I do, she'll see the guilt all over my face. "You don't need to be here for me, Bee."

"What does that mean?"

"It means you're his *wife*. Your job is not to take care of me."

In the reflection in the glass, she looks puzzled. "What if I want to?"

"You wouldn't if you knew—" I stop abruptly, realizing that I'd just said that out loud.

Bee pushes herself to an upright position and cocks her legs. "What should I know?"

I shake my head. "I can't."

"Is this about Dmitri reading you the riot act the other day for not telling him yourself about my father hijacking you in that department store?"

Of course, the first thing that jumps into my head is the ass spanking Dmitri promised me. "No," I mumble with a cringe.

She gets to her feet and joins me at the window. "He's a hot-headed bastard most of the time. But honestly, it's only because he's protective of the things he cares about. Don't take it personally, Wren."

"He threatened to spank me!" *Oh, God. I did* not *just do that!*

Bee doesn't look at all bothered by that revelation. In fact, she's got a saucy smile on her face that almost looks apologetic.

"Well..." Before she can get a word out of her mouth, laughter snorts out through her nostrils and she slaps a hand over her mouth. "Shit, I'm sorry. I don't mean to be laughing."

"Why *are* you laughing?" I demand, close to tears.

"Because you look so guilty," she explains. "And I don't understand why." I bite my bottom lip and Bee's eyes widen with realization. "*Ah*. You *like* the idea of him spanking you, is that it?"

"Bee—"

She holds up her hand and I find myself staring at her pretty, pink palm. "First of all, Dmitri's a handsome man. You also happen to be carrying his baby. It's natural that your feelings are a little… confused right now."

I gawk at her in disbelief. Justification was not on my bingo card. I wonder if she'll continue to justify me if she knew I've spent the last two nights getting off to endless fantasies of him. Most of which did, to be transparent, include a fair amount of spanking.

Either she's just *that* confident or she's the most understanding woman on the planet. No matter which way you slice it, I don't deserve her. I don't think Dmitri does, either.

"Bee, I swear, no matter how confused my feelings may be, I'd never, ever act on them."

She winks at me. "Don't worry about it."

Don't worry about it?

I don't have the faintest idea what she means by that. Don't worry, as in, *I know you're not going to make a move on my man?* Or don't worry, as in, *I don't care if you do?*

"Anyway, we're about to have dinner. Wanna join us?"

My insides roil at the thought of sitting down to dinner with Bee and Dmitri. Third wheel is one thing; homewrecker is a whole other ball game. And I already feel dangerously close to the line between the two.

"Um, I'm actually pretty tired. I think I'll just turn in early."

She sighs as though she knows the real reason I'm declining her dinner invitation. "Okay then. Get some rest. And remember, if you ever need to talk, I'm right here."

"Thanks, Bee."

She gives me a parting smile and heads out, leaving me feeling like the backstabbing little shit I am. There's only one way to combat this guilt and I'm going to have to be resolute. Determined. Unwavering.

I have to stay far away from Dmitri Egorov at all costs.

I can do that.

I *can* do that.

I can…

Fuck.

32

DMITRI

"Well?"

"She's fine," Bee reports as she enters the kitchen and props herself up on one of the high stools. "She just doesn't want to be around you more than she has to."

"Figures," I mutter. "Women. Why do you have to make things so difficult all the time?"

"You want to know why?" she hisses. "Periods." Jabbing a finger in my direction like a dagger, she says, "Periods *suck*. And pregnancy. And all the shit that comes after pregnancy. And menopause! The wonderland of fun that is menopause. Guys don't have to deal with any of that shit. But we do. Except that we're also working, bringing home the bacon, taking care of the households, raising the children, and juggling a hundred other things to boot."

"What do you juggle?"

The fire dims in her for a moment. "I have to juggle the reality of who I really am with the farce I'm supposed to live."

The raspy hollowness of her voice plants me right back down in my seat. "*Blyat'.* I feel like an asshole."

"As you should."

"Bee, listen, I—"

"Brazilians!" she interrupts. "Brazilian waxes. That's another thing you don't have to deal with that women do."

I sigh and fold my hands on the marble countertop in front of me. "Message received, Bee. I get it."

She grabs an apple out of the fruit bowl and crunches into it. "She's going through a lot. You need to be patient with her. You also need to be honest with her."

"What will that accomplish?"

"Oh, I don't know," Bee drawls sarcastically, rolling her eyes just in case I wasn't clear on that. "How about developing some much-needed trust?"

I snort. "Trust? She hugged Cian O'Gadhra, acted like they were the best of friends. No way I'm going to trust that shit."

Bee hurls her bitten apple right at my head. For a slender thing, she's got a hell of an arm, but I've got better reflexes. My arm flashes out and I snare the apple out of the air before it hits my face. Casually, I bring the fruit to my lips and bite into it.

Bee just glowers at me. "Why are men so stupid? So she hugged Cian. Big deal. She clearly has no idea who he really is. You're not coming from a place of distrust; you're coming from a place of jealousy."

I'm tempted to lob this apple back at her. "Fuck that. I'm not jealous."

"He said defensively."

I roll my eyes and try to pretend as though I'm not getting riled up, even though there's an itchy feeling running through me like ants crawling under the surface of my skin. "You're reading too much into this. Why do you insist on acting as though there's something going on between Wren and me?"

"Maybe because my fiancé threatened to spank our P.A."

Well, fuck.

"She told you about that?"

Bee smirks gleefully. "I don't think she meant to. It just kind of slipped out. You want to know why she's avoiding you? It's because she feels guilty."

I suppose that explains it. She probably thinks I'm an asshole who's attempting to use her to cheat on his future wife. For some reason, the fact that she might be thinking that makes me uncomfortable.

"You realize that you're going to have to co-parent with her, right? You can pull that alpha male crap at work, but it's not going to fly here."

"You underestimate me."

She snickers. "And I think you're underestimating her. There's shit in her past she's holding onto. I don't know what, exactly, but there are definitely lines in her head she doesn't want to cross."

"I think I know," I murmur softly, meeting Bee's curious gaze. "Her father left the family to marry another woman. He essentially replaced their nuclear family with a different one."

"That makes sense." Bee nods. "And she probably doesn't want to be the 'other woman' in this fucked-up scenario we've got going on. All checks out."

I drop my head into my hands and run them through my hair. "The spanking thing just sorta… came out."

Bee just wags her eyes at me. "Hey, I understand the fantasy. I wouldn't mind spanking her, too. Especially the way she looked in that little—"

"Enough," I growl.

Bee's eyebrows arch for a moment before her lips curl upwards. "And he claims he's not jealous."

"It's not that," I insist. I don't know why I'm digging my heels in so hard. The more I protest, the more I'm proving Bee's point. "It's the fact that she's carrying my child."

Bee pretends to believe me. "Uh-huh, I'm sure. Speaking of our little Bratva-bound bundle of joy, how was it, seeing the latest ultrasound?"

I exhale sharply. "It was… a mind-fuck."

"Of the good or bad variety?"

I toss the apple core into the sink and stare out at the view of Chicago beyond my window. "The surreal variety. I could see his little head, his body… He looked like a real person. Developing stages, sure, but still… a real person." When my gaze slides back to her, she's smiling widely at me. "What?"

She chuckles. "Sounds like you're getting the feels."

"I didn't think I wanted to have children. It was never something I thought a lot about. But now, it feels… right."

"I'm happy for you," Bee decides, leaning forward and placing her hand over my arm. "But if any of this is going to work, you're going to have to figure out a way to find some common ground with Wren."

"How?"

She shrugs. "Damned if I know. This is why I stay away from relationships. Fucking and forgetting is so much easier."

"Yeah, well, forgetting is a lot easier once the fucking is out of the way."

Bee's smirk stretches all the way from ear to ear. "Now, doesn't that statement speak volumes?"

"Fuck off. Stop analyzing me."

"Maybe you should fuck her. Get it out of your system?" she suggests teasingly.

"That's not what I was implying."

"Sure it wasn't." She laughs, flipping her hair over her shoulder. "Frankly, I'm surprised it hasn't happened already."

"She thinks that you and I are together."

"Riiight. All the more reason to tell her that you have a little too much penis for my liking. Although, come to think of it, maybe then she'll prefer me to you." Her eyes light up at the idea. "Wouldn't that be fun?"

I grimace playfully, but there's a subtle tremor of unease ripping through my body. Bee is relentless when she sets her sights on a woman. The thought of anyone laying a finger on Wren—that waiter fuck at the concert venue, Cian, even Bee —sends those invisible ants under my skin scurrying in every direction.

"Your jaw looks a little tight there, buddy." Bee jumps off her stool and saunters over to me. She wraps an arm around my shoulders and whispers in my ear, "Scared?"

I turn to her so that we're practically nose to nose. "I dare you to try."

There's a shuffle at the entrance of the kitchen and Bee and I turn at the same time. "Shit!" Wren yelps. Her cheeks burn pink as she backs out of the kitchen. "I just came for snacks. Sorry."

She disappears as suddenly as she came and Bee glances at me with raised eyebrows. "I'm not sure what your plan is, but one thing's for sure: you need one."

33

DMITRI

Once I've finished making dinner, I prepare a separate plate and carry it down the hall to Wren's room. I knock at her door, but there's no answer. Impatient, I barge in and set the plate down on her dressing table.

It's unsettling how unsettled this room makes me. The sight of Wren's clothes strewn around, the sheets mussed in the exact shape of her body, the air rich with her scent—I feel like I'm drowning in jasmine and vanilla.

I'm also hard as a fucking rock.

Just when I'm reaching my tipping point and every voice in my head is roaring for me to get out of here, this place where I don't belong, the bathroom door opens and Wren emerges…

Wearing nothing but a pair of black panties and a towel wrapped around her wet hair like a turban.

Her eyes are downcast, so she doesn't see me immediately. Then she notices the food on her dresser and she freezes.

Run, most of those voices in my head yell.

Stare, whisper the others.

Guess which ones I listen to?

Her breasts are fuller than they were before. And just like every time I let myself look at her changing body, I get a heady surge of white-hot lust. That's *my* baby doing the changing. *My* seed in her womb, owning her from the inside out, claiming her. The swell in her stomach is because of me. The glow in her skin is because of me.

Fucking hell—if my erection gets any harder, I'm going to pass out.

"What the hell are you doing here?" she shrieks as the spell breaks. She reaches out to snatch a towel from the foot of the bed and hold it up over herself. But it's too small to hide all of her from me. Those curves still peek out everywhere I look.

Teasing. Taunting. *Tempting*.

"I brought you dinner," I rasp. "I thought we could talk."

She bristles with indignation. "I'm naked here!"

"Put something on. I can wait."

She glowers at me as she flings her useless towel on the bed and storms into the bathroom. She has to turn to do it, which is fine by me, because Wren is as exquisite from the back as she is from the front.

Spanking isn't enough to work these urges out. I need hours to spend turning her skin pink as I bite and suck and lick my way across every goddamn inch of it.

When she stalks back into the bedroom, she's wearing baggy sweats and an even baggier t-shirt. But if she really wanted to repel me, she shouldn't have chosen my t-shirt to wear.

"Don't you freaking knock?" she demands, crossing her arms over her chest, which only makes it more obvious that she's not wearing a bra.

"I'm not in the habit of knocking in my own house." Not the best way to start off what was supposed to be a *let's-try-to-work-together* talk, but it's hard to think straight with the raging hard-on threatening to rip through my zipper. "Listen, Wren, I know it's not easy being here—"

"Oh, ya think?"

I grit my teeth. "—but we have to figure out a way to get along."

"Or what?" she scoffs. "You're going to threaten to spank me again? Or maybe you'll just barge into my room whenever you please to remind me that I have no privacy because this is your house? Then again, that logic doesn't exactly hold true, considering you barged into my apartment, too!"

"Only because you didn't listen."

"I don't have to listen to you when I'm off the clock. You're not the boss of my entire freaking life!"

I stride closer and glare down at her heatedly. "I've got news for you: that baby in your belly means that I am."

Fuck me—this is definitely not going the way I intended. Why won't my thoughts behave correctly? Why do I feel like I'm burning up with a fever?

I let out a sigh and steel myself. *Control*—that's what matters here. Control myself. Control Wren. Control the situation.

"We need to figure out how to deal with everything that's happening."

Her nostrils flare. "I couldn't agree more. *This* is how I intend to deal with it." She takes a few steps away from me. "From now on, you don't talk to me and I don't talk to you."

I snort. "That might be a little difficult, considering you work for me."

"We can communicate through email and text and if, God forbid, we do have to talk to each other, we keep it strictly business."

"Don't be ridiculous."

"Which part of that is so ridiculous? We can't seem to talk to each other normally, so why talk at all?" When I say nothing because all the things I want to say involve telling her how I'd rather show her with my body what she does to me than to use my words, she nods in triumph. "That's what I thought. Now, get out of my room."

Wrong choice of phrase there, princess.

I'd been so close to leaving. It's not a good idea for me to linger here. The longer I stay in Wren's space, the higher I feel. Drugged up on the scent of her body wash and the sight of her wet hair soaking into my t-shirt she's wearing. "Self-control" feels more and more like a vague, irrelevant concept.

But when she challenges me… when she defies me… when she pushes my buttons…

I have no choice but to respond.

"No, I don't think I will."

She gulps. I hear every millisecond of the sound. My senses have slowed time to a crawl, tuned into every little thing she does, every breath, every thrumming of her pulse.

"This is my room. And I want you to leave."

"You keep using that tone and you're going to force me to discipline you."

She pulls back her lips in a feral sneer. "What are you going to do?" she taunts "Threaten to spank me again? That's all you do—hand out empty threats."

Once again: very poor choice.

This little *kiska* has no idea who she's dealing with.

I grab her arm and spin her around, pulling her back against my chest. There's no way I can hide my erection now. It's practically digging into her ass. "Was that a challenge?" I ask, hissing into her ear. She struggles hard but the little gasps exiting her body sound half-hearted to me. "I'm not so sure it was. If you want me to leave, you're going to have to ask nicely. Otherwise… I'll show you just how empty this threat isn't."

I'm vaguely aware that I'm not thinking straight. Or rather, I'm thinking with my dick. Now, if she just backs down, I can walk away without crossing that—

"Fuck. You."

Something gives way in my chest. The last bastion of resistance goes crumbling down.

And all hell breaks loose.

I drop down on the bed and drag her over my lap. Her shocked cry is swallowed up in another gasp when I rip down her sweatpants.

I take those black panties down with it, exposing the still-damp curves of her ass. The first slap lands hard, a sharp thunderclap in the otherwise taut silence of the steam-filled room.

"Let me be clear," I snarl, spanking her a second time. "You don't call the shots. *I do.*"

Another slap. Another squeal.

Her ass has turned pink already. I see the five points of my fingers blooming there like roses. The sharp *thwack* echoes in my ears, encouraging me to go in for another and *harder* and another and *more*.

But if I don't stop now, I might end up with my face between her cheeks, curling my tongue into her pussy as she spasms and feeds me more of those delicious cries.

So instead of giving into my baser desires, I throw her onto the bed as she scrambles to pull her pants up.

"Order me around again and I won't stop there," I snarl before storming out of her room.

My boxers are wet with precum. Fuck, is that embarrassing. I'm a *pakhan,* a CEO, a thirty-five-year-old man who's managed to cum in his pants and alienate the mother of his child, all in ten seconds flat.

Is that what Bee meant by "having a plan"?

34

WREN

It should be illegal to feel this many emotions in such quick succession.

First came the humiliation. Red-faced, horrified, stunned.

Then came shock.

Then there was anger—lots of that—followed by a nice, juicy helping of excitement.

Unfortunately for me, the excitement is the only one that lasted.

I writhed in bed for hours after Dmitri left me there. I was shamefully wet, even as my butt burned where he struck me. Sleep was being stingy, so when midnight turned to predawn and predawn turned to morning, I finally gave into the urge and touched myself.

It took approximately three seconds for me to come harder than I've ever come before as I relived the moment in my memory. As the orgasm faded, that roller coaster of emotions took me for another spin.

Humiliation—shock—anger—excitement—need.

And then we did the whole thing again for good measure.

Except this time, the fantasy didn't stop with the spanking. It started to take on new life. It started to *expand*.

Suddenly, I wasn't just being thrown onto the bed, my pants ripped off. No, now, I was pinned beneath his naked body, bracing myself for the moment his cock ripped into me. Possessing me, owning me.

He owned me from above and below, inside and out. And not once, not even in my wildest fantasies, did I ever try to stop him.

It's only after I'm coming down off the high of my second orgasm that I remember Bee. And that's when the shame hits.

That one lasts every bit as long as the need does.

So for the three days that follow, I actively avoid Dmitri. Per the terms of the agreement I laid out—well, "agreement" is a strong word since he never actually said yes, but whatever—I don't look him directly in the eye and I don't speak to him unless I'm forced to.

I'm prepared for blowback, but to my surprise, he doesn't give me any. He even arranges for Aleksandr or Pavel to drive me to and from work so that we don't have to carpool.

It's what I wanted. And yet…

I hate it.

I'm back to feeling incredibly lonely. I'm not talking to Dmitri. I can't talk to Bee. I'm not allowed to talk to Syrah about any of this. My only solace is food. Which is why I've become a serial snacker.

A bag of Doritos will never let you down.

A tub of Ben and Jerry's won't freeze you out.

A carton of cookie dough will never make you feel powerless.

I'm in the kitchen, trying to finish my cup of green tea before Aleksandr shows up to escort me to the office, when Bee walks in. She's wearing a pretty floral negligee that dances on her milky skin.

"Morning!" she chirps. I manage only a tight smile in response before I bury my face in my cup. Bee sighs heavily. "Do you want to tell me why you've been avoiding Dmitri and me for days now? I thought we made some headway in our last conversation."

How on earth do I explain to her that Dmitri made good on his threat to spank me? How do I explain that I *liked* it?

Actually, I'm not sure I even need to. She basically figured that part out for herself. Still—it hadn't actually happened at that point.

Worse—I'd promised her it never would.

"I just, uh, can't talk right now," I mutter, abandoning my half-empty cup in the sink. "I've gotta get to work."

When I turn around, Bee's standing directly in front of me, blocking my path, arms crossed. "What happened?"

That's it. She's seen the guilt and shame all over my face. She knows that I crossed a line with Dmitri. A big one.

"W-what did he tell you?"

Bee's eyes go round. "Did you sleep with him?" She doesn't look nearly as outraged as she should be.

"No!" I gasp. "Of course not."

"Hm. Well, something happened. Dmitri's being annoyingly evasive about it, too."

"He's trying to control my life," I say, doing my best to summon up some indignation. "That's what happened. And any time I push back, he…" I trail off.

"He gets all controlling alpha douchebag on you?"

"In a word, yeah."

She nods. There's a slight smile playing across her face. Why isn't she more affected by this conversation? This is her *fiancée* we're discussing! "There's no point doubling down with Dmitri, hon. I appreciate your fire and your fight, but it won't work with him."

"For the love of God, what *will* work with him?"

"Play by his rules for a bit—" I open my mouth to object but she holds up a hand to shut me up. "It's not easy, I know that. But what's that old expression: you catch more flies with honey than with vinegar?"

"Ugh," I groan as my phone pings. I glance down with relief. "It's Aleksandr. He's here to pick me up for work."

Bee shoos me toward the door. "Go on then. Try not to let the bastard get to you."

Easier said than done. Everything he does gets to me at this point. Even his breathing gets my hackles rising.

Aleksandr tries to make conversation as he drives me to Egorov Industries, but I shut it down fast. I'm too in my own head to focus on the "epic night" he had with his buddies over the weekend.

It's a quarter to nine by the time I get to my desk. My first order of business is to prepare Dmitri's schedule, but while I'm combing through it, I'm beeped into his office.

I freeze uncertainly. He hasn't called me into his office at all since the spanking incident. So why now?

"God help us all," I mutter, grabbing the schedule and heading inside.

He's in his charcoal Tom Ford suit today. It's cruel how good he looks. Evil should be ugly, not this gorgeous.

"Ms. Turner," he barks, "your purpose in this office is to make my job easier, not harder."

The open hostility takes me back, but I hold my ground. "I wasn't aware I was making it harder."

He swings his computer around to give me a better look at what's drawing his ire. "What is this?"

I check the schedule on his computer with the one I just carried into his office. "It looks like you're double-booked today at ten."

"It does look that way, doesn't it?"

I check both appointments against my schedule. "Hold on—I didn't schedule the meeting with Japan."

"No, I did. It came up late last night and I was forced to make last-minute changes."

This is the most we've spoken to each other in three days. He's made no mention of what happened between us. Hasn't even attempted to apologize for it. Nor did he fill in Bee, which is proof that he knows it was wrong.

I feel the intense need to lob something at his head. There's a hole-puncher within arm's reach that would make such a delicious clunk if I could hurl it into his thick skull.

"I fail to see how this is my fault," I intone icily. "You can't make last-minute changes to the schedule without informing me."

"Are you forgetting who I am?" he says in a voice that's so viciously cold that I freeze in response. "I don't have to inform you about anything. It's your job to know. You're supposed to check my schedule every day and adjust it accordingly."

I probably should back down right about now. I have Bee in my head whispering about honey and vinegar and flies and God knows what else. But honestly, there's only so much a girl can keep in.

"Not if you make changes in the middle of the night!"

"I told you when I hired you that this job is twenty-four-fucking-seven."

"Yeah, this job seems to include a lot that I didn't sign up for!"

He scowls darkly. "Lower your voice." It's amazing how he can speak so softly and still have his words come across as powerfully as if he were screaming.

"I will not!"

"Wren." His voice cracks like a whip and for a moment, it's as though my skin is on fire. "We are in the office and the walls have ears. We need to practice discretion."

"*Discretion?*" I wish my voice had the same weight, the same presence his does. As it stands, he'll have to settle for my banshee shriek. "You put me over your knee like a spoiled child and you want *me* to be discreet? Well, fuck you! And fuck your *discretion*!"

His expression is hard to read. It's as though the black rage in his eyes has dissolved into nothing. And when I say nothing, I mean *nothing*. No emotion, either good or bad.

Then his gaze flickers past me. I turn slowly…

To find Vittorio Zanetti's filmy blue eyes fixed on me.

"It seems silly to ask if I'm interrupting when I so clearly am."

Shit. I was so riled up that I didn't even hear him enter. How much did he overhear? Is there any conceivable way to make a conversation about spanking sound like it's work-related? Just how fucked am I?

I'm sweating head to toe as Dmitri rises to his feet behind his desk. "You're not interrupting a thing, Vittorio," he says smoothly. "In fact, I'm just cleaning up in here."

I turn back to Dmitri, wondering what on earth he's talking about. Then I catch his expression.

Oh.

"Ms. Turner, you seem to be under the impression that your friendship with my future wife guarantees you immunity within Egorov Industries. Let me clarify one thing for you: you are not indispensable. You are not important. And you are not in any position to talk back to me." I want to look away from those dark silver eyes but I can't. "You have exactly ten minutes to pack your things and get out of my sight."

I flinch back as my jaw drops open. "Y-you're firing me?"

I probably should have seen this coming, but the truth is, I honestly didn't. I'm waiting for the wink. Surely there's a "gotcha" moment coming up, right?

Right?

Dmitri walks around to his desk and throws me a flippant glance. "You thought you could talk to me like that and everything would be fine?"

I swallow hard, trying not to look at the sneering Vittorio, who seems to be getting off on this exchange. "I-I need this job."

"You have a strange way of showing it." His voice is devoid of all emotion. Just like his eyes. He dials in a number and picks up his phone. "Aleks, get up here now. I need you to escort Ms. Turner off the property. Make sure you reclaim her lanyard and her security badge before she leaves."

I take a step towards his desk, but he stops me with nothing but a stare. "Save the pleading for someone it'll work on. You don't get second chances with me. Now, get out."

I bite down on my tongue to keep the tears away. I wish that I could turn back time and demand a do-over. Quite apart from needing the money, this job is the only reason I get out of the penthouse. Without it, I'm doomed to house arrest for… I don't even know how long.

I walk out of the office with my head held as high as I can manage. Vittorio's gaze follows me the whole time. He doesn't even try to make a secret of it.

I'm practically hyperventilating by the time I reach my desk. I grab my stapler and a box of paper clips before I realize how dumb I'm being.

"Fuck," I mutter, trying to breathe through the panic.

Dmitri had to have been joking. He was just putting on a show for Vittorio. This firing isn't actually going to stick.

"Wren?" Aleksandr appears from around the corner, looking concerned. "Everything alright?"

"Um…" My lips quiver and the tongue biting isn't helping anymore. A tear springs free. "He f-fired me."

He looks just as shocked as I feel. He glances at the door and exhales sharply. "Let's just get you home, okay?"

"V-V-Vittorio is in there with him."

He nods. "I know. I saw him enter the building. Come on." He gestures for me to walk over to him, but I just look at my desk helplessly. "My things… He told me to clear out my… my…"

"I'll handle that for you later, don't you worry." His tone is just gentle enough that I set down the office supplies, grab my purse, and follow him down the hall towards the elevators.

Spanked and fired in the same week. This has to be some kind of a joke.

As we ride down to the ground floor, Aleksandr eyes me warily. "It was just a fight," I whisper in a small voice.

He sighs. "Wren, no one fights with the boss."

I used to believe that. But that was *before*. Before I knew that he liked classical music and vodka. Before I knew he liked to wake up at the crack of dawn to use the gym. Before I knew he was a great chef who made the butteriest French toast I've ever put in my mouth.

For me, life is now divided into two swaths of time. *B.D.*—before Dmitri, when he was just my bosshole. And *A.D.*—after Dmitri, when he transformed into my nightmare of a baby daddy.

This is my fault. I'm the one who's grown complacent and sloppy. I've let our proximity cloud my judgment. I've fallen into the trap of believing that proximity equals intimacy.

Newsflash, Wren: it doesn't.

35

WREN

I'm in the kitchen trying to force down a sandwich when Dmitri gets home.

My knee starts bouncing and I drop the sandwich instantly. I'm not sure why I'm so nervous; it's not like he holds the moral high ground here. If anything, we're both to blame for the fight.

He storms into the kitchen with his jaw set tight and his nostrils flared. He spares me only a cursory glare before he goes to the fridge and yanks out a cold beer. He drains half of it before he slams the bottle down on the kitchen island so hard that I'm stunned it doesn't shatter.

He's looking down at the marble countertop when he speaks, but his words are directed at me. "You will never speak to me like that again. Not in private. Not in public. Is that clear?" Just like earlier, he's not screaming, but my eardrums ring from the harshness of his words.

My instinct is to just agree with him so that we can put this issue to bed. But my pride won't let me give in that easily. "If I agree, will you give me my job back?"

He glowers at me. "This isn't a negotiation."

"You're a businessman. I thought everything was a negotiation."

He rounds the counter and stands right in front of me. "Not when it comes to my subordinates," he spits. "And not when we're in my domain."

I throw my hands up in the air. "Everything is your domain! You've rigged the system and you expect me to be happy about it."

"You have every luxury—"

"Except freedom!" I exclaim. I can smell the beer on his breath. I've never been much of a beer drinker, but suddenly, I have this deep-seated craving to taste it. To taste it off his lips, specifically.

"You want to see the antithesis to freedom?" Dmitri growls. "Just look at Vittorio Zanetti."

The image of Bee's destroyed back jumps into my head and I flinch like I'm taking those same whiplashes myself. That old man is no joke. If he's capable of doing that to his own daughter, who knows what kind of pain he's willing to rain down on everyone else?

I bite my bottom lip. "I'm sorry. I shouldn't have spoken to you like that. Especially at the office."

He seems taken back by the sudden apology. "There's no room for weakness in a Bratva," he says in a soft voice that still manages to be urgent. "I can't be seen to be lenient on you. Especially not in Vittorio's eyes."

I gulp back my disappointment and peer down at my feet. "I need to find another job then."

His finger tucks under my chin and I freeze. He forces my face up with only the littlest bit of pressure. "There will be no need. I fired you from Egorov Industries, but you're still head of my Personal Management—"

"Which is still not a thing."

He ignores me. "Your salary will be significantly higher than what you made before."

I want to be excited. That would be great news if it didn't feel like a pity buyout. "It's not a real job."

He glowers at me and picks up his beer again, rolling it back and forth between his fingers. "Of course it is. The job description is simple—cater to whatever Bee wants from you; cater to whatever I ask of you."

I roll my eyes. "How convenient for you both. Except that you and Bee are barely at home. How is it a legitimate job if I'm expected to just sit here and twiddle my thumbs, waiting for you and Bee to throw me a bone and give me a task for the day?"

"You want real responsibilities—is that what you're saying?"

I grit my teeth and try to stay calm. "I'm saying I want to *earn* my salary. I'm not a charity case and I can't be bought."

He sighs noisily before turning and dumping the bottle into the recycling bin. "You want some real work to justify your salary? Fine. You are officially Bee's event coordinator."

"Hm. Okay. I can do that. What event does she have coming up that she needs my help with?"

"Our wedding."

I can practically feel the color drain from my face. "Y-your wedding."

I'm not sure why my body feels so cold and clammy all of a sudden and I really don't want to unpick that particular knot right now.

"That's why Vittorio stopped by the office today. He came to demand that Bee and I push up the date of the ceremony."

I'm waiting for even the faintest sense of enthusiasm on his face, but there's none to be found. "If you don't mind me saying, you don't seem very happy."

"Would you be happy if some old *mudak* was calling the shots on your life?" he snaps at me.

I shrug. "I mean, I've dealt with it pretty well, all things considered." The joke sinks in immediately and he offers me an impatient glare that has laughter snorting up through my nostrils. "You're right; it's not exactly the same. You're not old."

"Very amusing," he mutters without cracking a smile. "By the way, the wedding will be on the tenth."

"The *tenth*?" I gasp, all humor suddenly gone from the situation. "That's less than a month from now!"

He nods. "You wanted to work for your salary. So—get to work."

I place my hand on my stomach as he leaves. Life really is a cruel bitch, isn't she? Not so long ago, I was planning on having a baby that belonged to my sister and brother-in-law.

Now, I'm planning a wedding for my baby daddy who just happens to belong to another woman.

At least things can't get any worse.

36

WREN

There's something otherworldly about Chicago in the middle of the night. Lines of brake lights in the distance like inset rubies. Golden pools of streetlights. Windows lit, windows dark, silhouettes shifting amongst the indigo shadows.

You can't pick a wrong window to look out of in this apartment. But for my money, the living room has the best vantage point of them all. I load a plate with leftovers and settle into a seat on the floor so I can gaze out at all the lives unfolding around me.

I'm usually so exhausted that I sleep through the night without a problem. But tonight is the first time I've woken up in cold sweats, scared awake by a dream I can't quite remember anymore.

Hence the mini-mountain of food in front of me.

"Doors closing."

I sit upright, my mouth full of Häagen-Dazs. I so do *not* want to be caught snacking in the living room in the middle of the night by Dmitri. Quite apart from being embarrassing, I need some distance from him.

"Well, helloooo there!" a familiar voice croons.

I sigh with relief. "Bee. Where have you been?"

She rolls her eyes sloppily as she staggers in through the archway. "Out, Mom. *Jeez*." She takes a very zig-zaggy route towards me, bumping off several pieces of furniture on her way over.

"You're drunk," I accuse.

She scrunches up her nose. "You going to punish me, baby?" she asks in a tone that is very confusing to me. Is it meant to be seductive or is it just coming out that way by accident and she's too wasted to notice?

"Uh… no. Just asking a question."

"Cookie dough!" she blurts in delight, dropping down heavily onto her knees in front of me. She slumps to the side, her shoulder coming to rest against the glass wall, then reaches a clumsy hand over to swipe a finger through the mound of cookie dough on my plate and raise it to her lips.

She's wearing loud eye makeup in a glittery green and a sequined dress to match. What little fabric there is to the garment is strategically positioned to keep her more or less modest, though the nipple pasties are truly doing the Lord's work.

Crumbs tumble onto the carpet as Bee runs another finger in the dessert and attacks the lump of cookie dough like she hasn't seen food in months. There's a franticness to her that unsettles me. Her drunken giggles masking something a little deeper, a little darker.

"Bee…" I venture. "Are you okay?"

She flashes me a sardonic thumbs up. "Great," she says with a mouth full of food. "It was a *ggreagtnfucnfeindnight*."

"What was that?"

She swallows and starts over. "It was a great night."

I try to smile. Was her lipstick always smudged as if she was just kissing someone? "Yeah? Where'd you go?"

"New club downtown. Hellscape—so corny, right? Fucking amaaazing DJ, though. Hey, you got anything to drink?" I pass her my glass of water and she downs it in one gulp. "Fuck, nectar of the gods, am I right?" She doesn't wait for me to answer or agree. "She was playing all these sick beats and she was stupid hot. I'm talking curvy, sexy, tatted-up, with a smile like straight crack cocaine." She purses her lips. "You know, she kind of reminded me of you."

I point a finger at myself. "Me?"

Bee chuckles before unleashing a very unladylike burp. "Oops." She giggles some more. "Yeah, you," she says as she boops me on the nose. "She looked a lot like you. Same eyes. Same green."

"You got to see her up close then."

She gives me a salacious little wink. "Oh, I got up close alright."

What the hell is that supposed to mean? It sounds like she's implying that she got it on with the DJ. The female DJ. Which is weird, considering she's currently engaged to a man.

Not just any man, either. The manliest man out there.

Nothing is making sense right now. Unless of course I'm still dreaming and the Haagen-Dazs is nothing but a figment of my imagination.

"You should have been there, Wrenny!" she sighs, picking at the crumbs on her legs. "It was unreal."

I shrug and point to my belly. "Unfortunately, this little guy keeps me hostage most of the time. And when he's chill, your fiancé's not."

Bee grimaces. "Yeah, I know that feeling. A hostage in your own life. It blows." She blinks and the brightness in her eyes drains away without warning. "But sometimes, it's necessary…"

I frown. "What's necessary?"

"This," she says, throwing her arm over the living room like I'm supposed to know what the hell she's referring to. "All this."

She looks so out of it that I'm starting to get concerned. "Bee, how about I help you into bed? How does that sound?"

She wags her eyebrows at me. "Mm-mm. Is that a proposition? Are you prop-pop-sitioning me?"

"Okay, now, you're slurring. Definitely time to get you into bed." I get to my feet and offer her both my hands.

She stares up at me blankly for a moment. "Where are we going?"

In my experience, there are two types of drunks. There are the ones who drink to have a good time and then there are the ones who drink to numb themselves.

Right now, Bee's giving me strong Type B vibes.

"To your bedroom," I say firmly. "Take my hands." She slaps her palms against mine and I pull her forward until she's upright. "Lean on me if you have to." We stumble through the penthouse until we get to Bee's room. It isn't until we're right at her door that I realize Dmitri might be in there sleeping. "Uh, go on. I'll wait out here."

Before I can stop her, she's shoved open the door carelessly, causing it to crash loudly against the supporting wall. "Shit," I hiss. "Quietly, Bee!"

She just laughs. "Oh, don't be such a worrier. It's fine."

She doesn't remove her arm from around my shoulders, so I'm forced to walk into the room with her. It's very clearly empty, though. In fact, the bed's neatly made. Dmitri must still be in his office. Or maybe he's out as well, getting wasted and maybe-or-maybe-not seducing beautiful DJs with dazzling smiles. For a couple who seem to have such good vibes together, they spend a lot of time apart.

I sit Bee down at the edge of her bed and she teeters in place. Her eyes finally manage to focus on me and she tries to lift her hand but it drops as though it's too heavy for her to carry.

"You're so pretty," she mumbles.

I smile awkwardly. "Thanks."

"You're totally my type, ya know," she says softly. "But he got to you first…"

I'm spared from having to say anything when she flops back on top of the covers and starts snoring softly.

"Damn, Bee," I whisper. "You're a hot mess."

I grab her legs and hoist them into the bed. Then I drape a blanket over her and backpedal quietly out of the room. As I'm closing the door, it strikes me that, as nice as Bee has been to me, she hasn't been very honest, either.

There's no denying that she and Dmitri are close. But how close? Is her relationship with Dmitri just a marriage of convenience, or do they have real feelings for each other? The fact that I'm hoping for the former makes me sick to my stomach.

What is wrong with me?

37

DMITRI

Power gives you freedom.

Words my father lived by. Words he ingrained in me so young that power was the only thing I coveted.

It took me years of adulthood, of owning that power, to realize that he was just feeding me bullshit all along. It was all just a marketing strategy.

Power doesn't give you freedom; it breeds *enemies*. It gives you problems.

Right now, I have five.

One: my best friend and soon-to-be wife who is suddenly proving unable to commit to the farce we shook hands on.

Two: her bloodthirsty father, who is sniffing closer and closer to the truth beneath the duplicitous life we are living for his benefit.

Three: the Irish motherfucker who stole Elena from me and seems intent on making history repeat itself.

Four: the woman who's made it her mission to turn my life into a living hell without even trying. Oh, and she happens to be carrying my son.

The fifth and final problem is myself. For not getting my shit together and focusing on what's really important, which is marrying Bee and protecting my son. Wren shouldn't factor in at all. So why is she the loudest voice in my head right now?

Bzz. Bzz. Bzz.

Gratefully, I sit up in bed and grab my phone. "Aleks?"

"I know it's late, but something's happened."

"Spit it out, man."

"There's been an explosion at the warehouse in Burnside." I jump out of bed and start throwing on clothes blindly as he keeps rattling off details. "No casualties. But we have five injured men who were on the night shift. Two have been taken to the emergency room; the other three are being treated here as we speak. Pavel's doing a sweep of the place to make sure we know what's gone down."

I storm out of the apartment. "An explosion is what's 'gone down,' Aleksandr," I growl. "My warehouses aren't in the habit of self-combusting."

"Right, but we don't know who—"

"The fuck we don't!" I hiss. "This has his name written all over it."

"Brother, why would he do this now? The Irish have been quiet for years."

"Why do you think they've been quiet for years?" I demand. "That slippery fuck, Cian, has been biding his time, building up a plan. He's always wanted to take me down. You think the attack on Wren was a coincidence? You think his appearance at The Eclipse was a coincidence?"

"I'm just advising caution."

"Advice has never been your forte, Aleksandr. Stick to what you do best: following orders."

His breathing gets heavier. "Fine. I'll see you soon."

He's not one to get angry easily, but I know I've pissed him off. I've never cared before and I'm not about to start now.

By the time I get to the warehouse, the smoke has settled and I can see the full extent of the damage. The explosion has taken out the whole back end of the structure. Black soot clings to the walls and embers hiss as they crunch underfoot.

My head spins with the unwelcome sensation of déjà vu. This night feels far too similar to another night from my past. A night when I turned the whole fucking city upside down and all I got in return was her body. Blackened and charred, hardly recognizable.

It was the ring on her finger that forced me to believe it.

I breathe in the dark plumes of smoke and vow, not for the first time, that I'll avenge her death.

Pavel and Aleksandr jog over the moment they see me. "Do we know what caused the explosion?"

"A handmade bomb," Pavel reports. "Hidden in the back half of the warehouse."

"Have you checked the security footage?"

Aleksandr nods. "Three times over. Whoever planted the bomb took advantage of a blind spot at the back of the warehouse. The camera catches a shadow, but we don't have a face."

I smell blood and sulfur. "What about any suspicious persons loitering outside the warehouse in the last twenty-four hours?"

"We haven't combed over footage for the exterior cameras yet."

"Do it and report back to me immediately."

Pavel gets right to it while Aleksandr lingers behind. "No one died," he adds, as though that information is somehow comforting to me.

"If that bomb had been planted at the offices… or the penthouse…"

"There's no way that could have happened."

I glare at him furiously. "Didn't you say something similar to me the night Elena went missing?" I snarl. "What were your exact words?"

"Brother—"

"*'They won't target Elena. There's no way they'd be that stupid.'* Was it something like that?"

He flushes. "The Irish are a lot more powerful than they were a few years ago."

"So you're afraid of a fight, is that it?"

Aleksandr's mouth drops. "I'm not afraid of anything. But I do want to win. And we can't win by being impulsive."

I'm vaguely aware that he's making sense. The problem is the logical side of my brain is currently being overridden by huge amounts of adrenaline and testosterone. And there's a masochistic part of me that takes pleasure in it.

This isn't about the mundane politics of war—it's not about babies or marriages or weddings.

This is about taking *action*.

This is about the tangible thrum of battle—feeling a gun in your hands and knowing that, when you pull the trigger, someone will die.

This is about sweat and tears and bloodshed.

This is what I was truly built for.

"How long has it been since Elena died?"

"Dmitri—"

"Answer me."

"Six years. Just about."

I nod. "Six fucking years. So don't you stand there with a straight face and tell me I'm being impulsive. I can't let it happen again."

Aleksandr's forehead wrinkles up like it used to when he was a kid. "Is that what this is about?"

It takes all of my self-control not to take a swing at my own brother in front of all my men. "She means nothing to me."

"You just said—"

"She's carrying my son," I spit forcefully. He flinches back and holds up his hands but I keep going. "And as long as my child is inside her, I need to make sure that nothing touches her."

"I get it; I do," he reassures me quickly. "I just want to make sure we're hitting the right target."

"Who else could it be?"

"What about Vittorio?" He plants his hand on my shoulder. "He's suspicious about Wren. It might be that he's figured it out."

"I've got eyes on Vittorio. He may have his suspicions, but he doesn't have enough information to act. Nor is he going to."

"How can you be sure?"

"Because he wants us to move up the wedding." It's hard to say out loud, but the moment the words are out of me, I realize that a large part of my anger at this moment has been triggered by his unexpected visit yesterday.

Aleksandr eyes me carefully. "Shit. Uh, how… how do you feel about that?"

"Who are you, my shrink?"

He ventures a smile that dies almost immediately when I glare back at him. "I just mean, does it matter if you get married next week or next year? You're getting married either way, right?"

He has a point, one that makes me realize that the idea of marrying Bee wasn't always so unpleasant to me. In fact, not too long ago, it felt like the perfect solution to an inconvenient problem.

So what's changed in the last few weeks? What's made me so reluctant to go through with a plan that I set in motion myself?

"Gather some men," I order. "Half a dozen of your best. I need to pay the Irish a visit."

I head back to my car and start driving west. The last time I was in Irish territory was six years ago. To recover Elena's body. I take the same route I did back then—the masochist in me is on fire tonight.

I drive slowly, just to make sure we're seen in the area. If I know Cian—and I'm sure I do—he's going to have eyes everywhere. My men trail behind in a car almost identical to mine. We're impossible to miss.

I park outside O'Malley's, which is only dimly lit from the inside. I chose this place for two reasons: it's a known O'Gadhra mafia hang-out. And Wren mentioned it to me after our run-in with Cian at the concert. Nothing will send a clearer message than taking down a sentimental landmark.

As I get out of my jeep, my phone starts to ring. ***Unknown Caller.*** I snort—how predictable.

"Cian."

"Little late to be dropping in unannounced, don't you think, old friend?" His voice is gravelly, rough with sleep. Someone's clearly woken him up to tell him that I'm in his neck of the woods.

"I figured it was only polite, considering you just targeted one of my warehouses."

His shallow breathing slows. "I didn't target shit."

"Unfortunately for you and the building I'm standing in front of, O'Gadhra, I don't believe a single word that comes out of your mouth."

"Whatever you're going to do," he hisses, "I suggest you don't."

"If you're scared, you shouldn't have blown my property to bits. Might've saved us all the heartache."

"You do not want to start a war with me, Egorov."

I chuckle darkly. "Wanna bet?"

"I'll say it again: I had nothing to do with targeting your warehouse."

"Just like you had nothing to do with Elena's death. Am I getting that right?"

"Jesus Christ, Dmitri!" He actually sounds panicked and it's giving me life. This is what I came for. "If you do this, you will leave me no choice but to respond. Once this starts, there will be no stopping it until one of us is dead."

"I'll take that as a promise," I growl.

I hang up and give Pavel a nod. Seconds later, the embossed green sign that reads ***O'Malley's*** starts to glitter with light. The fire spreads fast, throwing off heat and color and swallowing everything in its midst.

Who knew that starting a war could look so beautiful?

38

DMITRI

Wren startles like a frightened deer when I walk into the kitchen. "I can leave," she offers quietly when she's got her wits about her again. But she doesn't get up from the high stool.

"No need. I won't be here long."

I grab one of the bottles hanging from the overhead bar rack and pour myself a hefty shot of whiskey.

"Why do you smell like a burning forest?"

I purse my lips after I down half the drink. "That's a very specific analogy."

"Well, you smell like smoke and your normal musk is really, like, stormy…" Her cheeks go beet red as she's talking. "But yeah, I mean, uh, mostly the smoke."

"There was a fire in one of my warehouses." I purposefully leave out the bomb. I don't want to stress her out. Because of the baby, obviously.

She gasps. "A fire?! Was anyone hurt?" Her eyes are wide with concern, her forehead puckered with worry. The fact that she cares so much right off the bat is annoying as hell.

No—it's *endearing* as hell. And that's what makes it annoying.

"A few men working the night shift were injured."

"But they're going to be okay?"

"Yes." The plan was to walk my drink out of here and enjoy it alone. But I find myself sitting down instead. As it turns out, I don't even need the drink to calm down. She does that to me all on her own.

"Well, okay. Good. That's good. You must be relieved."

How is it possible that she can still assume the best in me even after I've proved time and time again that I'm an asshole? Then again, she seems to think Cian O'Gadhra is a stand-up guy, so it's safe to say that her judgment is, to put it mildly, flawed.

"Sure. Relieved."

Wren tilts her head to the side. "Are you hungry?"

I'm not in the slightest, but I nod anyway. She promptly bounces up and starts fluttering around the kitchen, pulling things out of the fridge and the cupboard. "Fair warning: I'm not the greatest cook in the world, but I make a decent grilled cheese."

She radiates self-consciousness as she makes the sandwich. Her gaze keeps flickering over to me when she thinks I'm not looking back. I wonder if this is her attempt at an olive branch.

I almost wish she wouldn't, though. Being at odds with her makes it so much easier to justify the colossal secret stuck in my throat.

The aroma of melting cheese fills the air and it almost succeeds in driving out the wet smoke smell still clinging to my clothes. As she flips the sandwich on the griddle, my gaze slides down to her ass. *The soft cotton of those pajamas would be so easy to—*

I catch myself just in time. Right before the images in my head spin out into fantasies I can't control. Thankfully, she turns around a few moments later and presents me with a fat grilled cheese oozing from all four sides.

I take it and murmur a wordless grunt of thanks. She perches on the next stool over, closer than her previous seat. "Well?" she asks after I've taken my first bite.

"It's delicious," I say once I swallow.

Wren blushes, quietly pleased with my praise. "I perfected that sandwich over many late drunken nights. Not my drunken nights," she hurries to correct. "Rose went through a phase right before she met Jared. I'd force some food into her when she got home to sober her up."

I cringe. Why do all her stories involve her sister in some way, shape, or form? It's almost like she knows I'm hiding something and she's trying to draw it out of me.

As if realizing the same thing herself, her blush morphs and she hides behind the curtain of her hair. "Anyway. How, er… how'd you get into cooking?"

I take another bite of the sandwich. Now that my taste buds are awake, I am suddenly ravenous. "I wanted to impress—" I stop just short of saying Elena's name. I've got to be careful with this one; she has a way of lulling me into a sense of security and it makes me want to say shit I would never have otherwise said. "—Bee."

"Oh." A tremor runs across her face that looks suspiciously like sadness. But when she looks up at me, she's wearing a soft smile. "It clearly worked."

A fog of melancholia hangs over Wren's head tonight. If only I could see what's going on inside of her.

That had been so much easier with Elena. She told me everything she was feeling, everything she was thinking. And even when she didn't, she wore her emotions on her face, clear as day.

"Do you have a vision for the wedding?"

My gaze recoils to hers before I realize that she's talking about my wedding to Bee. I shouldn't be so surprised. I suppose it's taking longer than I would've expected to accept that Bee and I have only weeks left until we're husband and wife.

"Whatever Bee wants," I demur gruffly.

"You must have *some* opinions." Her knee is bouncing softly, but I have no idea why she would be nervous. "If I'm going to be planning this wedding, I want to do something you'll both appreciate."

"I don't have opinions."

It's not necessarily true. I might have had opinions—if this wedding was real. I did have opinions when it came to my marriage to Elena. She wanted my input for every single decision that was made. It was how we ended up saying "fuck it" to the elaborate ceremony we'd spent years concocting and did it all instead on the steps of Town Hall—me in a shirt, no coat, her in a knee-length white dress with daisies in her hair that I bought from a nearby florist a few minutes before the ceremony. Bee and Aleksandr were our witnesses and afterwards, we sat on the curb and ate churros and ice cream.

It was perfect.

I shudder and snap back to the present when I realize Wren is watching me carefully. "Well, I'll get them out of you in time," she threatens with a weak, wobbly smile to let me know she's joking.

I clear my throat. "What are you doing up so late?"

"I've been having trouble sleeping," she admits, glancing at the antique clock on the wall. "Aw, dammit, it's past two."

"Go to bed. You need your rest."

She pinches her nose. "I agree. But if I can't sleep, I can't sleep."

"I'll talk to Liza. Maybe there's something she can give us to help you sleep through the night."

Wren leans back scowling and the t-shirt stretches across her burgeoning belly. I'm overcome with this need to touch it. *It's about my son,* I tell myself. *It's not about her.*

"I don't want to take a pill to sleep, Dmitri."

"Must everything be a fight with you?"

She blinks, taken back. "It's not a fight. I just have different opinions than you do. And as far as my body is concerned, I get to have a say."

I drop the half-eaten sandwich in my fingers back onto the plate. "Are you getting at least eight hours of sleep each night?"

"Are you?" she retorts without missing a beat. "Honestly, I've never seen a couple more intent on avoiding sleep."

I stiffen. I know that Bee's late-night escapades have gone on unchecked, but I didn't know that Wren was aware.

"You're both night owls, huh?" she presses.

"You could say that." Wren squirms in her seat for a moment, darting little glances in my direction. "What is it?"

"Nothing."

"Wren."

She shrugs and sighs. "Well, it's none of my business, really. But Bee seemed kinda off when she got in a little while ago."

"'Kinda off'? Explain."

She flushes delicately. "I mean, she was really drunk, so maybe that was part of it. But she did seem kind of… sad. Almost like the drinking was a… a consequence of it. Or, like, a symptom. Or maybe a cure, I dunno." Unease has my extremities tingling with warning. "Then again, maybe she was just having a little fun?" Her gaze flickers to me searchingly. "She does get really flirty when she's drunk."

Fuck me. Did Bee make a move on Wren? Has Wren been sitting up trying to figure out the dynamic between Bee and me? She's getting dangerously close to the truth and it's making me uncomfortable.

"You don't need to worry about Bee," I reply curtly. "She's fine."

She opens her mouth to argue, then closes it again and exhales. "Oh, okay. Then again… you didn't see her tonight. You weren't around."

"I don't have to be around to know what's going on with my fiancée."

She flinches. "If you say so. I was just worried—"

"Well, don't be," I cut in. "It's not your business to worry about Bee. In fact, it's not your place to talk about her, either."

She reels back, her face falling instantly. The tentative truce of the last half hour falls away. Wren's jaw is working hard from side to side like she wants to say something.

Do it, I dare her silently. *Ask me. Have mercy and just fucking ask me so I don't have to hide this shit anymore.*

In the end, though, she doesn't. She climbs off her stool and makes for the exit.

The smart thing to do would be to let her go. But she's gone and ignited my rage all over again. Where there's smoke, there's fire—and I'm burning just like my building did.

So as she passes by me, I snag her arm and reel her into my side. She's eye level with me, and her green irises are flaming every bit as bright as mine are.

"Let's get one thing straight," I growl. "Just because you live here doesn't mean you know shit about Bee or me or our relationship."

She tries to free her arm from my grip, but I just dig my fingers in deeper. Her lips are pressed together in a hard line and she keeps her mouth shut very deliberately.

"You're here because it's not safe for my son out there," I snap, jabbing a finger toward the world beyond these four walls. "But if you want freedom, you'll get it soon enough. Once you push him out, you'll be free to go wherever the fuck you want."

She stops struggling. Stops moving altogether. "What is that supposed to mean?" she whispers hoarsely. "Are you threatening to separate me from my son?"

I like her proximity a little too much. Her body is giving off all kinds of heat. If I turn just a little bit to the right, she'll be standing squarely between my legs. "That's up to you. If you want to stay with our son, that means you'll have to stay put."

Her eyes crackle like fireworks. The emerald turns dark and I wait expectantly for her anger to burst all over me. "You fucking—"

"What's going on here?"

Both of us flinch in the direction of the kitchen entrance. Bee is standing in the open doorway in a pair of tiny shorts and a tank that reads, ***I'm great in bed—I can sleep for hours.***

Wren springs away from me as though we've been caught in the act. Weirdly, it feels like we have. "What's going on here is your fiancé is an asshole," she manages to spit. Then she darts past Bee and out of the kitchen.

Bee stares after her until her footsteps are swallowed back up in the silence. When she turns back, her eyes are narrowed with accusation.

I get off my stool before she can start in on me. "You look like shit."

She sighs and shakes her head. "You're making things so much harder than they need to be. You realize that, don't you?"

Yeah, I think miserably to myself. *I really fucking do.*

39

WREN

I wake up with two completely unrelated thoughts in my head.

The first is that I can't afford to alienate Dmitri, because he has the power to keep me away from my son.

The second: it's my birthday. More importantly, it's the first birthday I'm going to be spending without Rose.

Cue the crying.

I cry through my morning pee and my shower and, when I realize that I'm not in the least bit hungry, I skip breakfast so I can put my pajamas back on and curl into bed and cry some more. Fetal position all the way, because that's how God intended for His creations to cry.

Or so I assume.

I lose time to thought and, somewhere in the midst of my grief, I fall asleep. Not the restful kind—it's too tormented with old memories disguised as dreams for that.

I picture walking down sidewalks and every face is Rose's. None of them will talk to me.

When I wake up, feeling worse than I did when I fell asleep, my cheeks are sticky with dried tear tracks. I don't bother wiping them away because no sooner am I awake than do fresh tears start to fall along the same paths.

In some ways, it makes sense that I would lose it today. Right after I buried Rose and Jared, I jumped back into work. It was the first time I'd actually been grateful to Dmitri for being the Type A control freak he is, because he'd kept me so busy that I didn't have time to dwell with my pain. I could always feel it, hibernating deep inside me, but I was able to keep the lid on it.

Now, though, that lid has well and truly been blown the fuck off.

If this keeps up much longer, I'm going to be a dried husk of a woman. I'd go to the kitchen and guzzle some water if I wasn't so nervous about running into Bee and Dmitri. Today of all days, those aren't encounters I feel up to handling.

Death by dehydration it is, then.

As it turns out, I don't even have to leave the room to get exactly what I don't want. Around three in the afternoon, Bee raps on my door. "Wren? Is everything okay in there? You haven't left your room all day."

She sounds worried. But I'm sure that has nothing to do with me and everything to do with what she walked in on last night. Which was intense and confrontational in my eyes, but probably nothing short of suspicious in hers.

I glance down at my arm and find an indigo bruise blotching my skin from where Dmitri held me. "Happy birthday to me," I mutter darkly.

"Wren," Bee calls out again, "can we talk?"

I cringe. Talking is the last thing I want to do. I don't have even a fraction of the emotional bandwidth to discuss what may or may not be happening with Dmitri and me.

Especially not in a conversation with his future wife.

Whose wedding I just happen to be planning.

The term "shitshow" was invented for people like me.

"Wren, if you don't open this door right now, I'mma give it my best hi-ya and break it the fuck down."

I collapse back into bed and throw the covers over my head. I feel like a bitch for ignoring her, but I just can't face today. I'll sleep through it and deal with the consequences tomorrow. At the moment, it feels like a solid plan.

Or at least, it does—right up until I hear the lock turn in my door. I guess I shouldn't be surprised that they have a spare key handy. There's no such thing as privacy in this freaking prison.

Whatever. I'm just going to stay under the covers and pretend I'm alone.

That backup plan is shot to hell just like the others when Bee grabs the blankets I'm hiding under and tears them right off me. Flinching, I grab my last line of defense—the always-trusty pillow—and plop it over my head.

No dice. That goes the same way as the rest of them.

I groan, pressing my face into the mattress as colorless starbursts erupt behind my closed eyelids. "Leave me alone."

"I will not. If this is about what happened last night, I'll talk to Dmitri, okay? He was being an asshole and you have every right to be upset."

I'm not so far gone that I don't appreciate that Bee's here giving me the benefit of the doubt. I can't see her, but I feel the bed tilt to the side under her weight. "Can you please talk to me?"

I'm just so, so tired. Admitting that pretty much steals the last bit of energy I have left. I turn to the side, where Bee is looking down at me with pity in her eyes.

Her eyebrows hit her hairline when she takes in the hot mess that is my face. "Jesus, Wren. Who died?"

It's a serious question. So I give her a serious answer. "M-m-my sister," I sob, descending into more of the full-scale blubbering that's already consumed my whole morning.

Bee has no context for understanding, but unfortunately for her, I'm in no fit state to explain. To her credit, she doesn't ask me to. She leans forward and hugs me and I cry onto her shoulder, which is soaked in seconds.

What I learn then is that there's a big difference between crying alone and crying on someone else. A few wordless minutes later, I feel drained, but I also feel relief. Plus the full ache of resignation that comes with it.

"Shit," I mutter when I get my voice back. "I'm sorry."

"Don't be sorry," Bee chides gently. "You're having a bad day. We all have them."

God, I wish my growing love for Bee would cancel out my complicated feelings for Dmitri. But apparently, the heart doesn't work that way.

Pity.

I sit up and accept the tissue she hands me. "I didn't expect it to hit me so hard. It's just... twenty-nine years," I breathe. "And this is the first birthday I'm spending without her."

She ogles me for a moment. "Wait. It's your *birthday*?"

I nod half-heartedly. "Twenty-nine today."

"My God, Wren! Why didn't you tell me?" She jumps right off the bed, looking around like a parade of clowns or something is about to burst out of the walls at any moment.

I stare at her, a little perplexed. "Because it's not really important."

"Of course it is! It's your birthday! We have to celebrate."

This is so not where I thought this was going. She seems to have completely forgotten that I'm in the middle of a five-alarm meltdown over my sister being dead. "'Celebrate'? Bee—I have no desire to celebrate. My sister—"

"Your sister is dead, Wren," she says emphatically. The shock of that statement does a great job of shutting me up. Bee, however, does not take it back. "She's dead. But you're not. And if she were here, she'd want you to celebrate. She'd want you to be happy."

"I'll be happy tomorr—"

"Nuh-uh. Sorry. That's not an option. We're going out tonight to celebrate."

She starts to head for the door, as if it's decided. "Bee, for God's sake! I'm not in the mood to get dressed up and hit some lame club and pretend to have a good time. Plus, we don't have reservations anywhere and I—""

She holds up a hand to stop me. "I'm the future Mrs. Dmitri Egorov. That name holds weight in this town. I'll handle everything. Wear something sexy."

With that, she strolls out of my room, leaving the door wide open. I can't even crawl under the covers because she's taken them all with her.

Sometimes—this being one of those times—it makes perfect sense why she and Dmitri are together. They're the two most headstrong people I've ever met in my life.

After I've closed my room door, I end up pivoting in the direction of my walk-in closet.

Maybe going out tonight wouldn't be the worst idea? It beats crying into my pillow in a fetal position, at the very least. I can cry in a nightclub for a refreshing change of scenery.

I stroll through the racks of as-yet unused dresses draped from their hangers. I haven't had the opportunity to wear any of them and, now that I do, I can't find it in me to be excited about it.

But Bee is right about one thing: Rose would have wanted me to celebrate.

She was all about birthdays. I was the one who got all shy about making myself the center of attention, but Rose looked forward to hers. "I'm officially accepting presents," she'd announce when the calendar flipped to June. "It's my birthday month, bitches!"

I'm tugging at the hem of a pretty white wraparound dress with a halter neckline when Bee bursts back in. "Ah, perfect choice! I couldn't have picked better myself."

I drop the garment like it burned me. "I was just looking at it."

"Nope." She breezes past me and plucks the dress from the rack. "You're wearing it tonight."

I sigh tiredly. "Bee…"

I've never seen her look so determined. "I'm not playing today, Wren. You don't get to sit around and mope all day. I know I'm a poor stand-in, but I consider myself an understudy for your sister. I'm just doing what she would have wanted for you today."

"I'd like to point out that you never actually met my sister."

She waves that bit of logic away. "Details," she demurs, flinging the dress at me. "Now, put that on. How do you feel about letting me do your makeup? You love it? Great. I'm excited, too."

"Um, I wasn't planning on wearing makeup."

Her back is to me, but I can still hear her snort. "Think again." She bends down and frees a pair of black stilettos from the bottom rack of my open shoe display. "This pair will go amazing with your dress."

I squint at the heels with uncertainty. "Don't you think this is all a little… over the top?"

"There is no such thing. Now, go shower. I need a clean face before I apply your makeup."

I end up spending five minutes staring at my reflection in the bathroom mirror while the shower heats up behind me. I look the exact same way I did the day I found out about Rose and Jared's accident. My cheeks are blotchy, my eyes puffy, my nose red, and dried tear tracks that look like scars run up and down my face.

A nightmare, in other words.

Thankfully, the rinse helps me look decidedly less nightmarish. I can't quite get rid of the puffiness in my eyes or the blotchiness on my cheeks, but by the time Bee's done with me, I actually look quite good.

"There. Don't you feel better now?" Bee proclaims, wielding her makeup brush up like a battle ax.

I nod shyly. The truth is I actually do feel better. Somewhere between the blush pink lipstick and the cat eye eyeliner, I even start to look forward to a night out.

That lasts all of about ten minutes.

It goes up in smoke the very moment that Bee and I walk to the foyer to find Dmitri standing there in a crisp suit. Navy blue, pinstripes, Hugo Boss. He wears it on Tuesdays more often than not. It makes his eyes shine.

He's murmuring in a low voice to someone on the phone with his back to us. I freeze and clutch Bee's arm. "He's coming with us?" I hiss in her ear.

"Consider him more of an ATM than anything else tonight. Her smile is angelically innocent—or devilishly mischievous, depending on how you look at it. "We're going to the Rainbow Room, honey. Order whatever you want. He's paying."

That's funny—because right now, it feels like *I'm* the one who's going to have to pay.

doesn't have a back full of scars courtesy of him. She twists around in her seat to hail the waiter again right on cue. The dress she's wearing bears her back, but there's not a scar to be seen. It's only when I peer super closely that I can see the sheer, flesh-colored body suit she's wearing underneath.

I force a smile back on my face as she turns around again. "Did A.S.S.H.A.T. last very long?"

"Three dates and a couple of makeout sessions," Bee answers dismissively. "To be honest, he wasn't a great kisser." She leans to the left and grazes her fingers along Dmitri's cheek. "Not like my tamed beast over here."

Is it my imagination or does he pull back just a little? It's almost a flinch before he stiffens suddenly and resigns himself to letting her play with his ear and I'm left wondering if I imagined the whole thing.

"What about you, Wren? Any notable first boyfriends to talk shit about?"

"No one with a funny name, unfortunately," I say. "Tommy Sheridan was my first. We were both fourteen and on the track team. It lasted four months and ended because he got mad that I beat him in a cross-country race."

"Sounds like a prick." She raises her glass in a toast. "To pricks. Can't live with 'em, can't live... well, mostly just that one."

We clink our glasses together and laugh. Meanwhile, Dmitri continues to look pained. The only one who doesn't seem in the least bit awkward right now is Bee. That may also have a little something to do with the fact that her waiter has just delivered her second round in as many minutes.

"*Excusez-moi, garçon!*" She waves him over yet again and starts tapping on the rim of her cocktail glass. "Another, please."

Make that three.

Bee turns that megawatt smile of hers onto her sour-faced fiancé. "It's your turn, Dmitri."

"My turn for what?"

"We've both shared our first boyfriend experiences. Time for yours." She bats her eyelids at him expectantly.

I've got to hand it to the woman: she's got cojones aplenty. I wish I had a fraction of her courage to go jousting right at the surly ghoul shadowing our every move tonight.

Dmitri scowls. "You already know that story."

"Like the back of my hand," she confirms. Then she points her chin at me. "But Wrenny here doesn't."

His scowl darkens. "I don't live in the past."

"Coulda fooled me," Bee mutters under her breath, though it's not so low that we don't both hear perfectly well.

Instead of responding, Dmitri just gives her a pointed glare before excusing himself from the table. "I'm going to go get another drink."

Considering the waiter's standing only a few feet away from us, it seems like a pretty obvious attempt to get some space. Which is perfect, because I could use some space, too. Not to mention the freedom to let Bee have it for subjecting me to the intensely awkward vibes of the evening.

"What were you thinking, inviting him tonight?" I demand. "Are you on drugs?"

Her eyes get a little brighter at the suggestion. "No, but I could be." She winks. "I know a guy—"

"Bee!"

She laughs. "Oh, come on, I'm just joking. Obviously. Unless…"

"Was inviting Dmitri another one of your jokes? Because I've got news for you: it's not funny!"

She glances back over her shoulder. "I know he's being a giant grump tonight, but—"

"No, there's no 'but'! He obviously doesn't want to be here and you obviously made him come. And I am obviously uncomfortable."

She squints at me with something like pity in her eyes. "Come on, Wren. You're a smart girl. Do you really think that Dmitri Egorov does anything he doesn't want to do?"

It's the exact same question I asked myself earlier in the night. But what, then, is the answer? Of course he doesn't do anything he doesn't want to. That would mean that he *wants* to be here.

But…

"All you have to do is take one glance at the man," I protest. "He looks miserable sitting here between us talking about first boyfriends and pantyhose."

She giggles. "How about we talk about our periods next? Really get him squirming."

I laugh through my indignation. It really is hard to resist Bee. I may be surprised about a lot when it comes to the two of them, but Dmitri falling for her is not one. Hell, I'm as straight as they come and *I'm* half in love with her.

"Bee, seriously," I insist once I've got a handle on my laughter, "why did you invite him?"

"You want to know the truth?"

"Yes, please."

She squints at me over the rim of her third drink. "I didn't invite him. I told him we were going out for dinner to celebrate your birthday and he insisted on coming with us."

I'm having a hard time closing my mouth. "You're… Are you…"

She nods with a smug little smile on her face. "He pretends he's only here to 'protect us,' but I've known him a long time, Wren. You're the mother of his child. And he's here for your birthday."

Suddenly, I feel flushed. And restless. And sweaty under the armpits.

Bee leans forward and puts her hand on mine. "He may come across as an asshole, but he's anything but that. The only reason I'm even alive today is because he stepped in and protected me."

I gawk at Bee wide-eyed as I try to process what she's saying. But before I can get to any follow-up questions, Dmitri sits back down again with a drink so strong, I can smell it a foot away.

My thoughts are running rampant. *Let's just humor Bee here and pretend that she's right about Dmitri being here because he wants to be. Clearly, he needs a fuck-ton of alcohol to do it. And really, does that even count?*

"Wonderful!" Bee says suddenly, clapping her hands together. "We're all back together, we've got a little buzz going, the girls have had some laughs at the expense of the prince of darkness over here… I'd say the evening is going swimmingly, wouldn't you?"

"The time of my life," mutters Dmitri.

But even his acidity can't knock Bee's shine. "There's only one thing missing." Turning to me with that same wicked smile on her face, she asks, "Do you know what that is?"

"Uh…"

"Stronger liquor," adds Dmitri in another aside.

"Cake!" Bee squeals over him.

The moment she says "cake," I hear the hiss and spit of sparklers going off. From my peripheral vision, a whole armada of waiters appears, bearing a gorgeous cake decorated with a metric shitload of candles and a huge *2* and *9* wedged into the center.

"Bee!" I gasp, hiding my face behind my hands.

She cackles wildly. "Haaappy birthdaaay to—"

I grab her arm and jerk her towards me. "If you sing, I will take you down!"

Dissolving into still more laughter, she paws at my hands where I'm clutching her. "My goodness, kitty has claws. Meow!" She hisses at me for good measure, but at least she doesn't continue with the song, thank God. Dmitri looks more pained than usual but he does put his phone aside.

The waiters deposit the cake on our table and disappear. "You can at least make a wish and blow out the candles," Bee suggests.

I glower at the little instigator. "I don't believe wishes come true."

"Satan's right-hand man over here is poisoning you with his negativity." She scowls. "Will you just blow out the damn candles?" She keeps muttering under her breath and it sounds a hell of a lot like "don't know what I'm going to do with these two."

As I lean in towards my cake, I glance towards Dmitri, who seems to be trying very hard not to smile. It isn't until after I've blown out the candles that I realize I've wasted my entire wish thinking about him.

I cut three pieces of cake and plate them up for all of us. As I pass Dmitri his piece, I feel suddenly shy.

His fingertip grazes mine as he takes the plate and meets my gaze for the first time all night. "Happy birthday, Wren," he rumbles.

I'm embarrassed to say that my insides do a funny little dance. "Thank you."

My hand drops and I focus on the decadent chocolate cake in front of me. It still hurts that Rose isn't here with me. But I have to admit—with all this hubbub to distract me, this weird, three-pronged family-that-isn't…

It hurts much, much less.

41

WREN

Just after Dmitri pays the bill, Bee gets to her feet. "Need to use the ladies' room. Gimme a second, *por favor*."

Dmitri looks less than pleased at the delay, but he doesn't say anything as she wobbles away, a little unsteady after the rapid-fire parade of alcohol she just annihilated.

I, on the other hand, feel compelled to break the silence. "Thanks for dinner."

He shrugs. "Not a problem."

"And thanks for coming tonight. You didn't have to."

His eyes fall on mine as if by accident. "We're going to have to learn to get along," he says gruffly. "For our son."

He has a point; it's just a point that makes me extremely sad. "I'm really happy for you and Bee, you know."

I'm not sure why I say that. I'm probably compensating for the less-than-generous feelings I've had the past few days. The night Bee came home drunk was confusing, to say the least. But every day since then has just reinforced the bond the two of them have. I can't say anything about Bee without Dmitri jumping down my throat. What is that, if not love?

Dmitri doesn't bother responding. Just gets to his feet instead. "Bee's heading back this way. Let's get going."

I suppress a sigh and stand. I wish he could just have a normal conversation with me. Then again, the normal conversations we've shared are responsible for my current state of emotional turmoil, so maybe I'm better off without them.

The valet is driving up Dmitri's car as we step outside into the street. "Shit," I curse, my breath pluming white in the frigid air. "It's co—"

SCREEEEECH!

BANG. BANG. BANG.

I'm knocked off-center when Dmitri grabs me and shoves me behind him. My vision blurs behind panic. *What the hell was that?* I've watched enough action movies to recognize the sound of gunshots, but my brain is having a hard time processing them in real life.

How can there be gunshots *here*? We're in the nicest part of town.

I look up to find Dmitri standing huge right in front of me, shielding me with his body. His arms are raised as though—

BANG. BANG.

Yes, he is in fact returning fire. And he's not the only one. I can just make Bee out where she's taking cover behind Dmitri's car. But she's not cowering down in fear like I am.

No, she's got a gun in her hands, just like Dmitri does.

And just like him, she's shooting back.

As it sinks in, I become aware of the chaos raining down on us from all sides. I can hear the wail of sirens, the high-pitched screams of fear, the shattering of glass, the endless report of gunfire. I cup my hands over my ears and fall back on a soothing mechanism that I developed around the time Dad left us and Mom started going loopy.

"One." Deep breath. "Two." Deep breath. "Three." Deep breath. "Four." Deep breath. "Five."

More gunshots. Louder. Closer. I can hear them even over the sound of my terrified heart throbbing in my ears and my cupped hands. I feel like my pulse is in my throat.

Shadows converge around me. More huge men. I hear them murmuring, talking over each other in harsh, staccato bursts.

"How many more?"

"Emptied the clip, but…"

"Is she okay?"

I'm not sure who's asking. Aleksandr? Pavel? Bee? I can't even distinguish between real and unreal right now, much less male and female.

"Leave it. I've got her."

Strangely, *that* voice I can recognize.

I'm lifted off the ground and transferred into the back of a dark vehicle. I focus on Dmitri, on his bulk and scent. I grab his arm just before he closes the door on me. "Stay with me."

It's nothing but morbid fear that makes me ask. He glances to his left, then his right, and finally, he nods. He climbs in with me at the same time that Bee jumps into the front seat and punches the roof of the jeep. "Move out." As the jeep speeds off, Bee twists in her seat to look back at us. "Is she okay? Is she hurt?"

His hands pat me down, thorough but gentle. "She's fine. She didn't get hit."

But as I trail my eyes down his body, I realize he did. "Oh my God!" I gasp, pointing at his arm. "Blood."

He glances at his arm dismissively. "Barely worth noting."

"Y-you're hurt." A desperate sob leaves my lips. "You're hurt because of me." It seems very clear that he wouldn't be bleeding from the arm if he hadn't thrown himself in front of me.

He grabs my face firmly, forcing me to look him in the eye. "This is not your fault. Do you hear me? None of this is your fault."

Those silver eyes are so calming. All of him is, really. He's holding me tight, his arms wrapped around my body like he knows how badly I need the physical reassurance. I'm holding onto him every bit as tightly.

I should let go. I should put some distance between us.

But instead, I just cling on that much tighter.

I'm whole. I'm intact. The precious cargo in my womb is just as safe as I am.

"Your arm…" I whisper to him. Complete sentences aren't quite in my reach yet, but that's a start.

"Don't worry about me." He almost sounds irritated by the wound.

"Lots of… lots of blood."

He glances down at the drying scabs and the fresh blood trickling past his elbow whenever he moves or flexes. "Would you prefer I clean up? Are you uncomfortable around blood?"

I blink and a freeze frame of Rose's body appears behind my eyelids. She's lying frozen on that police table like a slab of meat on a butcher's counter. Her blood has dried on her skin and it is *everywhere, so much of it, so much blood…*

"I wasn't, until…" I choke on my own words. This is the kind of traffic jam in your throat that tears were invented to cure, but apparently, I wasted all my tears earlier today. Just when I need them most, I'm fresh out.

A part of me is relieved. Crying is exhausting business.

"Let me wash up." He heads into my bathroom and a moment later, I hear the tap start to run.

I'm not sure why I swing my legs off the bed and follow him gingerly. Maybe I just want to prove that I can. That I haven't lost the ability to function entirely.

I pause on the threshold. Dmitri is standing tall in front of the sink with his shirt off, using one of the hand towels to wipe the blood off from his torn bicep. His muscles ripple under the light even when he doesn't move. Little by little, the streaks of red disappear, though the towel comes away slick with crimson.

I wasn't the one to clean Rose's body. The coroner had taken care of that, partly because it was his job, but also because I was a little bit preoccupied with hurling up my guts in the hospital bathroom.

There are days when I still regret it. It felt like something a sister ought to do. God knows I'd spent so many days and nights combing out Rose's hair or forcing her to sit still while I practiced doing makeup on her. I ought to have been the last one to do those things, too.

With shaking fingers, I pick up another towel from the shelf and inch closer to Dmitri. He doesn't see me until I reach out to pass the towel under the running faucet.

When he does realize what I'm doing, he freezes. His hands still and fall to his sides.

I don't meet his eyes. The only sounds are our mingled breathing and the gushing of the tap. I focus on the blood he can't reach, smeared up the back of his arm.

I dab once. The towel stains red. His skin glistens clear. No one says a word.

There's a part of me that recognizes that Bee should probably be the one doing this. But the larger, louder part of me feels this possessive need to be here by his side. To take care of him the way he took care of me tonight.

So I wipe, and I wipe, and I wipe, until there's no more blood and nothing left for me to do. Only then do I set the towel down on the countertop, just as delicately as I've done everything else.

"Thank you," I murmur.

He twists around to face me. I flinch as he puts a finger under my chin and forces my eyes to his. "Are you okay?"

My lips wobble. "I… don't know."

His jaw pulses, but his finger remains tender and soft right where it is under the cliff of my chin. "I'm increasing security around the penthouse. Both inside and out. No one is going to get to you. Or Bee."

"Is she okay?"

"You saw her. She can take care of herself."

That almost makes me smile, just as much as the pride in his voice makes me want to cry. Not because I'm jealous, but because I'm never going to be that girl.

The girl who hears a gunshot and pulls out a gun of her own.

The girl who doesn't just freeze, but fights back.

I reach out to run a single fingertip down Dmitri's bicep, following the inked path of a tattoo. It swirls and spirals. He's so warm and solid to the touch, barely moving except to breathe. My own breath is still caught stubbornly in my throat.

Finally, I drop my hand and step back. "You should go see how Bee's doing."

His forehead creases. "Bee's fine."

"She's your fiancée. You should be with her right now, not me."

His lips flatten into a thin line. He nods without argument, grabs his bloody shirt, and leaves. I stand there, caught helplessly in the middle of their life, and try not to panic.

"One."

Deep breath.

"Two."

Deep breath.

"Three."

It doesn't help this time, though.

43

WREN

The world outside my rooms feels dangerous now.

It's not just the guns and the bullet wounds and the towels drying with crusted blood that I'm talking about, either.

Even more threatening is the minefield that is Dmitri, Bee, and myself.

I've managed to lock myself in a one-way love triangle and I need to get the hell out of it before the baby is born. Preferably before their wedding day.

It's weird how Bee just got on with life the day after the shooting. I'd walked into the living room the next morning to find her sitting on the floor with piles of wedding magazines splayed out around her. She told me to join her and started rattling off nonchalantly about fabric swatches and floral arrangements.

Even though I knew she was just trying to distract me, I let her. I'd spent most of the night dreaming about her fiancé, so it was a refreshing change of pace from half-remembered snatches of Dmitri picking me up, Dmitri stroking my chin, Dmitri looming over me like a smoke-scented mountain.

I didn't contribute much to Bee's rambling, though. I wasn't in the right headspace to be planning much of anything, let alone her wedding to him.

By the end of the day, it became clear to me that I wasn't the only one struggling. Bee's voice stayed level and carefree, but she kept pacing the living room in a way that reminded me of a lion at the zoo. When I asked if she was okay, she just answered with a manic, "Never been better."

I could not relate.

The next day was more of the same. Constant chatter, wedding planning, and lots and lots of pacing. For Bee, at least. I just sat there and watched her. If I never moved again, that'd be fine by me.

Now, for the third night in a row, I'm awake at three in the morning. And it's once again because I was dreaming about a man I have no right to dream about.

The fact that my panties are wet makes the guilt so much worse.

By the time I swap out my underwear, I'm wide awake and troubled with anxiety. I figure a walk to the kitchen for a glass of water might help calm my nerves. I've just stepped out into the hallway when I hear noises. A very familiar kind of noise.

I freeze. *What is that?*

I close my eyes, count my breaths, and will myself not to panic. The apartment is well-protected; Dmitri swore as much. If I can hear sounds, they're one hundred percent coming from either Bee or Dmitri.

Inching closer, I listen closely. What I first thought were low, worried whispers are in fact... *moans.*

Oh, God.

I peek around the corner of the archway that opens into the living room. Moving shapes writhe on the couch. At first, my still-half-asleep brain sees lions wrestling. But as my eyes adjust and reality sets in, I realize that what I'm seeing is two people, naked and joined together, breathing deeply, moaning loudly, completely wrapped up in one another and oblivious to the world around them.

I'm in hell.

I'm taut with shock. Frozen with horror from the tips of my toes to the top of my head. I need to turn away. I need to get the fuck out of here. But it's as though the masochistic part of my brain has taken over and it's forcing me to watch.

"Yeah... fuck, like that..." Bee's voice is half-strangled as she collapses back onto the sofa, out of my sight. Arching her head over the armrest, her hair drapes down to the floor like a curtain of silk as her lips part in pleasure and that other dark silhouette dives between her legs. "Eat me out, baby. Make me come... Make me..."

I have half a mind to slap my hands over my ears and run down the hallway screaming showtunes as loud as I can. As it stands, I don't want them to know I'm here. I don't want them to know I've seen them.

I retreat slowly, with my heart in my throat. I'm just about to turn away when something occurs to me. The legs coming off the far end of the couch, opposite of Bee… those legs are far too thin and delicate and feminine to belong to Dmitri.

And if it's not Dmitri having sex with Bee, then who…?

Instead of sneaking out like I ought to, I find myself creeping forward, further into the living room.

Pervy? Yes, absolutely.

Did curiosity kill the cat? Deader than a doornail.

But do I keep going anyways?

Why, yes, yes, I do.

I round the sofa, my heart beating harder, my eyes popping as I confirm that the face buried between Bee's legs is not Dmitri's. Hell, it doesn't even belong to a man. She's being eaten out by a spikey-haired blonde with a tattoo sleeve and a pierced nipple.

"Bee!" flies out of my mouth before I can realize just what an insanely stupid thing it is to intrude here.

Bee jerks away from the blonde, who screams and grabs a cushion to cover her breasts. "What the hell?" the short-haired blonde cries out, turning to Bee with her lips glistening in the moonlight slanting through the open windows. "You said there was no one else here!"

Bee is looking at me breathlessly. "Goddammit, Wren," she sighs. "You scared the shit out of me." She collapses onto the sofa next to the blonde, legs akimbo without an ounce of shame. "And you ruined my orgasm. I was just about to come."

The blonde looks at me with an arched eyebrow. "I can fix that," she purrs before winking in my direction. "Green Eyes can watch if she wants. Hell, she can *join* if she wants, too."

I stare at the blonde. "Who *are* you?"

She winces. "You the fiancé?"

"No," I snap. "The fiancé is a man."

The blonde whips around to stare daggers at Bee, who's looking pretty chill for a woman who's just been caught cheating. "A *man*? Seriously?"

Bee shrugs, plucks her silk robe off the floor, and gets to her feet. "Time for you to go, babe. Slumber party's over."

The blonde scowls in my direction, but she doesn't argue. She picks up her things, dresses quickly, and heads towards the foyer. Bee doesn't even watch her go. She cinches up her robe and saunters over to the bar.

"Want a drink?" she asks me casually.

"A drink?" I exclaim. "A *drink?!*"

She smacks her forehead with her palm. "Oh, right. You're pregnant. I keep forgetting."

"Bee!" I say, trying my level best not to judge. "What are you doing? This isn't like you!"

She pours herself some gin and throws me an amused look. "What do you know about what I'm like? You don't know me. Not really."

I can't say that doesn't sting a little. But it's also very obviously true. "I… You… I don't get it. You and Dmitri… you have such a great relationship."

"We do," she admits freely, taking a sip of her cocktail.

I shake my head, confused by my own emotions. Fucked up as it is, I do have feelings for Dmitri. And even though seeing Bee and him together hurts like hell sometimes, I don't want to see him wronged.

"Bee, he loves you so much. I can't believe you would do this to him!"

"Wren—"

"Cheating is one of the worst things you can do to someone. Trust me, I've seen more cheating in my life than I care to admit. My father did it to my mother and it destroyed her."

Bee balks, her drink-holding hand frozen in midair. "Are you judging me?"

I swallow my indignation and draw myself up tall. "No. I have no right to judge you. God knows I've got enough skeletons in my own closet." She squints at me questioningly and I feel compelled to go on. "Long story short, I was involved with this man. This *older* man. He..." I wince as those old feelings come rushing back, no dimmer for the time that's passed since they first consumed me. "He told me he was divorced but, as it turns out... he wasn't."

"Shiiit." Bee leans a hip against the wall and crosses her arms. "Go on. I'm on the edge of my seat."

"He had a wife, two kids, a mansion in the valley that he told me she got in the divorce. It was all lies. Well, not *all* lies. There was a mansion in the valley—but it's where they lived together, as a family."

The predawn gloom keeps me from puzzling out just what the emotion rippling across Bee's face might be. "Did you love him?"

"I… I don't know. I thought I did."

She nods. "I love Dmitri, Wren, I really do. But I'm not *'in love'* with him. Never have been. Never will be." That familiar, mischievous grin spreads across her face, albeit a bit shyly, as she adds, "He's got a bit too much Y chromosome for my liking."

I hesitate as it all snaps into focus. Like an optical illusion, where you've seen the whole picture the whole time, but you couldn't see the hidden image until someone told you where to look.

"You like women," I breathe out. It sounds stupid as soon as I say it, but it's undeniably the truth.

Bee abandons her drained tumbler altogether and picks up the whole bottle instead. "Bingo," she says. "For the record, I wanted to tell you all this ages ago."

Goosebumps erupt all over my skin. "Tell me *what*, exactly? What's going on here?"

"I'm gay, Wren. Dmitri was the first person I came out to. I was twelve; he was a little older. These scars on my back? They're a result of my 'conversion therapy,' courtesy of my sadistic fuck of a father."

My eyes pop out of their sockets. "Oh my God… He whipped you to turn you straight?"

"Bingo once again. But as you just saw, it didn't work. I'd rather staple my nipples to my stomach than go near a penis."

A crazed laugh slips out against my better judgment. "Sorry, that's not… None of this is really funny. This is your life, not some joke."

Bee puts her hand on my knee. "If we can't laugh, we cry—and I, for one, would much rather laugh. Dmitri's my lifesaver, Wren. My way out. Vittorio was planning on marrying me off to this old bastard who was as sadistic as he is. Hated people like me as much as Vittorio and he knew about my so-called 'perversions.' He would have killed me long before he converted me. That's why Dmitri stepped in and proposed. He likes to say that we're both getting something out of it. I get to live free, more or less. And he inherits the Zanetti mafia when the time comes. But the truth is, he would have done it regardless."

I exhale sharply and drop to a seat on the couch next to Bee. "Fuck, that's… I mean, that's a lot of information all at once."

She winks and pats my knee. "Hey, if it makes you feel better, I forgive you for ruining my hookup."

I manage a weak smile. "Why didn't you tell me all this sooner?"

She shrugs apologetically and tips the bottle of gin to her lips. "It was Dmitri's call. He thought it would be simpler this way."

Simpler? Maybe.

But for whom?

44

DMITRI

There's a disturbance in the penthouse. Something has changed.

I sense it the moment I walk into the kitchen after my morning workout and find Bee and Wren at the island with their heads together, whispering madly back and forth.

The suspicious part? They fall silent the moment they spot me.

Even as I assemble a breakfast, I'm vaguely aware of the secretive glances being traded behind my back. Neither one is particularly subtle, but at least Wren is genuinely trying to be. Bee couldn't give a shit less.

I finally slam the milk carton down on the marble countertop. "Okay, what the hell is going on?"

Wren glances down immediately. Bee just ogles me with that insatiable grin of hers. "What ever do you mean, Mr. Egorov?"

Scowling at her, I add a splash of milk to my coffee. "If you're plotting to leave the penthouse, don't bother. It's not safe out there just yet. I'll let you both know when you can have an outing. Fair warning: it will be a heavily guarded one."

"We're not plotting anything, darling. Don't you worry."

But the side smile she throws Wren is troubling. *Very* troubling.

Surely Bee wouldn't have crossed the line with Wren, right? Wren is her type, she claims—or at least, she claims in order to piss me off—but the situation is so complicated; she's carrying my baby, for God's sake. And Bee would never do that to me. Despite the fact that I've said repeatedly that I have no real interest in Wren…

Fuck.

No. No. I'm spiraling now. I can't afford to—

"You okay, big boy?" Bee inquires, sipping her coffee delicately.

"Yeah. Fucking peachy."

She just shrugs and turns to Wren. "Oops—sweetheart, you've got a little something on your mouth there. Wait, let me get it." She licks a thumb and brushes it over the corner of Wren's lips a little too sensuously for my liking.

The question bears repeating: *what the hell is going on?*

"Excuse me," Wren says awkwardly, jumping to her feet and trying to keep me from seeing how bright her cheeks are burning. "Gonna go, er, organize the seating chart for the wedding."

"I'm right behind you," Bee calls out as Wren disappears around the corner.

I wait until she's safely in her room before I storm around the island towards Bee. "I asked once and I'll ask again: what the fuck is happening?"

She rises off her stool and pats me on the shoulder. "Just a little woman-to-woman bonding, that's all. You should be happy. Don't you want your future wife and your baby mama to get along?"

At this precise moment, the honest answer would be a resounding "fuck no." I'd rather send them to opposite sides of the globe if it means never having to see Bee—or anyone, really—touch Wren like that in front of me ever again.

"Beatrice—"

"Whoa, whoa. Don't you full name me. You want to know what happened between Wren and me last night—if something did in fact even happen? Well, you'll have to ask her." She taps my cheek with an open palm and winks viciously. "You snooze, you lose, buddy. Just sayin'."

Then she's gone, switching her hips like she's sex walking.

Furious, I storm down the hall towards Wren's room. I'm so on edge that I barge in without knocking.

"Ahh!" she shrieks in surprise, twisting around from the window seat and nearly knocking over the seating charts laid out in front of her. "What the hell, Dmitri? You can't just bust in here whenever—"

"You better start talking and you better start talking now."

"I—"

"Right. Fucking. Now."

The sunflower pajamas she's wearing look ridiculous. So I have no clue why my dick perks up at the sight of her in them. Sometimes, it seems like just the two of us in an enclosed space is all it takes.

"Oh, *now*, you want to talk?" She plants her fists on her hips and glares at me.

I pause. I wasn't expecting quite so much attitude. I also wasn't expecting how my presence here doesn't seem to surprise her at all.

"Because," she continues, "I've been living here for over a month now and you haven't been interested in 'talking' before."

"Don't be a child."

"Me?" she hisses incredulously. "*I'm* the one being a child? Please."

I take a step forward and shove myself right in her face. She stands her ground and scowls darkly at me. "Don't fuck with me, Wren."

"Or what? You'll put me over your knee again!?" she demands. "Is that it?"

"I just might."

There's not an ounce of quit in her today. The green of her eyes is spitting at me like the sparklers on her birthday cake. "You want me to tell you things? To be open with you?" she asks, crossing her hands over her chest, which does not fail to draw my attention to her breasts. "Well, that's a two-way street."

"Have you been paying attention at all?" I snarl. "This is strictly a one-way street and it belongs to me."

"Right. Because *everything* belongs to you, huh?" she asks. "Me. This baby. Bee." *What is that tone? It's a little too knowing. Too scathing.* "Although, can we really say Bee belongs to you if she's out there sleeping with women?"

There it is.

Fuck. Me.

My eye twitches, but apart from that, I manage to keep a straight face. If Bee made a move on her last night, I'll kill her. I swear I will.

"What did she do?" I grit out slowly.

"It's more a question of *who* she did."

"If the answer's 'you,' there's going to be hell to pay."

For the first time, I feel like this conversation veers off the track Wren had laid out for it. She freezes, confusion blotting out her anger for a moment. "Wait. Pause. Rewind. Do you think something happened between Bee and me last night?"

"Like you said, Bee can be a flirty drunk."

"Meaning *what?*" She snaps back to being pissed off. "That if Bee had tried to get in my pants, I would've let her?" Jabbing an angry finger into my chest, she spits, "Apart from the fact that I'm not gay, you and Bee are together! Or at least, I thought you were—and there's no way in hell I'd have been party to infidelity."

"Okay, we get it," I reply sarcastically, knocking her finger away from me. "You have principles."

Wren looks like she wants to take my head off. Honestly, I'm kind of hoping she tries.

Give me an excuse to bend you over my knee again, I beg silently. *Give me one reason and I'll snap, I swear.*

"Where are *your* principles?" she fires at me. "Why didn't you tell me that Bee was gay, that you two aren't really in a relationship? That the wedding I'm planning is a total freaking sham?"

Her cheeks are flushed pink. In so many ways, she's never looked more beautiful.

I keep all of that inside, though. Outwardly, my voice stays cool and level as I answer, "Because it was none of your business."

"You made it my business when you knocked me up!" she screeches. Then her voice softens. "I deserved to know the truth, Dmitri. Do you know the kind of hell I've been through the last few weeks? I felt so damn guilty all the time. I couldn't sleep. I could barely eat. I could—"

"'Guilty'?"

All the indignation on her face curdles at once. The blotchiness on her cheeks gives way to a blossoming blush that says I homed in on exactly the right word. "What I meant is… Fuck, never mind."

"Oh, no." I advance on her, cornering her into the wall until my hips are very nearly flush with hers. "No, you don't get to tell me not to mind. Why were you feeling guilty?"

She scowls and tries to turn her back on me. I grab her arm and keep her pinned in place. "A piece of survival advice for you: don't *ever* turn your back on me." Her jaw clenches furiously and she still refuses to meet my eyes. "Wren. Answer the question."

Her eyes close. Her breath rattles in and out of her chest and I could almost swear she's counting silently.

"You spanked me," she says at last. Her voice is raspy and barely audible.

"And?"

"'And'?" she repeats as her eyes fly open and bulge. "It was entirely inappropriate! Especially because you were 'engaged'! I felt horrible about it. I almost apologized to Bee so many times. The only reason I didn't is because then I'd have had to explain what happened."

My mind keeps spasming off-course. It's saying, *I bet she's not wearing anything underneath those pajamas.* It's saying, *I bet her lips would be so soft and sweet if I claimed them with my own right now.* It's saying, *Maybe now is the time to find out.*

"You disobeyed me. I had to punish you. Simple."

Her cheeks are cherry red now. "Screw you. None of this has been 'simple.' That sure as hell wasn't 'simple.' It was…"

She fades away, so I prod. "Yes?"

"*Wrong.*" She spits out like it's a dirty word. "It felt like… like we were cheating on Bee."

It's so adorable that I almost laugh. "So you were turned on?"

"Let me go." She closes her eyes again and wiggles like that'll convince me to let her out of this position.

Unfortunately for her, it has the exact opposite effect.

"Not until you answer the question—and answer it honestly."

"Fine," she confesses. "I was turned on. But so were you! Don't even try to deny it because I felt you—and you know what? It wasn't the first time."

I pull her right into the same thing she "felt" last time and her eyebrows soar up her forehead. "I wasn't going to deny it." Her lips part in a silent gasp, but I'm not done yet. "Bee and I have never been romantic. Ever. This arrangement is simple: we parade as a couple, but in private… we fuck who we want."

Desire ripples across her eyes and I know for sure that we're on the same page. Whether she likes it or not.

"Now that you know I'm not hers… tell me you're mine."

Wren shakes her head desperately. "You're still her fiancé."

I grind my erection against her and she cries out softly. "You want to say no?" I challenge. "Go right ahead. I'm not looking for forever here. I'm talking about a good fuck. But if you want more—"

"I don't," she insists emphatically. "I don't."

"Then you're a coward?"

She pushes at my arm halfheartedly. We both know she isn't going anywhere. "I'm no coward."

"No?" I ask mildly. "We'll see about that."

45

DMITRI

I wasn't ready for *this*.

She comes at me like a hurricane, all pent-up anger and passion and frustration. Her lips are soft and relentless at the same time. It takes me only a second to meet her at her level.

I never thought I'd say this, but the wait has been worth it, if this is what was always waiting for us at the end.

I rip off those ridiculously, baggy pajamas she's wearing. I need her—no clothes between us, no lies between us, no facades or games or bullshit between us. Just her bare. Me bare. Her sweetness on my lips and her softness under my hands.

I strip my own clothes off as soon as I'm done with hers. Her nails dig into my skin as she attempts to help me, but she's shaking so badly that she can barely hold on. I know the feeling—every brush of her skin against mine feels like an electric shock. It feels like I'm a teenager again and this is my first time. I'm not sure it's ever felt this intense before. This urgent.

As our naked bodies grind together, I have to grit my teeth together to stop myself coming already.

We fall back onto the bed together. I'm tempted to step back a moment. I want to take my time, look at her, admire her. But my erection feels like stone and my balls are so damn heavy it feels like they're weighing me down.

"Dmitri, if you don't get inside me right now…"

Fucking hell. There goes one more notch of self-control. It doesn't help that her hands are still running all over my chest and she keeps mewling feverishly.

I bend and stick my tongue in her ear at the same time that I pass a finger through her wetness. She bucks off the bed and cries out my name again, one long, broken string of half-croaked syllables.

I grab her wrists and pin them to the bed while my cock inches closer to her dripping pussy. "I'm going to make you scream, baby," I growl in her ear.

Her stomach is small and understated, not yet an impediment to sex. But her breasts are full and heavy. *My baby is doing that to her body,* I think. *This fucking angel is carrying my seed.*

Nothing else has ever been hotter.

I circle her nipple with my tongue as she shivers and gasps beneath me. Her arms keep twitching to be freed, but I'm not about to let go anytime soon. I love this feeling: having her beneath me, completely at my mercy.

"Please," she whispers. "Fuck me… Just fuck me…"

I smile darkly and let her nipple pop free from my mouth for a moment. "Are you going to be a good little girl from now on? Keep your hands where they belong, where I tell you to keep them?"

"Y-yes!" She shivers. "Yes, I promise."

"Who do you belong to?"

She doesn't so much as hesitate. "You, Dmitri. Only you."

If I delay any longer, I'm going to come before I even make it inside her. So, gripping her wrists a little tighter, I shove myself into her pussy in one aggressive plunge.

She's so wet that I slide in easily, without the tiniest bit of friction. It takes only half a dozen powerful thrusts before she's screaming uncontrollably. I can feel her orgasm ripple around my cock, trying to coax mine out of me. I'd hoped that sex would get her out of my system, but what I'm feeling right now is not indicative of anything close to an end.

The only thing flashes across my brain now is *more, more.*

Fucking *more.*

I bite back my orgasm and ram into her. Over and over again, desperate to feel her come again. I want her walls clenching around me, milking out my pleasure like it's the only thing on earth worth having. I grab her hips and roll us over, forcing her on top. She doesn't need any instructions or encouragement. She takes off instantly, rolling her hips against mine while my balls keep slapping at her ass.

"You're such a fucking angel when you take me like that," I snarl up at her as her breasts bounce and moans flutter past her laps.

Her palms plant down on my chest as she bucks against me, wild and completely uninhibited, her hair flying everywhere.

More moans. Sweat and lust slicked between us. The air hot, vibrating, rich with her scent and mine.

I've got two thrusts left in me. Maybe three, if I'm lucky.

"Yes!" Wren cries. "Fuuuuck… Mmm…"

A trail of perspiration dives down her chest. I haul myself up so I can lick up that valley and run my tongue over the curve of her ear.

She tastes like heaven. Salty and sweet at the same time. The same thought surges through my head: *more, more.*

But the need for "more" is exactly what this was intended to prevent. There can't be more. There can only be this.

So when I finally come, exploding inside her, I tell myself that this will be the end.

Enjoy it now, motherfucker. This is one sin you cannot afford to repeat.

When it's over and we both return to our senses, I can practically feel Wren retreating from me in mind, body, and soul. She reaches for her pajama top, fingers and lips both wobbling. The sweat on my skin dries cold and sticky.

"I'm just, uh…" she mumbles. "Just gonna go shower. I'm… yeah. Showering."

She doesn't meet my gaze as she flees into the relative safety of the bathroom. I stay just long enough to see little curls of steam begin to flow beneath the crack in the door. All I want is to memorize this scent and this feeling. The way her handprints are still sizzling on my chest. How limp and sated and perfect I feel, and yet how much more I could still take. A minute of rest and I'd be ready to dive into her all over again.

That's why I have to get up.

I dress quickly and leave. I'm walking down the hallway, craving the comfort and silence of my bed, when I hear a little *tut-tut* in the direction of Bee's room.

She's leaning against the doorframe, her eyes trained on me expectantly. "I probably should be mad, but I'm not. You two really needed to get that out of your system."

I want to snort in disbelief. *If only that's what it succeeded in doing.*

"I don't want to hear it, Bee. Not today."

She grins, then she zips her lip and throws away the key. With a parting wave, she disappears into her room and I'm left to deal with the ramifications of what I've just done.

46

WREN

DMITRI: *Bee has a dress fitting today. Aleksandr will pick you both up at ten.*

I've been staring at the text ever since he sent it. Periods and complete sentences have never felt so cruel, so curt or hard or impregnable. There's nothing here to suggest that last night even happened.

Other than the smell of him on my skin.

It clings to the sheets, too, which is why I've spent most of the morning with my nose buried in them. As 10:00 A.M. draws closer, I reluctantly get dressed and meet Bee out in the living room.

Even though I know that she and Dmitri aren't really together, it still feels weird meeting her eye. Have I betrayed her? Should I have spoken to her first before what happened?

It's just that there had been no time to think about anything. One second, I was planning seating arrangements for their wedding—and the next thing I knew, Dmitri was right there in my face, being all hot and intense and... *urgh*.

"Yo, girl," Bee greets, giving me a little wink that I have no idea how to interpret. "Had a good night?"

Again, how the hell am I supposed to answer that? In the end, I decide not to. "You have a dress fitting this morning?"

She's busy applying a coat of deep fuchsia to her toenails. "Indeed. I'm going for dramatic yet simple."

I sit down opposite her. "I think that's an oxymoron."

"You calling me a moron?"

My jaw drops. "No, of course not—"

Bee's head floats up towards me, revealing a wicked grin. "I'm kidding, Wren. Chill." She goes back to her nails with a soft smile still playing on her lips. "I wanna make sure I get the right dress, so you're gonna have to be honest with me, okay? Can I trust you to be honest?"

The pressure builds like a volcano. I can feel my panic and guilt start to bubble over the top and it all comes out in one torrid, breathless stream. *"I'msosorrybutIhadsexwithDmitriyesterday."*

She freezes over her big toe, her gaze snapping to me, her lips parted. Is she pissed? Shocked? Annoyed? Hurt?

Then laughter bursts through her nostrils. She keeps going, having to set the brush down so she doesn't spray nail polish everywhere, and laughs until tears stud her eyes.

"Why are you laughing?" I ask incredulously.

Finally, she sighs and relents. "Partly because you looked like you were about to poop yourself if you held that in for a second longer. But mostly because you felt the need to tell me at all. I mean, quite apart from the fact that this has been brewing for a while now, I heard you guys loud and clear last night. Sounded like you two had an—" She gives me a cartoonish wink. "—explosive time."

"Oh, God." I bury my face in my hands. I might just stay like this forever.

"Never apologize for good sex, hon," she chides, rapping me lightly on the back of the head. "It's one of the few joys we get in this cursed life."

Mumbling between my fingers, I say, "I'm so, so sorry."

"Why on earth would you be sorry?" When I peek out, I see she has an eyebrow arched in amazement. "It's about freaking time the two of you got it on. The sexual tension was killing me."

"You're not… mad?"

"Wren," she says tiredly like she's talking to a small child, "you were there for the conversation where I told you that this whole wedding thing is a sham, right? I mean, that was you I was talking to?"

I protest, "Still, we didn't have a conversation about—"

"About what?" she interrupts. "Me explicitly giving you permission to fuck my fiancé?" I blush hard, but she just laughs at my discomfort. "Babe, seriously. There are a fuck ton of things to feel awkward about in this whole sordid affair. This is not one of those things. You wanna fuck Dmitri? By all means, go right ahead. He needs to be good and fucked. Hopefully, it makes him less grumpy. Win-win-win, baby."

I swallow. "Right. Yeah. Okay. I mean… thanks."

She snorts and goes back to painting her toenails. "No need to thank me. He was never mine to hand over to you. It was never my place to give you or him permission." She finishes up, checks her handiwork, and then kicks her feet up on the ottoman. "We can leave when my nail polish dries."

We sit there in silence for a moment. Then, suddenly, I'm laughing, too, and laughing, and laughing, and laughing. It completely dissolves the stress sitting on my shoulders.

"Let me in on the joke," Bee insists with an elbow dug into my ribs.

I shake my head. "I just can't believe this is happening."

"Yeah," she agrees with a chuckle. "Now, just imagine how *he* feels."

Then we're both laughing, and the world doesn't seem quite as heavy as it did just a little while ago.

47

WREN

"Well?" Bee asks, twirling around so that I can get a better look at the Caroline Herrera she's wearing.

"Beautiful."

"I sense a 'but.'"

"I preferred the Vivienne Westwood. The off-the-shoulder, crepe silk A-line."

"That was a good one," she agrees, turning to look in the mirror and check the angles. "But I think I want a more fitted silhouette. A-lines feel too romantic for me. I want *sexy*."

"Like you have to try."

She gives me an appreciative wink and raises a hand towards the saleswoman who, bless her soul, has spent the last three hours catering to Bee's every whim, of which there have been many, ranging from champagne and strawberries to a tiny silk robe for her to wear between fittings.

"Lemme try the lace veil again, Tanya." She weaves it onto the top of her head and turns to me. "Well?"

"Very pretty. Very traditional."

"Ew. Just say you hate it, okay?" Bee pulls the veil off and hands it back to Tanya. "Give us a moment, Tan. I need a breather."

After I've helped her out of the dress, she collapses onto the plush white sofa that faces the array of floor-length mirrors.

"Another glass of champagne?" I ask.

"Honestly, just give me the bottle."

I hand her the bottle and she takes a big glug straight from it, then wipes her mouth with the back of her hand and settles back again. "Being pregnant must suck."

"Because I can't drink champagne?" I ask, crossing my legs and leaning into the armchair.

"Well, that, obviously. And because, you know… there's an alien growing inside your body."

I pick up my glass of sparkling apple juice. "So I'm guessing you don't actually want to be a mother."

"Oh, hell no," she says adamantly. "I never wanted to get married, either. And yet here I am, trying on dresses like I'm some sort of Disney princess."

"You're not enjoying this even a little?"

Bee throws me a glare. "I like playing dress-up. Just not when it involves the shrinking of my life." She takes another mouthful of champagne and puts the bottle down. "Shit, I shouldn't have said that. I'm being ungrateful."

"I don't think so. You're being forced into a marriage that you don't want. To a man, no less. I'd say you have the right to feel… well, at the very least, uncomfortable."

"I'm not uncomfortable so much as angry," she corrects with a little sigh. "I guess a part of me never really thought it would get this far."

I hesitate before I speak up again. "Can I ask you a serious question?"

"Shoot."

"Why not just… run away?"

Bee smiles wryly. "It's not like I haven't thought about it. But my father would never just let me go. He'd track me down and, trust me, he'd find me." She leans back against the sofa and kicks her bare feet up. Those fuchsia toenails of hers stand out against the bright whiteness that's literally everywhere in this bridal shop. "And if he found me, he'd kill me."

A shudder runs down my back. "Would he really…?"

She doesn't even hesitate before she nods. "He's tried in the past. He walked in on me with one of the maids years ago. He forced me to strip naked before he whipped me—in front of all his *vors*."

My hands fly to my slack-jawed mouth. "No."

"Oh, yes. I was out of commission for weeks after that beating. When Dmitri bullied his way into the mansion, I was practically catatonic, staring off into space like a ghost."

I blink back the tears in my eyes. "Bee…"

"Oh, stop it. Stop that right now. Don't you dare feel sorry for me. If there's one thing I hate more than tears, it's pity. I'm no victim." Her voice is curt. "You know who told me that?"

"Who?"

"Dmitri, obviously." I smile and she returns to take another pull from the champagne bottle. "Is this hard for you? Seeing me trying on wedding dresses to marry the man you have feelings for?"

I squirm in place. "Are you always so blunt?"

"With everyone except my father."

Pretty sure my cheeks are turning red. Pretty sure it's all the more obvious considering all the freaking white in this room. There's an ocean of white, Bee's bright fuchsia toenails, and then me, ripening like a cherry tomato.

"It's much less hard than it would have been if I didn't know the truth," I admit sheepishly. "But twisted as it all sounds to me, I'm glad you're marrying Dmitri if it means you're safe from your father."

She smiles. "You're right… That is twisted."

Laughing, I poke her in the arm. But the laughter dies down almost immediately. "Bee?"

"Hm?"

"How is this going to work?"

She sighs. "You know what? More often than not, I have no clue. But don't you worry: Dmitri will take care of us."

"You're confident."

Pushing herself up onto one elbow, she levels me with a stern, solemn gaze. "I've known him for almost three decades, Wren. I *know* the man. He doesn't take shortcuts, especially not when it comes to protecting his own. He'll take care of us. Always."

Something warm spreads through me when she says that. She believes it. She believes *him.*

So maybe it's okay to let myself do the same.

The curtains draw apart and Tanya appears long enough to let Dmitri walk in. He looks pained at having to be here at all.

"Have you picked a dress yet?" he asks, throwing a cursory glance over at the rack of gowns.

"I think so." Bee hauls herself off the couch. "Need to talk to Tanya first. 'Scuse me. Champagne's coming with me, though."

The bottle dangles from her fingertips as she slips out of the dressing suite. I watch her go and then, just like that, I find myself alone with Dmitri.

He seems just as taken aback as I am. Or maybe I'm just projecting. Maybe he's not taken aback at all. Maybe he's just annoyed.

Is he going to mention anything about last night? Should I bring it up? Are we supposed to pretend it didn't happen?

The air around us is charged and crackling, like there's a silent conversation being had in the space between us—though who's participating in it and what they might be saying is way beyond me.

After a pregnant pause, he walks over and sits down on the sofa. But there's far too much space between us. Too much to assume that an honest conversation is forthcoming, at least.

"She's going to make a beautiful bride," I murmur, if only because I'm sick of the silence.

Dmitri doesn't respond. He just sits there, staring off at the rack of dresses like he can see through them.

Just when I've given up on him, he speaks without actually looking at me. "You'll need a dress yourself."

"I have dresses."

"A new one. An evening dress."

"That's okay. I don't—"

"Tanya will help you," he interrupts in the same lifeless monotone. "Pick one and put it on my tab."

I stare back at him. Even if he won't look at me, I'm not shying away from him. Not anymore. "Thanks, but no thanks. This is not about me. This is about Bee. And you."

It's hard to place it when I can only see his profile, but something ripples across his eyes. "You know that there is no Bee and me." His voice is just as soft and hollow, but for the first time, there's emotion in it. I can't place it any better than I can the expression on his face, though.

I swallow. "You know, I think what you're doing for Bee is amazing."

Scowling, he leans back, sweeps an arm over the top of the couch, and crosses one ankle over the opposite knee. "Marrying Bee means that I will inherit the Zanetti mafia. I'm doing this for me."

My eyebrows pinch together in a scowl of my own. "I call bullshit."

He looks annoyed that he has to finally look in my direction. "Excuse me?"

"You heard me. I call bullshit. I get that you need to maintain this big shot, alpha dog, Bratva don persona—but we both know that's not why you're marrying her."

His lips press together in a thin line. "Don't make the mistake of believing that I'm the good guy, Wren. You'll only get hurt."

"I know you're a dangerous man. God knows you insist on reminding me of that as often as possible. But… you can be a good one, too."

I turn away from him to hide my smile. Maybe Bee's right; maybe I don't need to know how this will work out.

Maybe I just need to trust that it will.

48

DMITRI

"The hell is taking Bee so long?"

"Wedding dress shopping takes time," Wren replies coolly. "It's a process."

"It's also a fake wedding." I run a frustrated hand through my hair. "It doesn't matter. I don't give a shit what she's wearing."

"Aw, I'm sure Bee will be so touched by that heartwarming, romantic sentiment." She shucks off her shoes, pulls her bare feet up onto the sofa, and wraps her arms around her knees. "You know you're not required to be here, right?"

She's got me there. Truth be told, the only reason I'm here at all is because of her. I spent most of the morning trying to keep my distance. That was a losing effort, as it turned out. I caved and came down, justifying my presence here as "extra security" and justifying the hundred-and-fifty miles an hour I drove here at as "not wasting my fucking time." Aleksandr saw right through the bullshit, if that douchey smile he cast my way was any indication.

"Aleks has shit to do for the Bratva. I had to take his place on the security detail."

Her eyebrows arch skeptically. She knows as well as I do that there are a hundred men I could have chosen to take Aleksandr's place.

"How're things at the office?" she asks instead.

I scoff. "Your friend gives me dirty looks every time I walk down her corridor."

She laughs. Why does it sound like music? "Syrah's just protective. But don't worry: she's all bark, no bite."

"That'll serve her well. Because I bite back."

She scowls. "Just when I think you're halfway decent—"

I interrupt her with a cruel laugh and lean forward to scoop a strawberry off the platter on the coffee table between us. "I make no pretense about who I am. You're the one who keeps insisting that I'm a good man."

Wren's face flushes red, but she doesn't reply. She pulls out her phone and pretends to scroll for a while, though I'd bet every penny I own that her mind is a complete and total blank right now.

Grimacing, I get out my own phone and start scrolling through messages. "Motherfucker," I mutter when a new email comes in.

"What?" Wren blurts before she can stop herself.

I glance up at her. "Nothing. Work things."

"I work for you, you know," she reminds me acidly. "Actually, 'work' is the safest conversational topic I can think of. Everything else is a minefield with you."

She may have a point. I sigh and let my phone drop down onto my lap. "New client. Wants to buy up a string of warehouse facilities with port access, all cash, but he's insisting I meet with him first."

"Who's the client?"

I peek down at my phone to check the name. "Deerfield something."

She goes pale almost immediately. The color drains from her face so fast that I'm afraid she's having some kind of heart attack. I lean forward and grab her arm. "Wren?"

She blinks fast, rips away from me, and launches herself to her feet. She looks like she wants to sprint out of here, but she settles for pacing back and forth in wild, random circles.

"What is wrong with you?" I demand.

"Th-the client," she stammers. "You said you haven't met him yet?"

I stand up and place myself in front of her. She doesn't even seem to notice. "Wren, what's going on?"

"Is his name William Deerfield? It is, isn't it?"

Even her lips are chalk-white. I want to bite them, if only to bring the color back.

"For fuck's sake, Wren, will you tell me what's going on?"

Her eyes flicker to me reluctantly. "We've, uh… we've… crossed paths in the past."

That's all it takes to put my heart in my throat. I can feel my pulse in my wrists and temples as I drag her toward the couch. "Sit down."

"I don't want to sit down."

"Sit down anyway."

Surprisingly, she listens. She lets me steer her to a seat, though she keeps chewing on the inside of her cheek the entire time.

"Talk to me. How do you know him?"

"I don't *know* him. Not really. Not anymore."

If I weren't so impatient to get this story out of her, I might've smiled. "You're carrying my baby, Wren. You've also made fast friends with my fake future wife. Like it or not, we're going to be spending a lot of time together. We may as well get to know each other."

She squints at me suspiciously. "I'll remind you of that the next time I want to know something about *you*."

She keeps scratching at her cuticles, that leg of hers vibrating up and down. I've never seen her so agitated before.

"Wren—"

"We were *involved*," she blurts out. Her lips press together like it disgusts her to even say the words. "We were… together. But I… He… Fuck, I don't even know how to say this. I found out he was married."

My pulse doubles, triples, pounding harder and faster through my veins. The fear on her face makes me sick to my stomach.

"I know this sounds like an excuse," she continues, "but honestly, I didn't know he was still with his wife when we were together." She grabs one of the fuzzy white throw pillows and hugs it to her chest. "He told me they were divorced. And I actually believed him. For a year and a half, I didn't suspect a damn thing."

I'm burning hot with a feeling I barely recognize. But as foreign as it is, I know the name of it.

Jealousy.

Jealous that this smug fuck ever touched her. Furious that he lied to her.

But that all pales in the face of what she says next.

"And then…" Her voice quivers. "I got pregnant."

"You got… pregnant?" I repeat slowly.

Her nod seems more like a cringe. "I was twenty-five. I wasn't ready, but I was… happy," she explains softly. "I was naïve enough to believe he would be, too."

It's hard to keep a lid on my rage. I want to gut this motherfucker. It's been however long since he put her through this and yet the horror in her eyes says it's as fresh now as it was on day one.

"What made you think that?" I rasp.

"He has two kids with his ex—" She stops short, her eyes going wide at her own misstep. "—with his wife, I mean. He gave me this whole sob story about how she took his kids when she left him. He was so broken up about it. He claimed that he loved them both to death and he just wanted to be a good father to them, but she was keeping them from him…" She trails off. "And I swallowed every single lie he fed me."

She looks so small. So afraid.

She glances at me uncertainly. "When I told him I was pregnant, he flipped out. He went from angry to panicked so fast that he blurted out that Candice would leave him if she found out. And when I pointed out that Candice had already left him, he just stared at me with all this self-pity in his eyes. He didn't have to say anything else. I knew I'd been played."

"What happened after that?"

She blinks and two fat tears squeeze out of her eyes. "Shit," she whimpers, wiping them away aggressively. "I won't bore you with the details. Bottom line: I got an abortion."

"Was it your choice?"

Her eyes snap to mine. She wasn't expecting the question.

Which is exactly why I can read the answer written all over her face. Everything I need to know is right there, painfully and blindingly obvious.

"That bastard," I hiss. "That fucking bastard. I'll kill him."

Her hand flies out and lands on my arm. "Listen, this is all ancient history, okay? Go ahead and make your deal with him. It won't matter to me. Especially because I'm not part of your company anymore."

No, but you are part of my family now.

"I'm serious, Dmitri," she continues. "I don't care if you choose to sign him. I just… I wasn't prepared. I didn't think I'd ever see or hear from the man again."

Bee chooses then to burst through the white curtains. "Okay, guys! I'm—" She stops short as Wren peels her hand off mine quickly. "Shit. Did I interrupt something?"

"No," Wren insists, getting to her feet. "Everything's fine. Did you pick a dress?" She's trying her best to act normal, but her eyes are too shifty and there's a wobbly catch in her throat.

"Yup, I'm going Westwood." Bee turns to me. "I put it on your tab, hubs. Thanks! How about lunch before we go home? Dmitri's paying."

Wren smiles tightly as she follows Bee out of the room. I pull out my phone and dial Aleksandr immediately. "Tomorrow's meeting with William Deerfield—is that still on?"

"Yessir. Confirmed it a few hours ago."

"Call him back and cancel. With prejudice."

"Seriously?" he balks. "We're nixing a contract worth millions? Why?"

"Because I said so," I growl. "Your job is not to question. Your job is to execute. So go fucking execute."

"Okay, jeez. Manners wouldn't kill ya. I'll cancel the meeting."

"And I want the fucker blackballed."

I don't have to see Aleksandr to know that he's surprised. "Um… are you sure?"

"Chase him out of the city. Anyone who so much as sells him a fucking hot dog will have to answer to me."

I hang up. It's not as satisfying as burying my fist in his fucking face.

But it'll do until I can get my hands on him.

49

DMITRI

"Care to tell me what's going on?" Bee asks the moment Wren disappears down the corridor towards her room.

"Nothing," I grunt.

"'Nothing'?" She casts her voice in a deep baritone like mine, stands up tall, and furrows her brow in a cheap imitation of what I apparently look like. I'm not sure which element of the impersonation pisses me off the most. "Nothing. *Nothing*. Please, Wren was quiet for the whole damn lunch—"

"I'm surprised you even noticed, with all that talking you were doing."

She ignores me. "—and you couldn't stop looking at her. Did you pick a fight with her again? Because that is not cool, Dmitri. She knows the truth now and you know what that means, right?"

"Not sure I give a—"

"It means we're a team. We—"

I put my hand on her face like I used to when we were kids and shove her away.

"Asshole!" she snaps at my back.

I don't mean to go to Wren's room, but that's exactly where I go, my body buzzing with a simmering adrenaline that's crying out for an outlet. The mix-up that landed her in my penthouse feels dangerously close to inconsequential now. The only thing that matters is that she's here; that she's carrying my son.

But there are a few other details that I can't ignore no matter how much I try.

Like, for example, the fact that her sister is gone because of me.

That detail had been easier to disregard before. Before I knew she didn't deserve the hand that life had dealt her. Before I cared about her happiness more than my own agenda.

Fuck.

Her room is unlocked, so I let myself in. She's standing in the bathroom with the door cracked open. Her back is to me so she doesn't notice that I've entered. I'm about to let her know that I'm here when she starts unbuttoning her blouse.

A gentleman would stop her now. Or at the very least, turn away.

Unfortunately for her, I'm no gentleman.

Her hair falls in messy waves down the curve of her bare back, marred only by the pinkish indent of her bra straps. When she peels off her pants, my semi becomes a raging hard-on. Her underwear is a sheer scrap of lace, and she has her thumbs hooked in the waistband to tug it down her legs when she twists around—

And that's when she spots me.

"Goddammit!" she yelps. One hand goes to cover her chest, the other where her thighs meet. I stride to the bathroom's threshold unapologetically. With every step I take, she gets more and more self-conscious. "You shouldn't be here."

I meet her eyes. "Keep going."

She bites her bottom lip uncertainly. "Dmitri…"

"It wasn't a question, Wren."

Her hands tremble as she forces them down to her sides. I have no idea why anyone would choose to hide a body like that. The woman is flawless. That swell of her belly only makes her more so.

"You're beautiful," I whisper into the silence.

She blushes, a tide of scarlet embarrassment that starts from her cheeks and spreads like wildfire to the rest of her body. Her eyes shudder the same way her hands do, but she stays perfectly still otherwise. She's looking at me as though I'm a wolf who's about to pounce.

She's not far off.

"Tell me: who were you thinking of when you were masturbating in the living room the other night?"

"You saw that?" she blurts out.

"I saw *everything*." I move closer still and place my fingers under her chin, forcing her gaze back up to mine. "Don't be embarrassed. I could have watched you forever."

Her lips part. Shock? Lust? Her dilated pupils say that, beneath the flushed cheeks, she's burning up with the same things surging through me.

"Tell me," I growl again. "Who were you thinking of?"

I press my fingers against her lips, turning them a darker shade of pink. So plump and juicy. So sweet, I'm sure—if only I'd let myself taste them.

"You," she says softly. "Only you."

"Tell me what you were thinking of. I want the whole fantasy. Every last detail."

Wren winces like I'm hurting her. She's leaning away from me ever-so-slightly, I notice—and we can't have that now, can we? So I grab her by the waist and march her backwards until she's pinned between me and the bathroom counter. Her breasts are heavy and warm against my chest and I can feel her pulse pounding beneath my fingertips.

"Dmitri…"

My grip on her hips tightens. That's all the warning she needs.

Wren's throat bobs with a taut, terrified smile. When she talks again, her voice is a barely audible rasp. "I-I… imagined you were with me…"

"Doing what?"

She swallows again. "T-touching my breasts…"

I reach up and fondle her breast, rolling the nipple between my thumb and my forefinger. It peaks immediately into a hardened point and she shivers, her words dissolving slowly into breathy moans.

"Go on," I encourage. "I can't have you be so easily distracted."

"You sucked on my… my…"

I scoop her up easily and set her down onto the counter. When I have her where I want her, I bend forward and suck her tight nipple between my lips. She bucks an inch before I lock her hips back down onto the marble.

"Keep going," I snarl as I glide my kiss across her chest to tease the other nipple until it's painfully hard.

"Then you, uhh… you… *fuck…* you moved down to my… my…"

Her shyness is fucking adorable. But it'll do her no good where we're going. Where *I'm* going, rather.

I slip down onto my knees and part her legs as wide as they'll go. When I shove the lace seat of her panties aside, she's wide open for me already and glistening under the lights.

My tongue lashes out, just the tip of it, for a long, teasing taste. Fuck, she tastes so damn good. Salty and sweet, and the way she twitches as I lap her up only makes it that much better.

One lick becomes two. I part her folds with a finger so I can explore every nook and cranny of her.

In the corner of my eyes, I see her knuckles going white as she clings to the counter's edge. But like a good, obedient girl, she stays right where I have her.

She comes almost as soon as I slide a finger inside of her, my tongue lathing at her clit the entire time. Sputtering moans rain down on me like manna from fucking heaven, something in between a breath and a word.

Her desire coats my chin when I finally rise again. I catch sight of myself in the mirror—tall, eyes aflame, lips shining with the evidence of Wren's orgasm. My tongue flickers out to catch a stray droplet.

I pick up the conversation right where we left off. "What happens next?" I press. "What came after?"

She swallows. Her eyes dart south of my belt before she wrenches them back up to meet mine.

"You fuck me," she says in a hiss, no longer ashamed to use the right words. "*Hard.*"

I nod in satisfaction.

Then, the time for talking is over.

I pull her closer to the edge, free my cock from my pants, and line myself up with her. There's a momentary pause as the tip of me nuzzles her opening. Our eyes are locked, her fingers laced behind my neck, mine on her hips. We both inhale a breath and hold it—hold it—hold it…

Perfectly in sync.

Like we'd have ended up here, in one way or another, no matter how many twists and turns it took to bring us to this moment.

Like this was always going to happen.

Like neither of us ever had a choice.

Then I dive into her and all thoughts of fate and purpose go out the fucking window. There is only Wren—her wetness and her heat and her whimpering as she clings to me and I fuck her like I'll never get to do it again.

It strikes me towards the end, as we both race towards our climaxes, that if I want to get Wren out of my system, fucking her is definitely not the way to do it. For that to happen, I might have to stop altogether. Go cold turkey.

And you could give me all the money, all the territory, all the power in the world…

But that's still not gonna fucking happen.

50

DMITRI

Nothing gets me in a bad mood faster than seeing Vittorio's name on my lock screen.

VITTORIO ZANETTI: 4 missed calls.

"Motherfucker," I mumble under my breath.

"Talking about my father?" Bee asks, poking her head from around the kitchen corner.

I join her in there and grab a beer from the fridge, angrily twisting off the cap and pitching it into the trash can. "Who else? He wants the wedding moved up again. Apparently, 'soon' isn't soon enough."

Her lip curls up like she's smelling something rotten. "'Motherfucker' isn't 'motherfucker' enough, either." Sighing, she sticks her plate in the sink and cracks her neck from side to side. "I'm heading out tonight, 'kay?"

"Bee—"

"I know, I know," she interrupts before I can begin expressing my frustration. "I'm not going anywhere overly exposed. Plus, I'm an expert at covering my tracks, so don't worry." She slinks past me, running a hand over my shoulders. "So tense. You should really find a way to work out all those knots. A massage, perhaps? Or maybe a little romp in the—"

"Fuck off, Bee."

Her laugh lingers long after she's gone.

I wish I had a better retort, but I'm on my last vestiges of willpower lately. Running on pure fumes.

The last three days have been an exercise in discipline. Only one fuck a day? It's like telling a man in the desert to content himself with a single drop of water.

One fuck isn't enough. Two wouldn't be. Nor would five, or ten. It takes me literal seconds from the time I finish to get hungry enough to devour Wren again.

It's becoming a problem. Well, more of a problem than it already was. So I'm going out of my way to spend as much time out of the penthouse as possible.

Between Egorov's normal business dealings and this burgeoning Bratva war with the Irish, I have plenty to keep my hands occupied. The same can't be said for my mind, though. Every spare moment I have invariably ends with me lassoed into a fantasy of Wren.

Her legs spread for me in invitation.

Those mossy green eyes as she crawls her way down my body...

I have never been the type of man to notice the irrelevant details. Freckles, birthmarks, this scar here or that way she moans when I touch her *there,* like *that.*

But suddenly, I'm noticing it all.

And every single thing is a stronger aphrodisiac than the last. I find myself hurrying to finish my work so that I can get back home, so that I can find an excuse to seek her out, to explore her body more and more. To discover new freckles, new marks on her body, new ways of making her scream.

I always figured the devil would come for me one day.

No one ever told me she would look this good.

"She's in her room, by the way," Bee chimes in as she walks back past the kitchen on her way to the exit. "She's been a little down all day."

"Down?"

Bee shrugs. "I asked. She didn't want to talk about it."

Before I know it, I'm on my feet and charging toward Wren's room. I don't even care about the knowing, smug look that Bee throws my way.

This time, I remember to knock.

"I'm okay, Bee, really. Just need a little space."

Space? Fuck that. I push my way into her room, proving once again that nothing good comes from knocking.

She looks up from the small scrap of blue fabric in her hands and freezes when she sees me. "Oh. It's you."

I walk over to the window seat and sit down opposite her. Something's off. Her shoulders are hunched and her eyes look swollen, like she's been crying.

"What's that?" I ask, gesturing to the fabric in her hands.

She passes it to me silently. It turns out to be a little blue blanket. Hand-knitted, if I had to guess, judging from the uneven, clumsy stitching.

I venture a guess. "You made this?"

"No. Rose did." She glances to the side, where a bunch of empty boxes have been stacked. I recognize them as the boxes I'd used to move Wren's stuff from her old apartment. "I was organizing a couple of things in the walk-in when I came across that."

I hate seeing that look on her face, but silently, I feel this strange sense of victory. She's finally decided to unpack.

I look down at the blanket. It's so small. More like a handkerchief than something for a human. "It won't go to waste," I remind her gently.

Wren smiles through her unshed tears. "It just feels so unfair. This baby was never meant to be mine."

I shift uncomfortably. *Tell her, asshole,* demands an angry voice in my head. *Tell her the truth. Tell her what happened to Rose.*

It's not the first time I've ignored that voice. It's not the hundredth or the thousandth time, either, and it won't be the last.

Because I just can't fucking bring myself to do it.

"'Meant to be' is one thing, Wren. 'What is' is a different thing altogether."

She rubs a hand on her stomach absentmindedly. "It's funny: Mom was always convinced that I would be the first one to have a kid. I suppose, in the end, she wasn't wrong." Her gaze drifts from the window to me, barely seeing anything in front of her. "It's weird to think she won't be here when I give birth, either. I'll be alone."

"You won't be alone," I rumble fiercely. "You'll have me." Her eyes brighten with surprise. "And Bee." The light in her eyes dims just a little bit.

She takes the blanket from my hands. "As far as the world is concerned, this baby won't be mine at all. It'll be yours and Bee's."

"Only temporarily."

Her eyes snap to mine. "What does that mean?"

Fuck. That wasn't meant to come out. There's more trust here than there once was, but this isn't about trusting her; it's about protecting her. She doesn't need to know the unsavory details of how my world functions. Nor does she need to know the lengths I will go to to get what I want.

"It means that this will work out. You just need to trust me."

She frowns. "Dmitri—"

I get to my feet and offer her my hand. "Come on. We're going out."

"Where?"

"This little hole-in-the-wall place down in Little Italy. They've got the best damn gnocchi you will ever put in your mouth."

She gives me a shaky, watery smile. "Well, how can I say no to that?"

∽

"This is the place you had in mind?" she asks as we walk into Stefania's. Her eyes rove over to me questioningly. "Doesn't really strike me as the kinda place you'd put so much as a toe in."

I arch my eyebrows. "And what is that supposed to mean?"

She flashes those pretty little dimples of hers. "Nothing. I mean, it just seems a little, shall we say… humble for you."

"I can be humble."

Wren just snorts. It's enough of a comeback all on its own.

We navigate to the back of the restaurant and I pull out a chair for her. A waft of her scent—citrus and sandalwood—rushes over me as she sits. Just like that, I'm hard as steel.

"I used to bus tables here when I was a teenager," I explain.

She twists around to gawk at me as I take my own seat. "You, bussing tables?"

"Don't look so surprised. Manual labor is not beneath me."

Wren snorts once again. I can't decide if it's more amusing than it is irritating, or vice versa.

"It was part of my father's plan to make a man of me," I add.

"Waiting tables is supposed to be some kind of initiation to manhood?" she asks in disbelief.

"No. Kicking me out of the house was." I gesture over to the tiny spiral staircase that winds upwards to the second floor. A lopsided **STAFF ONLY** sign hangs from one of the banisters, rusted with age. "I used to sleep in the storeroom upstairs."

Her jaw is practically scraping the table. "Why on earth would your father kick you out?"

"Honestly, he had plenty of reasons. I was a smartass. I talked back, questioned him constantly, refused to listen. I was trying to assert my dominance. Problem was, I wasn't the alpha."

Her eyes soften in what can only be genuine sympathy. "That must have been hard for you."

"No." I shake my head. "It was a way for me to prove myself. And I did. I showed my father that I didn't need his money or connections to survive."

"So he came back for you?"

"Walked in six months after I started working here and told me to pack up my shit and come home," I confirm. "He didn't say anything, but I knew he was proud."

Leaning back in her seat, she whistles softly. "And I thought *my* family situation was complicated. Yours is straight-up medieval."

Before I can respond, a new voice interjects. "There he is, my favorite busboy!" Stefania sashays up to our table in all her colorful splendor: a bright red dish towel hooked into her canary yellow apron, jet-black hair cascading down over her olive skin. When she sees Wren, her plucked-to-within-an-inch-of-their-lives eyebrows fly up her forehead. "And he brought a friend, to boot!"

I rise to my feet and greet her with a bump of kisses. Her waist has expanded over the years, but her cheeks have caved in. "How've you been, Stef?"

"Lonely," she retorts, swatting my arm. "It's been *months* since you last visited me. Months, I tell you!"

I place my hand against my heart. "My apologies. I've been busy. Stefania, this is Wren."

Wren smiles shyly. "I've heard amazing things about your gnocchi."

"A friend *and* a suck-up." Stefania winks back playfully. "Flattery will get you everywhere, *tesoro*. We've got pumpkin stuffed tonight. How about I get you two bowls? Sit tight. I'll be right back."

When she walks away, Wren stares after her curiously. "I'm guessing this is her restaurant?"

"She inherited it from her husband a few decades ago," I explain as I sink into my seat again. "The rumor is that he died of a heart attack—but personally, I think she offed him herself. He was a miserable bastard. She's happier now."

Wren blanches. "Jesus."

I chuckle at the horrified look on her face. "Don't worry; she's family."

"Family, huh?" She looks around cautiously.

"I didn't know what it was like to have a mother who'd kill for me until I met Stefania."

Her hand falls over her stomach tenderly. "It's an instinct that's becoming more and more familiar to me."

"I wouldn't worry about that. Leave the killing to me."

"You're not kidding when you say stuff like that, are you?" She leans forward and sighs. "That should scare me. But it doesn't."

Funnily enough, I'm experiencing the exact same sentiment. Sitting with Wren in this restaurant, talking about parts of my past I've only ever shared with the people closest to me—that shit should be scary.

But instead, it just feels right.

∼

By the time we're finished with dinner, the restaurant has mostly cleared out and Wren's got a permanent smile on her face. "That was a transformative experience. Like, I've died and gone to heaven. I am one with the universe, and the universe is a bite of pumpkin gnocchi."

Stefania laughs as she clears away our tiramisu plates. "I like this one, Dmitri. Bring her around more."

I'm annoyed when my phone starts ringing. Excusing myself, I step outside to take Aleksandr's call. "This better be good, man."

"Why? Am I getting in the way of your quality time with Wren?"

My teeth grind together as I look up and down the street. "Did Bee tell you I was with her?"

"Nope. This is just how you always sound when you're impatient to get back to her."

"For fuck's sake… why did you call?" I say before he can build up a head of steam on a topic I'm intent on avoiding.

He chuckles. "Just wanted to give you an update on O'Gadhra's movements. He's sticking to his territory for now. But he's been a busy little bee. He had five different meetings and that was only today."

"Anyone important?"

"Nah. Local gangsters in his area. Chumps, really. That's about it."

I hear the tinkle of the bell above the restaurant's entrance as someone steps outside. "Keep at it. Call me if you hear anything else." Cigarette smoke assaults my nostrils as I hang up and Stefania joins me at the curb. "I thought you quit smoking?"

She throws me a cheeky grin. "Gotta die of something. Might as well be something fun."

"You? Die? Doubtful," I snort. "You'll live forever."

She chuckles and takes another drag on her cigarette. "She's lovely, by the way. I approve wholeheartedly."

That's not why I brought Wren here. But the moment the words leave Stefania's mouth, I find myself wondering, *Why else would I bring Wren here?*

"It's not my imagination, is it?" adds Stefania. "She's pregnant?"

I grab the cigarette from her hand and take a puff. That's all the answer she needs.

"Mm. That's what I thought. And it's yours, yes?"

My eyes snap to hers, that itchy ferocity surging through my veins the way it always does when the thought of someone else touching Wren comes up. "Yes."

Stefania's eyes glow a little brighter as she takes back her cigarette. "Then you need to mark your territory." She takes another long drag and exhales a long plume of smoke. "There's a stray in there sniffing around your woman."

Instant hackles rising.

Instant fists clenching.

I burst into the restaurant to find Wren leaning away from a gangly young man, who's pulled a chair up to hers. She's smiling uncomfortably and shaking her head, but he doesn't seem to be getting the message.

Maybe he'll get mine.

He's so engrossed in Wren that he doesn't notice me until I've grabbed the collar of his shirt and yanked him right out of his seat. "What the—"

His exclamation dries on his tongue when he sees who's taken hold of him.

"Lost, little boy?" I snarl in his face, smoke wreathing every word.

"S-sorry!" he stammers. "I w-was... I thought..."

Wren gets to her feet, anxiety dancing across her face. "Dmitri, let him go."

"Oh, I wouldn't get involved, dear," Stefania advises as she steps back into the restaurant and starts drawing down the blinds. "Best to let your man handle it."

"The question is, can *you* handle it?" I spit in the *mudak's* face.

He shakes his head vehemently. "I'm s-sorry. I'll stay away. P-p-please!"

"Dmitri!"

I shove him away from me hard and he lands on his ass on the floor. He scrambles around immediately and races to the exit, his shoes sliding across the floor in a cartoonish escape. The door swings open and he's gone, leaving behind nothing but a cold draft from the threshold and an angry crackle in my knuckles.

Wren is staring at me with her mouth hanging open but Stefania looks not bothered in the least as she pulls down the last blind and heads over to the spiral staircase. "Enjoy the rest of your evening, kids," she says with a maternal smile. "Lock up before you leave. Wren, *tesoro*—" Wren turns to her distractedly as she finishes, "—it was a pleasure meeting you."

After she disappears upstairs, Wren turns her disbelieving expression on me. "What was that? It was totally harmless. He was just—"

I get in her face, my hand curling around her hip. "Nothing is harmless about a man flirting with you like that."

"Why?" she demands, bristling tall. "Because I'm yours?"

My lips curl up into a smile. A startled gasp escapes her lips when I push her backwards onto the table we just ate dinner off of. I shove her legs apart and pull her panties down as her pupils dilate.

"Precisely. because you're all fucking—" I thrust inside her hard, twisting her frown into a smile. "—*mine*."

51

WREN

Three days later and I'm still sore from the restaurant sex with Dmitri.

But that doesn't mean I'm not capable of walking on my own.

I rip my arm out from under Aleksandr's hand. "What's the damn problem? I'm just getting out of the car!" He tries to grab me again, but I swat him away. "Aleks! Seriously."

"Do not get out of the car until I come around with an umbrella," he orders.

Rolling my eyes, I unlock the door. "It's just a little rain. I'm not gonna melt if I—"

Blip.

"Did you just lock me back in?"

He shoots me a dirty look from the driver's seat and jumps out of the SUV. A few seconds later, the door opens and reveals him standing there with a black umbrella in hand.

"What is *with* you today?" I demand. "It was bad enough you wouldn't let me sit up front with you. This is excessive."

"Listen, it took a lot of convincing to get Dmitri to agree to let you have this lunch with Syrah, okay?" he says, eyes pleading. "He only agreed because I promised I would be here the entire time and I'd take care of you."

"He's not gonna care if I get wet."

Scowling, Aleksandr pulls out his phone and holds it up to my face. There's a single message on the lock screen.

DMITRI: *There's a storm coming in. Make sure she doesn't get wet.*

Well… I stand corrected.

My jaw drops. "Don't you think he's overdoing it just a little?"

Aleksandr just shrugs. "He's protective. To a fault, apparently. Now, come on—it's really starting to pour."

We walk into Serendipity and I breathe in all the delicious scents that filter through the air. The entrance of the restaurant is all persimmons and fresh lemon. And as we move into the dining area, savory fish and sizzling potatoes fill the air.

I'm so distracted by the smells that it's not until I sit down that I realize the restaurant is completely empty. "Since when are people in this city afraid of a little rain?"

As if in answer, thunder booms overhead and the silverware on the table shivers in place.

Aleksandr smirks. "I don't think it has anything to do with the rain."

I cock my head to the side. "What does that—?" There are three waiters standing off to the corner, looking at me as though I'm the belle of the ball. "Oh my God! Did he clear out the whole restaurant?"

"You may be right," he concedes with more of that same wry grin. "He does have a habit of overdoing things."

"How the hell am I gonna explain this to—"

"Wren!" Syrah squeals, coming up around the corner. Aleksandr throws me a wink and backs away as Syrah bulldozes right into me, squawking about how great I look. "You look hot. Seriously *hot*. Pregnancy suits you. Oh my God, are you wearing Prada?!"

Self-consciously, I look down at the caramel-colored knit dress I'm wearing. "Umm…"

She grabs my arm and pulls me closer. "He's paying you enough to buy *Prada*? Girrrl, you've got it good. Tell me everything."

I laugh awkwardly. "Don't I know it?"

I have to admit, it feels strange to sit here and talk to Syrah without actually being able to tell her anything. Every time she tries to ask about my so-called 'job,' I try to change the subject.

By the time we make it to the main course, I'm exhausted from the verbal gymnastics. "So how's the new client, by the way?" I ask tentatively, wondering if I even want to know.

"New client?" Syrah asks through a mouth full of lobster thermidor.

"I thought I heard that Egorov was signing Deerfield? That'd fall into your department, right?"

"Oh. Right. Yeah." She takes an unconcerned sip of her wine. "Didn't take."

I try not to look too invested. "It didn't?"

"Nope." She shrugs. "Apparently, the boss nixed the deal."

There's a buzz on my skin. Honestly, it feels better than alcohol. "Are you sure?"

"Mhmm. I spoke to Rogan about it a few days ago. Dmitri refused to so much as meet with him. Must be some bad blood there. Above my paygrade, though."

I'm too distracted by the warmth spreading through me to muster up a reasonable response. I know I told Dmitri to go ahead and make the deal, but it's only because I knew I didn't have the right to ask him to do anything else.

Except he'd made that decision all on his own.

For *me*.

"Wow, it's super empty in here today, huh?" Syrah asks, looking around cluelessly as if she's just now noticing. "Weird. I thought this place is usually pretty popular."

I fidget in my seat. "Um, yeah… weird."

"Definitely." She redirects her attention back to me. "So, come on, tell me about the job. You've barely said two words about it and I'm dying to know."

This is the third time she's circled back to the job. If I keep avoiding the question any longer, she's gonna get suspicious.

"Busy," I say vaguely. "Both of them have a lot going on. And… the wedding's coming up, too." The words taste bitter coming out, no matter how nonchalant I pretend I am.

"Shit, you're really planning their wedding?"

"I'm helping. Bee's got a specific vision about what she wants. I'm just the executor."

Syrah scrunches up her nose. "Blech. Is she a bridezilla?"

"No, no," I demur quickly, rushing to Bee's defense. "She's actually pretty chill. It's her father that's the demanding one."

"Weird. And what about the gray-eyed Adonis she's marrying? How is he with you?"

I swallow my awkwardness. "He's polite. And generous. I can't complain."

Except that I have a list of complaints seared in my head and the list is only getting longer.

He's a Bratva don.

He's marrying another woman.

He's controlling and possessive and entirely too demanding.

And the worst of all… *I can't stop thinking about him.*

Once we're done with our food, I put the bill on my "expense account," a.k.a., Dmitri's personal tab. We're heading towards the exit when my phone buzzes.

ALEKS: *I'm gonna bring the car around. It's still raining hard so wait for me under the awning. Don't be a wiseass.*

"Dammit," I mumble under my breath.

"Something wrong?"

I put my phone away. "No, no. Just work stuff."

We walk out of the restaurant and rain pelts us, sharp and frigid. "Gross!" Syrah says. "It's torrential out here."

The valet drives her car up first, so she gives me a quick hug and makes a run for it. She beeps goodbye twice and takes off just as Aleksandr drives the SUV around behind. There are three short steps before the pavement and despite what Aleksandr told me about staying put, I rush down, eager to get out of the cold.

Except I underestimate how slippery those three steps are. My heels slide across the last step and gravity betrays me. I start to cry out, but my scream is cut off when my head bangs hard against the top step, sending ripples of pain shooting through my body.

My vision goes blurry and my limbs go numb, and the sky seems intent on drowning me.

"Wren! Wren! Fuck, are you okay?"

The worry in Aleksandr's voice reminds me that his neck is on the line here. I want to tell him I'm alright, but I've forgotten how my tongue works.

It's the first time that I feel real fear. But it's not for myself.

"Fuck," he mutters. "Is that blood?"

52

DMITRI

"It's not happening soon enough!"

Vittorio reminds me of a petulant child. A petulant child with overgrown nose hair and saggy skin around his jowls. The only things he's missing are the foot stomp and a wobbly bottom lip, and the longer we stay here bickering, the more likely they are to appear.

"We moved up the wedding by six months, Vittorio," I growl quietly. "That isn't soon enough for you?"

Scowling, he taps his hand against my desk. "You've been engaged for over a year. You should have been married by now."

"Your daughter has a vision for our wedding and she wants it to be perfect."

"I don't give a flying fuck what she wants," he snarls. "I want the bitch married!"

I get to my feet slowly, pulling my lips back over my teeth. "What did you just call my fiancée?"

Those saggy cheeks of his pale. "I meant no disrespect—"

"If that were true, you wouldn't be here wasting my time. Respect goes both ways, Vittorio."

"Listen—"

"No. I'm done listening," I hiss. "It's time for you to pay attention. You want the spectacle of our marriage? Well, that requires a big show. This isn't just a wedding; this is a display of power. The Zanetti mafia and the Egorov Bratva, united under one banner. We have to give the people something to talk about, don't we? That requires time. Planning. Coordination. We need to make a statement."

He swallows, his gaze trailing over me with defeat. My logic is getting through to him but he's still not happy. Why not, though? His eagerness borders on panic and it's rubbing me the wrong way.

We're interrupted when my phone starts to ring. "You can show yourself out," I tell him as I walk out of my office. I only answer the call once I'm traveling down in the elevator. "Aleks?"

"Okay, don't panic but… we're heading to the hospital."

"The fuck? Who's 'we'?"

"Wren took a little spill outside Serendipity. She's conscious now but—"

I hang up furiously and resist the urge to slam my fist through the elevator walls. The moment the doors sweep open, I rush to the front of the building where my Mercedes is parked. I run through two red lights and nearly take out a herd of pedestrians before I pull up outside St. Joseph's Presbyterian.

As I walk through the luminescent corridors and the spotless bronze sconces dotting the walls, I curse Aleksandr out internally for bringing her to this place. I hate hospitals in general. But this one opens up the black sinkhole inside me that I usually only crack open when there's dark shit that needs repressing.

"Dmitri!" Aleksandr calls as I turn the corner and catch sight of him. "She's in here. She's totally fi—"

I grab the front of his shirt and reel him towards me. "She better be," I breathe in his face. Then I shove him aside and burst into the room.

Wren takes one look at me and her eyes light up. "You came."

The fact that she's surprised pisses me off. *Of course I came.* "Are you okay?"

She nods. "Took a bad spill. Knocked my head. There was a little blood, but the doctor said I don't even need stitches."

Her cheery mood does nothing to convince me that everything is alright. "The baby?"

"The doctor's on his way to check," she says, sounding decidedly less cheery. "Listen, Dmitri, don't be mad at Aleks. He took really good care of me—"

"If that was true, we wouldn't be in a hospital right now."

Her jaw snaps shut for a moment. She takes in my dark expression and sighs. "It was my fault, okay? I was supposed to wait for him under the awning, but I thought I'd make a run for the car and I slipped. It was stupid and—"

"You're damn right it was stupid," I spit. "What the fuck were you thinking, running in a thunderstorm?"

She wrinkles up her nose. "It was an accident," she says in a tiny croak. "It just happened."

"Excuse me." We both turn around as the doctor walks in. His face pulls me back in time—seven years, to be precise. I recognize him instantly. The same leathery skin, the same thin lips, the same receding hairline, though it's lost another inch since I last saw him.

He clearly recognizes me, too, because his eyes flare bright. "Mr. Egorov, how nice to see you after so long. Is Elena—"

"This is Wren," I snap, moving to the side so he can see her lying on the bed.

"Ah," Dr. Falco says awkwardly. "I apologize, ma'am. I mistook you for—"

"Doctor, if you don't mind, I'd like to make sure everything is alright with the baby."

He clears his throat and walks to Wren's bedside. "Of course. How far along are you, my dear?"

I fade backward, reeling from invisible blows. When I blink, I can practically see Elena's innocent smile beaming up at me from a hospital bed identical to the one Wren's lying on now.

I like when he calls me 'my dear.' Makes me feel precious.

I float to the window as Dr. Falco examines Wren. Every time I glance over my shoulder, I catch her peeking at me anxiously.

"Well?" I demand after a few minutes have passed.

"The baby's heartbeat is strong. Everything seems fine."

"I don't deal in probabilities, doctor. I want you to tell me that she and the baby *are* both fine. Not that they *seem* that way."

Dr. Falco fumbles his clipboard and sighs. "What I meant is they are fine. Both the baby and Elena—" He stops short and for a moment, I think he's on the verge of swallowing his own tongue. I'm right on the cusp of cutting it off so that it goes down a little easier. "I apologize—Wren. The baby and Wren are both fine."

"Good. Get out."

He scurries away like a beat dog while Wren looks at me, wide-eyed and accusing. "What the hell was that?"

"I don't like incompetence."

"He misspoke. You didn't have to be such a gigantic asshole!"

For fuck's sake, the woman has a concussion and she's still picking a fight with me. I stomp over to her bedside. "I wouldn't have to be an asshole if you listened."

"Oh, so now, this is my fault?"

"By your own damn admission, this is your fault!" I remind her.

She bites her lips. "It was an accident! I didn't want to fall and endanger the baby. What is your problem?"

"You!" I growl, slamming my fist against her bedside table. "*You* are my problem."

Her eyes have gone watery. At least she's not fighting back anymore. But that just makes it all worse.

For the first time, she reminds me of Elena.

"From now on, you're going to obey," I snarl, backing out of the room and nearly slamming into Aleksandr where he's standing guard in the hallway. "Get her discharged and bring her straight home."

Then I get the fuck out of this hospital.

Before more memories of Elena can drag me back under those dark waters.

53

WREN

I'm no therapist, but I'm pretty sure Dmitri's dark mood has something to do with Elena.

Whoever the hell *that* is.

From the way that Dmitri reacted to hearing her name, I've discerned that she was someone he cared about deeply. I'm hoping for mother or sister, but my instincts are telling me that that's not the case.

In my morbid curiosity, I end up siccing Syrah on the discovery mission.

WREN: *Any leads?*

Hours since I sent that to her, though, I still don't have an answer. Strange. Also, unsettling. I'm still frowning at my phone and begging for three dancing dots to appear when a voice slices in through the stifling silence.

"Hello? Anyone home?"

"In here!" I squeak back, voice rusty from disuse.

Bee rushes into the living room, where I'm curled up on the couch in a nest of blankets. She's looking like a hot mess in a sequined burgundy dress and four-inch heels. If I had to guess, I'd say she slept in her makeup, judging by the smeared mascara.

"Are you okay?" she asks, hurrying over to kneel in front of me and squeeze my calf tenderly. "I heard about the fall."

"I'm fine. Just a little concussion is all."

"Thank God. A little rattle of the brain is good every once in a while. Reboot ya, y'know?" She collapses onto the sofa next to me and kicks off her heels. "Dmitri sounded *pissed,* though."

Sighing, I pick at the edges of the cushion I'm hugging to my chest. "When is he not pissed at me?" Bee smirks and I eye her cautiously, wondering if maybe our friendship is strong enough to override her loyalty to Dmitri or if I'm about to make a terrible, irreversible mistake. "Although, I have to say, in this particular case, I think it was less about me and more about someone else."

"Oh? Who?"

"The doctor that examined me recognized Dmitri. I guess they have history. He mentioned a woman named Elena."

Bee's face freezes. "Oh. Uh… shit."

That tells me everything I need to know. "Who is she?" I ask in a whisper. "Bee, who is she?"

She fidgets in place, adjusting the hem of her dress as though she's suddenly conscious of how much leg she's showing, despite there not being another living creature within three floors of us. "She's, uh, well, you know... She's Elena. She's... someone Dmitri used to know. Before. Before you, I mean."

I bite down my frustration. "Yeah, I got that, Bee. Was she his ex-girlfriend? A friend? Sister?"

Bee chews on her bottom lip and gives me an awkward shrug. "I'm sorry, Wren. It's not my story to tell." She gets up as suddenly as she arrived, picks her shoes off the floor, and damn near sprints towards the open archway. "I'm glad you're okay."

Well. So much for that.

I don't think "interrogator" is a job title in my future.

Grimacing, I get up and start nosing around the house in the hopes that a clue might pop up. But I'm not any better at being a detective than I am at being an interrogator, because the only evidence of a relationship is Dmitri's fake relationship with Bee.

It's the same things I saw and noticed when I first stepped foot in this penthouse: shoes intermingled, his-and-hers clothes thrown here and there, that kind of thing. Although, now that I know the truth, I'm almost amused by how carefully placed it all suddenly seems. False evidence planted everywhere, almost *too* obvious to the casual observer.

When my phone starts ringing, I grab it eagerly. Sure enough, it's Syrah, thank the Lord. I rush into the privacy of my bedroom and make sure the door is locked before I answer.

"Did you find anything?" I breathe.

"Just call me Sherlock Syrah, because—"

"Well?!" I catch myself nearly shrieking and lower my voice. "What is it, Sy?"

"Jeez, someone's eager. Why do you care so much about your boss's ex-wife?"

I almost choke to death on my own spit. Even when I manage to avoid that grim fate, the surprise of those three little words is like a sledgehammer to the stomach.

I plummet to a seat on the floor, my back resting against the bedpost. "Wait, what? Elena was his ex-wife?"

"Yep-yep. According to Erica in H.R.—er, I mean, a source that shall remain nameless—they were married for a few years. She used to come around the office sometimes. According to my source—who is definitely not Erica in H.R.—she was a cute little thing. Blonde and blue. Innocent, sweet. They got married pretty young."

My vision goes blurry as I stare off into space. "I had no idea. Did he—did she... Was it a bad split?"

Syrah draws in a slow breath that sends nervous tingles running up and down my spine. "I... I guess you could say that. She died."

Oh, God.

I have three distinct and related thoughts in quick succession. The first: *That must have been hard on Dmitri.*

The second: *No wonder he's so damn protective.*

The third (and no, I'm not proud of this one): *How am I supposed to compete with his dead wife?*

"Wren?"

"I'm—" I gulp to wet my parched throat and try again. "I'm here."

"Is everything alright?" I hear the rustle of motion as she leans in closer. "Why do you care so much about all this?"

The *"it's none of your business"* part is implied.

"I was just curious, that's all."

"Oh. Okay." Another rustle. Another crackle of brief static. "Because for a second there… no, never mind."

"No, go ahead. Tell me."

It can't be any worse than what I'm already thinking about myself, so she might as well.

Syrah laughs awkwardly. "For a second there, I thought you might be catching feelings for Dmitri."

It feels like my insides are shriveling up. "Definitely not."

"Good. Because, I mean, he's taken. Like, extremely taken. There's no point pining after a man you can't have."

Cringe. It's total and complete, head to toe, inside to out. Devastating, really.

"Totally," I say in the breeziest voice I can muster up. "That'd be so dumb, right? Don't worry. I'm not. But, er, yeah, anyway, thanks for the info, Detective Mehra. Talk soon?"

"Oh, yeah, okay." She sounds taken back by the abrupt goodbye, but I can't keep up the pretense for much longer. I'm this close to a nuclear meltdown and I need to get off the phone *stat.* "Bye."

I let the phone drop to the carpet as I loll my head back against the bedpost and stare up at the ceiling. Is it weird that I'm so much more insecure about Dmitri's dead wife than I am about Bee? Maybe because, while his relationship with Bee is for show, his relationship with Elena was definitely not.

My instincts are screaming at me. They're saying, *There's no place for you in his world. He made space for a woman once, and she's dead now.*

Who are you to think you could replace her?

Who are you to even try?

∼

That evening, I'm in the living room pretending to read a book when the elevator doors announce Dmitri's arrival. I don't have to accidentally-slash-on purpose run into him, because he seeks me out first.

"How are you feeling?" he rumbles as he darkens the doorway. He keeps his distance, and the pathetic part of my brain immediately starts wondering if that's on purpose. If he knows what I've poked into and if he hates me for it.

"Fine," I say as flatly as I can. "I rested most of the day."

"Good. Do you need anything?"

The truth would be delightful, thanks. "Um, I was just gonna go get some water."

He tosses his coat over the nearby armchair. "Wait right there. I'll get it for you." He leaves me sitting on the couch, wondering—and again, I'm aware that I'm being pathetic and petty and stupid and ridiculous—if this was the kind of thing he did for Elena.

Did he take care of her the same way? Did he learn to cook for her? Was he as protective? Did they ever talk about having kids of their own one day? Did—

"Here you go."

He hands me the glass of water. I mutter a quick, "Thank you" and take it from him, careful not to let our fingertips touch.

I'm hoping he'll sit down, but he shows no signs of it. Instead, he retreats toward the hallway. "I've got some work to do. If you need anything else—"

"Who's Elena?" *Yeah, yeah, I know. Real fucking smooth.* I curse myself out internally and try not to be too terrified by the darkness spreading across his face. "I'm sorry; I know it's none of my business, but—"

"You're right," he spits. "It isn't any of your business."

"I just want to know you a little better, Dmitri," I rasp. "I want to understand."

Anger ripples across his eyes. There's no mistaking that that's what it is, but this is different than any anger I've ever seen him show before. It's scarier by miles.

"You want to 'get to know me'? What the fuck do you think is going on here, Wren?"

I push up to my feet so that I'm not craning my neck to look up at him. "I just think—"

"You think, just because we've fucked a couple of times, that means we're in some sort of relationship?"

I draw in a breath. In my head, I start to sing, *Sticks and stones may break my bones, but words...*

"Or maybe you think of yourself as my mistress? It seems to be a role you're comfortable with, historically speaking."

Never mind. Words can definitely hurt me. Those hurt worse than anything he's ever said.

My vision blurs behind a veil of tears.

"That's not fair." The heat of my words is lost in their tremble.

"What's not 'fair' is that I'm stuck having a baby with you," Dmitri snarls. From my peripheral vision, I notice Bee lingering at the entrance to the living room. I can't bear to look at her. Either Dmitri doesn't see her or he just doesn't care. "Since you seem to be confused, let me make this clear for you—"

"Dmitri!" Bee's voice is raised in alarm, but he ignores her as he advances on me, suddenly huge and broad and utterly terrifying.

"We are not friends. We are not lovers. And you are most definitely not my girlfriend. You are nothing more to me than an incubator for my son. And once he's born, I will have no more use for you." He pauses just out of reach and stares at my tears unflinchingly. "Is that fucking clear enough for you?"

I nod once, turn tail, and run. "Wren!" Bee calls desperately, trying to grab me. I push past her and take refuge in my room. Except it's *not* my room; it's his. Everything is his.

His apartment.

His world.

"What happened to 'ride-or-die'?" I drawl over the lip of my steaming coffee mug.

"It's precisely *because* I'm your ride-or-die that I get to tell you when you're being an asshole. And guess what? The time for that is now."

I set my mug down and shove it away. Even coffee as black and acrid as my soul isn't helping this morning. "She doesn't fucking listen," I growl. "She's constantly questioning me. Always picking fights, refusing to accept the fact that I know better."

"Christ on a fucking cracker, man! Do you even hear yourself?" Bee slams her palms down on the counter. "You need to stop comparing her to Elena. It's not fair, Dmitri."

I bristle defensively. "I'm not doing that."

"Like hell you are! *'She doesn't listen. She's constantly questioning me. She's always picking fights.'* Wah-wah-fucking-*wah*. You're like a little baby. All I'm hearing is that you're threatened by the fact that she's her own person. She's got opinions and thoughts and she's not afraid to voice them. I get that you're not used to being with a woman like that—but maybe, just maybe, it's a good thing."

I rise to glare down at her, the stool scraping and tottering behind me. "What are you trying to say?" I demand. "That Elena wasn't her own person? That she didn't have opinions or thoughts of her own?"

Bee recoils and the intensity of her venom recedes. "Now, come on, D. I loved her, too. And you know that's not what I mean."

"Really?" I walk around the counter to corner her into the cabinets. "Because it feels like you've been taking potshots at

Elena for a while now. It feels like you have something to say about her."

Cornered though she is, Bee's jaw drops indignantly. "That is so not true. I'm just forced to skirt around the truth because I know it's a sensitive subject for you and I don't want to hurt you."

My fists clench tight at my sides. "What 'truth' are you skirting round?"

She darts a glance at the kitchen entrance, no doubt checking for Wren. But the hallway remains empty. "You know I loved Elena," she says again in a quiet croak. "She was—"

"I know what she was," I interrupt. "I don't need you to tell me."

Bee clamps her mouth shut for a moment and takes a deep breath through her nose. "You know what?" she says at last. "I'm not jumping into the cesspool with you. When you're ready to have a real conversation about this, then—"

Bzz. Bzz. Bzz.

I look down impatiently at my phone where it's shimmying across the countertop. "It's Aleksandr," I growl by way of explanation as I answer the call. "Yeah?"

"Dmitri." His voice is somber. Something's not right. "There's been an incident. Some of our guys had a clash with the Irish." I rise to my feet. "We got two of theirs, but… they got one of ours."

"Who?"

"Akim."

No. My free hand balls into a fist. "Fuck. His girlfriend is pregnant, isn't she?"

"Yeah." Aleks sounds lower than I've heard in a long time. It makes sense: he and Akim were born within months of each other. They've been close since the cradle. "I, uh... I was over there only last week for dinner, and I... I..." He takes a breath. "Dmitri?"

"Yes?"

"I can't tell her. I just can't do it, man."

"You don't have to," I answer at once. "I'll take care of it."

I say my goodbyes and we hang up. There are some days when playing the *pakhan* weighs heavy. This is one of them.

But it's what I was made to do.

As badly as I want to do anything but this, I have to go break the news to Akim's woman. Bee stares at me balefully as I grab my things and leave without another word.

Just before I cross into the elevator, though, I feel a gnawing unease in my gut like there's a fishhook tethering me to the guest bedroom. I don't relish the thought of leaving without talking to Wren first. Of abandoning her to whatever hell I'm putting her through right now.

It's my first clue that Bee is right. I was wrong.

But right now, I don't have time to be anything other than what my men need me to be.

So I press the button and descend. *"Doors closing,"* chimes the voice.

So is a chapter in my life I never asked for.

Irina cradles her pregnancy belly as though she's scared it might disappear on her.

I had no idea she was this far along. Even her belly button has popped. I can see its indent through the fabric of the soft cotton dress she's wearing. It's been forty minutes since I knocked on her door and broke the worst news of her life to her, and I'm still not sure she's fully processed it. I can't bring myself to leave her in this state.

She's gazing off at the picture wall on the far side of the room. She and Akim smile out from frame after frame. Happy, young, radiant.

"I can't believe it," she repeats. "He can't be gone. I can't believe he's gone."

"I'm going to take care of you, Irina," I intone softly for the thousandth time, not that it's done a bit of good." You and the baby."

She doesn't take her eyes off the photographs. "Akim always spoke highly of you, Dmitri." Her voice shakes for a moment before she regains control of herself. Slowly, she turns to me. Her eyes are free from tears now. Scrubbed bright and clean like the sky after a storm. "But when he spoke about you, it was as *pakhan*, not as family. It's not your job to look after us."

"Akim died in service to me and the Egorov Bratva. The least I can do is take care of his wife and child."

"We're not married." A rattling, weary exhale escapes through her lips. "He brought it up a couple of times after we found out about the baby, but… I'm the one who kept putting it off. It's just a piece of paper, I told him. *God.* That sounds so stupid now."

She drops her face into her hands as her whole body shakes, though she still refuses to let a single tear fall. I stand uncomfortably in place. It feels wrong to sit here, in another man's home, comforting another man's wife. I can't even take care of my own household; who am I to take care of Akim's?

And yet I must. There's no one else to do what must be done.

"You and your baby will have a monthly stipend in perpetuity. And if you ever have need of anything else—"

"Don't condescend to me," she snarls suddenly, ripping her hands away from her face. Her cheeks are blotchy but her eyes remain bright. "I'll tell you what I need, Dmitri: I need someone to squeeze my hand in the delivery room and tell me everything's going to be alright. I need someone to take my kid to kindergarten on days when I'm too sick to get out of bed. I need someone to hold me at night and quiet my fears. *That's* what I need, Dmitri. Can you give me that? Can you give me *any* of it?"

Springing to her feet, she jabs one quivering finger in my direction. If it weren't for the coffee table between us, I almost believe she'd go for my throat.

And fuck... maybe I'd let her. God knows I deserve it for the least of my sins, never mind the worst of them.

"Akim was my only family. And now that he's gone—" She lets out a strangled, feral cry. "How do I do this without him? I'm alone... all alone..."

Why the fuck am I seeing Wren every time I blink? It's Irina, then it's Wren; Irina; Wren.

Both pregnant and vulnerable.

Both lashing out because there's nowhere else to go with their pain.

"I know it feels that way now, but I assure you, you're not alone. Aleksandr and I have your back, Irina. The Bratva has your back. Your child will want for nothing."

She shakes her head. "Except a father. Try giving me that, Dmitri. You can't."

My chest is taut to the point of bursting, but there's nowhere else for me to put any of the things inside of it. *I* have to bear them. *I* have to hold them.

It's only me against all this anguish. I can't afford to bend and break.

I place a hand on Irina's shoulder. "Aleksandr will meet with you to discuss funeral arrangements. Do whatever seems fitting. I will take care of all the expenses."

She nods, a tear slipping down her cheek at last. That lone tear wounds me more than if she'd shed a flood of them.

I bow once and step out of their home. The night is bleak and chilly as I make my way to Egorov Industries, though I leave the windows down, as if the cold air in my face can cleanse me of the blood on my hands.

On the way there, I call Rogan. "I need you to draft something for me. And I need it ASAP."

I'm not sure how to fix everything with Wren.

But this might be a start.

55

WREN

The subdued knocking at my door is a one-way ticket from my depressive state of catatonia back to reality.

I sit up, bleary-eyed, just as Bee walks in with a tray overflowing with crackers and cheese. Color-coordinated toothpicks spear through grapes like kebabs.

"Felt sorry for me, so you decided to come fatten me up?" I observe in a dry mumble.

She sets the tray down on my bedside table and promptly climbs right in the bed with me. "This is more of an *I'm-sorry-my-best-friend-is-an-ass* cheese plate than a pity cheese plate."

I force a smile. "Thanks, but I'm not hungry."

Bee sighs and pats my knee through the covers. "He gets really weird about Elena. I stopped taking it personally a long time ago."

"I might have not taken it personally if he hadn't made it personal."

Bee grabs a grape and pops it into her mouth. "Fair point," she agrees between crunches.

Frowning, I slump down against the pillows. "He must have really loved her, huh?"

"Yeah. He did."

Her eyes flash to me and then away again. The discomfort is obvious, but fuck it—we're all living various uncomfortable lies in this house, so Bee and I might as well both get used to it. Dmitri is the only one who doesn't seem to be affected.

But then again, maybe he is. He just has a very different way of expressing it.

A significantly angrier, crueler, more verbally violent way.

"You don't need to stay and babysit me, you know," I add. "I'll be fine."

She glances to the side. I follow her gaze and cringe at the mess I've created. In the hours since Dmitri spat in my face and stormed out, I've pulled down books from their shelves, cut into the feather cushions with sewing scissors, and taken those same scissors to the surface of the vanity. Just little signs of my tantrums everywhere you look. I'm embarrassed as Bee's eyes pass over all of it.

"I, uh, I felt the need to rearrange. Or redecorate, or whatever you want to call it."

Bee smirks. "You did a fantastic job."

"I'm sorry. I'll clean it up."

She puts her hand on my leg. "Don't you dare. You have every right to let out some steam."

The door swings open without warning and reveals the last thing I expected: Dmitri standing there in a midnight black suit, with a white envelope in his hands.

He doesn't comment on the mess I've made of my room. Instead, he just strides calmly to the foot of the bed. "Bee, give us the room, please. Wren and I need to talk."

My back straightens out. "I have nothing to say to you."

Bee gets off the bed. "Maybe this isn't the right time, Dmitri—"

"Bee."

His tone is terrifying, but also terrifyingly effective. Even Bee yields to it when he sounds like that.

She throws a defeated glance over her shoulder at me. "I'll be in the living room if anyone needs me."

She slips out of the room. I redirect my attention to Dmitri. Maybe, under normal circumstances, I'd heel, but not today. Not tonight. Not like this.

If he expects me to be a docile, obedient little house slave, he's got another thing coming.

"I have something for you." He holds the envelope out to me.

I take it curiously, but with my finger poised to tear it open, I pause. "What is it?"

"Open and see."

His face is neutral. No sign of the stormy rage from earlier. Frowning, I rip the flap off and pull out the thick stack of papers inside. It's quickly obvious what I'm looking at. What's not obvious is *why*.

"This is a contract?"

"You can read it yourself," he confirms, "but in summary, it states that the apartment below this one is officially yours." I tense up. *What the hell does* that *mean?* "All expenses for said apartment will be covered by me. Your monthly salary will continue to be remitted into your account for your personal expenses. And once the baby is born, that amount will be increased proportionally."

There's no emotion in his voice. There's no expression on his face. He might as well be reading the weather forecast from a teleprompter.

"You will be safe, you will be comfortable, and you will have your own space."

My heart is thudding painfully as I extricate myself from the covers and get off the bed. At the end of the day, he can "remit" anything he wants to anyplace he wants, but there's only one way to sum up what this means.

"You want me gone."

"I want to give you the space you so obviously crave." His eyes slide to the mess I've made of the room. "Clearly, you're not happy here."

It's honestly pretty ingenious how he's turning this around on me. Like *I'm* the one who needs space. Like *I'm* the one who doesn't want him digging around in my past.

She said sarcastically.

"I don't need a whole new apartment when I already have one of my own."

"This is a compromise, Wren." His eyes narrow dangerously. "It's important that my child stays close to me. This way, we both get what we want."

"Which is…?"

"Space. Lots of it."

I feel like crying. No, I feel like screaming. Does he think he's being slick with this B.S.? Does he really think that elevating me to the status of glorified mistress, held at arm's length, will make me think that this is a good idea?

He pulls out a little white box from his pocket and deposits it on the bed. "These are the keys and the access code to your new apartment. It's unfurnished at the moment, but that can be easily remedied if you so choose. Feel free to go look at it whenever you want." He stands there for a few moments longer, but when I don't say anything, he turns towards the door. "Bee and I have somewhere to be this evening, but if you need anything, Aleksandr and I are both contactable."

He leaves me staring at the white box on my bed. A key. A key to a whole new life, to privacy and safety and room to breathe.

How can something so pretty be so insulting at the same time?

∼

I ignore the white box for hours before my curiosity finally gets the better of me. Well, that and the fact that I can actually leave the penthouse without supervision. So what if it's only one floor down? Small freedoms are better than no freedoms.

Except that, when the elevator doors open into my own private penthouse, I realize it's not freedom at all; it's just another pretty cage.

And it's got "Dmitri Egorov" stamped all over it.

Quite literally, actually. He must have done a walkthrough earlier, because I can smell his smoky scent in the air. There's nothing to distract from it except the view. One floor lower, but otherwise, no different than the one I'd just left.

"God," I whisper to myself as I slide onto the floor and lie flat with my eyes trained towards the ceiling. "How is this my life?"

It's not the first time I've asked myself that question. The answer hasn't changed, though. By which I mean, the *lack* of an answer hasn't changed.

I keep reaching out to find some explanations for any of it— *why is Rose dead?* and *why did my father leave?* and *why did William lie?* and *why is Dmitri doing this to me?*

But I keep coming up empty. Grasping at nothing. Shadows passing through my hands like sand at the beach.

I close my eyes and take inventory of what I know, the things that I can hold in my palms and be certain of.

I'm pregnant with a dangerous man's baby.

If I stay, I'm going to have to live a lie right under his heel.

If I leave, I'll have to look over my shoulder for the rest of my life.

It doesn't feel like much of a choice. But then, I've made difficult choices before. I can do it again if I must.

"Wren?" I sit up when Bee walks into the empty living room an hour or so later. "Bingo. I thought I'd find you in here."

She's wearing a black dress and an elegant updo, like a stretched-out Audrey Hepburn. "You look nice," I mumble.

Her smile is half-hearted as she pulls on the folds of her dress. "This ol' thang? Thanks."

"Is there a reason you look like a Disney princess on her way back from a funeral?"

Her lips tug up at the corners in a reluctant smile. "Because I'm on my way back from a funeral, actually."

"Shit. I'm sorry, Bee." My cheeks are red with embarrassment.

Leave it to me to make a flippant joke that hits way too close to home. I'm on fire these days.

She waves away my apology. "It's all good. It was a Bratva funeral, not a personal one." She sighs before lying down on the wooden floors next to me. "Still sucks, though."

"I'm with you on that one."

Even now, I can't think of funerals without feeling the ghost of an itch down my torso. I have only one mourning dress and it scratched like hell. I wore it to Mom's funeral and then, years later, I wore it to Rose and Jared's. Even after they all left me, the itch from the zip remained.

Such a petty, insignificant reminder of days that hurt so much.

"You okay?"

I stop scratching and force my hand down to the side. "Yeah. Fine."

"Well," Bee concludes, "this is uncomfortable." She sits up with a low groan and stretches. "Why the hell are you lying here on the floor?"

"Because there's nowhere else to go."

She shoots me a pitying look. "You can talk to me. You know that, right?" *Do I know that, though? I'm not so sure.* "I know you're pissed at him, Wren, and you have every right to be. But he is making an effort—"

"'An effort'?" I laugh deliriously, pulling my legs up to my chest. "This? This bullshit? This isn't 'effort.' This is his way of controlling and manipulating me. You heard him the other night—I'm nothing more than a walking, talking incubator to him. Actually, scratch that: preferably not a 'talking' one at all."

"He regrets what he said to you, Wren. That's why he wanted to make this gesture—"

Cutting her off again, I shake my head vehemently. "Please. He gave me this penthouse under the guise of generosity, but it's really just a front for his own motives. He tells me that he's giving me space, but it's just smoke and mirrors. This isn't my space; it's his. It's *all* his." Bee opens her mouth but I shut her up by raising my palm. "I'm not interested in hearing from his spokeswoman right now, Bee. If you're gonna speak, I'd like to hear from my *friend*."

Her lips come together and she nods silently. Then she gets to her feet, dusts off her dress and offers me her hand. "Come on. We're getting out of here."

I'm not a huge fan of this empty penthouse. But the one upstairs isn't a whole lot better. "I'm not ready to go up yet."

"We're not going up. We're going *out*."

My eyes widen disbelievingly. "Where?"

"Somewhere that's not here." She gives me a reassuring smile. "You want some real space? Well, then let's go get you some."

56

DIMITRI

DMITRI: *Where the hell are you?*

BEE: *I stayed as long as I could. You know funerals aren't my thing.*

I grimace, but I can hardly blame her. I still remember the way she cried when her mother died. Big, loud, ugly sobs that aged her by years. She was only thirteen and completely unprepared to live her life without her mother. She nearly threw herself on that coffin as it was lowered into the ground.

Of course, Vittorio wasn't there. No one was. The Zanetti mafia weren't in the habit of mourning their don's former mistresses, so there was no one there for her but me. I'd clutched her around the waist as she screamed for her mother, wondering how it was possible to hold together a person who was on the verge of breaking.

A minute later, Bee sends me a picture of a sprawling hotel bed, trussed up in a pillowy duvet with the *Ritz Carlton* logo stamped on the linen. It's a bit of a departure for Bee. She usually tends to bury any negative feelings under retail therapy. Then again, it might be a little too late in the evening for any serious shopping.

Not that that's ever stopped her before.

Another picture pops up on my screen. She's lying on the bed with one arm thrown up to the side.

And she's not alone.

It takes a second before I realize that the woman lying next to her isn't some random cocktail waitress she picked up at a bar.

It's Wren.

My Wren.

DMITRI: *What the fuck are you doing? Wren's not supposed to leave the penthouse.*

BEE: *Chill. I'm with her.*

That doesn't make me feel any better. I home in on the picture, zooming in on Wren's face. Her eyes are closed and I'm not even sure she's aware she's being photographed. She looks so *sad.* Or maybe I'm reading too much into it. Maybe she's just tired?

Either way—I want to know.

I get to my feet, leaving the circle of men sitting around Akim's living room, exchanging stories about the man and drinking in his honor. Aleksandr turns to me. "Everything alright?"

"When's the last time *anything* was alright?" I demand. "Much less *everything?*" Aleks looks too inebriated to decipher my snarling. "I've got something I need to do. You'll hold down the fort here?"

"Of course."

"Make sure Irina is doing okay."

"Yeah, I—" He hiccups mid-sentence. "I will."

I head across town to the Ritz, unsure how to approach this situation. I mean, for fuck's sake, I made a peace offering and she throws it in my face by breaking the rules? I shoot off a quick text to Bee.

I need a room number.

Instead of texting back, Bee calls. "You *came*? My God, Dmitri, we need to talk about boundaries."

"I agree. The boundaries line up perfectly with the penthouse walls. You're the one who broke them."

"You're gonna have to wrap your head around the fact that Wren and I are not yours to command. You can't just boss us around like your little toy soldiers."

"Wanna bet?" I snarl.

She sighs dramatically. "Yeah, sure, throw your weight around; see how well that works. All that'll do is push her further away. She'll get suspicious of even the good stuff. Leave it to you to make gifts feel like punishments.."

I stop short. "The apartment was a peace offering."

"Did she seem happy when you gave her the keys?"

I'm about to answer when my mouth snaps shut. Truth is, Wren had been uncharacteristically quiet. She didn't look happy by any stretch of the imagination, but I'd assumed she was just processing.

"Wait—"

"For God's sake, Dmitri—Wren is not Elena! They're not the same person. You can't assume throwing Wren an expensive present is going to solve any of your problems, much less all of them."

"I didn't have problems with Elena."

"Because she worshiped you!" Bee hisses. "Unhealthily, in fact. If you'd told her to jump off the Brooklyn Bridge, she'd have done it. Wren is not gonna be as easy to manipulate."

"That's not what I'm doing."

"No? She wanted some independence, so you gave her the apartment below yours. *After* you told her that she was a walking, talking incubator. You gave her a tomb for a womb. Doesn't that just roll off the tongue, hm?"

"Fuck me," I mutter.

This is all turning to shit in my hands. I suppose it's what I get for trying to do a nice thing. It's all just getting thrown back in my face.

But that does pose a question: *was* I trying to do a nice thing for Wren? Or was the downstairs apartment really a gift from me to me? If I kept her locked up out of sight, I'd be in control of my life again. No insolence, no fiery temptations.

Who pays the bigger price for my inability to keep a lid on my own desires: Wren… or me?

"Just a heads up," Bee chimes in, "she's at the ground floor restaurant, picking up some food."

I shake my head to dispel the thoughts crowding in. "I'm taking her home."

"Did you not hear a word I said?"

"We need to sort this shit out before the baby comes. It's not like I have time to waste."

She sighs. "Fine. Do as you please, not that you need my permission for that. But just so you know, I'm staying. Can't let this perfectly good room go to waste. Oh, and Dmitri?"

"What?"

"For once in your goddamn life, don't be an asshole."

I hang up as I storm into the lobby. Almost simultaneously, Wren emerges from the sliding glass doors on the left with a tote bag of food slung off her arm. Her gaze is so fixed on the patterned marble floor that she doesn't even notice me slipping into the elevator behind her. It isn't until I've pressed the emergency button and the elevator lurches to a stop that she looks up.

"Dmitri?!" she nearly screams.

I shake my head. "What am I going to do with you?"

The shock on her face twists into disgust. "Oh, gee, I don't know. You could do what you do best: throw more money at the problem and expect it to go away. Maybe a second apartment so I can store all the gifts you're planning on bribing me with?"

I was so proud when I handed her those keys. *You're doing a good thing,* I told myself. *Put a feather in your fucking cap, you Good Samaritan you.*

Idiot. Goddamn idiot.

"I didn't mean to offend you—"

"Didn't you, though?" she interrupts venomously. "No, of course not. You meant to offend me right *before* then, when you said I was no better than your mistress. That's all I am to you, right? A cheap whore to be used and discarded at the pleasure of a powerful asshole with more money than decency!"

She makes a lot of good points. So I say two words I don't know that I've ever said before.

"I'm sorry."

Her jaw drops. "E-excuse me?"

I take a step towards her, but she just backs up against the elevator's padded back wall. "I'm sorry about what I said to you earlier. I regret it." I make sure to meet her eyes. "Deeply."

Her eyes scrunch up. "What's the catch?"

"There's no catch. I'm apologizing for being an asshole. You told me things about your past in confidence and I weaponized them. It was wrong." She holds my gaze tremulously like she's waiting for the other shoe to drop. "Giving you your own apartment was meant to be a gesture of goodwill. You wanted some independence, space of your own—and I was trying to give you what you wanted."

She blinks, her eyes sliding away from mine. "You think *any* of this is what I wanted?" Her voice is raspy, quiet, and shaky with emotion.

"I'm trying here, Wren."

She snorts derisively. "Well, clearly, you're not used to trying at all. With anyone! Do you even realize how hot and cold you blow? I can't keep up! One day, you're making me breakfast, watching me undress, and telling me how beautiful I am. The next day, you're looking at me as though I'm some sort of calamity that happened to you. A bag of burning dog shit that got dropped on your doorstep. How am I supposed to keep up?"

"I know it's not fair—"

She holds up a hand to stop me. "Spare me the lecture. I'm intimately acquainted with how *un*fair life can be, Dmitri. I lost my father to a whole other family. Then Rose and I lost our mother's mind to grief before we lost the rest of her to cancer. I used to think that every person had a quota of pain they had to endure. And after we buried Mom, I thought, *Surely, surely now we've reached our quota*—but no. Life wasn't even close to being done with me. It gave me *you* instead."

Ironically, as Wren speaks, it's Bee's words that start to sink in. *Wren is not Elena. They're not the same person.*

I've made the mistake of treating Wren the way I would have dealt with Elena. The difference is, Elena didn't have much of a life before she met me.

If I was ever cruel, I would apologize the next day by buying her something. She would accept my apology with a smile and a kiss. And that was it. There would be no conversation, no tears, no dramatics. I used to think it was one of the most wonderful things about our relationship.

But suddenly, I'm seeing it in a different light. Was it surgery or was it simply a Band-Aid over a bullet wound?

"You're right."

She exhales sharply. "Is this you humoring me again?"

sketches of her next great idea. Birds on a power line; waves breaking against a barnacle-clad rock; a dancer in flight, one leg kicked up, hands high over her head, a haunted look of bittersweet nostalgia on her face.

The pages have turned sallow, curling in at the edges. When I pick up one sketch, the paper feels like it's moments away from disintegrating in my hand. "You were so damn talented."

"You're biased."

"Not true. Your paintings made me *feel* things."

"Then why did you take them all down?"

I glance to the side wall, where dozens of her paintings sit propped up with their backs facing out, so all I can see is wood frames and the ragged edges of unpainted canvas.

"Because they made me feel too much," I admit.

A draft passes through the door, kicking up the acrid tang of acrylic and sawdust. I used to bury my nose in her hair at the end of the day and breathe that in. On her, the scent was beautiful. Now, it just makes me wrinkle my nose and wave it away.

"I created these paintings for you, you know. Everything I did, everything I was, was for you."

Moonlight spills across her empty canvases, casting dots of bright white that dance across the blank surfaces. If I squint, I can almost see her ghost sitting in front of me, paintbrush poised with the tip of the handle pressed against her lips as she thought.

"I know. And I couldn't do the one thing that I promised you I would do. I couldn't keep you safe."

She half-turns to me, enough to illuminate her profile in the moonbeam. That little cleft in her chin—I haven't thought about it in so long.

"You should have learned by now, Dmitri: don't make promises you can't keep."

"I was so sure I could do it. Even after I held you there, frozen and lifeless, I was sure I could bring you back through sheer force of will."

"You held me, yes. But you never cried for me. Not once."

"What would tears have changed?"

"Nothing. Except for the wall around your heart. Except for the dam you locked your grief behind."

"Some things are too painful to feel."

"Is that why you're so drawn to her? You see in her all the pain you've refused to let yourself process?"

I pluck up one of her sketches and move to the window. "She wears her heart on her sleeve and she doesn't apologize for it."

"Maybe you could learn a thing or two from her."

"Are you giving me your blessing?"

I glance to the side and for a moment, it really does feel like she's standing there with me; her favorite blue and white bandana holding back the donkey fringe she'd once referred to as her "quarter-life crisis."

"I think you should stop feeling so guilty for wanting her."

"You're my wife."

"I haven't been your wife for a long time, Dmitri. It's time to stop putting me on that pedestal. It's tiring work to stay up there."

Unease trembles across my skin. "Is that how you felt?"

"If you remember me as perfect, if you're remembering our marriage as perfect—then you're remembering wrong."

"*Blyat*," I mutter, my hand tightening around the sketch, crumpling up half of the too-thin paper. I drop it before I destroy the rest of it and drift past her easel to the nook in the corner.

It's a smorgasbord of patterns, shapes, and colors. A fat green sofa, a patchwork beanbag, a sleek glass table riddled with paint drippings, a color-blocked carpet with fraying ends. Nothing matches and yet it all goes together anyway.

Have I spent the last few years pining over a dream? Even worse, did I spend my entire marriage idealizing the woman I was married to? My mind picks away at raw memories that I've spent so much time suppressing until they feel distant and blurry. Every time I try to wrap my hands around them, they disintegrate like the sketches on the desk.

Was Bee right this entire time and I've just been too stubborn to listen?

"She's so damn different than you," I whisper.

"Maybe that's why you care so much about her."

"That doesn't make sense."

"She challenges you. She excites you. She doesn't put up with your shit the way I used to. You were a boy when we met and I was perfect for you then. But you're not a boy anymore, Dmitri."

"I feel like I'm betraying you."

There's a reason I've avoided this room for so long. There's a reason I took down all her paintings the moment she died and turned their faces away from me.

"You don't want to betray me? Then do me a favor, my love. Remember me as I really was."

I wish I could. But sometimes, it's easier holding onto dreams than reality.

58

WREN

Dmitri's dark circles are glaring when he walks into the kitchen the next morning, oddly underdressed by his standards in gray sweatpants and a plain white t-shirt.

"Coffee?" I ask.

He nods silently and takes the stool opposite me. I can feel the unspoken conversation he promised me hanging in the air between us.

"You look like you had a rough night," I say to break the silence.

"I was in her art studio. Didn't get much sleep."

I eye him from behind my mug. He hasn't mentioned a name, but it doesn't take a genius to fill in the blankets. It might take a mind reader to figure out why he's suddenly so open to discussing her now, though.

"Elena was an artist?"

He flinches when I say her name, but he shrugs just as casually as I asked the question. "I would say yes. She would object. She'd just say she liked to paint."

When he finally looks up at me, I see how red and raw his eyes are. I can't imagine him shedding a tear, but there's nothing else that wrecks a persons' face quite like grief pouring free.

"What did she like to paint?"

He picks up his coffee mug and gets to his feet. "Come and see for yourself."

I'm more than a little stunned. It's one thing to hear him open up about Elena; it's another thing entirely to have him invite me into her space. "Are you sure?"

He just gestures me forward and we walk to the east wing together. The door is slightly ajar and I can already smell metallic paints and aged wood. He swings the door open and stands aside to let me pass.

I hold my breath as I step inside. I see couches, bookshelves, windows with light streaming in, but my attention is drawn to the row of easels bearing mostly blank canvases.

I shudder—it feels like she's still in here, always just out of sight no matter which way I turn. Her paintings are everywhere. So are her books, her colors, her smell. I never once in my life saw this woman and somehow, I feel as though I know her already.

"It's beautiful," I murmur. For some reason, I talk softly. It feels as though we've entered sacred space. I wonder if Dmitri feels the same way.

"She spent hours in here every day," he rumbles from the doorway where he's leaning. "If she wasn't painting, she was reading on the sofa or knitting by the window."

I walk over to the table beside her easels and run a tentative finger along the paint-splattered edge. I'm scared to touch anything, scared to move anything, though even just the motion of us entering the room has sent the sketches fluttering across the desktop.

I turn towards Dmitri. He's still in place by the threshold, gazing around the room like he's not sure what to make of it anymore. "Thank you for letting me in here."

His eyes find mine. "The room's yours."

I gape at him. "Pardon?"

Uncrossing his arms, he pushes tall and walks toward me. "I've been holding her memory hostage in here. Refusing to let her go, refusing to move on myself. It's not what she would have wanted. Her paintings deserve to be displayed proudly, not hidden away as though they're something to be ashamed of."

I stand still. Dmitri watches me quietly. "I know what it means to love someone so much that the only way you can cope with their absence is to pretend they never existed in the first place," I whisper. "I know how much that hurts."

He looks me right in the eye and I feel something powerful pass between us. I can't put my finger on what, exactly, but suddenly, I don't feel as though I'm trespassing anymore.

"It's a losing battle."

I smile sadly. "Trust me, I know. But grief robs you of common sense." I step close enough to place a hand on his arm. "I appreciate the gesture, Dmitri, but you don't have to give me this room. It's hers."

"No," he replies firmly. "It *was* hers. I want you to have it."

"You already gave me a whole apartment, remember?" I'm trying for breezy and casual, but the wobble in my voice gives me away.

"That was a stupid decision," he admits with a sigh. "I wasn't trying to get rid of you, Wren. And I wasn't trying to erase you from our son's life. I was genuinely trying to show you that I was listening when you said you needed space."

My heart thuds in my chest. "I'd argue that a six-bedroom apartment is maybe a little too much space for one person."

He inclines his head in a silent concession. "Fair enough. Which is why we're standing in the happy compromise."

"I don't want to usurp her place in your life," I blurt out. "Not that I'm trying to replace her; not that I ever *could*… I just, um…" My words fade into awkward quiet. "Honestly, I'm not sure what I'm trying to say."

Dmitri raises a careful hand to pass his thumb tenderly over my cheek. "This isn't about replacing anyone, Wren. It's just time. I've never seen the point in shrines anyway."

I bite my bottom lip. "I wouldn't have the first clue what to do with this place."

"Then start simple," he suggests. "Pick a new color for the walls. Everything else will follow."

As he lets go of me and turns towards the door, I'm overwhelmed with the urge to tell him just how much this means to me.

A room is one thing.

Space is another.

Him opening up to me is another still.

And if that can happen…

Maybe "trust" isn't so far behind.

So I do the only reasonable thing I can do in this situation, really. I run after him—grab him—and give him a kiss that says all the things I can't find the words to say.

59

DMITRI

We collapse to the ground in a surprised tangle of limbs. If it hurts, she doesn't notice, and neither do I. I'm too busy consuming every bit of Wren I can get. She tastes like peaches and cherries. All sweet saltiness and soft heat.

The thin cotton of her white blouse is flimsy underneath my hands. I'm about to rip it clean off when she moves to straddle me, her nails digging into my neck. My hand slides from her hip to her ass, trying to guide her closer—when I become aware of something cool and sticky at my side.

She lets out a startled little gasp and breaks the kiss. Both of us snap around to see the upturned paint can beside us.

"Shit!" Wren gasps, jerking off of me. "I'm so sorry, I didn't see—" She lurches forward and pulls up the spilled can, only to upend another paint can with her foot. "God, Dmitri, I'm —fuck! Shit!"

"It's fine, Wren."

She doesn't seem to be listening. "Spiraling" might be closer to the truth. "No, it's not. It's really, really not. This is Elena's space and I just fucked it up and kissed her husband and —"

I shut her up by stroking my hand against the side of her face. Her eyes flit to mine, the blush subsiding, if only just a little. The paint on my hand leaves a streak of baby blue on her cheek. "This isn't Elena's space anymore. And I'm not her husband. I haven't been for a long time." I pull her closer until her soft curves melt against my body. "It's time to breathe some new life into this room. It's what she would have wanted."

"Are… are you sure?"

I answer by pressing my lips back down on hers. If I'm being honest, I like the paint. It feels right.

This room, this world, this heart of mine… it's all been sterile and sealed for far too long.

I'm in the mood to make a mess of it.

Wren lets out a startled yelp when I drag her down onto the floor. My fingers find the end of her blouse and tease it up over her growing belly. My God, it's such a turn-on knowing that that's my child inside her. If I get any harder, I might explode.

I peel off her clothes as she lies there and lets me, panting heavily, her eyes sparking and lips fluttering wordlessly every time I touch her. Her legs part to make room for me and she bites her lip when I touch the wet heat between her thighs.

I happen to glance down at her bare chest and see something that makes my mouth twitch up in a smirk—daubs of bumblebee yellow paint arcing around the curve of Wren's breast.

That, too, feels right.

Marking her. Claiming her. In streaks of yellow and blue paint, in lovebites and nibbles scored along the curve of her neck.

Inside and out, she's mine.

Head to toe, she's *mine.*

And if that's not enough, when Wren sees what I'm seeing, her eyes light up with a spark of mischief. She plants a hand in the puddle of paint oozing around us, reaches up, and marks me just like I've marked her. A handprint of yellow stamped right in the center of my chest.

I'm hers every bit as much as she's mine.

That, too, feels right.

We fuck—slowly at first, then harder and faster. I don't look away from her and she sure as hell doesn't look away from me. She's a writhing, moaning mess of yellow and blue and bright green eyes in the midst of it all.

She comes and I come, though fuck if I know the order or the way in which it happens. I just know that I'm losing myself in Wren Turner and there's not a chance in hell that either of us can turn back now that we've come this far.

"God," she breathes at last, rolling off me. "We've made a mess."

"Worth it."

She smiles self-consciously, looking down at her body. There's evidence of my work all over her. Her hair is a disheveled mess knotted up in a rat's nest on top of her head, marred with more streaks of paint. She looks well and truly fucked. It's the most beautiful I've ever seen her—and if I've said that before, then sue me, because it's true every time.

I get to my feet and offer her my hand. "We'll need to wash off quickly before the paint settles and you look like this forever."

I guide her to the shower, holding her up so her trembling legs don't give out beneath her. When we step under the hot shower spray, I keep my hands on her, smoothing them over the paint streaks again and again until the water drips clear.

Wren's eyes have lost some of their luster when I circle back to look her in the face, though. I frown. "Everything okay?"

Her lip wobbles for a fraction of a second before she sucks it between her teeth. She steps up and folds herself in my embrace. "What are we doing, Dmitri?" she murmurs softly.

The moment the question leaves her lips, I see ghosts. A whole damn horde of them, lurking just beyond the frosted glass of the shower, staring balefully at me in reminder and accusation.

Rose. Jared. Elena.

How cruelly ironic that the losses that helped bring us together might be the same ones that tear us apart.

But only if she finds out.

"I don't know," I confess quietly.

Her fingers run from my abs to my chest, then back again. "I'm scared."

My hand curls around her waist protectively. I know I have to tell her. This is too big a secret to keep hidden. But at the same time, I wonder if maybe that's exactly why I should shield her from it.

Some truths are too big, too dangerous, too heavy to hold. Especially if the goal is to put them behind you and move on.

"I can protect you, Wren."

"That's not what I'm talking about." She shudders. "After… after everything, I vowed that I'd never be another man's mistress. And somehow…" Her eyes travel up to mine. "… I find myself making excuses to be yours."

I tip her chin up with the crook of my finger. Those eyes are flush with longing, with desire, and yes, there's fear there, too. Fear most of all. "You already are mine," I tell her firmly. "There's no going back now."

But even as I say it, I can't help but wonder…

Am I trying to convince her—

Or myself?

60

WREN

"This is the freaking *life*."

Syrah is spread out on one of the freshly unpacked lounge chairs in my newly christened den, a fluffy white towel keeping her hair up, sliced cucumbers over her eyes, and her mani-pedi still gleaming as it dries.

Chuckling, I tuck my blanket in around my legs. "Glad you're enjoying my baby shower."

She sits up straighter and removes the cucumbers from her eyes. She pops one into her mouth, ignoring my look of utter disgust, and peeks towards the door cautiously.

"Where's Bee?" she asks in a low voice.

"Still in the kitchen, apparently."

"She's super nice."

"You seem shocked," I observe with a laugh.

"Well, I mean, I kinda am. I didn't even realize you guys were that close until you told me she was hosting a baby shower for you."

I eye the small tower of presents beside the coffee table that Bee had warned me against touching until she came back. "It took me by surprise, too. We've gotten close since I've been living here, but I didn't expect… all this."

Syrah eats the remaining cucumber. "Tell it to me straight: is she your number one now? Are you leaving me for her?"

I giggle. "Don't be ridiculous. You'll always be my work wife. Even if we're not technically working together anymore."

She sighs and settles back, only temporarily sated. "Honestly, I wouldn't even blame you. I mean, look at all those gifts. I've never been great at math but even I can solve this equation. There are exactly two guests at this party and there are at least two dozen presents. And since I bought only one—"

"It's not a competition, Sy."

"Of course not. She wiped the floor with my ass!"

I snort and reach for my glass of lemonade. "Stop it. I love you both. And since the two of you get along great, I see no reason why we can't all—"

"Have a three-way relationship?"

"Sure, that's exactly what I was thinking."

Syrah gives me a salacious little wink. "Great minds, huh?"

"Great. Dirty. Depraved. Whichever adjective you wanna use."

Giggling, Syrah glances over her shoulder and then lowers her voice even further. "I'll be honest. I thought this setup was hella weird. But seeing you here with Bee... I dunno. It works."

That familiar sense of guilt creeps up all over again. I so desperately want to tell Syrah the truth about our little live-in arrangement—but every time I practice the conversation in my head, it sounds so outlandish that I scrap the idea altogether.

I fidget uncomfortably. "Thanks. We're still figuring it out."

"And how are you getting along with him?"

Ah. *Him.*

The answer to that question has been pretty simple of late. Because things with him have been great. And I'm talking capital G-R-E-A-T, great. Since our little paint sexcapade three weeks ago, life with Mr. Egorov has been the smoothest sailing.

More often than not, he spends the nights with me, sleeping and also lots and lots of not-sleeping. He usually comes home late, but I either wake up to him the next morning or I get a midnight, mid-dream interruption in the form of his tongue between my thighs.

It is so, so worth the broken sleep.

The best part—well, second-best after the mind-blowing sex—is that he hasn't been as closed-off as he used to be. We don't sit around, gossiping about our hopes and dreams or our deepest, darkest secrets or who has a crush on who, but he isn't so averse to mentioning little tidbits about his past or his life anymore, either.

I knew that he had a lot of respect for his father, but "love" wasn't really a word he associated with the old man. I knew that he had a fierce sense of obligation to his *vors* (another term that he has only recently introduced me to) and that his Bratva functioned like an extended family, albeit with a hierarchy and a specific set of rules, but I didn't know just how far that sense of loyalty extended.

It feels like I'm putting together a collage, grabbing greedily at the little scraps he offers me and pasting them into a clearer, more complete picture of Dmitri Egorov.

And as it turns out, it's much easier to forgive the possessive, stubborn side of his personality when you see how deeply he cares about the people in his life. Bee, for one example.

Elena, for another.

Some of his wife's paintings are now hanging around the apartment. That was more my doing than his, though he didn't stand in my way for a second. He helped me hang them himself, actually.

It isn't that I'm not jealous of the love he had for her; I'm not quite that enlightened yet. I'm just mature enough to understand that a man who's capable of that kind of loyalty and care has enough to go around.

Enough to give to a woman who's maybe just a tad bit insecure, but very earnest. A woman who's clumsy but well-intentioned, deeply romantic but terrified of being hurt. A woman who's falling deeper and deeper in love with him with every passing day.

To a woman like *me*.

"Wren?"

Jeez, I'd totally spaced on Syrah. "Sorry," I mutter. "Um, things with him are fine. We get along great." I cringe inwardly. Is that maybe a little too much? "I mean, we get along good. Fine. Fine and good."

I want to smack my palm against my forehead and shout a successive stream of *Idiot, idiot, idiot.*

"Fine *and* good, huh?" Syrah asks, eyeing me suspiciously. "Sure sounds like it."

She's no fool; she senses that I'm not telling her everything. But I know my friendship with Bee is throwing her for a loop. She knows me well enough to know that I would never betray another woman by cheating with her man, particularly not a friend, so maybe she's just chalking up my awkwardness to a harmless crush.

Luckily, the focus is pulled from my guilty conscience when Bee careens her way back into the den with a full-on food cart, one of the ones you get in fancy restaurants where they serve your meals under silver cloches and pronounce "confit" and "sauvignon" correctly.

"Okay, ladies!" she announces. "It's time to stuff ourselves to the gills and start opening presents!"

"Finally!" Syrah exclaims, clapping her hands together. She throws herself onto the soft white carpet that forms the base of my sitting area and props her elbows on the wooden coffee table. "Which present are you going for first?"

Bee laughs. "Ah, I see the order has been reversed. So be it! Gifts now; food later."

I reach for Syrah's gift first. It turns out to be a double whammy: a gift for the baby (a set of three onesies) and a gift for me (a sexy leather bustier).

"That's for your post-mom bod," Syrah explains as I hold the bustier up to my chest. "You're gonna have to find that baby a father at some point, right? Well, this will reel him in hook, line, and sinker."

I'm glad she doesn't notice the look Bee shoots me from across the coffee table. Blushing furiously, I thank Syrah with a flying kiss and reach for the next present.

Most of them are for the baby, all of which are expensive and smell of artisanal perfumes, but some are for me. Like a set of poetry books that I mentioned once to Dmitri I'd seen in a bookstore in London but was too broke to buy. I also get a sprawling collection of French creams and perfumes from Bee.

"You've done too much, Bee," I protest. I'm giving her the full credit, all the while knowing that Dmitri is responsible for at least half these presents and the ideas behind them.

I'm not the only one who's been catching spare scraps and assembling a collage, it seems.

"Nonsense! I've done just enough."

"Wait!" Syrah says urgently, pulling up a thin red envelope wrapped in a dainty silver ribbon. Amidst all the excitement and chaos of unwrapping, it must have slipped under the coffee table. "You missed one."

"Who do I have to thank for this?" I ask, looking between Syrah and Bee.

Syrah holds up her empty palms. "Sadly. I can't take credit."

"Neither can I," Bee agrees. "Not sure I even noticed that one when the bellboy brought up all the goodies."

I grin from ear to ear. The envelope has Dmitri's fingerprints all over it; I'm just hoping it's not the deed to another apartment. I pull out the glossy papers inside.

... Pictures?

My brain feels like it's short-circuiting for a moment when I finally take in what I'm seeing. They're not the glossy, professional prints I was expecting. They're grainy and pixelated, zoomed in from afar. I'm looking at shady freeze frames from CCTV footage of a dark street in what I'm pretty sure is Chicago.

I catch sight of a street sign and confirm—definitely Chicago. As a matter of fact, that's the street where…

And why does that car look so familiar…?

"Wren? Is everything alright?"

Is that Bee asking, or Syrah? My heart is hammering so hard against my chest I can't distinguish between their voices.

I move to the next picture. This one is different. Clearer. I can see the two people sitting in the driver and passenger seat of the car that I could swear is the same one that—

My blood goes cold instantly.

That's why the car looks so familiar. When I remember that old Ford Focus, I see it only the way it looked after the accident. Nothing more than a glorified tin can, crushed and bent like the body of an accordion.

"Oh, God…" I whisper.

"Wren, what's wrong?"

Bee moves to take the pictures from my hands but I rip away from her before she can. Despite my seven-month stomach, I lurch to my feet fast and run straight for the bathroom, taking the pictures with me. I slam the door shut and flip through the photographs I haven't seen yet.

I was wrong; Dmitri had nothing to do with this envelope. Which begs the question: why would someone send me pictures of Rose and Jared's crash?

I freeze on the fourth photograph in the bunch. My fingers are trembling so hard that I almost drop them all.

No. No. No.

But it's not a trick of the mind. It's not Photoshop. It's not doctored.

It's Dmitri.

He's standing on the curb, gazing at the Ford Focus. He's got a gun in his hand and his arm raised, pointed straight at the car.

Straight at my sister.

This should be a happy moment. But how can it be? Dmitri has stolen everything from me—including the joy of this miracle pregnancy. Even that is called into question. How "miraculous" was it, really? What strings did he pull?

Knocking pounds at the door. Hard and angry.

My jaw tightens with determination. Bee can knock 'til she's blue in the face; I'm not opening the door and I'm sure as hell done talking to—

The lock turns. I feel the protest in my throat but before it has a chance to come out, the door swings open.

It's not Bee on the other side.

It's him.

Dmitri's gaze slides from me to the array of pictures on the floor. I'm hoping to see something other than cold impassiveness, but he's got his poker face on. He walks into the bathroom and kneels down in front of me. I pull my legs in tight and try to make my body as small as possible. If he touches me, I'll scream bloody murder, I swear I will.

"Wren—"

"Don't you fucking dare—"

I don't really know what I'm trying to say. *Don't you dare lie to me? Don't you dare touch me? Don't you dare make me care about you?* He's already done all of that. The sins have been committed. The damage has been done.

"Let me explain."

Tears pour down my cheeks as I stare back at him. "Those pictures are real, aren't they?"

"Yes," he says. I flinch; it physically hurts. He didn't even hesitate. "Yes, they're real."

I probably shouldn't close my eyes in front of a cold-blooded killer, but then again, what is even the point? He's already got me in his lair and under his control. The last several months have been a masterclass in manipulation. He didn't have to force me into anything, not truly. I just offered up my bare neck to him like an idiot lamb at the slaughter.

And what was I doing while he lulled me into a false sense of security?

I'd been daydreaming about his silver eyes. The sharp square of his granite jaw. The way his muscles rippled with every movement.

I let him seduce me… this monster who killed my sister in cold blood.

"Sh-she was perfect," I stutter, sobs wrenching from my chest. "She was kind and beautiful and bright and brilliant and you murdered her!"

He doesn't so much as blink. "If I knew then what I know now, I would have spared her. I wouldn't have punished her for her husband's crimes."

I'm so lost in my own shock and grief that I almost miss that last part. "'Husband'? '*Crimes*'? This is about Jared?"

"Jared and the men he decided to get in bed with, yes."

I squint at him furiously. "I knew Jared. He didn't move in the circles you do. He was a good man. He was a decent man."

"He may have been—once upon a time. But even decent men do desperate things sometimes. And Jared was desperate enough to go to the Irish."

The Irish? "Are you talking about—"

"The O'Gadhras," he fills in bluntly.

"Cian?!" I exclaim. "That's impossible; he's a good guy. He's—"

"At the time, he was brother to Cathal O'Gadhra, boss of the Irish mafia. You spent some time with Cian; surely you noticed the wolfhound tattoo on his right arm. That's the mark of the O'Gadhra mafia."

"Impossible. Cian and Jared were friends. He used to come over for dinner, for fuck's sake!" I shake my head, even as a snapshot memory of Cian rolling up his sleeve at the table to reveal the snarling wolf on his forearm floats into my mind's eye. "It was normal…"

"There was nothing normal about it. Jared cut a deal with Cathal and Cian was in charge of enforcing it. He didn't just come by for pot roast, Wren; he was coming by to make sure Jared kept to his end of the bargain. Which he did."

I'm quickly approaching information overload but I swallow and try to concentrate on his face without looking directly into those silver eyes. "Why should I believe you?"

"Because I have proof." He rises to his feet, looming impossibly huge above me. "And if you come with me, I'll show you."

I stare at his stony face. Say he does show me something, and say it does look like proof. How could I possibly trust it? Trust *him?*

As if he's read my mind, he sighs. "I understand you might not trust me right now, Wren, but the honest-to-God truth is that I had no clue who you were until after I found out you were pregnant."

"You really expect me to believe that?"

"It's the truth. What you believe is up to you."

I use the sink counter to pull myself upright. When he tries to help, I cringe away from him. "Don't touch me."

He drops his hands wordlessly and strides out into the den. My stomach twists when I look around at the space that he helped me create the last few weeks. I thought I loved him for it. Now, it just feels like more deception, more manipulation. More cruelty in the form of kindnesses I never should've accepted.

"Sit down," he instructs, gesturing to the sofa.

I'd expected him to take me somewhere else—his office, maybe? Is that where these kinds of conversations normally take place?

But it's just as well that we do it here, because I'm not sure how much longer I can stay on my feet. I sink onto the cushions and beg myself to remember how to breathe.

He sits on the brown leather armchair and withdraws a small recording device from his pocket. He places it on the table next to a dark brown file.

"January 14th, 2017. Does that date mean anything to you?"

I swallow to keep my jaw from shaking. "That was the date that Rose and Jared started their first round of IVF."

Dmitri nods. "The first of five rounds."

"Five? No, that's wrong. Rose only tried twice." I'm actually relieved that his information is incorrect. It proves that he doesn't know what the hell he's talking about. And if he doesn't know what he's talking about, that means he's wrong about Jared, he's wrong about Rose.

Maybe he's wrong about all of it.

Dmitri's expression doesn't change. He gestures to the dark brown file. "Go ahead. Open it."

My fingers tremble as I reach for it, desperate for answers and at the same time, terrified of what I might find out. I hesitate before I open the file. "What's in here?"

"Nothing graphic," he assures me.

I open the file and find—"Medical records?" I whisper as my eyes home in on the names at the top of the page. "Rose." My finger drags across those four perfect letters. "Jared."

"Those are copies of your sister's medical records, starting from January 2017. As you can see, she's signed every page. Along with her husband."

One glance and I know those signatures are authentic. "I don't understand," I mumble, staring at the dates of each round of IVF. I was aware of the first and second round of IVF—but the last three?

Why would she keep that from me?

I shake my head and slam the file shut, refusing to believe what I've seen with my own eyes. "No. Why would she lie to me about this?"

"Because she couldn't explain where she and Jared were getting the money for all these rounds of IVF without telling you the truth."

"And what is the truth?" I demand.

"That Jared cut a deal with the Irish. Cathal O'Gadhra signed off on it himself. If Jared did something for Cathal, Cathal would give him as much money as he required until Rose was pregnant."

I feel sick. I haven't felt like this since my first trimester. I swallow the bitter bile and try desperately to concentrate. "I don't understand... Where do you come in?" I'm sweating profusely under my arms. Fuck, I'm sweating in places I wasn't even aware you could sweat from.

"Cathal wanted a gun for hire. Someone who couldn't be easily traced back to him." Dmitri's jaw clenches tight and the silver in his eyes grows dark. "Jared was the weapon he exploited to get back at me."

"How?"

A shadow ripples across Dmitri's face. "Elena."

That's all he says.

Just her name.

But it hits me like a slap across the face.

"No..."

"Those photographs you saw are only one part of the bigger picture. They may be true, but they lack context. The story didn't start the day Rose and Jared died; it started the day Elena died."

I'm not even aware that I'm shaking my head until my head starts to spin. "R-Rose would never have agreed to that... never—"

"I don't know if your sister was aware of the particulars of the arrangement. Maybe Jared kept that from her. I don't know, and I'll be honest: at the time, I didn't care. All I wanted was revenge. All I wanted was to do to Elena's murderer what he did to me—rob him of the woman he loved."

"God!" I explode as tears fall fast down my cheeks. "I can't believe this… I can't believe this…"

Dmitri leans forward and nudges the recorder towards me. "All you have to do is press play."

My lips tremble so wildly I'm afraid I won't be able to get the words out. "I'm not s-s-sure I w-wanna h-hear what's o-o-on there…"

He stares at me unblinkingly. "You wanted the truth, Wren. That requires knowing all of it."

My finger trembles over the play button. I take a deep breath and press it. Immediately, there's a faint scratching sound and then a series of muffled breaths set against a backdrop of whirling wind.

Then a voice rips through the white noise, clear and breathy and trembling and so painfully recognizable. "You killed her… Rose… Rosie!"

I start shaking. I have to grip the edges of the sofa to keep from completely unraveling. The recorder keeps playing, cruelly oblivious to my borderline hysteria.

"I want you to know that she didn't have to die." Dmitri's voice cuts through me like a knife, sharp and ruthless. "But you made a choice."

"I did n-nothing!" Jared screams desperately. "I don't even know you!"

"But you knew my wife."

White noise rushes in to fill the gaps in their fevered conversation. And then—"Oh God... She was your wife..."

"I want to hear you say her name."

All I can hear after that are heavy sobs, panicked pleas. "P-please... I was desperate—*we* were desperate! Rose wanted a baby... I would have done anything to make her a mother—"

"Including murdering an innocent woman?" Dmitri demands.

"I-I didn't know w-who she was!" Jared stutters. "I swear, I—"

"Say her name. Say her name. Say her *fucking name!*"

"Elena!" Jared wails. "Elena... oh, fuck... I'm sorry... I'm so sorry..."

His whimpers fade to nothing. Metal hisses in the background as it cools. Dmitri's voice on the recording is soft when he speaks again. I have to strain to hear him. "She was pure... so fucking pure. And you robbed the world of her. You robbed *me* of her."

"I d-didn't know... I was given a name and a face. I-i-it was the only thing he asked of me."

Dmitri's laugh is like a bolt of lightning, sudden and otherworldly. "And where is he now? Buried six feet in the earth, rotting away to nothing. Was it worth it?"

Jared's breath whistles as loudly as the wind. Maybe what I can hear is fire raging in the background? I can't be certain. A small part of my brain registers that somewhere in the background of this frozen recording, my sister's body lies, freshly dead.

"Please," Jared begs. "S-spare me…"

"I made my wife's corpse a promise. I promised her that I wouldn't rest until I killed the two men responsible for her death. The one that ordered it and the one that carried it out."

The tape crackles with the sound of hisses and spits. Definitely a fire, though I knew that already. Jared's body was covered in burns when he was found.

"Time to fulfill that vow."

The report of the gun makes me scream.

I clap a hand over my mouth as my eyes fly to Dmitri. It feels like this is all happening in the present. For me, in a way, I suppose it is.

Dmitri leans forward once more and switches off the recorder. The silence that follows is oppressive after the chaos of that recording. If only I could switch my mind off so I don't have to replay it again and again…

And again…

And again…

"I know that was hard for you to hear. And I understand that you hate me right now. But I spent so long trying to track down the man who killed Elena. When I finally found him, I wasn't capable of acting rationally. Or compassionately. All I wanted was to do to him what he did to me."

I blink, pushing the tears out of my eyes. I feel strange. Like I might break apart, limb by limb. The only thing that keeps me chained to reality is the soft fluttering inside my belly.

Dmitri stands and I flinch away from him despite the fact that he's several feet away from me. "I never meant to hurt you, Wren. For what it's worth, I am sorry."

Then he leaves.

I hear the door close behind him and when I look up, he's gone. So is the recorder. I tuck my feet up, put my head down, and curl up on the sofa with my face pressed into the cushion so I don't have to see anything but black.

My tears soak the pillows beneath me.

I close my eyes and pray for oblivion.

62

DMITRI

"Dmitri?"

I lift my head and find Bee standing on the threshold of my office door, the whites of her eyes bright against the darkness.

"What do you want?"

"I just want to make sure you're okay," she explains gently. "Can I put a light on? It feels like Dracula's lair in here."

Before I can answer, she starts to reach for the switch. "Don't," I snarl. "Leave it."

I've had enough time to adjust to the darkness. The thin ray of moonlight streaming in from the gap in the blinds is more than sufficient for me.

The outline of her arm freezes in midair. After a pause, she withdraws it and crosses the room to sit on the couch, far closer to me than I would've preferred.

"How are you?" she asks.

"Stupid question."

Usually, any snappiness on my part unleashes the corresponding bitch in Bee. But tonight, she doesn't allow me to trigger her. "You're right. That was a stupid question." She gives my leg a pat. "I'm sorry, Dmitri. That must have been a hard thing to discuss."

"Those pictures…" I growl. "There's only one person who could have sent them."

"You can deal with that tomorrow," Bee insists. "You don't have to—"

"I made a mistake in letting the Irish scum multiply," I interrupt viciously. It's the first time I've spoken in hours, so my voice is hoarse and jagged. "I should have snuffed them all out with their don. I cut off Cathal's head, only for Cian to take his place."

"Cian is manageable—"

"That's what I thought, too. I thought wrong."

She sighs and slumps back, though her fingers keep twitching like she wishes I'd let her give me comfort. "Dmitri, right now, perhaps you need to focus on the home front."

"What are you asking me to do? Patch things up with Wren? Make it all hunky-fucking-dory?" I scowl darkly. "She wants nothing to do with me after tonight."

"She just found out," Bee tries. "Give her time. She needs to process and grieve. It's not an easy thing to wrap your head around the fact that the man you love is responsible for killing your sister."

I cringe away from her. "*Love*. What the hell are you talking about?"

She squints at me through the darkness. "Don't play dumb, Dmitri. It doesn't suit you. Wren clearly has feelings for you."

"Feelings are one thing; love is another. And even if she did have feelings for me, learning that I murdered her sister and brother-in-law in cold blood will have certainly taken care of that."

"Not if you do damage control!" she cries out. "Not if you—"

"Enough, Bee," I spit. "I'm done talking about this. It is what it is and there's no going back now."

I swing my legs off the sofa and get to my feet, then walk over to the bar and pour myself a strong drink. Bourbon. It was always Otets's drink of choice after a failure or a particularly harrowing day. Seems like the time is right to make it my drink of choice as well.

"Wren was a distraction that I should never have indulged in." I take a long sip, relishing the burn, the sting in my gut. "I should never have allowed myself to blur the lines between us."

"She's carrying your son!"

"And that remains her purpose for the time being. Her *only* purpose."

"You don't mean that."

"I assure you I do."

"Dmitri!" Bee exclaims. "I understand that this has been an absolute shitstorm of a day, but you're giving up. And you only ever give up when you're afraid to get hurt."

I whirl around to glare at her. "You realize that the wedding is in a week, right? I don't have the time to convince Wren to forgive me. Maybe it's better that I don't have her forgiveness. It makes things simpler. Black and white. No more shades of gray."

"Right," Bee scoffs snottily. "Because it'll be much easier to keep her at arm's length that way, huh?" I knock back what remains of the bourbon and pour myself another glass. I have every intention of finishing the bottle before the hour is up. "For God's sake, Dmitri, you can't just let her slip away!"

The burn of alcohol is only marginally comforting. Even beyond the immediate distraction and the growing fog it provides, I still feel those fucking *feelings* lurking. Shadows in the dark. All the worse because I can't hit them back.

"She was never supposed to be part of the equation," I rasp. Bee stomps over to the bar and grabs the bottle of bourbon as I'm reaching for my third refill. "Goddammit, Bee, hand it the fuck over n—"

"She's perfect for you!" Bee yells, dangling the bottle out of reach. "I would go so far as to say she was perfect for you in a way that Elena never was."

I make a grab for the bottle, but she pulls it further away from me. "You don't know what the hell you're talking about."

"Yes, I do. I was *there*, Dmitri. Elena was a wonderful girl, but she lived to please you. She was a street urchin and you were the handsome prince who swept her off her feet. She idolized you in a way that wasn't healthy for any relationship."

"Hand over the damn bottle, Bee," I order through gritted teeth. "I'm not in the mood for this shit."

She ignores me. "Did you know that she hated Russian food?"

I stop short. "That's not true."

Bee nods fervently. "It is true. Remember the *salo* you used to import? Yeah, she'd throw it out the minute you left home. And the *pirozhki* you spent hours making, just for her? She used to pack them up the next day and take them to the Southside to distribute to the homeless. I know! I used to go with her some days."

Her eyes are bright and her cheeks are inflamed enough to radiate even in the gloom.

"She didn't like going to your charity galas, either. She'd have much rather stayed in the apartment and painted. She put on the pretty dresses and the dazzling smiles because it was important to you. Oh—and as for babies, she did want to have a child; she just didn't want to have one with you because she was terrified—and I mean *terrified*—of the lifestyle you lived. In her mind, you saved her and she was determined to devote her life to you in return. That wasn't fair to her or to you, Dmitri. How can any healthy marriage be so one-sided?"

She's full of shit. Spewing lies. She has to be, because none of this shit she's saying makes any goddamn sense.

I lunge forward again, but this time, instead of reaching for the bottle, I grab Bee by the upper arm and reel her in toward me. My fingers furrow harshly into her skin.

Nose-to-nose, I snarl in her face, "Get. The. Fuck. Out."

Then I snatch the bottle from her grasp and let her go.

She stumbles away from me, her face twisting with emotions I've never seen her show before. Not fear—that would be understandable. So would anger, but that's not what I'm seeing, either.

It's *pity* shining in Bee's eyes as she looks at me. Sympathy. Melancholy.

She looks infinitely disappointed in me.

"I'm pushing the wedding back by a couple of weeks," she says abruptly.

I can't muster up the energy for anything more than an obvious observation. "Your father won't be happy."

"I don't give a shit," she barks. "We need to make sure Wren is okay before we go through with this stupid shit. You can pretend not to care about her—but what about your son?"

I ignore my empty glass and just drink straight from the bottle. The bitter alcohol is starting to take the edge off, but it's too little, too late. Still, I need all the help I can get to drown Bee out.

She walks to the door but stops at the threshold to look back at me over her shoulder. "You lost Elena, Dmitri," she says softly. "There's no reason you should lose Wren, too."

63

WREN

As it turns out, that second apartment comes in handy.

When I asked Dmitri for space, I didn't anticipate how much space I would actually need. This revelation doubled that need, tripled it, raised it to the power of a billion.

Not that any amount of space can make me forget that *he's* the reason my sister's gone.

Walking into my newly furnished living room, I find Aleksandr lounging on the sofa. He's got his feet kicked up on the coffee table and he's nursing a cold beer in one hand.

"'Sup?"

"You don't have to be here every damn day, Aleks. I'm too pregnant to make a run for it."

He gives me a guilty smile. "No one thinks you're gonna run. I'm just checkin' up on ya. Yo, wanna get lunch?"

I frown. "With who?"

"Uh… me?" he answers, looking around confused as if someone else might pop out of the woodwork.

"You're really offering to let me leave the apartment?" I snort derisively. "There's definitely a catch there somewhere."

"There's no catch!" he insists. But the color in his cheeks begs to differ.

I plant my fists on my hips. "So you're not gonna surprise me with a surprise lunch guest? Your murderous brother, for example? Or his backstabbing fake fiancée?"

"'Backstabbing' is a little harsh, don't you think?" I swivel around to see Bee standing at the entrance of the living room. She looks flawless in a white vest and matching slacks over black Louis Vuitton heels.

Instantly, my eyes narrow into violent slits. "You."

I haven't seen her in a week. Not since I told her to fuck right off when she came over to make amends with a massive sheet cake with the words *"I'm so sorry"* scrawled on the top with pink frosting. She was lucky I didn't throw the cake at her.

"Me," she agrees with a weary sigh. "Can we talk?"

"No."

As much as I don't want to see or speak to her, as much as I don't want to see or speak to her killer of a best friend, I have nonetheless wondered why he hasn't even tried to make the effort to fix things.

Is it pride? Or anger? Or guilt?

Maybe he just doesn't care. Either way, I haven't seen him in nine days and counting.

Aleksandr throws Bee a hopeless look and pulls his feet off the coffee table. "Listen, Wren—"

"Don't even think about it," I spit before he can get a word in edgewise. "You so much as try to speak for either one of them and I'm kicking you out, too."

He holds up his hands in surrender and mimes zipping his lips closed.

I nod with satisfaction. "Good. Now, you can show Beatrice out of my apartment."

Aleksandr gets to his feet reluctantly, but when he approaches Bee, she pulls out a switchblade knife and holds it to his throat. "Touch me and you die," she hisses.

We both know the knife is all for show, but Aleksandr still throws me an apologetic look and backs away. Bee struts past him and perches herself on the edge of the coffee table in front of me. She crosses her legs primly, purses her lips, and fixes me with an unflinching gaze.

"You have every right to be pissed."

"Thanks for the permission," I drawl.

Her grimace screws up tighter. "I'm sorry," she says fervently. "I'll repeat it a thousand times over if I have to."

I cross my hands over my swollen belly. "If you repeated it a million times over, it still wouldn't be enough."

She throws a defeated look over at Aleksandr, who's standing off to the side, watching this whole exchange awkwardly. "He knew, too," she accuses. "How come you're not as mad at him as you are at me?"

"Because you pretended to be my friend!" I cry out. "I trusted you. I really thought you had my back."

"I *do* have your back, Wren. And we *are* friends. You mean so much to me."

"Let's face it: no matter how much you pretend to care about me, you're always going to choose Dmitri first."

"It's not about choosing sides, Wren. We're all on the same side here!"

"It would make your life a hell of a lot easier if I fell for that bullshit, wouldn't it?"

She takes a deep breath to steady herself. "He's not in the habit of killing innocent people, Wren. He regretted killing Rose immediately after he did it. He was just so destroyed over Elena's death; he was so consumed with getting even. He thought that avenging her death would help him move on. But he didn't get the peace he craved… not until he met you." She's blinking up at me earnestly. "So how ironic, how cruel, that after you came into his life, he realized that you were the sister of the woman he killed in retaliation for Elena's death."

I'm not gonna lie—I've spent as many sleepless nights tossing and turning over Elena's death as I have over Rose's. Neither one of them deserved to die the way they did.

Over the last week and a half, my grief has been clashing constantly with my sense of compassion. Because the twisted part is, I understand why Dmitri did what he did. And if it had been anyone but my sister, I might have been okay with it.

Well not *okay*-okay. But I would have been able to wrap my head around it a little easier.

I squint at Bee through my tear-studded eyelashes. "I am sorry about Elena," I whisper. "I just can't imagine…" A shudder races up my spine. "I can't believe Jared was capable of something like that."

"Sometimes, you don't know what you're capable of until your back is pushed to the corner."

I shake my head. "But this? We're not talking about taking out a second mortgage. This was murder, Bee! And he chose to do it."

She nods. "It's hard to accept that you don't always know people as well as you think you do. Especially not the ones you love."

"I've been driving myself crazy all week trying to figure out if Rose knew about Elena or not." I exhale sharply. "Was she in on it, too? Was she so desperate for a child that she was willing to kill for one?"

Bee shifts uncomfortably, the coffee table beneath her groaning with the motion. "I'm afraid I don't have the answer to that question."

I close my eyes and a tear slips down my cheek. I'm actually surprised—I figured I'd used up my quota of tears for the month. For my whole life, actually.

When I open my eyes again, Bee's looking at me sympathetically. "The last few years before she died… she got more and more erratic," I admit softly. "More and more desperate."

Bee nods. "So you do have doubt?"

A little sob bursts from my lips against my will. "Three rounds of IVF, Bee. She kept three whole rounds of IVF from me. All those miscarriages she had… they weren't natural pregnancies like I thought. She was getting treatment, and she was using dirty Irish mob money to pay for them!" I wipe my tears away and run a hand over my face. "I remember sitting up with her one night after one of those miscarriages…"

"I can't keep doing this, Wren… I can't keep losing babies… Every new loss feels like my chest is being wrenched apart."

"Then stop. Take a break. Stop trying," I told her. It was the first time I'd made the suggestion out loud, after over a year of trying to sheathe my tongue.

Her face was blotchy with tears. I remember she looked so much like our mother at that moment. Not the way Mom had been when Dad was around, but the way she looked after he left; after the cancer ravaged her body, stolen her youth and most of her beauty.

"I can't stop. I can't give up. I owe it to my future self, to Jared, to keep trying no matter what. I'd do anything, anything, *to become a mother."*

Those were charged words even then. But now, viewed through a different lens, they strike differently. It makes me shiver to think just how much of her morality she compromised along the way.

In the end, it was the very thing that ended her life.

"I keep turning over everything in my head," I tell Bee. "I keep searching for clues in my memory, something that will help make things clearer about how much she knew. But I…"

Bee leans forward and puts her hand on mine. "My advice?" she asks gently. "Stop thinking. Stop searching. She's gone,

Wren. There's no point dragging up her corpse and demanding answers from it. The dead don't speak."

I look down at Bee's hand on mine. I want so badly to let it comfort me. But in the end, I pull away. "No, but *you* do. Or at least, you could have. But you chose to keep silent to protect Dmitri."

She sighs. "You've seen my back; you know the lengths Dmitri went to save me from that monster I call a father. What would you have done in my place?" I hate how obvious the answer seems when she puts it that way. "That is not to say that I wouldn't do the exact same thing for you."

"I would never need you to."

She accepts that with a small nod. "Because you're a better person than either Dmitri or me, Wren. Maybe you're a better person than even your sister and brother-in-law were."

I stop the trembling in my jaw by biting down on my bottom lip. "It's so weird. I feel like I've lost her all over again. It feels like—"

"You've lost the person you thought she was."

My jaw goes slack when I realize that's exactly what I'm feeling. I believed that Rose shared everything with me—but clearly, there were large chunks of her life that she deliberately kept hidden.

Probably because she knew what I would have told her: if you have to work that hard for something, maybe it's not meant for you.

Even when I remember her now, I remember mostly the good stuff. The way she carved our initials into the swing

Dad built for us just before he left. I remember the way she stroked my hair at night when I had a nightmare.

I actively avoid thinking about the last few years. The desperate attempts at conceiving, the hours she spent in churches because she thought finding God would help her get pregnant. The endless tears, the fits of anger and frustration. The time I watched her press her hand against a hot skillet just to "feel something other than heartbreak."

"Wren." Bee's voice cracks through my fractured thoughts. I glance towards her; she's looking at me with kohl-rimmed eyes, bright with sincerity. And I can't help thinking, *Can I really afford to be an island?* "I know I've hurt you and I'm sorry for that. The only thing I can do now is promise to be as honest as I can from here on out."

I peer towards Aleksandr, who's still doing his best to pretend like he's not eavesdropping. Somewhere deep in my chest, my anger is butting heads with my loneliness.

"Is this about me?" I ask bluntly. "Or is this about the baby I'm carrying?"

Her brow drops. "What do you mean?"

"I mean, is that little speech you just gave sincere? Or are you just trying to manipulate me now because you know that, in order for us to raise this baby together, you need my cooperation?"

Her mouth twists downwards and hurt flickers across her eyes. I've never seen her quite this raw before. I want to believe it's not an act, but the cynical part of me just can't handle being lied to yet again. "I don't blame you for wondering—and I'll admit, it would make things simpler. But that's not why I'm here. That's not why I'm trying to make peace with you." She sighs deeply. "I'm here because you're my friend and I care about you."

I take it all in. I can't deny that beyond my suspicion, I am touched. I'm also desperate not to be alone in this. Especially since it seems clear that Dmitri isn't going to make the effort Bee is willing to.

"Okay," I say at last. It comes out in a breathy sigh.

She gasps, her jaw dropping and her eyes going wide with relief. "Okay?"

I nod and she launches herself at me, wrapping her arms around my shoulders and tackling me back against the armchair.

I'm laughing snottily as she pulls herself off me and retreats back on the coffee table. "Does this mean I have my wedding planner back?" The smile drops off my face and Bee's expression sours, too. "Shit, sorry. That was a stupid thing to say."

"It's okay. I, um… I actually forgot about the wedding. Wasn't it supposed to be this week?"

"I pushed it back," Bee admits. "I wanted to sort out things between us first. I didn't want to walk down the aisle with a maid of honor who hated my guts."

I stop short, completely taken aback. "I'm sorry—did you just say what I think you said?"

She gives me a cautious, self-conscious smile. "You can totally say no. I'll completely understand. But I am asking."

"Because you have no other friends?"

Aleksandr full-on snorts with laughter and Bee flips him the bird. "I have friends," she insists. "Just none that are privy to all the skeletons in my closet."

I stare at her incredulously. "And I am?"

"Well, let's put it this way: there's nothing I wouldn't tell you." She holds up her pinky finger. "Pinky promise."

Smiling, I can't resist looping my pinky through hers. "Oh, alright, screw it. I'll be your damn maid of honor."

Aleksandr takes that as his cue to sidle over to the lounge area and sit down. "Aw, look at you two. One big, happy family."

I glare between Bee and Aleks harshly. "Let's get one thing straight right now: I may be good with the two of you, but that does not mean I'm okay with Dmitri. I have no desire to speak to him and the feeling seems mutual. So let's just keep it at that."

Bee throws Aleksandr a worried, wordless glance.

"What?" I snap. "And considering the promise we just made, I'm expecting an honest answer."

Bee pushes her hair back behind her ears. "You are carrying his baby. You can't ignore him forever."

I get to my feet and grin viciously. "Wanna bet?"

64

DMITRI

"Come on, baby," she goads with a seductive smile. "Smile for me."

I have to fight every instinct in my body to keep from scowling. I can't believe she talked me into a fancy dinner at Sakura tonight.

Bee leans in and breathes in my ear as she drapes a hand around my neck. I have the urge to cringe away from her smoky breath, but there are a dozen pairs of eyes on us at the moment and at least half of them will report every tiny micro-expression back to Vittorio.

"Seriously," she murmurs. "Everyone's watching."

I press my lips to her neck and she laughs girlishly. It's amazing how she can keep her smile in place even when she's irritated as hell. And she definitely is. I can tell from the way her nails dig into my arm. I can feel each talon through my shirt and jacket.

"You are impossible." The inflection is flirty, but the words are anything but.

"I told you I didn't want to come out tonight."

She glides her hand down my arm. "Oh, suck it up, buttercup. If I can be seen in public with this hideous stomach—" She looks down and runs a palm lovingly over her fake belly. "—then you can handle one public dinner with your fiancée before we walk down the aisle." Her smile falters for only a second. "Besides, Vittorio already pitched a hissy fit when I told him I'd pushed the wedding back by two weeks. He's suspicious now and we need to convince him everything's just fucking peachy between us." She smiles a little wider, displaying her pearly white canines. "We need to play the happy couple."

"Fine." I swallow and adjust my collar. "How's the wedding planning going?"

"Fine."

She's been holed up with Wren in the lower apartment for five days straight. Obviously, Wren's stopped freezing Bee out. I would have asked how Bee managed to thaw out the ice princess if I wasn't so intent on pretending like I didn't give a fuck.

"Everything's organized then?" I press.

"Yup."

"Seating charts?"

"All done."

"Menu—"

"Because I want you to do something about it!" she cries out, letting her poker face drop in the heat of the moment. She picks it back up almost immediately and places her hand on my forearm where it rests on the white tablecloth. "You need to fight for her, Dmitri."

Something urgent and overwhelming rises inside me, desperate for traction. *I need to fight for her?* Fuck that. I've been fighting my entire life. Meeting Elena was the one thing I've ever done that felt easy.

Our relationship was easy. She was easy. So when we fell into our roles as husband and wife, it felt like I was finally getting a break from the constant war.

I see now what a seductive lie that was, though.

Nothing is easy. Nothing can ever be easy.

Anything that's too close to me and my world is in danger.

My gaze slides down to Bee's fake belly. I press my hand to it tenderly so that the whole restaurant can see. "The only thing we need to be concerned with right now is being the perfect family."

She shifts uncomfortably beneath my touch. "Dmitri…"

"We knew the cost of this charade," I remind her quietly. "This wedding has to go smoothly."

Her lips purse with determination. "For that, you're gonna have to talk to Wren. Or are you planning on ignoring my maid of honor through the whole ceremony?"

My jaw flexes furiously. "You asked her to be your maid of honor?"

She smiles. "Sure did. I had a special dress custom-made for her, too. Her belly has really popped in the last week. She's glowing."

She's rubbing my face in the fact that I haven't seen Wren in almost two weeks. I have been keeping tabs on her of course—just from a distance. Dr. Liza keeps me updated on every checkup, so I know my son is healthy. I know he's the size of a butternut squash. I know that he's been kicking feverishly for the last few weeks at all hours of the day and night.

Fighting. Just like his father.

"Have you felt the baby move?"

Bee's face softens instantly. "Yeah. It's trippy. There's an actual person in there," she murmurs in awe.

I'm gripping the armrest of my chair so hard that my knuckles have turned white. How is it fair that she gets to experience what should be my right as the baby's father?

"You planning on avoiding Wren even after the baby's born?" Bee asks curiously as though she's read my mind. "Because that's definitely gonna be a challenge."

"Less so than it is right now."

Bee just sighs and runs a hand up and down her belly. "Hope the little one doesn't inherit your stubbornness."

"Wren's every bit as stubborn as I am."

"True," she concedes. "Like I said, you two are made for each other."

I bite my tongue to keep from snapping at her again. The woman whose sister I murdered is the one that's made for me? It's a farfetched notion even by Bee's standards.

So why the fuck can't I get her out of my head?

~

The apartment is eerily quiet.

I'm extra cautious as I assemble the shelves along the wall that faces the crib I just put together. In a matter of hours, the space has transformed. I've accomplished everything I set out to do when I walked in here a handful of hours ago in the dead of the night.

But still, I can't bring myself to leave.

"Bee?"

Oh, fuck.

Wren walks into the nursery and stops short when she sees me. Her eyes go wide with shock and her cheeks flush scarlet. There's no way in hell she was expecting it to be me in here, which I know only because Wren would sooner jump off a bridge than voluntarily let me catch sight of her in that whisper-thin white slip she's wearing.

Bee was right: she is glowing. Something pale and beautiful and ethereal in the midnight gloom.

The shock on Wren's face gives way to indignation. "Coming in here whenever you want defeats the purpose of giving me my own space."

"You weren't supposed to know I was here."

Her eyebrows pinch together in a frown. "I suppose it makes sense. What I don't know won't hurt me, right? Isn't that your philosophy on everything?"

"I was just—" I run my hand over the crib before sighing and slumping towards the door. "I was just leaving."

"Wait."

I freeze, caught in no-man's-land in the middle of the room. Wren's not looking at me, though—her eyes have floated past to see the work of the last few hours.

"That wasn't there before," she whispers. She's staring at the rocking chair I sacrificed a thumbnail to build. It's toying back and forth gently in the breeze from the fan overhead, bumping with a tiny thump into the padded footrest I constructed to go with it. "And you put up a swing?"

I swallow. My throat is suddenly dry. "You mentioned once that you had fond memories of the swing you used to have in your backyard."

She nods without taking her eyes off it. "My father installed it with Rose and me. We loved that damn swing. Rose carved our names into…"

She trails off as she drifts closer, noticing that unlike all the other pieces in the nursery, this one's not shiny or new.

"Oh my God." She drops to her knees in front of the swing and snatches it up in both hands. Even from where I'm standing, I can see her fingers passing reverently over the two names etched crudely into the surface.

Rose* + *Wren

No one breathes for a few long moments. Then she looks up at me with her mouth hanging open. "This is our swing," she rasps. "This is *the* swing. You… What… How?"

"I went back to your old neighborhood," I admit quietly. "The new owners kept the swing up, so it was just a matter of convincing them to let me take it. I had to replace the rope, of course, but I was able to salvage the seat."

She gulps hard and turns back to stare at it. "I can't believe it." She keeps running her fingers over Rose's name again and again.

I don't move. The clouds outside the window part and let in a brief blip of moonlight that catches Wren's cheeks and shows me tears glistening there like diamonds.

Slowly, slowly, she gets back onto her feet. Her stomach has grown since the last time I saw her. I want so badly to touch it and feel my baby boy moving inside of her.

But I keep my hands to myself.

Wren looks at me, solemn and still. "Thank you," she whispers. "I don't even know how to—just, thank you."

"You're welcome." I turn for the door. "I'll see myself out."

I'm halfway gone when she speaks again. Just my name at first, barely audible over the whirring fan blades. Then: "This doesn't change anything. It… it can't."

Fight her, bellows that voice in my head. The primal voice, the warrior's voice, the voice I've always listened to. *Go to battle to prove she's wrong about you. Wage war to show who you really are.*

It's the first time that the instinct has come up so fast and so fierce that I can't deny the need, the desire to fight for her, for the baby she's carrying and the family we could be building together.

But the truth is, I've reserved all my fight for my business and my Bratva. I don't have the faintest notion of how to fight for a woman or a relationship.

The problem is this: if there's one thing I learned about war, it's that you never get out unscathed. Everything you bring to the battlefield can be lost if luck turns against you. So to fight for Wren, I have to risk losing her. To fight for my son, I have to risk never holding him in my arms.

I can't do that.

So I take the coward's way out. I yield the battle before it's even begun.

I nod.

And I leave.

65

WREN

"Vera Wang was never meant to be worn with a belly!"

Bee has a legitimate point. The gorgeous, strapless Vera Wang gown hangs off the back of the walk-in closet's door. The seams have been taken out at the waist for the sake of her fake pregnancy and the dress has a sad, deflated look to it now, like a wrinkled balloon with all the air sucked out.

"You're still gonna look beautiful," I insist.

My comfort is lost on her. She tosses the huge prosthetic stomach onto the bed and sinks onto the carpeted floor. "This sucks. It totally freaking sucks!"

I join her on the floor and take both her hands. "Is this about the dress or is this about the fact that you're marrying a man you're not in love with?"

"It's both!" she pouts. "Also, it's about marrying a man, period. It goes against my principles, Wren!"

I bite my lip, wondering how on earth I'm supposed to help her here. I'm way out of my depth and the one person who can maybe help is the one person I want to avoid at all costs. Especially since his move with the swing, which has made it extremely hard to hate him in the last few days.

Goddamn him for that.

Goddamn him for everything.

"Shit, I'm sorry," Bee whispers, looking directly into my eyes. "I'm being a selfish bitch, aren't I?"

"What? No, of course—"

"Here I am, complaining about my fancy wedding, while you have to deal with watching me marry the man you're in love with."

I drop her hands like they're on fire. Pretty sure my cheeks are on fire, too. "I… That is… I am not in love with him!"

Bee wrinkles her nose with embarrassment. "Shit. Sorry. That slipped out. I'm on a roll here, apparently."

"Do you really think I'm in love with Dmitri?" I demand.

The nose scrunching only gets worse. "Well, aren't you?"

"No!" I practically scream. "He killed my sister and my brother in law. He basically kidnapped me and kept me prisoner in his home for months. He… he…"

He cooked meals for me. And massaged my swollen feet. And bought me my very own apartment.

And tracked down a silly childhood swing just because I told him it meant something to me.

Goddamn him for all of that, too.

"Oh, God," I explode, trying to scramble up to my feet so that I can breathe a little better. "You're getting in my head," I accuse Bee. "You're trying to confuse me!"

"Oh, honey…" She gets to her feet, too, although far more gracefully than I did. "If you're confused, it's not because of me."

"I'm not in love with him, Bee. I'm just not."

She nods calmly. "Okay. You're not."

I frown. She's just placating me, telling me what I want to hear. My stomach twists as I try to put my finger on exactly why I feel so damn horrible right now. Because I have to admit: I felt horrible *before* Bee mentioned anything about my definitely-not-feelings for Dmitri.

It's hard to put a finger on anything when I can't get some air in my lungs, though. I'm wrapped in a thin silk robe but I may as well be wearing a cinched corset, based on the way my breath keeps getting stuck in my chest. "Urgh…"

I'm pacing back and forth when Bee steps in front of me and grabs me by the shoulders. She looks me in the eye and gives me a little shake that snaps me out of my panic. "Listen to me, Wrenny. You don't have to feel guilty."

"Guilty? Guilty about what?"

"About loving the man who killed your sister."

Shiiiiit.

There it is. That's the feeling I've been battling with all these weeks, wrapped up in a succinct little sentence. Guilt and shame and embarrassment.

Because, despite what I know, no matter the justification, I still haven't been able to put my feelings for Dmitri to bed.

Bee looks me dead in the eye. Her grip on my shoulders tightens. "You love him," she emphasizes slowly.

It's not a question. "Y-yes," I sob. "God, how can I still love him… after everything that I know…?"

"Because love isn't a switch you can turn on and off, Wren," Bee chides. "You know now that Rose kept things from you. Maybe she even lied to you. You may be angry with her for that—but it doesn't mean you love her any less, does it?"

"N-no…"

"Then why should Dmitri be any different?"

"Because!" I insist without anything substantial to back the word. I shake my head. "Because he—goddammit, I don't know anymore. I don't know…"

Bee guides me to the bed and coaxes me into sitting down. "It's a lot. You're carrying his baby, but you're going to have to watch him get married to another woman. Even if that woman is physically repulsed by men in general, it's going to be hard."

A tear slips down my cheek. I just want to curl up into a ball and go to sleep forever. Is that so much to ask?

"It shouldn't be," I squeak in a small voice. "It's clear that he doesn't care enough about me to so much as try to make this right."

"That's where you're wrong, Wren. He does care. He cares a lot. That's exactly why he's pretending so hard not to."

"That makes no sense."

66

WREN

"What the fuck is taking so long?"

I yelp in surprise as Vittorio storms into the room like a jackal foaming at the mouth. My pulse races up when I realize that Bee's prosthetic stomach is lying by the side of the bed where she'd flung it on the way to the bathroom.

I sidle to the side and kick it under the bed as subtly as I can manage. "She's in the bathroom," I say nervously. "Last-minute jitters."

Vittorio storms to the bathroom door and slams his fist against it twice. "Beatrice Zanetti!" he roars. "What the hell do you think you're doing?"

"For fuck's sake, Papa!" she screams right back, her voice only slightly muffled by the door between them. "Can't a bride pee in peace on her goddamn wedding day?"

"You're choosing this moment to piss?"

"I'm nervous! There's a thousand people out there!"

"Which should suit you fine. You've always loved being the center of attention!" He pounds on the door again and the frame vibrates dangerously. For a moment, I genuinely think he's prepared to break it down.

"Give me five minutes!"

Spit flecks the door frame as he snarls, "Don't you dare embarrass me further, you little—"

"Mr. Zanetti." He twists around as though he's only just noticed I'm here. I move away from the bed so as not to draw attention to his future "grandchild" underneath it. "This is a big day for her. It's only natural that she's nervous. Just give her a few more minutes. We won't be late, I swear."

As his eyes narrow on me, I feel like an idiot who's caused a distraction so that the prey can get away—only to become the prey myself.

"Ah," he croons as a fake, oily smile spreads across his saggy face. "The little assistant." I don't like how he says it. As though there's a giant question mark stamped over the title. "I've heard you've become indispensable to my daughter."

I refuse to let my fear break through. "Just doing my job, sir."

His gaze falls to my stomach. "How lovely you look. Beautiful enough to take attention away from the bride, almost."

"No one will be looking at me with Bee in the room," I say with an anxious gulp. "I'll be invisible."

I freeze when he reaches out without warning and drags a single fingertip over my stomach. I wish so badly I could slap it away; self-preservation is the only reason I stay my hand. "You and Bee aren't far apart at all, are you?"

"No."

"How interesting that you will have your babies within weeks, perhaps even days, of one another."

I shrug. "This isn't my baby. I'm a surrogate, remember?"

"Oh, I do remember. I remember *everything*." His voice ripples with warning. Then, in a sudden blur of motion, he snatches my upper arm and pulls me back towards his unnaturally white teeth. "I'm gonna find the truth sooner or later, little bird. And when I do, there will be hell to pay."

His grip on my arm tightens. But just as the scream rises to my throat, Aleksandr walks into the room.

"Don Zanetti, you're needed in the ceremony hall." His tone is just harsh enough to get his point across. It's bizarre to hear all the laughter and joy ironed out of his voice, to see his face violent and grim. It's like another person operating Aleks's body. I don't think I like it, although it's suddenly easy to understand why Dmitri trusts him so much.

Vittorio keeps his eyes fixed on me as he curls a lock of my hair through his fingers. He pulls it up to his nose and gives it a sniff. "Hmm. So sweet… so innocent… He definitely has a type, doesn't he?"

He turns away just before my gag reflex kicks in. "Five minutes," he growls. "And not a second more."

He slams the door on his way out and Aleksandr's taut expression falls flat. Now, he just looks tired. "Bee!" he says urgently, hitting the door. "He's gone."

The door opens and she appears, clothed in her white bridal underwear and non-traditional black leather garter because she can't do anything purely traditional if her whole damn life depended on it—which, in this case, it actually does.

"I can't do this!" she whispers in terror.

I rush forward and grab her hands. "Bee, look at me." I squeeze tight. "I'm gonna be right there with you, okay?"

She doesn't look convinced. "If I do this, he wins, Wren. He *wins*."

"No, he doesn't. He doesn't win, because you still get to live the life you want—"

"In the shadows," she corrects desperately. "How can you call that 'living'?"

"Jesus, Bee!" Aleksandr sags against the wall. "We're down to three minutes and it takes at least two to put that stomach on!"

"Shhh!" I hiss at him, pushing my palm in his face. "Go get the prosthetic and let me handle this." I turn back to Bee and force her to meet my eyes. "Beatrice Zanetti, from the moment I met you, you have been a badass bitch. Don't go soft on me now." Her nostrils flare and she chews her bottom lip. I take the stomach from Aleksandr and help her strap it on. "Your father's suspicious of me now, too. If we don't see this through, my baby and I are in danger. For all our sakes, this wedding has to go off without a hitch. Watching you marry Dmitri is gonna be one of the hardest things I've ever had to do. But to keep this baby safe, I'll do it a hundred times over. And if I can do that, you can certainly get through this ceremony."

My little speech works. She nods once and the fear leaves her eyes, and just like that, the Bee I know is back again.

Once the stomach's on, Aleksandr and I help her ease into her dress. I give her a tight hug and then she heads out, with Aleks and I trailing at her back.

The moment she turns the corner, the music starts up and Vittorio twists around from his position in front of the church double doors, his scowl softening just a little.

"You did good back there," Aleksandr whispers to me as we prepare to follow Bee and Vittorio into the ceremony hall. "That was very impressive."

"If you repeat a word of what I said to Dmitri, I will kill you."

He winks and grins. "Understood." He offers me his arm and I link my hand through it. "Although I will say—and don't take this the wrong way—Bee's not the only one who's a badass bitch."

67

DMITRI
THIRTY MINUTES EARLIER

"I've got good news and I've got bad news."

Aleksandr shuts the door on my private suite. I grab my cufflinks and start to fasten them in place as I turn to him.

"Is Wren ready yet? Does the dress fit?"

He blinks in confusion. "Which dress are you asking about? As far as I understand with the way these types of things normally go, Bee is the one who will be wearing the wedding dress."

Goddammit. I exhale through my nose and tell my idiot brain to get its shit together. We can't afford to slip up today. Things are so tentative, so fragile. Dangling on the edge of a cliff.

"They were two separate questions," I say coolly.

Aleksandr looks unimpressed with my pitiful attempt at saving face. "Ah, Freudian slip, as the good doctor would say. Explains a lot."

"I'm not in the mood, Aleksandr. What's the news?"

He claps his hands. "Good news first: the dress fit perfectly, fake baby bump and all, and Bee looks gorgeous. Bad news: she's no longer in the dress. She's in the bathroom right now either puking or shitting out her nerves. She didn't really specify which when she pushed me out of the way, and I kinda figured I'd let her get away with going light on the details this time around. Because, like, does it really matter which end it's coming out of, y'know? Like, if we…"

He keeps rambling as I glance at the Rolex on my arm. We're already forty-five minutes behind schedule. I haven't even seen Vittorio yet, but I know without even having to ask that the old bastard is almost certainly prowling the ceremony hall like a restless lion.

"I'll go back in and check on her in a minute," Aleks is concluding when I tune back in. "I just wanted to see how you were holding up first."

"I'm fine."

"So you keep saying. Aggressively."

"The moment this wedding is done, that old fuck Zanetti will be bound to me," I snarl. "Together, we can finish off the fucking Irish once and for all. That is my only priority right now."

He winces. "You really think doubling down on the war is a good idea?" Aleksandr ventures cautiously. "I mean, think about it, brother. You have a baby on the way. You have Wren to think of."

"I *am* thinking of Wren—"

"Are you?" he interrupts quietly. "Because the fact that you haven't even tried to talk to her yet seems to indicate otherwise."

"Goddammit, *brat*," I grumble. "Not you, too."

"Yeah, *me, too*," he sasses back. "You owe it to her and to that baby to at least fucking try."

I recoil in surprise. He's the same carefree puppy dog of a man as always, but there's something new behind his face, and I can't help but wonder how long it's been there. A melancholy, a sort of gloom just below the surface.

Did I miss that? When did it come? Why?

"The baby? Why do I owe the baby?"

"Because your refusal to be a decent human being is depriving your child of a happy, functional family."

"That's—"

"She's good for you, Dmitri. She's sweet and pure just like Elena was, but she's not some naïve little wallflower, either. She can handle this life. She can handle you."

I let out a weary sigh and plant both hands against the back of the chair in front of me for support. Standing suddenly feels like the hardest thing I've ever done. "You and Bee conspiring against me or something?"

He smirks. "I take it she's been giving you the same spiel?"

"Endlessly." I scowl. "You're disqualified as my best man."

"Too late for that by far." He slaps me on the back. "I'm gonna go check on the girls. Think about what I said."

I turn back to my reflection and try to erase the conversation from my mind.

But all that does is leave more room to think of her.

∼

By the time I step up towards the altar, it hits me hard—this is really happening.

A thousand pairs of eyes are fixed on me right now. The ceremony hall is bursting with roses, lilacs, and baby's breath, color blossoming in every single nook and cranny.

The sheer scale of this event stands in stark contrast to the day I married Elena. We'd driven down to Chicago City Hall in a vintage Cadillac with Bee and Aleksandr as our two witnesses. Elena wore a white cotton sundress, I wore a shirt with the sleeves cuffed to my elbows, and it was perfect.

Well, we thought it was perfect. If memory serves, Bee called it "a fashion travesty of the highest proportions." Needless to say, we ignored her.

The ceremony itself lasted thirteen minutes, including the time spent waiting for the clerk to gauge if we were truly serious. When we'd finally convinced her, we exchanged rapid "I do's" and then walked to the nearest corner and bought churros and ice cream.

I've never felt farther from that day than I do right now.

The orchestral music crescendos and then the bridal march starts up. I glance towards the harpists congregated in the far right of the hall, all dressed in white like overgrown cupids.

Then the doors open.

This is it.

My heartbeat rises. Why the fuck do I feel as though I want to jump right out of my skin? I've known for years that marrying Bee was the only real way to protect her. Hell, marrying her was my idea in the first place.

So why are my palms sweating? Why do my eyes keep roving over every window, every door as if I could throw myself out of here? Why do I keep glancing at those harpists in white again and again, like one of them will take my place and set me free?

Bee and Vittorio appear at the double doors and everyone rises to their feet. She looks beautiful—radiant in white, hair laced with a diamond-studded veil, the train of her dress swooping elegantly behind her.

But it's all wrong. Her head is bent in a way that belongs to a much shyer, much more self-conscious woman. Bee is not that and it's horrible to see her this way.

And then I see Wren and Aleksandr appear at the doors behind Vittorio and Bee. How *easily* my eyes stray from my bride. How *natural* it feels to admire Wren. She's wearing a floating, lilac-colored dress that matches the flower petals strewn down the aisle. The fabric ruches and drapes strategically over her stomach, making it hard to notice that she's eight months' swollen with my child.

Hard to notice for anyone else, that is.

But me? I can't look at anyone but her.

Even as Bee steps up to the altar, I take her hand with my eyes locked on Wren. It requires quite a bit of effort to tear my gaze away from the maid of honor to the bride.

Maybe it's the heightened urgency of the moment. Maybe it's the utter ludicrousness of standing here, opposite the best friend who'd rather punt me into Lake Michigan than marry me with any ounce of sincerity. Maybe it's simply long-suppressed instinct.

Whatever it is—it puts things in perspective. It makes one harsh truth undeniable.

Wren matters to me.

I can try to deny it—and fuck knows I have. I can pretend all I want. I can lie convincingly—to her, to the world, even to myself. But it doesn't change the fact that I'm standing here, wishing that Wren was the woman standing in front of me instead of Bee.

Based on the anxious frown on Bee's face, she seems to have come to the same conclusion.

"Are you okay?" she mouths to me. I nod as the officiant starts the ceremony. But Bee doesn't seem satisfied with my answer. She inches closer and pulls her eyebrows together. "Seriously, are you okay?" Except this time, she doesn't mouth the question; she whispers it. Loud enough that the officiant stammers to a stop and looks between us questioningly.

"Uh, should I continue?"

"Of course," I snap, shooting Bee a glare.

She shrugs and gestures over her shoulder with her chin in Wren's direction. My nostrils flare but she doesn't seem to get the hint. "Fix it," she mouths.

Suppressing a sigh, I nod. That's the only way I'll get any peace—both peace within my household and within my own tortured head.

The officiant clears his throat, clearly confused as hell about the two of us. "It is now time for the bride and groom to recite their vows."

There's an audible and collective gasp as someone rises from the throng of guests at the back of the hall. "Can I go first?"

I know that voice.

I know that fucking voice.

Both Bee and I whirl around in the direction of the tall figure striding up from the back of the hall. "O'Gadhra…" she whispers.

Cian O'Gadhra is wearing a black tux and a resigned look on his face. Behind him, the harpists rise to their feet and pull automatic weapons from their instrument cases and the folds of their white robes. A dozen guns quiver in my direction like black eyes.

"I vow to make this shit end today," he intones.

That's when all hell breaks loose.

68

DMITRI

Wedding guests part like the Red Sea. Screams echo throughout the chapel.

The throng of Irish gangsters start shooting mercilessly, but I've completely lost sight of Cian. My men converge around us like a human shield, brandishing weapons of their own, but we're outmaneuvered, outnumbered, insufficiently prepared for an invasion from within.

Three Bratva soldiers go down in explosions of blood. I can't smell the flowers anymore—it's just gore, gunpowder, and fear sweat drenching the air.

My first instinct should be to protect my blushing bride. But Bee is neither blushing nor very bridely as she pulls up her skirts and whips out a gleaming pistol of her own. Her eyes are alight with excitement; there's even a smile curling around the corners of her mouth as she aims through the gaps between the shoulders of my men and starts shooting.

"Aleksandr!" I roar. "Get her out of here!"

I don't have to specify which "her" I'm talking about. I meet my brother's eyes for only a second before he grabs Wren's arm and starts to pull her off the raised platform we're on.

He doesn't get far.

"Fuck," he hisses as more Irishmen burst through the back doors of the ceremony hall, hemming us in on the altar.

"I'll clear a path for you," I roar, shooting over Aleksandr's head and taking out two men in the process. "Wren, stay down!"

I whip around and assess. My men are doing as good a job as possible at keeping the Irish at bay. And we have the additional support of the Zanetti mafia. Speaking of which…

Where the fuck is Vittorio?

I try to scan for the old Italian don, but he's disappeared into the chaos of the fight. Wedding guests are hurtling this way and that, wailing in terror. Women cower beneath pews and crawl under tables as bullets scythe through the air over their heads. The aisles and doorways are crowded with one body after the next. Gowns drip heavy with sticky crimson blood.

It's a snapshot of complete and utter turmoil. Nothing makes that clearer than Bee in her wedding dress and her fake pregnant belly, popping off rounds like a trigger-happy maniac. Crazed bubbles of laughter escape her lips with every report of the gun.

When she sees me looking at her, she winks. "What a wedding, huh?" she says with zeal.

"You're supposed to be pregnant," I hiss, trying to pull her back.

She shrugs me off. "Pretend I'm the kind of pregnant chick who's not afraid of a good time."

I look back over my shoulder to make sure Wren is okay. One stray bullet and I could lose her; I could lose my *son*.

Bee follows my gaze and nods grimly. "Go," she urges. "Go protect your woman. I can handle myself."

One of the Irish manages to breach the steps. I send a bullet straight into his forehead and his eyes roll into death just like the rest of him.

"Get the girl!" another behind him shouts. "The pregnant one!"

We're swatting flies at this point. Every time one Irish soldier dies, two more sprout up to take his place. It's a mass of writhing limbs and flashing muzzles. Through it all, I see Aleksandr looming over Wren in the shadow cast by a vase full of flowers almost as tall as she is.

I charge over, clearing my way with a hail of bullets. When I finally reach her, she's ash-pale and trembling violently. I clutch her face in both hands and look her in the eye. "Don't worry. I've got you."

Her features dissolve for a moment and suddenly, I'm not seeing Wren; I'm seeing Elena. I made the same promise to her once, a long time ago.

We all know how that ended.

Wren's hands ring around my wrists and I'm caught captive by those perfect green eyes. "Please don't leave me," she whispers.

"I will find you," I promise her. "I swear, I will find you. Always."

Her eyes flicker past me before going wide with panic. "Behind you!" she screams.

Grabbing her by the waist, I fling her to the side, just in time to avoid our attacker. While we're still turning, I shoot twice, catching him once in the hip and once in the spine. He falls to the floor limp and spasming violently, bloody foam frothing up at his lips.

Aleksandr rushes back over. "We have to move fast. There are more men coming."

I nod and shove Wren towards him. She falls against his chest but her eyes are stuck on me, her arm reaching out desperately. "No. Wait! Dmitri…"

Hearing her say my name like that after so long gives me the eleventh-hour push I need. "Take her, brother. Keep her safe."

More men zig-zag in every direction. So fucking many of them. I can't tell friend from foe from innocent, terrified bystander.

All I have the presence of mind to do is watch Wren go and fire at any man who even glances wrong in her direction.

And then I see *him*.

An Irish soldier, neck marred with the sigil of the O'Gadhra clan, his tongue stuck out between his teeth in fierce concentration. He sees me looking at him—and then, when I can't stop myself from peeking once more at her, he follows my line of sight and understands instantly that she is the one thing I cannot bear to lose.

Then he starts to make for her.

I'm dumbstruck for only a moment before I start sprinting to intercept him. But in the end, it's that wasted moment that makes all the difference.

He leapfrogs a pew, and then another. I slip in a puddle of blood, hit the floor, throw myself right back up, keep running.

He withdraws a gun from his belt and loads a fresh clip as he keeps moving.

I stumble again. Get up again. A flying elbow catches me in the face, but I shrug off the blow and keep staggering toward Wren.

The whole world has shrunk down to a pinpoint. Wren in a lilac-colored dress and the man in black chasing her down.

When I get the tiniest of opportunities, I raise my weapon and shoot. He ducks just in time to dodge the bullet and plows onward to her.

He's too fast. I'm too sluggish and wrong-footed and my head feels like it's stuffed full of cotton.

Another flash in the corner of my eye. This one is white and blonde—my bride, leaping down the steps when she sees where I'm headed.

A foot whips out and catches me around the ankle. I fall again, and this time, I strike the corner of the altar steps on the way down, cracking my skull hard enough to see stars. That foggy, full-of-cotton feeling intensifies. The pinpoint shrinks.

I see Wren.

I see the Irishman.

I see Bee.

I see it all happen, and I'm powerless to stop it.

Bee raises her gun to cut down the enemy. She has a pure line of sight and she never misses—but the gun fails her. As she goes to pull the trigger, her weapon jams.

The Irishman grins in delight. He lifts his own gun and levels it off—not at Bee, but at Wren. His teeth, even from here, are yellowed and broken.

Bee's jaw drops, then sets with determination. I know before it even happens what she's going to do. I want to scream to tell her no, stop, don't do it—but even if I could, it wouldn't do any good.

She's never been much good at following orders.

The Irishman redoubles his grip, flicks off the safety, and pulls the trigger. His muzzle sparks and spits. A bullet emerges…

And Bee throws herself in its path.

It's the sight of red blossoming on Bee's wedding dress, dead center in the middle of her stomach, that clears the fog in my head. All of a sudden, I can move again. I shove myself upright, leaking blood of my own from the temple, and cross the final distance.

Bee is lying sprawled on her side as the red spreads and spreads and spreads. The Irishman who shot is dead already, killed by God knows who, drooling his last breaths onto the tiled floors. I turn my back on him and kneel in front of my fake wife.

I reach out to touch her too-pale cheek. It's still hellfire and chaos around me, but all I can think about is how cold her skin is already. Life shouldn't fade from a human that fast. It isn't right.

Not like this.

It can't happen like this.

69

WREN

Aleks drags me backwards as Bee's name rips its way out of my throat. Of all the things that have been torn from me in this life, losing her like this might hurt the worst.

"The fuck—" Aleksandr gasps as he tries to grab a hold of me.

I'll be honest: I'm not thinking straight. I'm not thinking at all right now. It makes zero sense to turn back around and run towards the fighting, but that's precisely what I do. Because all I can think is, *My friend needs me*.

My friend needs me, and I won't let her die alone.

I wriggle free of Aleks's grasp and get a few steps away before I trip on my skirts and go sprawling. At eye level, the red smeared all over the black-and-white tiled floors looks almost unreal. Like spilled paint, not something that just ran in my best friend's veins.

It's mesmerizing, almost. I touch a dumbstruck fingertip to it, drag it through the puddle and hold it up to the light.

It looks so wrong.

Before I can get to my feet, I find myself being pulled upright. I try to fight off whoever has decided he has the right to touch me, but then I hear Aleksandr's voice snap at me urgently. "Fucking hell, Wren, what do you think you're doing? I have to get you out of here!"

He starts dragging me towards the door behind the altar. "But—but—Bee!" I cry out stupidly. "What about Bee?"

"How is you getting shot gonna help her now?" he demands, tightening his grip on my arm.

"I have to make sure she's okay. I can't just leave her!"

He whips around, his expression incensed and borderline manic. "You can't do anything for her. She would want you—"

BANG!

Aleksandr flies off to the side, blood sprouting from his arm. "Go!" he bellows, panic chasing the anger off his face. "Just fucking *run!*" Wincing, he pulls out his gun with his good hand and starts shooting blindly.

As if in agreement with Aleksandr, my baby kicks hard against my stomach, reminding me that my life is not the only one at stake here. It snaps some sense into me and self-preservation kicks back in. I rush for the one unblocked door that remains and go careening into a huge, empty corridor. It's so quiet here, in stark contrast to the chaos of the ceremony hall just on the other side of the door. I can hear my own heartbeat thudding in my ears.

When I hear gunshots down the hall, followed by running footsteps, I take off again without any idea of where I'm going. I just have to find a quiet, safe place to hide. I have to stay out of sight. I have to—

I race around the corner and run right into the arms of a man in a black suit. He grabs hold of me and I immediately begin to thrash and scream. "No! Let me go! Let me—"

"It's okay!" he hisses. "I'm with Dmitri. I'll get you out safely." I stop struggling as hard, but I still don't feel calm; I definitely don't feel safe. The fact that I haven't ever seen this man before doesn't help much. "Come with me."

He half-carries, half-drags me down the corridor, into another hallway that branches off perpendicularly. An exit at the far end shines with a rectangle of light around the borders. Outside. Freedom.

We get closer and closer, and then we're outside, and the air no longer smells like blood, and I can breathe again.

Then he shoves me sideways.

I go tumbling into the arms of another man. One of several, actually, all of whom are clad in black and grimacing down at me.

"No—!"

I twist around, attempting to rush back inside, but the bastard who told me he worked for Dmitri catches me with one thick arm around the waist. "There's no running now, pretty lady," he whispers in my ear, his hot breath tinged like rotten fish.

I scream again, but he just scoops me up and tosses me effortlessly into the back of a waiting van. The doors slam shut, engulfing me in darkness.

When my eyes adjust, I realize I'm not alone back here. A silhouette hunches in the corner. And as the engine purrs to life, it speaks. "Funny seeing you here, Wren."

A light kicks on overhead. Cian O'Gadhra looks back at me. He's gaunt and pale, his jaw clenched tight, his hands tucked out of sight in his lap. I know who he is now. What he's done. What he made Jared do.

But it's still hard to look him in the eye and not see the man I thought he once was.

I scurry back into the corner of the van, as far away from him as I can get. "W-what do you want from me?"

"Have no fear," he says in a soft, meek voice. "I don't plan on hurting you. That was never the plan."

I'm a mess of sweat and dirt and blood. Bee's gown keeps flashing in my mind's eye. So much red on all that white. The shock of her blond hair, its curling ends dipped into her own blood and drinking it up greedily.

"What is the plan?" I ask cautiously.

"*Peace.* I wanted peace. Ceasefire. Dmitri's been a cold bastard these last few weeks with his attacks, one after the next after the next. So many dead men. I want it to stop."

"You overestimate my influence," I blurt.

He shakes his head, his expression softening and morphing in ways I don't understand. If this is his big villain speech, it's all coming out strange and wrong. He doesn't look proud or vengeful; he looks sad. Almost overwhelmed.

"Oh, I don't think so. I think I've got the measure of the situation just right. That baby in your belly is his. And Bee is just the con he's using to get the Zanetti mafia on his side."

He glances up at my face, which is a struggle to keep neutral. "Have I got the gist of it?"

"I'm not involved in any of this," I lie. "Not one bit."

He laughs sadly. "Oh, yes, you are, sweet Wren. You were involved by association the moment Jared walked into O'Malley's that night seven years ago and asked to speak to Cathal."

My God.

So it is true.

I thought I believed the story already—but hearing Cian confirm it removes that one iota of doubt that's been percolating unconsciously in the back of my head. "Please, Cian. Please don't do this. I'm… I'm pregnant—"

"I meant it when I said I wasn't going to hurt you, Wren." He shakes his head again. "I won't."

"Then why take me at all?"

"Because there's no reasoning with Dmitri Egorov." For the first time, his voice prickles with a lash of anger. "The only way to get him to listen is to *force* him to listen. Of course, that will be harder now, what with Beatrice being shot. That… that was definitely not part of the plan." He runs an anguished hand through his hair as though he genuinely regrets it, and again, I wonder what the hell is going on. "Which is why I had to take you with me."

"I-I don't mean as much to him as you think I do." I wish I could say I was lying boldly, but the truth is that I have no idea what the truth is anymore.

I don't know who loves me.

I don't know who wants me dead.

And I don't know what's going to happen in the next five minutes, much less the next days or weeks or years. Everything is a mess and a mystery, and I'm powerless to dictate the course of my own life.

Cian sighs. He sounds tired beyond belief. "I suppose we'll find out soon enough."

70

DMITRI

There has been only one other time I've seen her so helpless.

It was years ago, while Elena was still alive. Bee showed up at my front door bundled up in a massive winter coat despite the fact that it was the height of summer. The coat was white, I remember. As white as her wedding gown is now.

"Can I stay with you for a few days, Dmitri?" she asked. *"Please."*

I knew then that it was serious, that something had gone very wrong. Beatrice Zanetti never begged anyone for anything. And she sure as hell never left the house without a full face of makeup.

But here she was, on my doorstep in her coat, sweat mixing with the tear tracks running down her bare face.

It was when she stepped inside and shrugged off the coat that I saw what had happened.

It took everything in me to keep my hands to myself and not touch the fresh iron marks seared into her skin. Just like they're doing now, my fingers hovered in the air between us, as if, if I only tried hard enough, I'd be able to erase the damage.

"He did this?" I growled.

She shook with sobs that never quite broke through before collapsing onto the floor, her body wracked with pain as she tried to blubber words through her hysteria. I shushed her, picked her up, and carried her to one of the guest bedrooms. I stayed with her until she fell asleep. I vowed that night to protect her.

And yet here I am, holding her limp body in my hands, searching desperately for a pulse. It's the same fucking scenario playing out all over again.

The same failure.

The same pain.

I'm vaguely aware of someone calling for a retreat. The chaos dissipates all at once, the exact same way it started. One moment, there is mayhem in every direction—the next, we're alone.

"Pavel," I croak, "we need a fucking ambulance. Now!" I turn back to her where she's shivering on the floor. "Bee… Bee, come on… Don't you fucking dare…"

"Those Irish fuckers," Vittorio snarls as he approaches us. The devil only knows where he's been. "Is she alive?"

He leans in but I throw out an arm to keep him away from her. "Stay back," I order. "I've got this."

He scowls at first—but then his eyes flit to something else, and his scowl freezes.

I follow his line of sight in growing horror. It takes me only a moment to realize what he's seeing.

Fuck.

The bullet caught her hair in the stomach, dead center in her bodice. The blood has spread out from there, sloshing in every direction, but the force of the shot's impact ripped the seams to pieces. A piece of fabric is lolling down like a dog's tongue, revealing…

The undeniably plastic curve of her prosthetic stomach.

His jaw drops when he puts the pieces together. "What the fuck is this?" Before I can do anything, he knocks my arm aside, drops to his knees by his daughter, flicks open a switchblade knife, and plunges it right into the plastic bulge.

It dangles ludicrously from the blade when he draws it out. "I knew it," he proclaims. "I fucking *knew it!*"

I grab his wrist and squeeze until he lets go of the knife again. The belly wobbles on the floor with sickening jellied noises.

Behind me, I'm vaguely aware of Pavel rushing from the back to examine the damage to Bee's abdomen. I'm too busy looking at Vittorio, though, as he goes from red to purple to ashen with pure rage.

"You fucking lied to me," he accuses. "The pregnant whore is carrying your spawn; this traitorous bitch of a daughter of mine never was."

Between the shootout and my dying best friend, I've never given less of a fuck. Which is why, the moment he's done talking, I slam my fist into the side of his face, sending him reeling towards the floor with limbs flailing ungracefully in every direction.

I rise to my feet and tower over him. "I warned you once before. When it comes to the women in my life… watch your fucking mouth."

He scoots backwards on his ass, drawing trails in the pooled blood like a slug. Alberto hisses at the Zanetti men crowding us to stay back and let the don handle his business.

Breathing raspily in his chest, Vittorio hauls himself upright with the help of the nearby pew. His tongue darts out to lick the blood from his split lip.

"That was a mistake, Egorov. A big, big mistake." His tongue flits out again. It disgusts me. All of this pig of a man disgusts me, every last hair on his head and pore on his face. He's rotten all the way down to the marrow of his bones. I see that now.

"I would have given you everything," he continues. "An entire legacy, handed over on a silver platter. I gave you my daughter… and you couldn't even fuck a baby into her." He looks down at her with venomous contempt in his eyes. "What kind of man do you call that? Not a real one."

I step forward, right in Vittorio's bloody face. "A real man doesn't whip little girls."

"A real man," he counters, "knows how to do what must be done." He glowers at me for one moment longer, then whips around and walks down the blood-soaked, flower-strewn aisle with Dante, Alberto, and Valentino close at his back. "Take Beatrice. She's coming with—"

"No."

He freezes on the last step and glances at me over his shoulder. "No?"

"She is staying here. If you want her, you'll have to kill me."

As I speak, my men converge behind me. They're bloody and battered, but loyal to the death.

Vittorio's eyes snake from side to side, the whites of his eyes darkening with rivulets of red veins. "You know what?" he decides. "Keep the whore. What do I want with a defective daughter? She'll die soon enough anyway. That bullet didn't leave much room for hope." He raises one wrinkled finger into the air and wags it in my direction. "I'm coming for you, Dmitri Egorov. I'll make sure you join Beatrice in hell soon enough."

Then he storms out of the ceremony hall with his men trailing along in his wake. We watch him go and we keep watching, even long after the doors have slammed shut and the echo of the clang has died out.

"Dmitri!"

I twist around when I see Aleksandr come limping through the door at the rear of the altar. His clothes are an absolute ruin, but his arm is even worse. It's barely attached at the shoulder and it weeps endless rivers of blood.

"Aleks!" I call out, lunging toward him. "What the fuck happened?"

"I'm sorry, brother," he pants heavily. He winces and splutters in pain as he leans against the door frame, unable to come any farther. "I… I… don't know where she is. I was attacked; she ran. I don't know where she went…"

Before he's even finished speaking, I'm rushing towards the exit. But the sound of panicked yells brings me crashing to a stop.

"Hurry!" someone screams. "She's going into cardiac arrest—"

"We're losing her—"

"Fuck!"

My head is pounding with worry. Every heartbeat throbs and aches. A heavy sense of failure hangs over me like a flock of vultures, just waiting for me to give up so they can come down to pick at what's left of my bones.

First, I lost Elena.

Then I lost Wren.

And now, I'm losing Bee.

And here I am—caught in the middle, drenched in blood, surrounded by death. My hands are tangled and the chains are pulling me in every direction. Soon enough, they'll tear me to pieces.

Fate will either kill me first…

Or it'll kill everyone I love and make me watch them go.

One, by one, by one.

TO BE CONTINUED.
Dmitri and Wren's story concludes in Book 2 of the Egorov Bratva duet, TANGLED DECADENCE.
Click here to keep reading!

Printed in Great Britain
by Amazon